The Rock Star of Vampires

MIMA

iUniverse LLC
Bloomington

The Rock Star of Vampires

iUniverse books may be ordered through booksellers or by contacting:

iUniverse
1663 Liberty Drive
Bloomington, IN 47403
www.iuniverse.com
1-800-Authors (1-800-288-4677)

ISBN: 978-1-4917-3280-9 (sc)
ISBN: 978-1-4917-3281-6 (e)

Library of Congress Control Number: 2014907269

Printed in the United States of America.

iUniverse rev. date: 04/28/2014

Also by Mima

FIRE
A Spark Before the Fire

To learn more go to **www.mimaonfire.com**

Acknowledgements

I just wanted to express my endless gratitude to all the people who have supported my writing career from the beginning. I'm fortunate to have so many positive and encouraging people in my life.

I wanted to give a special thanks to Mitchell Whitlock for collaborating with me on the back cover synopsis. Mitchell is a talented and insightful writer who was able to take a limited explanation of my book's plot, to help create a terrific summary.

Thanks also goes out to Esther Murphy and Jean Arsenault, for making the editing process a little less of a nightmare.

I would also like to dedicate this book to the memory of my friend, Nadine Bujold. I miss you, sweet angel. This one's for you.

Chapter One

She could smell him. His fragrance was so strong that it became apparent to her from the moment he walked through the door. It didn't matter that she was in a crowded grocery store, full of Saturday afternoon shoppers. It didn't matter that vulgar odors surrounded her—cheap perfume, poor hygiene, laundry detergent—Ava Lilith caught his delicious aroma the second he arrived. It was sweet and refreshing, heavenly and intoxicating. She felt a bounce in her step as she glided up and down the aisles in search of this rare treat. At first, rushing—but suddenly self-conscious, Ava slowed down to a normal pace. There was no need to draw attention to the excitement that bubbled inside of her.

But oh, she was excited! Her heart raced in anticipation. It wasn't the fact that his breed was uncommon. Finding their kind in the western Canadian city of Vancouver was the tricky part. They were rarely found in a grocery store. Ava mostly discovered them in college bars, malls and movie theaters—but they were always surrounded by friends, and often difficult to separate from the others. She hoped he was alone. It would be much easier if no one were around to cause a distraction.

The intoxicating smell grew stronger which meant Ava was getting closer. People didn't notice anything unusual about a young woman walking mindlessly through the aisles, an empty green basket in hand. They couldn't

1

recognize that her caramel eyes were fading to a softer version. Nor could they see her cheeks becoming flushed as she moved closer to the scent. Electricity ran through Ava's body but no one was aware that her eyelashes were flickering twice as fast, as they always did when she recognized this scent. It was an aphrodisiac to her kind—those who were drawn to blood.

It wasn't so much that vampires enjoyed the taste of blood. Well—some did. Most saw it as nothing more than a supplement to their diet. However others, like Ava, simply craved the *feeling* of drinking blood. It was the warmth as it surged to the back of her throat, how it energized her in a way that food never could, making her feel centered and complete. It wasn't like a drug that gave a high, but a boost that was needed exclusively by mortal vampires; blood had the power to lift and sooth her spirits even on the most wretched of days.

Of course, some of the tenants living in her downtown apartment complex—made up entirely of mortal vampires—insisted taste was relevant. This included her older friend Benjamin Clarkson, who would arrogantly ramble on for hours about the many different varieties. He compared their consistency and potency as if he were speaking of fine wines.

In his imperious British accent, he claimed that eastern European blood was far superior to that of the North American. "There are some *obvious* exceptions," he would boast to anyone in the apartment building lounge that would listen, his dark eyes studiously avoiding those around him, almost as if to not be aware of their reaction. "But clearly I can't let you in on *all* my secrets." Benjamin always ended his senseless comments with smug laughter, as if everyone was sitting on their chair's edge, waiting for him to go on. And although no one did, he still rattled on like they were all entertained by his tales.

As irritating as he was condescending, there was something about Benjamin that intrigued Ava. His stories were so pronounced: he could create an entire scene with a few carefully selected words, often pausing as if he were mentally digging through an old chest of words that described his thoughts perfectly. There was comfort in his tales, regardless of how cryptic they were in details. Even when telling the darkest story, Benjamin didn't give the gruesome details, but often surprised his listeners by speaking from his heart.

He was one of two people that helped Ava to better understand her status as a vampire, which was still relatively new. He talked about the complicated layers that many didn't understand, going to great lengths to remove the myths created by imaginative writers over the years. He explained how mortal vampires were just regular, everyday people that lived, for the most part, normal lives. There were, of course, some distinctions and their physical need for blood was one of them. It was like vitamins to their kind.

The most desirable of all blood was that of a virgin. Not to be misunderstood—vampires did *not* feed on that of children or adolescents. It was unheard of in their community. Not only was it taboo to touch either, it was distasteful. In fact, a vampire's senses were at such an advanced level that it was vital for one of five to be alerted in order to even entice their interest. Children had such a vagueness that they were barely on their radar. With his deep, British accent, Benjamin *often* could be heard making the joke "I can always hear the little *bastards* long before I can smell them!"—and then he would pompously laugh at his own clever remark.

As for teenagers, her more sensible friend Landon Owens insisted that the upheaval of hormones made their scent unpleasant. In fact, Ava could usually tell when someone going through puberty was close at hand because they made her nose burn. There was an unpleasant musk that was completely revolting.

"You know how they always say that if you take someone's virginity, you're taking away their innocence?" Landon presented this question to Ava shortly after she became a vampire. She had been both confused and curious, desperately seeking guidance from one of her kind. Landon had more knowledge after doing a lot of research in this area. He was very inquisitive and unlike some of the other vampires, he felt it was necessary to understand all the details involved. Although only in his early 30s, Landon carried the intensity of someone who had lived for centuries.

"Yes?" Ava raised an eyebrow as she listened carefully, almost in fear. Her new strengths ironically made her feel powerless in the early days of her change because she had not yet learned how to keep them under control. She felt as though she were rediscovering herself. It was one of the most difficult stages of her life.

"It's not because of an average, everyday person having sex with a virgin. That's normal. It's a rite of passage." He shrugged, pushing aside a strand of dirty blond hair from his amber eyes. "The term 'losing innocence' originates from hundreds of years ago and it refers to vampires having sex with a virgin."

Ava slowly began to nod but had to interject. "But isn't it sort of taking away someone's innocence, regardless? Don't people see from a different set of eyes after they lose their virginity?"

"Somewhat," Landon nodded thoughtfully. "But losing your virginity is normal, however 'losing innocence' is a direct reference to losing it to a vampire. That's why teenagers instinctively want to cross it off their list while they're young. It's a built in biological reaction that they aren't even aware of, it is there to protect them from vampires. That's part of the reason why people got married when they were like 15 or whatever, hundreds of years ago. It was for fear of becoming a vampire."

"A normal sexual encounter is powerful but it doesn't even touch one that includes a vampire and therefore make them more vulnerable," he slowly continued. "Plus, the virgin's blood is so intoxicating that the vampire can easily lose control and make them one of us. And as you know, that's highly discouraged."

Ava tilted her head and averted her eyes, her thick chocolate tresses almost successfully covering her face. She didn't respond. Her experiences of becoming a vampire were bittersweet, at best.

Landon spoke softly. "Vampires have a different level of overall strength *because* of the fact that they drink blood, which alone can create a more intense encounter. However, it's the animal instincts of a vampire, combined with their strong senses that make the entire experience…. quite amazing." He paused for a moment. "But then again, we are our own kind of animal."

And he wasn't exaggerating. Although they had the conscience of any other human, mortal vampires had the instincts and senses that surpassed that of the average person.

"Vampires want virgins," Landon explained carefully. "It's because they are pure. It's like drinking fresh spring water rather than that full of chemicals. They're delicious to bite into and they give you a high, a surge of energy that no one else can match." He paused for a moment. "And they are inexperienced so they aren't aware that it isn't necessarily normal to be bitten during sex." His eyebrows rose slightly at the end of his sentence, almost as a subtle warning to Ava.

"I was not a virgin," Ava quietly remarked, her voice edged with frayed emotions. "Did he think I was one?"

At the time she had considered herself so lucky. Tall, with shiny blue eyes and dark blond hair, Bryan Foley's features resembled that of someone on television or in the movies—and it was probably after many comments to that effect, he would later successfully pursue such a career. But he was also charming—*very* charming, and appeared to know the exact words to cause an insecure young girl to drop all her defenses.

God! How could she have been so naïve? How could she have been so *stupid?* Did she seriously think that someone *so* perfect would seek her out for anything serious? Did she really believe *anyone* could fall in love with her? These were the questions that tore her soul apart again and again, in the dead of the night.

There had been such a strong hunger that flowed between her and Bryan. One of the reasons she became a vampire herself was because of those powerful moments together. They made her feel alive where she once had felt so dead inside. It was the feeling of dread every morning when her alarm went off, not wanting to get out of bed to start the day. It was the uncomfortable heaviness in her heart that pulled her down on a regular basis, causing her mind to race uncontrollably and her thoughts to nag at her constantly. There was something gripping inside of her and the only thing that seemed to take those feelings away was her time with Bryan, so she assumed that becoming a vampire would change her life. She was wrong.

And now she was trolling the grocery store for virgins. To most, it would be pathetic. To vampires, it was understandable. There were many different points of view on the matter but Ava was past caring. Life had given her an abundance of reasons not to have any feelings at all. Some friends insisted that she would see her calling very differently someday, but she wasn't there yet. And honestly, didn't understand what they meant by such a vague prediction.

It was in aisle six by the dog food section that Ava found him. *He smells magnificent!*

Putting on her most innocent face, she made her way in his direction. Her intense gaze automatically made him sense Ava's presence and he turned around. The animal magnetism hit them both as he met her eyes and froze, until his cheeks turned bright red—something that caused her mouth to water. She pushed her own natural insecurities aside and focused on her target.

He was tall, lanky and definitely young. Not *too* young. Ava guessed him to be 19. He wore a pair of jeans, a white t-shirt and a jean jacket. He wasn't going to get an 'A' for his fashion sense, but he smelled so good that she could overlook his choice of clothing.

Large, innocent eyes timidly watched as she approached, his mouth pursed in stunned silence. His hair was thick, overflowing with messy curls and as Ava got closer, she noticed the distinct smell of hair gel. He smiled nervously and she suddenly caught whiff of a cheap, musky scent that resembled deodorant. He was anxious and starting to perspire.

I have him right where I want him!

"Hello!" Ava made herself seem cheerful and approachable. The inexperienced ones liked that kind of thing. She gave him a confident smile, her eyes gazing up at him very sweetly in an effort to win his trust. Batting her eyelashes, Ava glanced at the bag of dog food in his hand. "I wouldn't recommend you buy that food."

"No?" His eyes were full of naivety. His mouth gently fell open after he spoke and she could see the tiniest drop of saliva on his bottom lip. The scent was intensifying.

"No," she purred, reaching in front of him, so that her petite body was in his line of vision. Grabbing the first bag she saw, *whatever it was*, Ava moved back slightly but made sure she was still in his personal space, while showing him another kind of dog food. It was store brand.

"See this stuff here," she spoke in a little girl voice. "It's just as good as the most expensive brand. All these other companies are ripping you off." It was bullshit, but it was irrelevant at that point. She could smell those natural fragrances that told her that a man wanted her and Ava continued to smile. "I *highly* recommend it."

"By the way," she extended her hand, "My name is Ava."

"Hi ah...hi Ava." he stuttered, taking her hand. She noted that his palms were sweaty. "I'm Sheldon."

"Hi Sheldon," she gazed into his eyes. "Do you really need to do this shopping right now? Would you have time for a coffee or something?"

"Ah, well my mom—"

"Don't worry about your mom," she interrupted in a gentle and soothing voice, then licked her bottom lip slowly, something that didn't go unnoticed by Sheldon. "I'll get you home before dinner."

Chapter Two

"So I hear that you've wrecked *another* one," Benjamin Clarkson's pompous laughter filled the apartment building's lounge area as he sat beside Ava, and across from Landon Owens and his girlfriend, Chloe Wallings. It was the afternoon following Ava's encounter with Sheldon from the grocery store and until that moment, no one had mentioned it. Most vampires made it a point to mind their own business and expected the same courtesy. Benjamin was an exception. Mainly because his wife, Olivia spent most of her days sitting in front of the window, watching the coming and goings at the apartment building.

"I guess there are no secrets around here," Ava commented uncomfortably while Benjamin either ignored or didn't notice Chloe's dark glare. Being in the apartment next to Landon's, Benjamin had occasionally made a few inappropriate remarks regarding the couple's personal life. At one time, Chloe had even looked into having this 50 year-old man booted out of the building. However Samantha, who was one of the co-owners of the four-story complex, insisted that her hands were tied and made every attempt to defuse the situation.

"Not at all," Benjamin responded good-naturedly and gently patted Ava's shoulder, while Landon appeared to be suppressing a grin. "So what virgin have you *ruined* this time, my girl?"

Ava cleared her throat, trying to rise above her embarrassment. Sure vampires were known to be promiscuous while they were single—she certainly had a stellar reputation compared to some of the other tenants—but Ava was still relatively new to the vampire lifestyle. "I found him at the grocery store."

Benjamin let out a hearty laugh. "At a *grocery* store! You really are the ingenious one, aren't you?" Shaking his head with a smile, he had a strange faraway look in his eyes, his cheeks glowing a rosy red. "Very clever, my dear girl. You never know where you'll find virgins these days. So did you break the little bastard, or what?"

"Well I'm not sure what you mean by 'break' exactly," Ava replied calmly after taking a deep breath. At times, Benjamin was difficult to tolerate but at the end of the day, he meant no harm. She knew he was only teasing her. If nothing else, he added a certain element to their conversations. "But I believe I made an impression." That was putting it mildly.

"Oh, did you bite him?" Chloe leaned slightly forward; the combination of her straight black hair and heavy, charcoal eye makeup made her look deathly pale. Seeing the overly made up young woman with her boyfriend Landon was a bit strange, considering he was so down to earth and average in his appearance. Unlike some male vampires, his style was casual and his demeanor, quiet. Opposites really must attract, she noted. Of course Chloe was the newest vampire in the building, so everyone was intrigued.

"Virgins just *fulfill* you in the most amazing way." Her dark eyes would've easily been haunting to most people. Ava felt she was being too dramatic—it was vampires like Chloe that put them all in a vulnerable situation because she *didn't* want to be mainstream. In fact, Ava believed that Landon's girlfriend wished for people to suspect her status, as her style was Goth and it seemed like she tried to act and speak how many fictional vampires did in books and movies. It was unsettling to those like herself that wanted to keep their existence a secret.

"But of course!" Benjamin decided to answer for Ava. "Taking home a virgin and not biting into him would be ridiculous! It's like being presented a gift and choosing not to open it."

"Was that late yesterday afternoon, Ava?" Landon spoke gently, as if he were calmly waiting to get a word into the conversation. "Cause I could smell him from my apartment, but I had the window open so I just assumed the scent was coming from outside."

"Late afternoon," Ava confirmed shyly, slightly uncomfortable with his question. She suddenly recalled telling Sheldon that she would have him home in time for dinner. That didn't happen.

"Did he realize that you were a vampire?" Landon gave her a subtle warning look. She knew he didn't approve of her actions. Although he was probably only five years older than her, there was something powerful about his presence that Ava always found intimidating. Ironically, she thought it was his tranquil presentation that made her feel so awkward around him. His gaze was intense yet nonthreatening, while his voice was smooth and gentle.

"No," Ava shook her head. "He had no idea."

"They just think you are into biting," Chloe leaned forward in her seat, a pearly, white smile crossing her crimson lips, her eyes glowing, increasingly darkened as she spoke. "Unless you go overboard and kill them, that is."

"I wouldn't do that," Ava said with some irritation in her voice. She had heard stories of vampires going completely overboard and draining their victims during intercourse. It was rare and something most wouldn't even consider, but it *did* happen. Their victims became the missing people whose photos were plastered in public places and yet, they would never be found. "Besides he probably thinks I just bit him and didn't drink any of his blood."

"The last thing you want him to know is that you're a vampire," Landon reminded her. Secrecy was an unwritten law that was absolute. In fact, there were some vampires that worked diligently to make sure that their kind weren't discovered—attacking online message boards, ridiculing the entire concept of vampires, anything that made the general public feel secure that vampires were only a myth. "Most keep our secret. Bryan Foley is probably the exception. And he won't be making *that* mistake again."

All eyes landed on Ava because they knew the story. Bryan was someone she had once hoped would fall in love with her. It wasn't until after learning that he was a vampire that she would find out why he was so intrigued by her. It was confessed to her during a weak moment, otherwise she never would've known the difference. Of course she had been so entranced that Ava begged him to make her one too. He finally granted her wish but it wasn't the magic key Ava sought. Bryan didn't love her and she was still miserable in her own life—her expectations fell to disappointment.

"I will say that people have some *odd* ideas about what *we* are," Benjamin either didn't notice or was attempting to relieve Ava's discomfort in the situation, by taking over the conversation once again. "Craziness about garlic and such! They could throw those little balls of garlic at me all day and it wouldn't faze me in the least! Such silly ideas! And holy water is another one. I'd like to know what makes it so *holy* to begin with, such ludicrous nonsense that people choose to believe."

Ava noticed Landon giving her a small, possibly apologetic smile from where he sat, while Chloe seemed engrossed in what Benjamin was saying. Landon was not a fan of Bryan, but she knew he hadn't meant to embarrass her in any way.

"All those stupid books and movies have made us into something we *never* were. My favorite is the belief that we sleep in coffins," Chloe gave a seductive smile and gently touched Landon's leg. He merely glanced in her direction and they made intense, if brief, eye contact. "Can you imagine? Why would we sleep in coffins?"

"Because my dear, they want to make us as abnormally freakish as possible," Benjamin insisted. "They say we don't sleep at all, that we fizzle away in the sun and roam at night, killing anyone and anything for blood."

"The sun thing makes sense but it's exaggerated," Ava spoke up, happy to not be the center of discussion. "Ever since I turned, my eyes are much more sensitive. If I don't have my sunglasses, I can't stay outside." She noticed everyone nodding in understanding. They all dealt with that situation but the fables created around vampires were mainly untrue. Most people could work or be friends with a vampire and never know the difference. "But I can't imagine *not* sleeping or eating. True, blood is like a vitamin that I need to feel like myself, but it's hardly like the stories I heard about vampires when I was a kid."

"It's under the assumption that no vampire is human," Benjamin insisted.

"We *all* are humans—just a very *different* kind of human." He swung his hand around dramatically, indicating everyone in the building. "However that isn't the case everywhere. There are both mortal and immortal vampires."

Ava felt her eyes widen. She glanced at Landon who exchanged concerned looks with her. Did *he* lie to her? Was she the only one who didn't know this fact? Hadn't Landon told her that all vampires were just regular people with some exceptional traits? All around her, they nodded in understanding. Ava suddenly felt incredibly naive. "W-what are you talking about? I thought all vampires were mortal?"

"*Most* vampires are living among us and someday, will die," Benjamin replied to her question. "But there are an elite few that are immortal and they'll live forever. Unlike us, they don't age and really, you could say they rule the world. They are some of the most powerful people on the planet."

"Where are they?" Ava immediately shot the accusing question toward Landon, her heart racing in excitement. Had he purposely deceived her regarding this topic?

"They aren't in Canada," Landon answered swiftly, Ava noticed. "They stick to the largest cities in the world. Immortal vampires aren't small town folks because people ask too many questions in smaller areas, especially when they aren't aging and everyone else around them is" Landon carefully monitored her expression. "Not that we would know where they are located, it's a secret."

"A very guarded secret," Benjamin jumped in, speaking to Ava. "Trust me, my little lady, I've been all through the bloody world attempting to find them but it's impossible. They hide very well, but it's rumored they are in Europe."

"You've been all over the world looking for them?" Landon raised an eyebrow, looking slightly amused at Benjamin's eccentric ways. "Why would you want to be *this* for the rest of your life?"

"To be immortal and live forever?" Benjamin smoothed out his pant leg as he responded. "I could only dream! But ah, I'm old; it seems like a wasted journey to even look now. Olivia and me aren't spring chickens anymore, but at one time if I could've found that fountain of youth, I would've jumped in with both feet. But now I'm just an old man."

Of course he was probably a little older than he appeared. Vampires aged a bit slower than average people. Ironically, it was mostly because of their simple diets and restful sleeping patterns rather than anything magical.

"Ava, you don't want to be an immortal vampire," Landon spoke as if he were reading the thoughts racing through her head. She felt a jolt run through her body as their eyes met, and quickly looked away. "It's a secret life. It's not easy and as beautiful as some would lead you to believe."

"With all respect Landon, I disagree." Benjamin studied his face while Chloe nodded enthusiastically. "It would be amazing to live forever. To be young, beautiful and have all the time in the world to see and do everything you dream about. As humans, we simply don't have the time to live all the adventures that we wish we could. And by the time you start to make sense of your life, it's half over."

"Not everyone wants to be 'normal' like you do," Chloe gently reminded Landon and he briefly glanced in her direction. "Being a vampire isn't a bad thing."

"To you, maybe," he sniffed. "But you've had a chance to be normal and even more so, you had a *choice* to become a vampire. I was tricked into it. I find it repulsive that drinking blood is the only way to feel strong and complete. I understand and accept it, but I don't have to like it."

Landon had actually done extensive research to see if there was a way he could *not* be a vampire. Ava assumed that was why he discouraged others from following the same path. But he had always been a friend, there to answer her many questions after she turned. Bryan had been expected to 'baby-sit' her for at least six months after the change in order to help Ava adapt. He was gone after a couple of weeks. Landon had stepped in during this emotional and confusing time.

"I've been one for so long, I almost feel as if I were born to it," Benjamin pointed out. No one really knew his story and oddly enough, he hadn't volunteered it.

"I must get upstairs. Olivia got us some lovely blood from VP yesterday." Ava recognized the name of the underground organization that sold human blood to vampires, known as Vampire's Plus. There were other such places that catered to vampires (or a vampires wanna-bes) but it was the most highly regarded. They bought blood from pre-screened sources and sold it at a substantially higher price to vampires like Benjamin. Not everyone could afford it.

Landon raised his eyebrows but didn't say anything. Ava knew that he got his blood through a smaller, more local company, but as rarely as possible. He felt it was wrong to take human blood in most situations. Chloe probably would go for any kind of blood, at any time—she seemed more open and had no qualms. Ava mostly found it in casual affairs with non-vampires especially--virgins, although mortal vampires drank each other's blood too. Landon warned her regularly to be careful, that it was a dangerous game she was playing, but there was a part of her that thrived on that very thing. After all, wasn't this the life she wanted?

After Benjamin returned to his apartment, Ava felt like the third wheel with Chloe and Landon: especially when Chloe started to rub her boyfriend's thigh. Although it probably would've been a bit of a turnoff for most people to witness in a public place, it had the opposite effect on Ava. It made her think of the hours she had spent with Sheldon the previous day. And early that same morning, and-

"See you later guys," Ava jumped up from the couch and hurried upstairs to her second floor apartment. Unlocking her door, she rushed into the entrance and looked around. She could smell him. He hadn't left yet. Walking toward her bedroom, Ava saw him stretching, exhausted.

"Finally, you are awake!" A grin spread across Ava's face. "I didn't think you would ever wake up after last night."

He responded with a shy smile. "I'm still here."

Benjamin was wrong. She hadn't *completely* broken him.

Chapter Three

Feeling slightly guilty for indulging in her primal appetites, Ava was only too happy to drive Sheldon home on Sunday evening. This idea was further encouraged when she caught him looking at her with his infatuated, puppy dog eyes. Was that how she once looked at Bryan Foley? Moments like this put her conscience in a battle with what was right—and what was *wrong*.

At the same time, Ava couldn't help but grin as she watched him run up the steps to his family home, while an older woman—whom she assumed was his mother—peeked suspiciously out the window. How would he explain leaving home on a Saturday afternoon as an awkward and self-conscious 19 year old, then returning Sunday night as a confident and secure man? There was no way his mother *wouldn't* see the difference in Sheldon. It practically screamed its way into their family home.

She felt powerful for an instant but within seconds, her thoughts shifted and guilt reappeared. Ava did her best to push these feelings aside. Glancing in the rearview mirror, her soft brown eyes carried a sadness that she hadn't expected. Pushing a strand of her dark hair behind her ear, she quickly looked away.

Traffic was light on that October evening. There was an eerie stillness in the night, which allowed her mind to wander into some dark places.

Unfortunately, the high from getting blood was always temporary and in the end, she continued to feel an unfulfilled emptiness in her soul. It was during those times that her thoughts automatically took a downward spiral, as she once again reviewed her 'doom and gloom' checklist. And for some reason, it always weighed more heavily on a Sunday evening, perhaps with the anticipation of a new week.

As a receptionist at an accounting firm, Ava dreaded going to work every Monday morning. She hated the professional front that was instilled in her in order to impress big clients: it consisted of fake smiles, insincere pleasantries and what Ava considered to be glamourized hostess duties, as she served tea, coffee and sometimes food. Often she felt more like an insignificant servant than a receptionist. But she also thought her abilities were limited and any ambitions to search for another job were often overpowered by her own apathy.

Realistically, the job was a supplement to her income, giving the impression that she was in the same financial position as everyone else her age. In truth, most of her bills were covered by her parents' hefty life insurance policies and other funds left in their wills, something she usually hid from people. However her fear of running out of money made her very careful regarding her spending.

Ava had lost both her parents in a plane crash when she was ten. It was the most devastating period in her life and she spent the next few years in a somewhat robotic state. She felt confused, frightened—and very isolated. Rather than finding comfort from other relatives, Ava was given to her hesitant grandmother, whom made it pretty clear that this grandchild was *not* her responsibility. However her attitude swiftly changed after learning how much money Ava was worth to a guardian. There was a clear stipulation in both her parents' wills that if they were to die, the person who took care of their only daughter would be financially rewarded. Even as she thought about it on that dreary Sunday night, her heart filled with anger—until grief took over.

She had no one. Her parents were dead and her grandmother was indifferent. Bryan used her and threw her aside and friends were pretty limited. The world was a cold place. Feeling like she had been snubbed by life was brutal. It filled her with a resentment that made her have less of a conscience about using someone like Sheldon and quickly discarding him.

But there was an even darker side.

Shamefully, she thought about harming people—an instinct that never existed pre-vampire day—it was an animalistic nature that she assumed her kind struggled with regularly, mostly during spells of anger. How many times had Ava stood face-to-face with a belittling boss and fantasized about shoving her down a stairway? What if the older, Chinese lady had known that she was a vampire? Would she still speak to her in such a demeaning manner?

How many times had she thought about harming her own grandmother? This was brought on by memories of temper tantrums that took place following her parents' deaths, causing her to refer to Ava as 'the devil's child'. The combination of mourning both parents and an unwelcoming new home created a series of screaming matches between the two. There was no compassion. There was even less affection. It made her tough. It made her lonely.

The one person that kept her from crossing that line was Landon Owens. He was her conscience. His opinion mattered because he was the only person since her parents, who had willingly taken care of Ava. This happened shortly after becoming a mortal vampire; back when she thought Bryan would fill this role, until he suddenly left the country for an ambiguous acting job. At first Ava had believed his assurance that she was fine on her own. Learning to be a vampire was a piece of cake. The belief that you needed a 'guardian' for a specific amount of time after the change was just a legend.

She kind of knew what to expect. Bryan warned that her senses would be heightened, her physical desires increased and that an intense weakness could overtake her body when she didn't consume blood. And for the first few days, it really hadn't been such a big deal. Ava even mentioned to Bryan that she felt *pretty* much the same as before, except her senses were slightly elevated.

"See, told you it wasn't a big deal," Bryan casually remarked, giving her an impish grin. His blue eyes danced about and he built Ava up to believe that it was *her* inner strength that prevented the outcome from being too overwhelming. He had her assuming that the worst was over, she was fine and when he left the following Monday for an acting gig in Europe, Ava would quickly and easily adjust to her new life.

He allowed her to stay in his apartment while he was away. Who knew it would be the same building she now had her own place in? For a day or two, Ava was naively in a state of bliss. She was in love and things were only about to get better. Maybe life *did* provide happy endings for people like her after all. Bryan would return from his job in a few weeks and everything would be perfect.

She predicted wrong. That did not happen.

Everything changed. It began with her hearing.

One night she suddenly awoke in a state of panic, as the sounds from throughout the neighborhood bombarded her at the same time. Police sirens down the street, two cats fighting a block over, drunken friends wobbling home after a night of partying and the couple across the street having sex—everything hit her like a brick. Not realizing her bedroom window was only opened a smidgen—all she needed to allow the night sounds to seep in—Ava panicked.

Covering her ears and curling up in the fetal position, her heart raced at an elevated level. Why was everything so loud? It was like turning the volume up on ten television sets and having them stuck at that setting—Ava felt as though she would lose her mind.

After a few hours of this obnoxious cacophony—some stopping and new ones joining—she *hoped* to die. It was too much. Too overwhelming. Did vampires have to deal with *this* everyday or was she having a different reaction to her change? Who could she ask? The only vampire Ava knew back then was Bryan—and she was having trouble getting in touch with him. At the time she hadn't yet known that his building was actually *full* of those who knew exactly what she was going through—people who could've reassured her that this was completely normal and that she wasn't going insane. This was the usual transformation: and it was the transformation that required her creator to be by her side.

Ava spent the next few days crying, fearful of this curse that had overtaken her body. Unable to sleep or leave the apartment, she sat in the corner, shaking with both hands over ears and feeling like a crackhead coming off her poison. She cried and begged God to make it stop. Ava would dig her own nails into her arms in anxiety, squeeze her eyes shut tight and hope that it would come to an end. After a week, it seemed more tolerable. She wasn't sure if it was because her senses had grown used to it or if the noise levels had subsided?

She hadn't even considered that this wasn't the only drastic change about to take place in her body. Her sense of smell was about to be altered.

If Ava dared to open her window, she was invaded by every odor in the neighborhood: food cooking, the dumpster behind the apartment building and the scent of every person that walked past her window. Even some that *weren't* walking past her window. At times, a sweet fragrance that Ava would later learn was the 'virgin scent' would flow through the room and arouse her like she never had been before. Other times the obnoxious stench from rotting garbage would cause her to vomit. In fact, her urge to throw up greatly outnumbered the alluring effects of virgins in the neighborhood. Most scents were strong chemicals that burned her nose and throat and above all, were repulsive. This combined with her immaculate hearing was overwhelming. It was too much all at once. She felt trapped in a body where she had no more control.

And just when she started to get through a few days of not vomiting after inhaling the many odors around her, Ava discovered her taste buds had changed. Food that was modestly enjoyable before was absolutely divine. Fruit, vegetables, all natural foods were exceptionally pleasurable and there were times Ava over ate simply because she was amazed by how tasty something as simple as an organic apple was, compared to the chocolate she used to enjoy.

Fruit and vegetables were crisp, fresh and delicious. However sugary and salty foods were repulsive. Donuts, cookies, cakes—they all made Ava gag. Potato chips and even something as simple as crackers, caused her head to ache immediately after the salty junk passed her lips. Processed food was next to impossible to consume. Food would never be the same again.

But most notable at this stage, was the fact that she now craved blood. It wasn't even the taste that she longed for, but the warmth and soothing aspect of this enriched fluid. She instinctively knew it was what was needed to feel fully alive, in a way that wasn't possible with any food or drink. It surprised her that this craving crept up and suddenly became a preoccupation. And although she was aware that becoming a vampire brought on such feelings, it never fully sank in until that day. Her understanding was that it was an occasional need, not an overpowering feeling. Had Bryan stuck around, she would have learned that it was normal in the beginning stages of being a vampire to have more intense need for blood—it was a way for your body to adapt to the physical changes and balance things out on its own—but in the early days, this craving frightened her. What had she become?

Then her vision became sharper.

Ava could see the smallest print on a sign across the street. Things she shouldn't have been able to see were visible. A piece of salt on the floor would grab her eye. It was remarkable. Among all the overpowering senses, this was one she appreciated. Life had never been so beautiful to her. Every detail in nature suddenly felt like a miracle. If everyone could see as she did, Ava decided, they would never litter or pollute the world again. She could see the effects of pollution all around her. It was the slight tinge of dust that others were unable to see with the naked eye and it was especially apparent after it rained.

It was also overwhelming—too much and too soon. No one had prepared her for how to deal with all these changes and get accustomed to them. That was Bryan's job and her desperate attempts to get in contact through email or a disconnected phone only led to frustration—then depression. Ava felt lost and alone once again. It brought her back to the day her parents died.

Then one night, she snapped. After being awakened by yet another overwhelming combination of sound and scents, Ava grew furious and angrily punched her fist into the mattress before collapsing in tears. Feeling lost in a fog, she pushed the covers aside and rose in the dark room. Looking outside to what she once would've observed as a quiet night, Ava decided she couldn't take it any longer. Quickly sliding a tank top over her bra and pulling on a pair of shorts, she crossed the floor to exit her apartment.

Slowly turning the knob, hesitating only briefly to take a deep breath, she walked into the hallway and quietly pulled the door shut behind her.

Absently climbing the stairs to the building's roof, Ava already knew what she had to do. There was no one for her in this world. Weeks of no phone calls or replies to her emails confirmed that Bryan was gone. Vanished like her parents who left one night for a trip to Hawaii, only to die on their way. She was always alone. She would always *be* alone. And this belief combined with all the transitions of becoming a vampire was simply too much for an already unhappy young woman.

Ava made the last step to the building's rooftop. Shivers ran through her spine and she hugged herself while tears dripped off her cheeks. Who would even notice she was gone? Her grandmother? Bryan? No one.

Walking toward the ledge, she looked over the side. There was no way Ava would survive this jump. Vampires couldn't fly—could they? She suddenly began to sob uncontrollably, realizing that she didn't even *know* the answer to that question and whom would she ask? Trapped in a body she didn't understand was her definition of hell on earth. She glanced over the side once again, before taking a deep breath and starting to climb on the ledge. An unexpected voice sent chills through her spine.

"That's not the solution." His words were soft and gentle, causing Ava to abruptly swing around to see a stranger sitting alone in the dark. Confused, she wondered if he had he been there all along? Through her tears, she watched as he approached her; his glowing eyes seemed to see right through Ava's fragile body. She noted that he was close to her age and was slightly taller than her, with a face that was serene and showed no judgment. There was a certain honesty set deep in his eyes and his words comforted her. "Don't do it."

Too shocked to say a word, she didn't respond. Ava felt chills seeping underneath her clothes, sending the cold air through her body. She began to tremble.

He continued. "Didn't I see you with Bryan? Are you his girlfriend?"

Like a frightened child, Ava wiped tears from her face and nodded at the same time. Feeling shame, although she wasn't sure why, she avoided his eyes.

"And he turned you into one of us, didn't he?" The stranger eased closer to her while his voice remained calm, soothing a fire deep inside her heart. "I can tell. I can sense your fears and desperation. He left you. Did he even tell you that you *were* a vampire?"

"What?" She barely managed to whisper. *He turned you into one of us.* Was this stranger a vampire as well? Was that why he had an unusual scent? Could he answer her questions? A sense of hope ignited in Ava but she feared to completely embrace it.

"You're a vampire, right?" He moved closer to her and she continued to watch him in silence. Frozen on the spot, Ava didn't move an inch. Slowly reaching for her hand, he grazed it with his fingers, causing a flicker of warmth in her body. "Bryan turned you, then left you. Am I right?"

"How did you know?" She felt hot tears start to flow down her cheek once again; but this time, they were full of relief. Her voice was small, childlike. "What do you mean? I don't understand." Ava found herself instinctively reaching out to hold his hand, while he moved her away from the ledge. Face to face with him, her heart raced and her body felt weak. Ava's legs were trembling uncontrollably and yet, her desires set a fire inside from the simple touch.

His lips curved upward into a small smile, his eyes filling with compassion. "Everyone in this building is a vampire. I'm assuming you knew Bryan was as well?" He asked again then waited for her to nod. "I know you are one cause I can sense it. I can smell it. And once you are one a little longer, you'll be able to spot one of us as well."

She was shaking now. It was the first time in ages that anyone had understood her or even tried. Heart wrenching pain shot through her body and another flood of tears flowed down her cheeks. The next thing Ava knew, his arms tightly embraced her body and she felt an unexpected feeling of contentment as she pressed against this stranger. It felt good. Electrifying. Her heart began to race, causing blood to stampede through her veins. He smelled so wonderful, enticing. She wanted to taste his skin and feel the sensation of it beneath her tongue. She wanted to run her hands over his naked flesh, allowing them to roam to places that sent pleasurable sensations through his entire body.

Suddenly Ava wanted him so badly that she couldn't control her breathing. Overlooking any shyness, her lips carefully touched the stranger's neck and abruptly moved to his anticipating lips. Their kisses were full of hunger, unlike *anything* she had ever felt before. An erotic sensation burned through her entire body and every time he touched her, the heat only intensified until she felt her head fall back, allowing a loud gasp to escape her lips. She felt out of control to her physical needs. His hands were everywhere and trailing behind them was a sensation that was completely new to her. Was this really happening? Was she dreaming?

Leading her into the dark stairway, he quickly closed the door behind her. Their mouths met again while he coaxed her body down onto the steps, he began to unzip his jeans. Ava worked to pull down her shorts, which he quickly grabbed and threw aside as he sat down on the step, drawing her down on his lap. Ava reached out and grabbed onto the railing, winding her arm around his neck, as he thrust into her. Ava's head fell back and she let out a loud, lascivious moan, while he panted uncontrollably over her. Within seconds she had the most intense orgasm of her life—it flowed throughout her body with waves of pleasure that was unlike anything she had ever thought she *could* experience. Pulling onto the railing, Ava was alarmed to find that her wrist hurt from the tight grip onto the piece of steel.

The stranger's dark gaze met with hers as he gasped for air, almost as if he had just run a marathon. He continually caressed her body. She could feel the heat like steam from his body, while his masculine scent filling her, as he removed himself from between her legs. He turned to see her letting go of the railing and gently massaging her wrist with her other hand. "You managed to get a grip?"

An embarrassed smile lit up her face. "I felt like I had to hold on to something because things were very -."

"You're a vampire. Your physical reaction to touch is stronger than the average person, so sex is," He stopped to take a deep breath while pulling up his underwear then pants. "Umm…. yeah it's a…it's at a completely different level that others generally experience."

Ava slowly started to stand up and hunt around for her shorts. Feeling slightly uncomfortable for several reasons, she shook her head while watching him zip up his pants.

"You *really* didn't know that?" He looked slightly alarmed as she quickly pulled on her shorts. Her legs felt wobbly and Ava sat back down on the stairs. When she shook her head no, his eyes became dark and frustration filled his face. "You should've been told this stuff."

"I wasn't." Feeling slightly disorientated for a moment, she barely managed the words. Ava felt humiliated by her rash behavior and ignorance. Bryan did tell her there would be a difference but perhaps she simply had not really understood.

He gave her a sad smile and looked down at his shoes then back into her face. Perspiration ran across his forehead and she could smell the intensity of the moment they had just shared. He reached out for her hand to help her up from where she limply sat and drew her into his arms.

"That's not right. That's not the way it's supposed to be when you turn. In fact, you shouldn't have become one of us at all."

"I didn't know," She barely whispered. Her leg still felt like they were about to give out, after standing up for only a few seconds. "I thought I was okay at first."

"And now you feel as if you are losing your mind?" He quietly asked while, gently caressing her fingers.

"Yes."

His stare was intense and although she tried, she couldn't read his reaction. Was he angry with her? As the dust settled from their powerful encounter, she felt her body calming down and she was more relaxed. His eyes continually probed her while neither of them said a word. She felt awkward and looked away.

He finally spoke. "You need guidance," his voice was smooth and tender. Squeezing the hand he had enclosed, he looked deep into her eyes. "I will help you."

Ava didn't break eye contact and managed a shy smile. "Thank you. I have so many questions."

"That's fine."

He gave her a compassionate smile and started to lead her downstairs, then stopped and turned around.

"By the way, my name's Landon, and you are?"

Chapter Four

"I hate my boss," Ava made the impromptu announcement during a lunch break. It was a few days after her fling with Sheldon and already, her energy levels were fading. "I need a new job."

Across the table sat Mariah Nichols, who took in these words with one raised eyebrow, while silently nodding her head. Her friend's sultry, brown eyes seemed to radiate a perfect combination of innocence and sinfulness, while sunlight flowed through a nearby window of the restaurant, gently touching the highlights in her long, sleek hair. For a moment, she appeared stunning, if not angelic. Her face didn't really show any compassion but yet, something told Ava that she was in her corner

Plus this was not a new topic of conversation for the two vampires, who originally met one year earlier in the lounge area of their apartment building. Both worked as receptionists in Vancouver's downtown area and met for lunch whenever possible, usually to gripe about their day. Unlike Ava, Mariah didn't have as much patience with her employers and had a tendency to sometimes find herself fired. Currently she was a receptionist at a doctor's office and seemed reasonably content—well, sometimes.

"I need a new *life*," Mariah spoke bluntly before continuing to sip on her second glass of red wine, something she had no conscience about consuming during her lunch break. In fact, two glasses of wine meant she was probably having a half decent day at the office.

"I swear to God," she spoke dramatically with both hands up in the air to convey her frustrations. "I'm about one whiny patient or screaming baby away from writing fake prescriptions for myself. Must everybody be so fucking intolerable? I'm starting to think that Ashley had the *right* idea." A small grin curled Mariah's lips, while humor sparkled in her eyes. Knocking back the last of her wine, she quickly scanned the room for a waitress.

Ava couldn't help but laugh. Ashley was a former tenant of their building who had made a huge leap from working in a clothing store, to working *it* on porn set. She explained that her life coach encouraged her to think about something she loved to do, then try to find a way to make it a career. She took the advice to heart.

On the day she dropped the bomb, Mariah gave her a sardonic nod while Ava sat in a stunned silence until she walked away, then turned to her friend and asked, "Is she fucking serious?"

"Oh, I think she is." Mariah grinned. "Very serious."

As it turns out, the beautiful red head with long legs and ideal body got the last laugh. A well-known American porn production company quickly hired Ashley and she reportedly had already gained a large fan base: not to mention the income to match. Meanwhile, Chloe moved into her old apartment.

"You know what?" Ava cleared her throat and took another drink of water while observing her friend, as she signaled to the waitress for another glass of wine. Her haunting eyes scanned the room before returning her gaze back to Ava's face. It was almost as if she were taking inventory of everyone in the restaurant. "We thought she was nuts at the time but she was clearly onto something. Now she works for like, two days a month and gets paid a shitload of money."

"Do you know what? I don't know why you are working at *all*," Mariah began to speak as the waitress rushed back with another glass of red wine, interrupting briefly to see if Ava wanted anything else. She smiled and said no, then returned her attention to Mariah, as the waitress rushed off.

"I have to work."

"No you *don't*," Mariah grinned as she rose the glass. The red wine was camouflaged with her cherry colored lipstick and quickly slid with ease into her mouth. Leaning forward, her eyes grew large and piercing. "You have all that money, remember?"

"I do but I still need a little extra income," Ava insisted with a loud sigh. "I don't want to drain my savings account while I'm young, plus I do need some kind of work experience for my resume."

"Oh come on," Mariah said while sitting down her wine glass, although only briefly. "Take some time off. Decide what you *really* want to do. Get away from that fucking accounting bitch." She referred to Ava's boss. "That's what I would do, if I were you. There must be something that interests you—or would you like to follow in the same path as our friend, Ashley?" she teased.

"No, I don't think that would be a good choice for *me*," Ava admitted with a giggle, but briefly considered the idea. Many of the top porn stars were known to be mortal vampires. Their sexual appetites combined with their 'anything goes' attitude made it an ideal position for their kind. "I'm actually checking job posts online and have a few ideas."

"Find what interests you, then look into it. Take a course."

"I don't know," Ava sighed. "I just don't feel like I can focus right now. Ever since my...change, I just can't get my head on straight. I can't concentrate. My thoughts just flip flop around, so it would be useless to try studying something right now." Ava paused. "Is that normal?"

"It's only been what? A year?" Mariah's question appeared to be more of a gentle reminder. "It's difficult to get a leash on everything. You're still more evolved then I was at that point. It's been over 10 years and I barely have my thoughts together *now*," she admitted while finishing another glass of wine. Ava couldn't help but wonder if perhaps her appetite for liquor may have blurred the lines more than being a vampire. She wasn't even sure if her friend had goals: the only thing that she ever discussed regarding the future either involved men or something frivolous, like shopping.

Blinking rapidly, Mariah's eyes scanned the empty glass in her hand as if she hadn't expected its contents to be gone so fast. "It's a slow process. Give yourself a break," she insisted, while smoothly pushing her glass away. "The first years are about learning balance. And to be honest, even if you weren't a vampire, chances are you would be just as confused about life. Being in your 20s isn't always the non-stop partying that everyone thinks it is."

Knowing that Mariah had turned 30 earlier that year, Ava assumed she probably had a good point, but still wondered how to end her restlessness.

"You'll never be the same girl you were before becoming a vampire," Mariah quietly reminded her of something Landon had told her on a few occasions. "But don't turn it into a bad thing. Focus on your powers not on your shortcomings. That's the mistake that a lot of people make."

Ava watched a thoughtful smile curve Mariah's lips and she knew her friend was right. Perhaps she was just looking for excuses to avoid making any decisions. She had made a choice and for better or worse, it was time to accept it.

"If I were you," Mariah leaned in toward Ava and glanced around to make sure no one was listening; fortunately vampires had such advanced hearing that neither had to speak very loud in order for the other to hear. "I'd quit my job, figure out what I wanted to do and in the meanwhile, I'd find that guy you did all weekend and totally feast on him. So what if he isn't a virgin anymore? I'm sure his blood is still pretty pure compared to most of the others." An evil grin passed over her red lips and she winked at Ava.

"Oh please! Sheldon will barely leave me alone as it is," Ava gave her friend a relaxed smile while her fingers played with her napkin. She could feel every last indent in the pattern of the disposable material, right to the warm spot where she had wiped a drop of water from her lips. When nervous, she found herself constantly touching everything, feeling each little shape and texture. For some reason, it made her relax. "He's sent me numerous texts today alone. I think he could be a problem if I don't cut him off now."

"What about," Mariah tilted her head down while her eyes cast upwards, as she carefully studied Ava's face. "What about Landon? You guys were pretty hot and heavy when I first met you. There was one time I thought you were going to drive everyone in the building crazy with that overpowering and distinctive smell of animal sex."

"Come on! You're senses aren't that strong," Ava insisted. Even *she* couldn't smell that kind of thing through the tightly closed doors in her complex. It was also her preference not to either. "Stop teasing me."

"Okay, I confess I'm teasing you a bit," Mariah giggled while leaning back in her chair. "But you have to admit that things were pretty intense for a while."

"Yeah well, that's history," Ava spoke casually but was unable to hide the sadness from her voice.

It was after Bryan disappeared and the two had met on the rooftop, that Landon had become an important person in her life. He helped ease her into the vampire lifestyle, while the two also had a very passionate relationship. Landon had a more intimate understanding of her vulnerable side. In many ways, he had saved her life. That alone would always give them a strong connection regardless of the status of their relationship.

"So?" Mariah thoughtfully tapped her long, red fingernail on the table. "Let it be intense again."

"He's with Chloe now and besides," Ava shook her head in defeat, "I don't think he wants to be with me anymore."

"Chloe?" Mariah rolled her eyes while turning her head in the same direction. It was no secret that she hated Landon's girlfriend even though she had never really gave an explanation as to why. "What is he doing with that Goth ditch pig anyway? She hardly seems like his type. Maybe she is a demon in the sack, cause she isn't winning him over with her intelligence or personality."

"I don't know." Ava considered the catty comments and although not a friend or fan of Chloe, she didn't feel they were necessarily justified.

"You mean she hasn't hit on *you*?" Mariah referred to the fact that Landon's girlfriend was bisexual. "Cause she's hit on me."

"That would be kind of weird, considering," Ava quietly remarked while making a face. Unlike her friend, Ava did find Landon's girlfriend attractive and *did* see what was physically appealing about her. There was something in her mannerisms that said she was fearless, that nothing was off limits. In fact, Mariah would be offended if Ava pointed out that her and Chloe were actually a lot alike in many regards. They were both aggressive about their opinions and passionately took on the role of a grand seductress.

The only difference is that Mariah preferred to do so with a silent allure as opposed to Chloe's blatant need for attention.

"I still say you should look into the Landon thing."

Ava merely smiled and quickly changed the subject.

"Hey Mariah, have you ever heard of immortal vampires?" She eased into the topic that had been on her mind since the weekend conversation with the other vampires. "Landon and Benjamin were talking about them a few days ago. I didn't even know they existed outside of movies. I thought all vampires were mortal, like us."

"I have heard something about that," Mariah wrinkled her flawless forehead as if in deep thought. "I think they reside in Europe, if I'm not mistaken. Although I've never heard for a fact that they are there or even if they *really* exist, for that matter—why do you ask?"

"I don't know," Ava lied and shook her head while briefly avoided eye contact with Mariah. "I was just curious. I thought we were *it* for vampires."

"Are you thinking you'd like to become an immortal?" Mariah bluntly asked but showed no judgment.

"It's crossed my mind," Ava replied truthfully while her fingers ran up and down her glass of water. "I don't know why, but it intrigues me."

"I'm surprised considering all the issues you are having adjusting to being a mortal. It just strikes me odd that you would be interested in making yet another change." Mariah glanced up to see the waitress approach to drop off their bill. Glancing at it, she quickly returned her attention to across the table.

"I know," Ava admitted and knew she had a very valid point. Why did the idea of being immortal appeal to her so much? Yet something coaxed her to learn about this dark cousin to her kind. There was something missing inside her heart and she felt that this could be the answer. Why else would she be thinking about it non-stop since the weekend. There was obviously a reason why she was unable to let it go.

"All I know is that I heard something about their thirst for blood being much stronger than ours," Mariah replied while grabbing her purse and searching through it. "And it is my understanding that they have less of a conscience about how they go about getting it."

"Really?"

"Well, that's what I've heard. It doesn't necessarily mean it's right," Mariah admitted. "It could be just a legend. It's like I said, I didn't know if they really existed at all, so I never really paid attention."

"Landon said that I wouldn't want to be one. He seems to think it would be the worst fate in the world."

"To Landon, it would be." Mariah pointed out with a humored expression on her face, momentarily glancing at an attractive stranger who passed by. "After all, he hardly has accepted the lifestyle he has now. He certainly wouldn't want to be an immortal. And it's like I said, he probably assumes that with the challenges you had to deal with, that you wouldn't want it either."

"What about you," Ava asked curiously. "Would you?"

"If given the chance?" Mariah considered the option. "I don't know. I would have to investigate it farther. However something tells me that it's rarely a choice. I suspect *they* choose you, not the other way around."

"Maybe."

"Probably." Mariah finally pulled out her credit card and glanced at her watch. "We have to get going."

Ava followed her lead and rose from her chair.

"I will do some investigating, if you wish?" Mariah glanced over her shoulder as they headed for the cash register.

"Could you?"

"Most definitely. I might know someone abroad that would have the answers for you," Mariah insisted. "It's no problem at all."

"Thank you."

Ava felt a sudden burst of happiness and her body felt light as she followed Mariah to the cash register.

Chapter Five

Sometimes the normalcy of her life caused Ava to forget that she had some exceptional powers. And the danger of forgetting her strengths, occasionally led to some serious consequences.

Then again, sometimes it was pure ignorance on her behalf.

One such incident happened on a Friday afternoon, following a particularly long and frustrating week of dealing with her boss. And it all began with an email in Ava's work account on the previous Sunday afternoon. It was an email she decided to ignore. After all, wasn't it bad enough that she had to deal with Ann Lee five days a week?

Sure it was part of her job to be alert to emergency work messages, but maybe Ava wasn't near her computer that day. Maybe she forgot to check her email. Maybe her computer was broken. Maybe she was busy. *Maybe* she didn't care.

Not that it mattered. Ava's boss called her on Sunday evening.

"Didn't you receive my email?" Ava sensed tension in her voice and found it ironic that Ms. Lee was irritated with *her*. After all, who interrupted whose day off? She was *just* a receptionist, for Christ sakes.

"What?" Ava decided to play dumb. "What email?"

"I sent an email of great importance to everyone in the office and you're the only one who did not respond," Ann's voice was hostile and accusing. "There is a meeting in the morning before we open. We meet at 7 am!"

Ava rolled her eyes. These 'emergency' meetings rarely had anything to do with her job, but Ms. Lee insisted that she must show up because she was part of the 'team'. Failing to do so would most likely be held against her.

"Ah…okay," she slowly replied and was about to ask what the meeting was regarding, when Ms. Lee abruptly disconnected the call.

The following morning, Ann Lee announced that it was *vital* everyone put 110% into their work because some *key* people from head office were planning a visit in the near future. This included the company's CEO, Derrick Johnston.

Not that Ava cared.

She listened to her boss rant about how any mistakes made at Anderson & Smith that week, could result in terminations the *next* week. Ava's face grew hot with embarrassment when her boss automatically looked in her direction, while making this comment. Some of her coworkers followed Ms. Lee's eyes and Ava lowered her head in humiliation.

Things didn't improve as the days moved forward. Ann Lee was constantly on her ass about everything from a misspelling, to returning five minutes late from lunch. It just seemed like the woman wanted to find reasons to fire her and although Ava hated her job, she certainly didn't want to suffer the humiliation of being forced out. She felt her resentment grow throughout the week and found she was constantly fantasizing about the middle-aged Chinese woman falling down a flight of stairs. Her menopausal bones were probably not very strong and well, wouldn't that make her less likely to walk away unharmed?

What was wrong with having a little fantasy?

As it turned out, Ava wasn't the only one who was growing frustrated. She could sense the tension among her coworkers. People were very tense and clearly ready to snap at the drop of a hat. There was a great deal of concern over why the company CEO would bother to make a visit to their office because it was considered most unusual to do so. People feared that it meant bad news and braced for the worst.

By Thursday morning, everyone was starting to wonder if the CEO and others were still intending to visit their office at all—or was this merely a threat to keep everyone on their toes. Ann Lee certainly wasn't becoming any calmer as the week progressed; while Ava did everything she could to avoid her boss all together.

On Friday morning, most of Ava's coworkers were starting to relax. After all, the week was almost over and everyone assumed nothing would happen that close to the weekend. Meanwhile, Ann Lee seemed much like a disappointed child who had her favorite toy ripped from her arms. Ava almost felt sorry for the pathetic little woman and in some ways, she related to that emptiness.

While everyone else gave a sigh of relief, Ava continued to anticipate the visitors. She knew they were coming that morning. Her instincts were all but screaming out the prediction, but Ava herself could not say a word. Not even when they arrived on the fourth floor and were walking off the elevator, when the strong scents of both arrogance and money overpowered the hallway and seeped under the door. And there was something else that she did not recognize. It almost felt like a smell she was familiar with but it was somewhat *off*, causing her nose to twitch.

Three men entered the office wearing very expensive designer suits and barely uttering a simple 'hello' to Ava, while she felt obligated to stand up from her seat and give them a warm and friendly welcome.

"Good morning gentlemen!" She faked a huge smile while quickly scanning each of their faces. The first of the three was a very unhappy and unfriendly man who appeared to be in his late 30s or early 40s, barely glancing in her direction before surveying the waiting area. The second man was older, probably well into his 50s and appeared to have led a difficult life. His face had a couple of prominent scars and Ava noticed his tanned complexion to be somewhat oily in appearance. His dark eyes almost stared through her and there was something unsettling about this man that she automatically recognized, but yet she forced herself to ignore it. *This can't be possible. Isn't this the CEO, Derrick Johnston?*

She quickly turned her attention toward the Japanese man that followed the other two, the first and only one to smile at Ava and say a simple hello. But even as the two exchanged pleasantries, she still felt the overpowering sensation of the CEO focused gaze. He only stopped when Ann Lee flew out of her office and to the front desk.

"Ava, you should've told me that the gentlemen were here," she softly scolded the receptionist before turning her attention back to the men. Ann offered to show them around, but with a strong British accent, the CEO declined. He insisted that they did not have time and that it was necessary to start their meeting as soon as possible. After Ava was told to make coffee and order food, almost everyone seemed to escape into the conference area.

When she was finally able to collapse in her chair and think about what had just happened, Ava was overwhelmed. Her body felt as though electric currents were running through it, especially her arms—but she ignored the strange sensation. Her mind was racing too fast to concentrate on her physical discomforts.

Ava glanced toward the conference room door and even though it was closed, she could feel the dark eyes of the CEO still glaring in her direction. She recognized the strong scent that the average person would miss, not to mention the slight glow in the back of this man's eyes. There was a darkness that seemed to follow him into the room, a chill in the air that was unlike anything she had experienced before and yet, an odd silence that most human ears could not recognize. The feeling was almost overpowering to Ava and a part of her wanted to get up from her desk and run out of the building. But she didn't. She stayed. And thought.

Was it really possible that Derrick Johnston—the CEO of Anderson & Smith—was also a vampire?

But yet, he wasn't one of *them*. There was something distinctively different about this man, when compared to all the vampires that held residence in her apartment building. His presence was not as ordinary or average in comparison. It was intimidating. It wasn't even so much what she smelled or saw, but the weakness that automatically filled her body upon him entering the room.

She would have to discuss it with Benjamin after work that night. She was anxious to pick his brain on the matter.

Ava attempted to ignore her anxieties and work on rescheduling that day's appointments. Carefully watching the clock, she was relieved to see that the meeting had not ended before her lunch break. Dashing into the neighboring office, Ava quickly let the intern Nisha know that she was heading out for an hour. She wanted to get as far away from that building as possible. Ava assumed that the meeting would end sometime while she was still out for lunch.

But she was wrong.

In fact, the meeting was just concluding as she stepped back into the reception area of Anderson & Smith. Ava noted that Nisha was showing signs of nervousness as well and appeared relieved that her coworker had returned. When everyone departed from the conference room, Ava noticed that her boss looked pale and physically drained, especially when compared to how she appeared that morning. What exactly had taken place during the meeting? The door was completely airtight, so she was unable to eavesdrop.

Sliding behind her desk and diving into her work, Ava was hoping to go unnoticed by the head office guys as they departed. But luck wasn't on her side. She could feel the Derrick Johnston's cold glare once again, and Ava noticed the pen in her hand start to shake, while her heart raced frantically. The power behind this man's eyes was nothing short of astronomical and it sent waves of fear through her body. Did he know she was a vampire? Was she correct in believing he was one too?

But it was just as they were finally about to leave, that single moment when Ava felt her body start to relax, that everything came crashing down. Derrick Johnston directed his full attention toward Ava and announced to Ann Lee that he wanted to have a 'brief meeting' with the company's receptionist in the conference room.

Ava felt her eyes widen in horror, as she exchanged astonished looks with her boss. Ms. Lee possibly appeared even more concerned than Ava actually felt at that moment. Had the situation been different and the CEO had *not* been a vampire, then perhaps she would've relished this moment—if for no other reason than to worry her boss. But that was not the case. Ava wondered if there was any polite way to say no, but quickly realized it was out of the question.

She silently headed toward the conference room while butterflies filled her stomach. Derrick Johnston followed her, quietly closing the door behind them. Feeling all the color drain from her face, Ava turned around and felt her heart pounding wildly, while she looked into the CEO's black eyes. He gave her a small, curious smile and signaled for her to sit down. He did the same.

"So Ava, I'm going to get right to the point," He continued to watch her and she briefly wondered how anyone could *not* see that there was something very unusual about this man? He was very unnerving to be near and she felt her hands start to shake again. Sitting at the end of the table, Derrick looked much more relaxed than he had with her boss, only minutes earlier. He studied her face, folding his perfectly manicured hands together. She felt her throat grow dry and sweat forming underneath her bra. "I know you are a vampire."

Ava didn't respond one way or another. She just sat and stared at him. Frozen.

"Just as you know that I am one also, except I am immortal." He hesitated, as if briefly waiting for a reaction. She had none. She was too stunned and felt her eyes widen in size. *So that was the unusual scent I was picking up on.* "And I don't have a problem with that. However, I do have a problem with this hex that you put on Ms. Lee."

"Thh-the what?" Ava stumbled over the words. "I put a- I did what?"

"You certainly have put a hex on your boss!" His lips curved into a slight grin. "And although I can understand why you have done so, I need you to remove it right away. Ms. Lee's well-being is of no interest to me, however, her position here is very important and I need it to be consistent."

Ava was stunned. How the hell did she put a hex on her boss? And how was she supposed to remove it?

"I-I will try."

"You have to more than try," Derrick curtly remarked. "You *must* remove it. Do you know how to do so?"

Ava shook her head no.

"How long have you been one of us?" He leaned closer to her and she felt faint.

"One year." Her voice was small and pathetic.

"And since you are a new vampire, I doubt you even are aware that you put hexes on people." His tone was almost soothing and Ava felt intoxicated by his stare.

She shook her head no.

"New vampires are always clumsy and uninformed," He spoke of mortals as if they were idiots. "So many change for the wrong reasons. They want to live like the fictional vampires in the movies and books, completely unaware of the responsibilities involved."

"They want to enjoy the sexuality but live like humans," A grin crossed his face. "Not realizing that it's a life changing decision. Not looking into their powers in advance. It's very stupid. Idiots! "

Ava wanted to convince Derrick Johnston that she had no idea about the hex or how to get rid of it. But at the same time, she feared his reaction.

A sudden commotion in the outer office abruptly ended their conversation. They both rose from their chairs and rushed toward the door to see what was going on. Nisha was running frantically back into the office with panic on her face.

"Ms. Lee fell down the stairs!" She cried out as she grabbed for the phone while people either ran out the door or gathered around Nisha, to learn more information. Even the two men who had accompanied Derrick Johnston that day had a glimmer of concern in their eyes. Beside Ava, the CEO gave her a dark gaze.

"She said she needed air and was going outside with me but just as we got to the top of the stairs, Ms. Lee tripped and fell. There's blood on her face and OH MY GOD, I'-

She suddenly stopped, to answer the 911 operator's questions. Ava bit her lip and exchanged looks with Derrick. He slowly shook his head in disapproval.

Chapter Six

Ava's boss broke her ankle. The doctors weren't certain of the extent of damage but since she was in so much pain, they speculated that it could be weeks before Ann Lee would be able to return to work.

However, it was immediately after the accident and before this diagnosis, that Derrick Johnston discretely pulled Ava aside.

"You're enjoying this, aren't you?" He hissed, just as the injured party was being taken away by ambulance. Stunned by the news that she had any part in the accident at all, Ava didn't know how to respond to that question. To be honest, a part of her *had* enjoyed watching her boss suffer. But was it possible that this incident was the result of a hex? A hex, which was caused by nothing more than her own cruel fantasies and hatred toward Ann Lee? Was that even believable?

"I told you, I don't know how I did it." She spoke honestly and felt her heart lurch in fear. Was she in danger? Was it possible that this man could kill her? After all, Mariah had recently told her that immortal vampires had little in the way of a conscience. Considering Derrick, felt that Ann Lee was an essential part of Anderson & Smith and her absence would affect the office, it was easy to see how Ava could be blamed for any disruptions.

"You naive little wench!" His darting eyes caused her body to freeze in terror, while Ava's stomach did flip-flops. A cold sweat broke out on her forehead and for a moment she felt tension crawl through her shoulders, as she anticipated him to pounce on her. She had never seen such a look of fury in anyone's eyes. And there was one thing Ava knew for certain—if Derrick Johnston wanted her dead, then dead she would be.

His eyes were glazed over and he slowly started to move away from her and silently gestured for the other two men to follow him, which they did. The three headed toward the exit and the Japanese man muttered something about being in touch soon. Then they were gone.

Ava felt like her entire body would crumble to the floor and she quickly slumped over in a waiting area chair. No one had appeared to notice her conversation with the company's CEO, nor her reaction to his departure. In fact, everyone was so busy discussing the events of the day, that they weren't answering their own phones or returning to work. Ava momentarily considered that perhaps this was the reason why Derrick Johnston was so concerned about the office's well being, if Ms. Lee wasn't there to oversee things.

Eventually, everything got back to order. Ava felt slightly robotic for the remainder of the afternoon, as fear for her life continued to plague her. Would she be found dead somewhere between that evening and Monday morning? It hardly seemed fair to be blamed for Ms. Lee's accident—but fair or not, it was *her* that Mr. Johnston blamed. Had there been a way she could've prevented it?

She finally decided to push her fears aside and focus on work. There had to be a solution. She would simply discuss the situation with Benjamin after returning home. He was the one person who seemed intrigued with the immortals and might be able to shed some light on the situation.

The clock had never ticked as slow as it had that afternoon. When her day was finally over, Nisha approached Ava to see if she would be interested in visiting Ms. Lee in the hospital sometime that weekend. Of course the idea held no appeal for Ava, but she hurriedly insisted that Nisha contact her the next day and they would work out something. The two girls said their good-byes and Ava rushed out the door and flew into the elevator, happy to get as far away as possible. She had to get back to the apartment complex and talk to Benjamin.

But when Ava returned to the building, he wasn't there. She didn't see him in the lounge area and there was no answer at his door. Her face was flustered from all the rushing; a silent tornado ran through her veins and pumped fear into every inch of Ava's body. Leaning against the door, she felt exhausted and upset. What could she do now? Grabbing her cell phone, she sent a text to Mariah: it was the third since the entire hex incident from that afternoon and Ava wasn't too sure she'd receive a reply. Although she was a wonderful friend, Mariah wasn't exactly famous for checking her Blackberry on a regular basis. She also had a way of disappearing on the weekends.

Feeling overwhelmed, Ava slowly turned toward the elevator. Lost in a volatile combination of thoughts and fears, she jumped when someone said her name. It was Landon's voice.

She slowly turned around to see concern in his face, as he leaned partway out his apartment door. It temporarily slipped her mind that he and Benjamin were neighbors. This was the closest she had come to his door since their romantic relationship ended. It had been at least six months.

"What's going on?" He studied Ava's face. Her exaggerated heart rate filled up the silence of the hallway. Landon tilted his head and reluctantly continued. "I can actually smell your fear. What's wrong?"

"You can..smell my fear?" Ava suddenly felt defeated. The connection they shared often made her uncomfortable. His stare was making her feel weak, crushed and because of their history, full of shame. Sometimes she felt as though the past was well behind her while other times, such as at *that* moment, she felt it would haunt her forever.

"Yes," Landon gave her a compassionate smile and hesitantly stepped back, gesturing toward his apartment. "Do you want to come in for a few minutes? It might be more comfortable than talking in the hallway."

Ava nodded and silently walked past him through the doorway. She was surprised when her libido made a surprising reappearance as soon as she stepped foot into the apartment. His overpowering presence in the room was stronger than she had remembered and when Ava turned back to glance at him, she thought she saw lust in his eyes. Clearing her throat, she sat on the couch while he closed the door.

"What's going on?" Landon slowly crossed the floor and sat down beside her. He was too close. Heat surged through her body and quickly distracted Ava from her fear. It was hardly the first time they had been alone together since ending their affair months earlier, yet it *was* her first time in his apartment. Perhaps stepping into the main location of their affair brought back the old physical memories. It was confusing and she struggled to understand.

"I-ah," She couldn't look in his eyes but instead looked intently down at her own legs. Although it was hardly visible, they were trembling. "I had a weird experience at work today and I thoughts maybe, since Benjamin seems to know a lot about vampires and the immortals, he might be able to help me." She shyly glanced in his direction.

"What exactly happened at your work to bring this up?" Landon's eyes showed no sign of emotion but studied her face. "Did you have some kind of strange reaction to something?"

"Well, yes and no," Ava reluctantly admitted.

"Ava, I know I'm not Benjamin, but clearly I know a few things about this subject." He spoke calmly and she noticed that he moved slightly closer to her. It was almost completely unnoticeable, but she could feel her body's reaction to his presence grow. Could he tell that she wanted him? She quickly looked away and took in the apartment that was almost identical to her own. "After all, I've been researching this for years, trying to find a way to get rid of this curse. Along the way, I'd like to think I learned a few things. So what happened?"

Ava sighed and began to explain. "The CEO of the company arrived in our office today and to make a long story short, I recognized him as a vampire."

"Wow! Your CEO actually went by your work? That's weird. They usually prefer to stay clear of the people actually *doing* the work," Landon attempted to make her laugh but it was clear that she was immersed in discomfort and unable to see the humor in his comment. "You know, it's not that odd that a CEO would also be a vampire."

"Yes, but you don't understand," Ava rushed to explain and without meaning to, edged closer to Landon. The heat that had already spread throughout her body was only growing now. "I mean he's an immortal."

Now, Landon looked alarmed. His eyes widened and his entire body appeared tense. "How do you know this?"

"He had a slightly different scent, but I didn't think anything about it at first 'cause I thought I smelled it before," Ava shrugged nervously. "A lot of vampires have different scents." She sighed. "He took me aside and told me he was an immortal. Then he asked me to take a hex off my boss."

"What?" Landon suddenly seemed lost. "You have a hex on your boss?" A small grin almost crossed his lips but seemed to stall. "You know *how* to put hexes on people?"

"I didn't think I did," Ava quietly admitted. "I-I kind of found out by accident."

"It's something that we usually don't discuss," Landon acknowledged, his hand running through his short hair. Even watching him touch himself in such a casual way created a fire that raced through her thighs and she briefly had to look away and change the direction of her thoughts. Why did he have this influence over her? Other vampires did not. It was discouraging to know how powerless she felt in the moment. "Most vampires aren't able to put a hex on someone unless they know how, and I didn't think you did."

"That makes two of us."

He slowly nodded. "You must really hate someone and sincerely wish them harm in order for it to happen. It's a little more complicated than that, I confess, but essentially that's what it comes down to."

"I guess I really hated her then," Ava admitted. "Because she had an accident today. She fell down the stairs."

"Wow!" Landon's mouth fell open ajar.

"And now this CEO is blaming me for taking her out of his office. He apparently needs her and I fucked it up," Ava hurriedly continued her story, while shaking her head. "I'm scared. What if he hurts me?"

"I don't think he'll hurt you."

"He was really angry," Ava confessed, searching Landon's poker face. "I think he might."

"He won't." Landon was adamant. "So basically he's concerned that no one can replace your boss? Or am I misunderstanding, and he's concerned about her personally?"

"No, it's totally about the office." Ava maintained. "Not about her."

"Then don't worry," Landon insisted, sitting back in his seat. "He'll find someone. The vampire community is a resourceful one when it comes to problems that need solving. He certainly cannot blame you for doing something you hadn't realized you could do."

"He was really mad and he *is* immortal. Don't they play by different rules?" Ava quietly asked, momentarily forgetting the sexual tension she felt between them.

"Yes and no," Landon's voice was smooth and soothing. "But chances are, his anger won't prevail. Vampires rarely hurt their own, especially for something so minor and easily fixable. I don't think you have a reason to worry. But just curious, what is this man's name?"

"Derrick Johnston."

Landon slowly nodded, while the tension in his face seemed to dissipate. "You have nothing to worry about."

"Landon, I'm not so sure," Ava turned slightly, accidentally touching his knee with her own. A shot of electricity flew through her body and this time, she could tell their desire was matched. Although he attempted to hide it, his breathing suddenly became slightly labored and she could see some minor, physical reactions with of his body.

"You will be okay," He cleared his throat and seemed to moved away marginally. "He won't harm you, I'm positive."

"But how do you know so much about immortals?" Ava felt desperate to understand the truth about their kind. How could Landon be so certain that she wasn't in danger? "Can't you tell me what you know? Maybe I could deal with this situation better."

"It's not necessary," Landon rose from his seat and as if to dismiss her, walked toward the door. "I have some things to do, Ava—if you don't mind. I promise you that you're safe and encourage you to not worry about this for another minute. This man probably already has the problem solved and has long forgotten your role in the issue."

"Oh, I-okay," Ava rose from her seat, managing to keep her legs steady as she headed toward the door. Glancing at the clock, she realized that Chloe would finish her job at the tattoo parlor soon and was probably going right to Landon's place, on her way to her own apartment. Like Ava, Landon finished work earlier in the day. "I want to learn more though. Eventually?"

"There's nothing to learn," Landon sounded very casual as he watched her stop at the door. "There's really nothing, don't worry about it."

Ava didn't believe him but quickly left. She'd find out on her own.

Chapter Seven

"I was looking for you yesterday," Ava sang out as she approached Benjamin in the lounge area. It was the afternoon following her conversation with Landon.

Sitting alone in the usual spot, he had a national newspaper opened to the business section. Glancing up at Ava, his eyebrows rose slightly and a mischievous grin crossed his face. Slowly lowering the paper, he gave her a curious stare.

"You were looking for me? What an oddity," He appeared amused by her confession. "Whatever would possess you to look for me, of all people?"

Ava sighed and sat across from the older man. Taking a deep breath, she launched into the entire story about Derrick Johnston, the hex and finally what Landon had said about the whole situation. She noted that the longer she talked, all signs of humor evaporated from Benjamin's face.

"I see," he finally remarked after she had finished her story. "You had an eventful day."

Ava felt slightly defeated by his response. It wasn't that she had anticipated him to be upset over the events of her Friday; however, Ava had expected more of a reaction. Especially considering Benjamin had openly discussed his attempts to locate immortal vampires during his youth. Wouldn't this information be of some value to him? Why were Benjamin and Landon both so dismissive about this entire situation? Was it just her imagination that this was sort of a *big* deal?

"That's putting it mildly," Ava muttered while attempting to search Benjamin's face for some kind of reaction, but just like with Landon, there was none. She shuffled uncomfortably in her chair. "I wanted to talk to you yesterday because I was worried of what Derrick Johnston would do to me. Also I knew you were also interested in immortal vampires and thought maybe this information would be of interest to you?"

"Oh, and it is," Benjamin gently folded his newspaper and sat it on the couch. "But it would've been of more interest when I was younger. Now tell me this Ava, what do you know about this Derrick Johnston?"

"Nothing," Ava shrugged while shrinking in the chair. She was getting the distinct feeling that other than herself, no one else really cared about her discovery. "I could immediately tell he was a vampire, but it wasn't until he told me that he was immortal that I had any idea."

"Are you sure he was being truthful?"

Ava had never considered this question. What if he was lying? What if Derrick Johnston had sensed her naivety and saw his ability to intimidate her? But no—there had been something distinctly different about her company's CEO. She had known it even before he walked through the door. "No, I'm sure he was telling the truth."

"And you think you are in danger?"

"Well maybe," she hesitated for a moment. "But when I spoke to Landon, he didn't think so. He insisted that I would be fine because vampires rarely turn on their own—but I'm not so sure."

"Landon said this?" Benjamin asked, looking at her intently. His forehead seemed to wrinkle slightly, while the rest of his face began to relax. "Well then, I would say Landon is probably right."

What?

"J-just, I mean," Ava began to stumble through her words awkwardly. Why was Benjamin now following Landon's lead and also dropping this topic abruptly? She felt frustration fill her body, followed by fear—did they both know something that they weren't telling her? What if Derrick Johnston was very powerful and they both didn't want to reveal the horrible truth—that her death was unavoidable? Worse yet, what if neither Benjamin nor Landon cared what happened to her? Why was she being dismissed? "I don't understand? Why am I the only person who thinks this is a big deal?"

"Because you are in the middle of the situation and aren't able to see it clearly," Benjamin reminded her and Ava had to admit that his point was a valid one. He continued to study her face quietly before saying another word. "Ava, you have nothing to fear. After all, both Landon and I have been vampires for a great deal of time so if we both assure you of your safety, then there's nothing to worry about. Do you really think we would let another vampire come along and hurt you?"

She didn't answer.

"Of course not," Benjamin made a funny face in an attempt to lighten the mood. "It would never happen with either of us around. I assure you that this Derrick character was speaking out of anger and being a dramatic fool and nothing more."

"But aren't you interested in the fact that he is immortal?" Ava asked again. This didn't make sense. It hadn't been long ago that Benjamin had spoken of his curiosity regarding the immortals. In fact, he had sat on that very couch and talked about his longing to be one in his youth. Even if he no longer wanted to turn, wouldn't he still find the information fascinating?

"Oh yes, it is of interest to me," Benjamin nodded apprehensively. "I just am very surprised that he admitted this fact to you. As I mentioned to you before, I had a great deal of trouble finding one of the immortals in my own searches. No one was talking and they were carefully hidden away. That's why I questioned whether or not this man was telling you the truth. It just seems rather odd to me that he would be so open with a stranger."

That was a good point. Ava was starting to wonder the same thing. "I guess to scare me?"

"Once again," Benjamin's face seemed to relax. "Just another reason why I question his honesty. He might've just wanted to frighten you."

"But there was something very different about this man," Ava thought back to the powerful scent that announced Mr. Johnston before he even entered the room. It was the penetrating stare he gave her as they sat together in the boardroom, while his voice sent shivers through her spine. The only other vampire that ever had such a strong presence with Ava was Landon, and that was a completely different scenario.

"Well, perhaps you are right then," Benjamin considered her point. "Maybe he is an immortal. Again, I just find it odd that he would reveal the truth to you. Very odd."

Ava silently agreed and finally decided to return to her apartment. She felt the same disappointment that had followed her conversation with Landon the previous afternoon. There was an emptiness in both their reactions that was unsettling to her, but she was unable to articulate the origin of these feelings. Was she simply being a drama queen? Neither had been able to eliminate her fear.

The remainder of the weekend was pretty uneventful. Ava spent most of it lounging around her apartment feeling despondent. For some reason, events such as this brought out all her harbored depression that never stayed hidden for very long. It was the dark, self-hating side of her personality that constantly reminded her that she was very alone in the world. Everyone had family: she had a grandmother that showed her no comfort. Everyone had a romantic partner: she had a string of meaningless affairs and none of which loved her. Everyone had at least one close friend that was only a phone call away: she had Mariah, who usually wasn't prompt to return her calls.

In fact, it was late Sunday evening when Mariah finally got back to the text messages that Ava had sent early on Friday. After receiving the latest updates stating that Landon and Benjamin didn't think she had anything to fear, Mariah merely agreed with them and said the two would meet for lunch sometime that week.

Nisha was the first person Ava saw on Monday morning. Cringing, she remembered her half-hearted promise to visit their boss at the hospital during the weekend. Fortunately, her coworker quickly commented on how Ann Lee wasn't actually admitted and she seemed embarrassed that she had jumped to such a conclusion. Nisha also had some interesting news.

"Mr Johnston found someone to replace Ms Lee while she is out." She shot Ava a brilliant smile, while her warm eyes shone brightly. "He starts sometime this week. I guess he's highly regarded."

"Really?" Ava felt the tension that had lived in her body all weekend, slowly start to melt away. She was surprised to find herself still feeling slightly ill. The news should've made her happy but something told her that she wasn't completely off the hook. "Who is it?"

"I'm not sure," Nisha confessed. "They didn't give us a name, just said that he's to start this week. Apparently Mr. Johnston is arriving later this morning to have a meeting with everyone regarding this news."

Ava was the exception to 'everyone', but she certainly didn't mind. Of course she would be in charge of ordering in food, making the coffee and being the servant/receptionist for the morning. Even Nisha, who often shared duties with her, would be attending the meeting.

It was an hour later when Ava once again picked up on the distinctive scent that filled the hallways and drifted under the door. She briefly considered Benjamin's question about whether or not the vampire was immortal and quickly dismissed it. There was no way he was mortal. The fragrance was almost overbearing—in fact, it didn't at all resemble that which filled her apartment building. And she realized that perhaps it wasn't so much the unusual smell itself, as the reaction it had on her body. Was this just because of her heightened senses, or did those who weren't vampires feel the effects as well?

There was an unmistakable presence that surrounded the company's CEO as he entered the office. It was an air of confidence and strength that Ava greatly envied. And behind him stood a tall, attractive man who appeared to be in his early 30s. With an olive complexion and large, chocolate eyes, the stranger offered her a warm, friendly smile, while Ava momentarily wondered what it would be like to run her hands through his shiny, black hair. He was gorgeous and his fragrance was rich and superb, but one she was unable to identify.

"Miss Ava Lilith," Derrick spoke to her in such a kind tone that she felt her eyes widen in shock: not to mention her surprise that the company's CEO even remembered her first name, let alone knew her last. "I would like you to meet Ms. Lee's replacement for the upcoming weeks. This is Matthew Crole."

"Hi Ava," his intoxicating eyes seemed to dance as he reached over and shook her hand. She could feel the intense charge as they touched and automatically knew that it was going to be difficult to work with such an incredibly handsome man. His scent filled the room upon arrival and it was invigorating. However, it was pretty clear that he was not a vampire. "It's very *nice* to meet you."

She noted a slight change in his voice when he uttered the word 'nice' and slowly nodded and smiled. "You too."

"Matthew, I will show you to the board room. We're a bit early but the meeting will be starting shortly."

The two disappeared and Ava felt herself exhale.

Wow

Before she could reconnect with a feeling of ease, Derrick returned to her desk and leaned forward, as if to tell a secret.

"I just wanted to apologize for my harsh words last week." He spoke sincerely, managing to throw Ava completely off guard. His eyes displayed an unexpected softness this time and his voice was warm and friendly. "I was completely out of line speaking to you in that manner."

Ava was stunned and opened her mouth to say something, but couldn't speak.

"I was caught up in an angry moment that had nothing to do with you and I overreacted," A slight nervousness entered his voice and Ava was stunned. "Please forgive me."

"Ah, sure.."

"Thank you." He nodded and reached over the desk to briefly touch her hand. And with that, he turned and marched back into the boardroom. Ava was shocked.

Chapter Eight

"Are you *serious*? All this happened since last week?" Mariah's eyes were huge as she listened to Ava's account of the weekend, followed by the Monday morning conversation with Derrick Johnston. It was the first time the two spoke since the whole immortal vampire issue surfaced.

"And we're what? Wednesday?" Mariah grabbed her Blackberry and hit a button, while Ava eyes scanned the restaurant that had become their usual hangout. All around them, other guests were sharing stories, laughing and appeared fully engaged in their specific conversations. It was a pleasant atmosphere.

"Yes, it's Wednesday," Ava replied and caught Mariah staring at her a phone a little longer than necessary to simply check the date. Quickly hitting a few buttons, it was obvious she was browsing through her text messages. Normally Ava would've been a little annoyed by her lack of consideration, but there was something in her friend's face, suggesting that something was just not right. "Is everything okay?"

"What? Ah, yes. Everything is fine," Mariah made eye contact with her once again, appearing slightly disorientated, while clearly trying to mask it with a smile. "I'm sorry, Ava." She cleared her throat and shook her head as if to shake out the thoughts that were trying to invade her mind. "That's terrible. I'm really sorry that I wasn't in contact with you sooner. I had no idea things were *that* insane. Your messages were kind of vague, so I guess I underestimated the situation."

"It's fine. There's nothing you could've done anyway." Ava heard herself commenting, even though she secretly was disappointed that her friend took so long to get back to her. At the time, she really could've used someone to help extinguish her fears. Then again, how many friends did Ava have; was she really in the position to start ostracizing one of the few people in her life?

"I know, but I must not seem like much of a friend," Mariah slowly slid her Blackberry away from her and reached for the glass of red wine she had barely touched. "So, it sounds like Landon and Benjamin were trying to dodge your questions. And why was this Derrick guy kissing your ass on Monday?"

Ava watched her friend take a long drink of wine just before beckoning for the waitress to come over. By the time she did, Mariah had emptied her glass.

"I expected as much from Landon, but not Benjamin," Ava confessed after the waitress left. She was picking at her Caesar salad but stress along with the repulsive odor from the next table, gave her little desire to eat. Mariah seemed more intrigued with her wine than the sandwich she had purchased. "I thought he'd have a million questions since he claims to have looked all over the world to find immortals. But he didn't seem to care. Made light of it, as if it was nothing. Both of them did."

"As for Derrick Johnston," Ava continued, using her fork to move a crouton around her plate; the lettuce tasted bitter and the dressing had too much salt. "I don't know what's his deal is. He was ready to rip my head off on Friday and totally apologizing on Monday. Since then I've been waiting for the other shoe to drop, but so far there's nothing."

"Weird," Mariah's face seemed to be in deep concentration but Ava wasn't so sure it was over her problems. The waitress returned with another glass of wine and her friend seemed to snap out of her daze. When they were alone again, she took a long drink then added, "I don't understand."

"Me neither."

"But at least you got rid of that old cunt of a boss," Mariah raised one eyebrow and sipped on her wine. "And a hex? Wow! I might need you to do me a few favors if you can put hexes on people. The world would *not* be a safe place if *I* could do it." Her lips curved into a malicious grin, while her fingers slid up and down the stem of her glass. Her eyes were dark and lifeless, even though she attempted to fake a smile.

"I don't even know how I did it the first time," Ava chuckled sheepishly. "Oh and get this—on top of everything, Ms. Lee's replacement is super hot."

"Really?" Mariah leaned forward in interest.

"Gorgeous," Ava nodded. "He's...beautiful." Ava recalled the handsome man that all the women at her work were swooning after like teenaged girls. And although he was clearly a very attractive man—with his alluring smile, friendly eyes and expensive suits—there was just something about him that didn't appeal to Ava. He was attractive, outgoing and perfect—so, what was wrong with her?

"I'm intrigued," Mariah beamed and slowly started to become herself again. "You'll have to get a *leg* up on that, as they say."

"He's my boss," Ava reminded her, laughing at her friend's predictable reaction.

"Just till 4:30," Mariah insisted in a singsong voice while finishing her second glass of wine. The two women shared a smile and Ava shook her head as Mariah continued. "Not that I am opposed to having sex during work hours. Although," she hesitated and her eyes shifted toward a nearby bar and back again. "That did get me fired once."

Ava briefly recalled the details of that story and somehow doubted Mariah showed any more shame for her actions at the time, as she did when giving the details to her friend afterward. It was easy to envy her courage and her willingness to live life on her own terms, regardless of the consequences.

The rest of the afternoon slid by with ease. Ava was relieved to finally go home, but surprised to find Landon sitting in the lounge area of the apartment building. It wasn't unusual for him to be there, just not during that particular time of day. She momentarily considered ignoring him, but guiltily changed her mind. He automatically looked up as she approached.

"Hey," her voice sounded small and weak, like that of a frightened child. She hadn't expected it to come out that way and was quite surprised when it did.

"Hey," his amber eyes scanned her body while his lips curved into a smile. Landon was in his office attire, which consisted of a blue, pinstriped shirt and dress pants. He worked at a telecommunication company that had a pretty liberal dress code, but he preferred to look professional. "What's up?" He tilted his head slightly, inspecting her face.

"Not much," Ava said while continuing to stand in front of him. For some reason, she felt overly exposed in her pencil skirt and heels, even though it wasn't the first time Landon saw her dress in this fashion. "How's work?"

"The same. You know, just convincing people to buy things they don't need or want." He referred to his job in the marketing department, while giving a boyish grin that caused her to briefly look away.

Ava nodded uncomfortably. She couldn't stop thinking about the last time they were together in his apartment. There was definitely some discomfort between them again today.

"So, ah, thanks for your help on Friday," Ava spoke clumsily, pushing through her fears of vulnerability. "I appreciate it."

"I didn't really help you that much." He cleared his throat and for the first time, looked away from her face. "I just calmed you down. That's it."

"No, you did more than that," Ava insisted shyly, nervously playing with the zipper on her purse. "You were the voice of reason; I guess I kind of overreacted."

"Well sometimes vampires like this Derrick guy like to push their weight around," Landon glanced back in her face but this time, he seemed to avoid eye contact. "You know, just like everyone else. You can't let them get to you."

"It's a little different with an immortal vampire," Ava reminded him. "He could kill me."

"Well, yes and no," Landon ran his fingers through his hair and Ava automatically thought of all the times she had done the same. His hair was so inviting to touch: soft and silky. This memory led her back to their intimate times together and she quickly changed her thoughts, although she noted his eyes were once again searching her face. Could he read her mind? She *really* hoped not. "Why don't you sit down, Ava." He pointed at the seat across from him.

"Oh, yeah, okay," she clumsily did so, her fingers nervously playing with the strap of her purse. Although he was being very kind to her, she felt completely tongue-tied.

"See, this is the thing," Landon chose his words carefully watching her reaction. "He could've killed you, but really, so could anyone. He was trying to frighten you. And as you know, a lot of the things that you see or hear about vampires are untrue. Even immortal vampires aren't as vicious as they are made out to be on television or in books."

"Yeah, but they have less of a conscience," Ava reminded him. After all, hadn't it been Landon that told her that at one time? Or was it Mariah?

"Yeah, that part is true," Landon seemed hesitant to agree. "They aren't as in control of their impulses as mortal vampires but they aren't complete animals either. They're more likely to kill for blood than they are to out of anger." He paused. "And even that is pretty unlikely. He wasn't going to kill you over an error. I'm sure he later thought about your predicament and realized that you had no idea what you were doing. And even if you had Ava, it clearly would've been too late to change the course of that situation."

"True," she certainly wasn't as concerned about the situation as she had been a few days earlier, but one thought did linger. "Do you think I am capable of putting a hex on someone again? I mean, do you think I can control this power?"

"Just be aware of it, but chances are you won't again unless someone really brings out that much anger and passion in you." He glanced down at some mail that was sitting on his laptop bag before continuing. "I think now that you know it's a possibility, you will have a better handle on it."

"Yeah," She looked down at her fingers, which continued to nervously play with the strap on her purse.

"So, have you had any other issues with this Derrick guy since we spoke?" Landon asked, shoving the mail into his bag. He eagerly looked in her direction.

"No, he actually showed up at my work again on Monday," Ava started to explain and noticed Landon's eyes widening in interest. "But it was only to introduce the replacement for Ms. Lee."

"Wow, replacement already?" Landon confidently smiled, then nodded. "What did I tell you? I knew it wouldn't take long."

"No, you were right about that," Ava replied suspiciously. "But he also apologized for being so rash with me on Friday."

"Nice!" Landon raised his eyebrows and his face beamed. "That's perfect."

"I was surprised."

"I bet."

"But I'm glad," Ava rushed to continue. "Although I didn't really trust it, especially at first."

"It's natural to be suspicious," Landon insisted. "Especially where he did a complete 180 in a weekend. But it's a good surprise. He obviously doesn't want to get on your bad side. You might give him the evil eye next." Landon joked.

"Please! I still haven't figured out how I did it last time," Ava felt her mood begin to finally lighten. "I will admit that it is a bit empowering to know that I can do it. I don't know if I ever will again, but it's still a nice piece of knowledge."

"I bet," Landon, continued to grin as he rose from his seat. Ava felt a little disappointed that their conversation was coming to an end. She really missed their talks. They rarely spoke now, unless they both happened to be in the lounge at the same time. Even then, he appeared to avoid her unless Chloe was with him, which changed the whole dynamic.

"Yeah," she stood and followed him to the elevator. Feeling a little nervous, Ava started to say things that really weren't necessary. "I still don't completely understand it all. It was just so weird."

"Don't worry about it," he said, hitting the elevator button then turning toward her, as they waited for the door to open. He gazed intently into her eyes for a little longer than necessary, and then quickly looked away. A lump formed in Ava's throat. It was her own fault that he always backed away from her. It was something she needed to address, even though she feared using the wrong words.

"You know, I wanted to—"

But she was abruptly cut off when the elevator door slid open and something grabbed both her and Landon's attention. Inside, with his perfectly tanned face and bright blue eyes, stood Bryan Foley—grinning from ear to ear.

Chapter Nine

Ava froze on the spot and stared. Her heart was pounding so furiously that she was certain every vampire within in a five-mile radius could hear it. A chill ran over her and a huge lump formed in her throat. Meanwhile Bryan smiled as if nothing out of the ordinary had occurred—as if he *hadn't* turned Ava into a vampire a year earlier, then deserted her—just as huge transformations took over her body. He exited the elevator with such ease, as if ignorant of the obvious tension that clearly surrounded him. Perhaps, Ava considered, he just didn't care.

"I can't believe I've been gone for so long!" He looked into Ava's eyes and attempted to express some innocent charm, displaying his signature smile that had helped to launch a moderately successful acting career—it didn't work on either her or Landon. She couldn't move. Her throat was dry and Ava wanted nothing more in that moment than to completely disappear from the room—maybe even from the world. But why was this so difficult? Why was she having such an intense reaction to seeing Bryan again?

A loud, frustrated sigh beside her brought Ava's attention back to Landon. She was surprised to see his eyes turn dark as he looked in Bryan's direction. In fact, there was no way that his contempt for the man that had turned Ava into a vampire could be missed. Landon's entire demeanor had completely changed in the last few minutes: from casual and relaxed to one of ferocity and rancorousness. In fact, if Landon were a wild animal of any kind, that would be the moment that Ava would've ran away before any bloodshed had occurred. Given the circumstances, she was prepared for Landon to hold some anger toward Bryan—but there was an unmistakable level of rage that she *hadn't* anticipated.

Either from attempting to ignore the obvious or complete naivety, Bryan continued with his good-natured charm and his pearly white smile. "I'm very *thankful* for the Internet at times like this, 'cause I don't know how else I would've sustained my apartment and-

"Ava, would you mind leaving us alone." Landon's words were cold and abrupt and came out more as a command than anything else. His voice sent an involuntary jolt through her body, even though she was well aware that any anger was being directed elsewhere. She opened her mouth to respond but nothing came out. Instead, Ava silently rushed toward the elevator. Feeling ill, her hand shook as she reached out to hit the magic button that would take her away. It glowed orange with her touch; the door immediately opened. Rushing inside, she ignored both sets of eyes as she quickly hit the button that would take her home.

She felt a strange sense of relief as the doors gently tapped together, but then her body felt like a balloon that was losing its air. She was weak, while her emotions were erupting to the surface. She had just managed to finally get her footing and move ahead in life—only to have him return and pull Ava back to where she had been a year earlier. She was once again the insecure, lonely girl– the girl who was so desperate for love and acceptance, that she invited the dark lifestyle to her door, and then lovingly invited it in to stay.

Why had he returned? His apartment had been vacant for almost 12 months after Ava left. Early on, there had been rumors that relatives of Bryan's were paying the bills and expected to take over the lease—but that never happened, nor did anyone else move in. The tenants just assumed there was some kind of arrangement between him and Samantha that allowed the place to sit empty.

Once Ava was back in the safety of her own apartment, she felt bombarded with emotions. Barely inches away from the door, she was unable

to do anything but fall to the floor and weep. Suddenly, all the memories from the past year came rushing back with such fierceness that it was almost impossible to breathe through her angry sobs. Ava thought of the nights full of despair when her transformation as a vampire left her with so many questions, fearing that she would lose her mind. And how many times had she waited, with false hope for Bryan to return to her? To swoop in and hold her hand when she needed someone the most? She felt resentment for the lies he had told her and then angry with herself for being so gullible.

Finally she stopped crying. Rising from the floor, Ava stood up and locked the door. Turning off the lights, she headed into the dark kitchen and poured herself a glass of water and quickly gulped it down. Standing quietly, staring through the darkness, she felt frozen. She didn't want to move or even blink. It almost felt like making any move at all was somehow telling the universe that she was ready to take on the next moment, that she was accepting whatever lay ahead of her—but that wasn't true. She wanted to stand still in that spot forever and not have to accept the future as it faced her—one second at a time—just stand quietly in the silent room and not even blink. Finally, a shiver ran through her spine and the high-pitched moans of one of the vampires upstairs having sex jolted her back to reality. She slowly walked into her bedroom and closed her window in order to cut off all sounds.

Removing her clothes and putting on her most comfortable pajamas, she crawled into bed. She didn't care that it was early in the evening, that she hadn't eaten dinner or even checked her email, because Ava didn't want to face anything more that night. It didn't matter if it was good or bad, she couldn't handle one more thing. Nothing.

Her mind began to run in circles uncontrollably. She thought of the encounter between her, Bryan and Landon downstairs. The unmistakable anger in her friend's face contrasting the completely guiltless charm in Bryan's eyes, as if he were clueless in what role he had played in her life. Ava couldn't help but wonder what had taken place after she left.

But maybe that was the actor in him coming out; after all, it *was* his profession. Obviously Landon was furious with Bryan for turning her into a vampire then immediately leaving the country. It had been the wrong thing to do and Landon had been pretty vocal on the subject on countless occasions. Ava knew that whatever had been said to Bryan wasn't pleasant. In a way, she was relieved that Landon had been there. How would she have reacted to a surprise encounter with Bryan, if she had been alone?

But another part of her felt very attached to the man who had made her a vampire. It was something that she hated to admit to herself and Ava wasn't sure she would ever be able to tell anyone else. Well, maybe she would tell Mariah. But even then, Ava felt confused by her feelings. There was a part of her that would've welcomed him back into her life and bed without a second's hesitation—and it was a part of herself that she hated. Why were humans never completely in control of their feelings, even when they knew that the specific emotions were bad for them? Nothing good could ever come out of her attraction to Bryan.

But how could she care about him at all? Bryan had left her right before the most serious of changes had occurred. He was like the man who showed compassion toward his pregnant girlfriend, only to disappear three months into the process and not return until after the child's birth. He had been careless and thoughtless. Yet, Ava couldn't help but wonder if Bryan had even realized what he had done. After all, wouldn't there be some hint of remorse in his eyes? Wouldn't he try to avoid her like the plague rather than look friendly and approachable? It didn't make sense. Nothing made sense.

But what role had she played in this situation? Ava wanted to be a vampire. She had *begged* for it. So, was this her fault? Did she and Landon have any reason to be angry with Bryan? Should she go downstairs to talk to them together? But no, she had been asked to leave.

It was just as confusing to see Landon's reaction to Bryan. Sure, he was angry but there were times that Ava felt he couldn't care less about her—so what difference did it make if she had been left in a mess? Maybe, she decided, he was resentful of the fact that he was left babysitting Ava for six months after the change. That would make sense, she sadly decided. Realistically, she didn't think Bryan or Landon really held any true feelings for her.

As she wrapped up comfortably in a blanket and closed her eyes, Ava found her thoughts travelling back to a night in August, a year earlier. It was a night that had given her a false hope that still made her bitter, to that very day. It was a night that would change her life.

At the time, she had been working at a pub in a seedy area of the city. It wasn't exactly the worst neighborhood, but it was far from the trendy and more secure areas most people preferred to frequent. However, Ava was determined to supplement her finances and at the time, it was the only job she could find. Her shifts rarely ran late, which enabled her to catch the bus home and not have to pay for parking. All in all, it wasn't that bad.

Everything was changing around the time she met Bryan. Ava was growing tired and frustrated with life, causing her position as a bartender to become even more taxing. The summer had just flown by and her job consisted of serving people who were happily gathering with friends, families and lovers, having fun and enjoying what the season had to offer. Conversations and laughter filled the pub, always reminding her that she was on the outside, looking in.

Ava wanted to be part of one of the happy couples that were cozy in the corner, sharing intimate discussions and flirtations. She wanted to have a circle of friends like the women dropping in after work, dressed in beautiful clothing bought in high-end stores, sipping on mixed drinks that cost almost as much as Ava made in an hour. And she wanted to be the daughter that had a weekly lunch date with her parents. But she wasn't any of these things.

And each night she returned to her grandmother's lonely house. And each night, she would cry in the shower before falling asleep in front of the television.

There was one particular night when she wanted to quit. It wasn't because of a specific event or a customer, but something inside of her seemed to be fading away. Her body felt heavy, her eyes were burning and she felt desperate as she changed into her street clothes before leaving the pub.

Light drizzle intimately touched her face when Ava walked outside, accompanied by a gentle gust of wind that welcomed her into the enigmatical night. She felt automatic disappointment seeing the bus she had intended on taking, as it drove right past its usual stop, long before she was able to dash across the street to catch it. Frustration filling her body, Ava slowly dragged her feet all the way to the bus stop where she was prepared to wait for at least 20 minutes for the next one to pass.

It seemed symbolic almost, she had considered. Ava always missed the bus in one respect or another; it was possibly God's cruel way of constantly reminding her that that in the grand scheme of things, her life was irrelevant. It was an unpleasant lesson she had learned long ago, but yet fate insisted on constantly reminding her. Sighing, she glanced around and finally decided that there was little to do—just wait.

Her mind drifted over the details of the day. They were all the same now; her routine, like clockwork.

She was so caught up in her thoughts that Ava almost didn't see him approach. In fact, it wasn't until almost the last minute that his shiny blue eyes grabbed her attention. In the darkness of night, Ava nearly hadn't recognized the beautiful face that watched her closely as he approached: but she soon would. Bryan Foley had been one of the most sought after seniors in her junior year of high school. He was popular for his athletic ability as well as his good looks, specifically known for his participation in high school football. Not that he ever noticed she existed. That's why she was surprised when he started talking to her. She doubted he recognized her now. After all, it had been a few years since high school.

"Excuse me, but do you know what time the next bus comes?" He now stood next to her, innocently tilting his head. He wore a black, leather jacket and jeans. His blond hair was slightly damp from the rain—something that didn't take away from his general appearance in the least. A hesitant smile slowly curved his lips.

"I-I'm not sure, I just missed the last one," Ava attempted to explain but felt almost too nervous to talk. He was perfection. And there she was, wearing a hooded jacket, probably smelling like greasy pub food and alcohol. In a small voice she continued, "Hopefully not long."

He slowly nodded and continued to gaze at her. At the time, she hadn't realized that he was taking in her scent. She hadn't realized that he was wondering if she was a virgin. She hadn't realized that he was on a mission to get her into his bed, so he could taste her blood. It had never occurred to her that he would even notice her existence. At that time, she hadn't realized he would change her life.

But he had. And he talked. In fact, he talked and joked with her until the bus arrived several minutes later. And then he talked to her some more, on the almost empty bus. He was very sweet, approachable and attentive. He knew to handle her with kid gloves. He knew how to get what he wanted.

But somehow, he managed to get her telephone number. And somehow he managed to get her email address—even though she couldn't remember giving it to him. Their whole conversation was so hypnotic that she forgot most of it by the time she got home. He said and did all the right things, including asking her on a date. And that's where Ava's dark journey began.

Chapter Ten

Ava was disappointed when a restful night's sleep did little to help her forget the demons that frantically clung to her soul. As soon as she woke, all the memories of the previous afternoon quickly returned, and she was reminded how Bryan's charming smile still managed to cripple her.

It was ridiculous and in a way, embarrassing. How could she be so stupid? This was a man who probably slept with hundreds of women. Bryan had casually turned her into a vampire and when she was at her weakest, he thought nothing of disappearing for a year and leaving no means to contact him. His cell phone was disconnected and her emails to him only bounced back suggesting that there was 'no known address'. If it had not been for Landon, Ava had no doubt that she could've ended her life on that terrible fall evening. Yet instead of feeling anger toward Bryan, Ava experienced the same intimidation as she felt for a teenaged crush. It was pathetic.

She was in a fog for the entire day. Her movements at Anderson & Smith were mechanical, while heaviness seemed to overtake her body. People talked and while her eyes searched their faces with interest, her thoughts were a million miles away. And although she managed to get her work done, it was the bare minimum of what she should've accomplished. In fact, had Ms. Lee still been at the office, Ava wouldn't have heard the end of it. Fortunately, Matthew Crole was new and had absolutely no issues with either Ava or her work. But not even his handsome face could distract her from the insecurities that were taking over her heart and mind.

By the end of the day, Ava began to understand where her sense of lethargy came from in the first place. The return of Bryan in her life made her world even less stable. A part of her still wasn't prepared to deal with the confusion and disappointments that she had managed to neatly tuck away a year earlier. Now, she had to ask him the questions that she was scared to ask; the questions that may have answers she wasn't prepared to hear. It was one thing to make assumptions and quite another to receive the difficult truth. She had come too far to have her emotional scabs suddenly ripped off.

But that wasn't where most of her disappointment existed. It was the feeling of rejection that crumbled away at her soul. Why was this becoming a theme? Ever since her parent's death, it felt as if she couldn't hold people in her life. They all left, only sticking around long enough to find a reason not to.

Was she unlovable? Was she saying or doing something that offended people? Did she come across as too needy? Clingy? Horrible.

Relief filled her body when Ava finally arrived back to her apartment complex after work. It was time to hide in her bedroom and escape the world. It was there she did not have to pretend or put on a pleasant face, but just sit in silence, alone. Ava briefly considered contacting Mariah, but chances were that her friend would not be available if she did—and like the previous week, probably wouldn't get back to her—so, why bother?

However, all plans to return to her apartment and suffer alone were abruptly put on hold when Ava found Landon waiting for her in the lobby. She could see his dark eyes searching her face from the moment she entered the building—they were full of compassion and warmth, something Ava hadn't expected to see again. And for a split second, she thought there was a hint of forgiveness; but that only lasted for a moment and then, it was gone. She robotically approached him at the exact same spot she had the previous afternoon.

"Hi," she muttered, taking a deep breath. Unsure of what to say next, Ava chose to say nothing. Her eyes quickly looked down at the floor. Familiar voices of other residents in their building could be heard chattering away, as they arrived home from work. She glanced in their direction but Landon quickly recaptured her attention.

"Ava, I didn't mean to take over yesterday." She looked up just in time to see him show some hesitation while carefully watching her face. His voice was gentle and warm, reminding her of the early days when they met. Back when there was an element of trust and respect in their relationship—before she had destroyed it.

Ava's smile was uncertain and uncomfortable. She felt more intimidated by his eyes when he was showing her compassion. She suspected that if he had started to yell at her, in some ways it would put her at ease. Not that Landon ever had raised his voice at anyone; it simply wasn't in his nature. But something told Ava that he had *not* shown the same restraint with Bryan on the previous afternoon.

"It was crucial that I let Bryan know that what he did to you was unacceptable," Landon's voice fell flat while his eyes grew darker by the second—at one point, Ava thought they turned completely black. It was the only time she had ever seen him this way. A chill ran up her spine, clenching her shoulders and shooting pain through the back of her head. "I assure you," he hesitated for just a moment and Ava thought she could've heard a pin drop on the floor, "he knows better now."

At first, Ava believed she was the only person who could feel frostiness in the building, until she overheard another resident suddenly comment on 'a chill in the air'. When she slowly began to glance around—ignoring Landon's intense eyes—Ava noted that many of the vampires who had just arrived home were staring in their direction. They weren't looking alarmed or upset; but each had a knowing expression on their face. Everyone except for Ava, who didn't understand what had just occurred and she had no intentions of asking.

"Okay. . .thanks," she hesitated then suddenly felt an urge to walk away. Feeling slightly faint, Ava began to move slowly toward the elevator. Glancing beside her, she suddenly realized that Landon had caught up and was gripping her arm.

"Sorry, I didn't mean to frighten you." His voice was melting inside her ears and it was as if something had taken over her body. No longer feeling like she was in charge of her own limbs, Ava continued to move toward the elevator and patiently waited for it to open. Moving inside, Landon was still with her as the door closed behind them both. Everything was an echo—his words that she couldn't understand, the sound of the elevator moving floor to floor and her own heart beating.

However once arriving on her floor and stepping out, she suddenly felt alive again. A cold sweat pushed her anxieties away and Ava was refreshed. It was much like the feeling she had after blacking out, then returning to consciousness. Except, she *hadn't* passed out.

Arriving at her apartment door, Landon led her inside and to the couch. His touch was tender and comforting, sending glowing warmth throughout her body, alerting all her senses.

"Are you sure you're okay? You seem a little shaken." He sat beside her and suddenly all discomfort was replaced by the usual physical attraction that she felt when they were alone together. Ava wasn't sure which was more excruciating. She glanced at his face and noted that he continued to speak as if nothing were unusual, so it was her assumption that the temptations were only on her side.

"Having Bryan return is pretty upsetting. I understand." he continued. "That's why things are a little weird right now."

"But why?" Ava found herself sounding like a whining child. Sitting up straight, she took a deep breath. "This happened a year ago. I thought I was over it."

"It is normal to feel this way, regardless of the passage of time," Landon carefully explained while leaning forward to be at her eye level. "He is the one who turned you and all things considered, it makes sense that you would have some kind of reaction to seeing him again. Bryan could go away for 20 years and the first time you see him after that, you would feel as uncomfortable as you were last night."

"Did I act really strange?" Ava suddenly felt paranoid. Had she looked so obvious? Pathetic? It was one thing to feel discomfort within one self: quite another to have others be witnesses. Personal anguish should remain a private thing, unless chosen to be otherwise.

"I could sense it as soon as you saw Bryan, but I doubt he did," He spoke very matter-of-factly and Ava instantly felt stupid. Of course he could sense it! Every vampire in the building probably could sense it. "I knew you were upset, which was another reason why I wanted you to return to your apartment. I figured you needed time alone. Plus I wanted to speak with Bryan regarding his broken promises to look after you, while your body was making the changes."

"What did he say?"

Landon's eye twitched and he glanced away. "He's aware of what he has done."

She thought about his words.

"But what about you? What happened when you were changed?" Ava wasn't sure if the question had sprung from true curiosity or if she was simply trying to stall the conversation, so she could spend more time with Landon. The attraction she felt for him rippled through her body in a way that was similar to the days when they were involved in a physical relationship. "Does the person who made you this way, have the same effect on you?"

He quietly studied her face, searched her eyes and was so close that Ava had to fight off the impulse to lean forward and kiss him. Finally he shook his head. "It's not the same thing, Ava. I was practically born into it. In a way, it is more sinister because you have no idea what the rest of the world considers being 'normal'. It's almost like you have to learn what comes naturally to others."

"Oh." She knew he wouldn't go into any more details. He never did. His secret was well guarded and he refused to share it with anyone. Many vampires were the same and didn't want to discuss how or why they had turned, often because many dark secrets were linked to their decision.

"When you are turned, it's a bit traumatic," Landon's voice was soothing, enticing and sweet. He could've talked about anything in that moment and Ava would still be under his spell. "When most people decide they want to become a vampire—something that really should be discouraged—they rarely understand what it does to their entire body. It's a huge transition to adapt to in the physical sense, let alone the emotional and spiritual side of it. That's why you often have many issues, Ava. You've only begun to scratch the surface of your new life."

She wasn't sure what that meant.

"I've been thinking a lot about immortals." She carefully brought up the topic, knowing that it wasn't going to be taken well, but she wanted to reveal the truth that was bursting inside of her. "I think that's my calling. I think that is what I want to be. Right now, I feel like I'm half in one world and half in another."

"That's because you are," Landon's voice continued to wash over her in the most comforting way, but his words were not what she wanted to hear. "Trust me Ava, you don't want to be an immortal. You would be living a fake existence, it's more work than it would be worth. The way you are now just requires you to become accustomed to your stronger senses, drinking some blood on occasion and otherwise be a human being in every other way."

"Of course, there are many moral dilemmas to consider. You would be essentially living a lie, never really able to be completely honest with anyone. There are other things to think about as well, such as whether or not to have children." Landon continued and seemed to break her out of her current trance, which she had invited. "As an immortal vampire, it would be impossible." He gave her a sympathetic smile.

He suddenly rose from the couch. Landon always seemed to leave just as she felt at ease with him and when their conversations grew relaxed. It was like having a bucket of cold water thrown in her face. She wanted to be carried away in the moment while they spoke, pulling them closer both physically and emotionally. But watching him walk toward her door, she was suddenly reminded that Chloe would probably be home soon. Disappointed, there really wasn't much she could say.

"Okay," she hesitated, dragging her words out. "I just want to thank you for everything you have done for me. Especially your help yesterday."

"I didn't do much," he turned as he reached for the doorknob. "Oh." He stopped. "Don't worry about Bryan. He's gone out of town for a couple more weeks to promote some indie film he did overseas, so you have time to prepare for his return *this* time. I had a pretty serious discussion with him so he won't be giving you any kind of hassle."

Ava wasn't sure what kind of hassle Landon expected from Bryan, but merely nodded in silence. As usual he had given her a great deal to think about and within seconds, he left Ava alone with her thoughts.

Chapter Eleven

"So, how's your week going?" Mariah asked, sipping on her glass of wine. The two had barely ordered lunch on a dreary Friday afternoon and already, it was clear that Ava's friend was having a bad day. The dark circles beneath her eyes could not be hidden with makeup, while Mariah's body carried a general look of defeat. It was for this reason that Ava didn't feel it was the best time to bring up her own problems.

"Fine," she replied while scanning the menu: not that it mattered, she always ordered Caesar salad rather than try anything new. Her appetite had been greatly altered since becoming a mortal vampire. Ironically, she enjoyed garlic despite all the myths suggesting the two were a lethal combination. "Just the usual shit."

"Really?" Mariah suddenly was very alert, her chocolate eyes dancing in excitement. "Is that how you categorize Bryan's return home? You just consider it a normal event in your week, even though you've not seen him since he turned you?"

Oh.

"I just thought that..." Ava hesitated for a moment as the waitress returned and took their order. When she left, Mariah was watching Ava closely, so she continued. "I guess I just didn't want to think about it. Plus you have your own problems, without having to listen to mine."

"I would rather listen to your problems than think about my own," Mariah confirmed, and even though she made reference to them, it was clear that Ava's friend was not about to get into any details regarding the issues that were weighing her down. "So I take it you spoke to him?"

"Not exactly," Ava hesitated then went on to describe the surprise meeting with Bryan in the apartment building lobby, followed by her discussion with Landon over the entire situation. She noted that Mariah appeared to get a slight lift from hearing her story, so it didn't feel as if she were unloading all her problems. "It was a bit overwhelming, to say the least."

"It always is when you see the person who turned you," Mariah repeated Landon's comment from earlier in the week. She gave a half-hearted smile, her eyes showing some signs of compassion. Her attention was momentarily taken away when the waitress brought another glass of wine and sat it on the table. Ava hadn't even noticed Mariah finishing the first one. "I guess I didn't think he would return or I would've mentioned it to you. Also, I haven't seen mine in years, so I guess I kind of forget how emotional it can be."

"Where is the one who turned you?" Ava tilted her head slightly and attempted to search her friend's face. Mariah was very secretive, rarely disclosing much about her life. Ava always felt that it would be like a Pandora's box, if she ever did. "When did it happen?"

Mariah quickly averted her eyes and shook her head. At first, Ava thought she would refuse to answer, but after a moment or two, she finally spoke. "I don't know where he is and I don't particularly care, to be honest with you."

"Oh," Ava suddenly felt that she entered a forbidden zone. Maybe she shouldn't have asked. "I'm sorry, Mariah. It's none of my business."

"No, it's fine." Her eyes met with Ava's while her fingers tapped on the stem of the wine glass, as if she were contemplating what to say. "It just was a really difficult time in my life." She cleared her throat and glanced around, lowering her tone substantially so that only someone with immaculate hearing would understand a word. "I didn't have a choice in becoming a vampire. It just happened."

And the topic was closed. Mariah didn't volunteer any further information and Ava sensed that she wouldn't have received anything if she had asked. It made Ava somewhat nervous when considering Mariah's words, but she completely understood how a passionate sexual encounter might possibly lead to a vampire's partner becoming one of them. Still, there was something very unsettling in Mariah's voice that worried Ava.

"I'm sorry to hear that," Ava quietly replied, unsure of what else to say. There was definite tension at the table and she certainly would not push the issue. After taking a sip of her water, she continued to note the darkness that covered Mariah's face and decided maybe she should reveal a few more details. "It was pretty emotional for me. I had no idea I would feel so terribly after all these months. Fortunately, Landon was around to sort things out."

"Really?" Mariah raised an eyebrow while taking a sip of her wine. "I heard he was *not* very happy with Bryan. I think he probably tore a strip off him for turning you, then taking off with no contact info. That's a big no-no, as you know."

"That's what I've been told," Ava nervously confirmed. The anxiety that overwhelmed her the last few days had made sleep almost nonexistent. Unlike the first night after seeing Bryan, she spent most wide-awake, her mind flying vigorously in every direction. "Then Landon was stuck looking after me; I'm sure that probably pissed him off."

"I don't believe he was ever really *stuck*," Mariah's eyes lit up and her lips curved into an impish grin. She took another large gulp of wine. "I think he wanted to do it."

"He probably would disagree with you now," Ava quietly countered.

"I think *you* are way too hard on yourself," Mariah said, continuing to smile. "I think he had feelings for you and maybe he still does. Why else would he be so angry with Bryan?"

"Because he was stuck looking after me," Ava let out a short laugh and attempted to hide her sadness, by glancing around the half-empty restaurant. Her eyes returned to rest on Mariah, who had a very complex expression on her face—it was a combination of seriousness and confusion. "Come on, look at how awfully that situation turned out. I'm sure he merely tolerates me now. Besides, he has a girlfriend. He loves her. I assure you, I don't fit into the picture at all."

"I think you are probably jumping to a conclusion," Mariah lifted her glass once again and let out a loud sigh. "Having a girlfriend means fuck all these days. Everyone has to hide behind someone or something so they don't seem vulnerable, and I believe that's the case with Landon. As long as he hides behind that *person* he is dating, then he can pretend he doesn't still care about you."

"Maybe you are romanticizing the entire situation," Ava couldn't help but roll her eyes. She knew better than to think that any man held such high regards or strong feelings for her.

"I think you are too hard on yourself." Mariah repeated compassionately.

Ava didn't reply. Luckily, the waitress returned with their food right at that moment, making it easy to change subjects and move on to something else. Fortunately, Mariah had a bit of news to share with her after the waitress left.

"I almost forgot," her warm eyes widened substantially and for a moment, actually appeared to lighten in color. "I have some important news for you."

"Really?" Ava attempted to show some interest as she bit into the lettuce, but it simply was not coming through as her voice droned in response. Very little could've really captured her attention at that point, especially in light of the last few minutes of their conversation—at least, she didn't think so.

"I found out some information," Mariah leaned forward and her voice fell to a whisper. "About the immortal vampires."

"You did?" Ava automatically perked up. Now *this* was something that interested her, even though it shouldn't have. It was like Landon had pointed out—she had enough trouble adjusting to her new life as a *mortal* vampire—why did she think that becoming an immortal would be more suitable? However, something told Ava that this could be what would fill the void in her heart. She needed it.

"I knew that would grab your attention!" Mariah grinned as she unwrapped her pita and inspected it carefully before continuing. "I was talking to an old friend of mine recently and since he is from Europe, it occurred to me that he might have more information. I mean, after all, Benjamin is always going on about how the immortals are in Europe, right?"

"And?" Ava asked excitedly, her full attention on Mariah.

"And he came through," Mariah confirmed as she ran her fingers up and down the wine glass stem. Once again leaning forward, her voice lowered. "He said that at one time they were all believed to reside in Europe, but now with the Internet connecting the world, it has become apparent that this is no longer the case. It seems that immortal vampires live everywhere but tend to prefer more populated areas because it makes it easier to mix in with different kinds of people. No one asks questions in a big city."

"I think Landon kind of said something like that once," Ava felt her enthusiasm deplete. Was this it?

"Oh there's more," Mariah insisted, her eyes widening again. "He said there is a leader for all these vampires. All the immortals report back to him, but very few actually know his identity. And most would prefer not to at all. He's very powerful and not someone you want to cross. For example, someone like Bryan who was so casual about turning you and leaving immediately after, could be a loose cannon."

"Why would this leader care about what mortal vampires do?" Ava asked.

"Because we are still vampires. We still carry the secret," Mariah reminded her. "This is something that regular humans cannot know about. They've worked way too hard to convince people that we are just a myth and not real. We have top people all over the world who eliminate any signs that we exist."

"So, if for example, a scientist were to find proof that vampires are real and wanted to share his knowledge with the world," Mariah's voice seemed to lower further. "He would be dead within hours. He would *never* get the information out and it would be destroyed. There are some vampires at the top and that's what they do. They make sure that the rest of the world thinks we are just a product of stories and completely fake. It's not other mortal vampires that looks after this kind of thing, like we originally thought."

"So, like, the CEO of my company?"

"He's one of them. Immortal vampires are very powerful people who make it to the top," Mariah's voice was steady but Ava could feel her own heart pound furiously. This was it. This was what excited her. She was convinced that nothing would ever captivate her quite like the concept of being an immortal vampire. The idea made her feel powerful and fearless. More than anything, Ava wanted to be a part of this world. She wanted to be one of the elite few who experienced everlasting life and eventually be included with the others, who guarded the vampire secret from the world.

"Your CEO got where he is because he's immortal and has had centuries to learn about the business world, plus they tend to have few scruples, which would make him a natural as a CEO. As a vampire, he is entrusted to keep the secret and help the others whenever a problem arises." She continued. "That is his job. Many of the most powerful people in our world are vampires, we just don't know their identity."

"So like, just any powerful people?"

"Apparently, they are often in the science community, politicians, the CIA, people who are in *great* power so we're not talking the shift supervisor at Burger King." She hesitated for a moment and offered a mischievous smile. "Then again, you never know."

"And now with the Internet, there are many vampires monitoring what people are searching for online, websites about vampires, that kind of thing. They try to see if there is any area for concern and act accordingly." Mariah finished the last of her wine and appeared reluctant to continue. "That means if someone is too close to the secret, they may suddenly go missing or in a lot of cases, are found after 'committing suicide'. Apparently there is a great deal of murders manipulated to look like suicides. They go as far as to create fake Google searches, emails, texts, anything to discredit the victim's mental health. Basically, anything they know the police would look at when investigating."

"Amazing," Ava couldn't help but to be impressed. It was like a secret organization that was carefully guarded. It almost made her feel safer to be a part of it.

"And it gets better," Mariah's eyes lit up once again; a huge smile crossed her face. "As I said, there is one guy who's the leader. He's the one who runs the show. He's been around forever, probably hundreds of years and always manages to adapt to the times. Very smart man, apparently he appears very young—that is according to those who have actually seen him. He lives in secret and is said to be always moving around the world."

"What does he do, exactly?"

"He oversees the vampires. The scientists, CEOs, all those people report to him on a regular basis to make sure everything is kept in order. I don't know much more about him, that is something my friend really wasn't able to help me with. He just said this guy wasn't to be fucked with, so I guess you can take that however you wish."

"No name? Location? Anything?" Ava was intrigued. For the first time in days, she was truly filled with excitement and enthusiasm. This information gave her reason to wake up in the morning and something to work toward. Becoming an immortal vampire was her goal. She wanted to escape to this underground world and start over again in another existence.

"No, it's all very hush-hush." Mariah continued to grin, letting Ava know that there was another tidbit of information that she was dying to share. "But there is one more fact that may interest you. Apparently since this guy is technically over a hundred years old, maybe even older, his sexual appetites and prowess is supposed to be through the roof. He's a legend and women who have been with him, rave about his abilities. They say he spoils them for any other men."

"Really?"

"In fact, there is a special name for him," Mariah's eyes sparkled, and her smile grew with each word. "He's called the Rock Star of Vampires."

Chapter Twelve

"...the rock star of vampires.."

The words echoed through Ava's head, long after her lunch with Mariah had ended. And even as she lay in bed that night, Ava felt her brain dancing between this revelation and the possibility of meeting that vampire in the future—the idea intrigued her.

What would he look like? Mariah seemed pretty sure that his appearance was still that of a young man, but yet he had years—*years* of experience. Was it wrong to be curious about a stranger: a man she didn't know? It didn't make sense at all, but yet the fantasy took her away from the realities of her life. In fact, the *entire* immortal lifestyle took her away from the realities of her life. She wanted to escape—run away to their world, and never come back again. It was what she desired.

Unfortunately, Mariah had tapped out her source on this topic. He did not have any more information to share. If only Ava knew where to begin her search, it would be much easier. If she had a name, a location, any information to go on, it would seem more possible to find him. But she didn't. And he was so powerful that it seemed impossible that Ava would. But what if—what *If*, she could find a way that he would seek *her* out? Attempting to figure out a method to do so put her into a deep sleep. It was a sleep that brought with it a series of bizarre dreams. But Ava would only remember one of them.

The dream was a sequence of confusing fragments that were both erotic and mystifying. It started with a conversation with Landon that took place at her kitchen table; but she couldn't understand a word he was saying. And every time she repeated the question, "What?" the more infuriated he appeared to get toward her.

But the dream was about to get a great deal stranger, starting when Landon rose from the seat across from her, only to suddenly disappear.

Rising from her own chair, Ava began to mindlessly wander through the apartment, as if she were searching for him. But it was dark, very difficult to focus on anything and after awhile, it felt more like an unfamiliar setting rather than her home. For some reason, she had a strong sense that he wasn't that far away, but finding him was another matter all together.

Cautiously moving her feet forward, Ava made several clumsy attempts to both find and turn on a light switch, but to no avail. Her heart began to race and she felt like the rooms were becoming quite narrow as she moved ahead, uncertain of what she would find next. Finally, she made it to her bedroom and that is where she found Landon: on her bed, naked.

Showing no signs of modesty as he lay against some propped up pillows, fully displaying his lean body with the dim lighting of a nearby lamp. His eyes carried a hint of seduction while his face was relaxed, unassuming and his chest rose slightly with each breath he took.

Stunned by this presentation, Ava found her feet frozen to the ground and her heart jumped around with excitement. Holding his body motionless, Landon's eyes perused her without even blinking. Eeriness surrounded her and Ava opened her mouth to speak, but the words weren't coming out.

"Aren't you going to come to bed?" He asked casually, as if they still had an intimate relationship and she was the one acting unusual. He appeared confused as to why she was even hesitating. "What are you waiting for?"

Opening her mouth, Ava was attempting to reply, but again the words wouldn't come out. Instead, her body flowed across the dark room, while a chill ran up the back of her shirt and caused her to shiver. Slowly easing onto the bed, she felt Landon's arms reach out and pull her body on top of his with such vigor that Ava almost didn't see it happen at all. Immediately, she felt intense desire building up for him.

Beneath her, Landon's heart raced at an alarming rate. Temperature rising, his breath increased dramatically in a matter of seconds and she instinctively felt her lips reach for his, but instead she found them on Landon's neck while his pulse beat wildly against them. She found the entire experience increased her arousal even further, as his hands continued to roam her suddenly naked body. Then a voice behind them alerted Ava's attention. She reluctantly took her lips from Landon's neck and turned to see Bryan standing beside the bed.

"Mind if I join?" He began to quickly remove his clothes before Ava could respond. Although a part of her was hesitant to even be in the same room with him, let alone bed, another part of her was enticed. The thought of having sex with two men at once sent a spark of excitement throughout her body and it ended with an intense heat between her legs. Before she could answer, Ava felt Bryan's body climb over her own as his teeth sunk into her neck, causing Ava to moan loudly in pleasure. Both of the men were touching her everywhere, clearly anticipating the eruptive conclusion to this encounter—and so was she. Her senses almost couldn't handle every sensation that traveled through her, right to the tip of her toes.

And then she was awake. Wide-awake, and sitting in her bed: alone.

Throwing the covers off her body, Ava sat up and welcomed the cool air that surrounded her. Perspiration ran down her back while her heart raced at a frightening pace. Her mind probed why she had such a bizarre dream, especially about two men whom she was unlikely to ever have sex with again. Feeling confused and frustrated, Ava decided to go to the rooftop to refresh her body and clear her mind. Pulling on a sweater, she grabbed her apartment keys and headed into the quiet hallways. Rushing up the stairs, she was relieved to find the rooftop empty. It was not unusual for vampires to go there late at night for various reasons, but mostly to look out at the Vancouver skies.

A light rain fell on her and she welcomed it, while a slight chill enclosed her body. Taking a deep breath, Ava again wondered why she had such an inexplicable dream? Was it indicating that things weren't finished between her, Landon and Bryan? Was it a fantasy of hers to hook up with the two of them? Did it mean nothing at all? She started to recall every detail and found herself wondering if a threesome with both vampires would be as exhilarating in real life.

But all the excitement from the dream slowly caused her spirits to drop. When all was said and done, it actually made her kind of sad. After all, Landon clearly had some contempt for her, barely tolerating her presence while Bryan never took her seriously for a moment. Right now, she considered, Landon was probably in bed doing Creepy Chloe and judging by her appearance and overall attitude, odds were their sex life was out of this world. And Bryan—chances were he was somewhere having his own threesome. And here she was, standing on the rooftop—alone. And soon she would return to her empty apartment and bed. And so, what started off as an erotic dream that was exciting now turned her emotions raw and tears began to run down her face.

It really wasn't fair, she decided. Ava noticed that other girls were fake, unattractive and in some cases, overall bitches—and yet, the men in their lives didn't seem to care at all. But for some reason, she just wasn't enough of anything to have her faults overlooked. She wasn't attractive enough. And definitely, no one would accuse her of being too smart or successful either. Never the nicest girl in the world—a nice girl doesn't do hurtful things, like what she did to Landon or put hexes on their boss. Was she held under stricter guidelines than other girls? Was more expected of her and if so, why? Why did the world always feel that Ava Lilith didn't measure up?

Eventually she wiped the combination of rain and tears from her face. Exhausted, she decided to just go back to bed. It wasn't helping her if she fixated on the disappointments in her life. All she could do was focus on what she wanted—and what she wanted was to become an immortal and escape this world.

As she turned to leave, the stairway door slowly opened and Ava was surprised to see Landon walk onto the rooftop. He didn't appear to be shocked to see her, but raised his eyebrows slightly.

"Well, fancy meeting you up here again," his face showed signs of friendliness, much to her relief. Landon's amber eyes softened as his lips curved into a relaxed smile. She already knew what he was thinking. The last time they were together on the rooftop, was the night she was planning to jump and he saved her. It was the night they had sex in the stairway.

"Yeah, I needed some fresh air," Ava explained, pulling her sweater tightly over her body. "I woke up and couldn't sleep."

"I see." Landon replied as he moved closer to her, his eyes full of curiosity. "Me neither, actually."

For a moment, Ava thought she heard a hint of seduction in his voice, but quickly realized that her dream was probably clouding her judgment. "Yeah?" She replied, giving him a sheepish smile. Ava self-consciously ran a hand through her hair and suddenly remembered that she was standing in her pajama pants: how embarrassing. He wore a blue and grey t-shirt along with baggy gym pants.

"I.. um, had an argument with Chloe," He spoke slowly, carefully picking out his words. "I figured it would be a good idea to make an escape for a few minutes."

"Oh, I see," Ava secretly wondered what their argument was about but wasn't about to ask. "Sorry to hear that." A lie.

"Yeah, well it happens," He shrugged casually. "And you couldn't sleep?"

"I, yeah, I had a weird dream and couldn't get back to sleep." Ava almost couldn't look him in the eye as she explained. "Not a big deal."

"It's been a long time since I've seen you come here." He brought up this point again, she noticed.

"I usually don't."

Their conversation seemed to hit an awkward pause and Ava debated leaving all altogether, when Landon spoke up.

"By the way," he cleared his throat. "I hate to tell you this, but Bryan is heading back to town this weekend."

"For Halloween?" Ava knew it was his favorite holiday.

"Ah no, actually, someone in his family passed away," Landon replied. "So I guess he's coming back early. I just wanted to warn you in advance."

"Thanks." She suddenly thought of her dream from earlier that night and quickly looked away from Landon's probing eyes. It was embarrassing to her, even though he obviously knew nothing about it.

"No problem," Landon hesitated until she looked back into his face. "Just let me know if he gives you any problems."

"Okay."

"So, um…I also hear you've been asking a lot of questions lately," Landon sounded slightly awkward as he broached another subject. "A lot of questions about the immortals."

"Yeah," Ava felt no shame in her reply, while at the same time, she wondered if it was Mariah that had told him about it. As far as she knew, the two didn't really socialize. "I wouldn't say *a lot* of questions, but a few."

"Ava, you really don't want to make that change," Landon insisted. "It's not a life that you would want."

"You keep saying that, but it's *my* life to do what I choose," Ava couldn't help feeling slightly rebellious. Why did he keep insisting that this wasn't for her? What did he know and why did he even have a say in the matter? "I want to learn about them and to be honest, I want to be a part of their world."

"But why?" Landon shook his head slowly, and she sensed all the calmness he expressed earlier quickly disappearing. A gentle rain continued to run down his hair and face, creating a certain allure that was hard to miss. "Why do you want to learn about them? Why do you want to have anything to do with that kind of life? What's wrong with your life as it is?"

Ava felt like screaming. What exactly was *right* about her life as it was?

"I don't like how it is now. There's something missing," she held a hand to her heart. "And it's not something that I can get here, as things are now." Her hand waved in the air, as if to indicating the city. "This isn't for me. I know I'm in the wrong place, living the wrong kind of life."

"Doesn't mean you have to become an immortal, Ava." He quietly maintained.

"But I think it does. I just feel it in my heart, it's not something I can explain."

"I think you should avoid it. Things will get better," Landon calmly tried to convince her. "They always do. If you become immortal, you can't change back. You can't become mortal again. It's done. It's finished. There's no turning back."

"I know that," Ava replied and cleared her throat. "That's what I am hoping."

"Ava, please, just think about what you are asking," Landon's eyes seem to plead with hers and she couldn't help but to be angry. What did he care what she did? He was barely a part of her life at all. "It's permanent."

"I know," she replied, although Ava honestly hadn't considered this aspect of immortality at all. Of course she knew there was no turning back once she crossed that line, but had she *really* thought about what that meant?

Shaking his head, clearly frustrated with her, Landon didn't reply. He finally rubbed his eye and looked back into her face. "How exactly do you plan to do this? I mean, what *do* you know?"

"Not a lot," she admitted, and then rushed to continue. "But I'm determined to learn all I can."

"It's not easy, from what I hear." He shoved both hands in his pockets.

"I'll find a way," Ava stubbornly insisted. "The next time the CEO to my company is around, I'll talk to him."

"I guarantee, he won't tell you a thing."

"He was pretty open about the fact that he was an immortal, so maybe he will," she spoke optimistically.

" 'K," Landon nodded and looked toward his feet briefly. "I hope you change your mind before it's too late."

Gesturing toward the stairs, Ava walked ahead of him and slowly opened the door. She could hear him breathing loudly on the back of her neck and attempted to ignore it. Was he thinking of the time they had sex on that very stairway? The idea tempted her in the moment, but she fought it. When they reached her floor, he briefly touched her arm before Ava entered the hallway.

"Just please, don't do anything drastic. Maybe look at other options that will make you happy?" Landon gently asked. "And please discuss it with me before you do anything rash?"

She slowly nodded but knew she was lying.

Chapter Thirteen

"Another one!" Mariah shouted over the multitude of voices that also competed for the bartender's attention. She impatiently shook her empty wine glass in the air.

The two stood amongst a collection of witches, demons and pirates at a popular nightclub on a busy Halloween night. Ava had chosen to dress up as a nun, while Mariah sported a skimpy schoolgirl costume that showed off all her voluptuous curves and left little to the imagination. Ava wasn't sure if it was for that reason or simply because of Mariah's intimidating eyes, but the two women were served immediately, despite the fact that others continued to wait.

"Thank you!" Mariah exchanged seductive grins with the bartender, as he handed them both their drinks. "It's a pleasure doing business with you."

Ava looked away and smirked, amazed at her friend's ability to charm men with a simple smile. It was one of the things she most envied about Mariah.

The two women quickly moved away from the busy bar and to a quiet corner to observe the other customers. It humored them both to see what Mariah referred to as the 'resurrection of the vampire costume'. This was of course, in direct relation to recent books and movies surrounding the popular topic. Suddenly, everyone was fascinated with growing fangs and drinking blood.

"It's really the sexuality that intrigues people," Mariah was quick to point out, as the two stood aside and watched the collection of vampires that overwhelmed the room. Ava sipped on her wine and listened. "And it's the dark, underground world where all the deviants and loners feel they have a home. So, of course the vampire world is popular." She stopped and sighed loudly. "But if only they knew."

"If only they knew," Ava took over. "That a huge part of our lives is a secret and less exciting than they think."

"It's never how it appears on the outside," Mariah slowly shook her head caressing the top of her wine glass with the tips of her fingers. Her head was leaning slightly, her eyes glazed over as she observed a group of guys without costumes, as they passed by and checked her out. "Fortunately, the longer you are one of us, eventually it becomes normal."

Ava agreed.

"I smell one," Mariah abruptly looked away from the group of guys and her eyes travelled around the room. "Do you?"

Ava knew she was referring to a virgin. And just as she began to shake her head 'no', she hesitated. "Yeah, you know what? I think I do. I just can't tell where it's coming from."

"Hmm…" Mariah's head swung back and forth anxiously, her nose twitching in midair. Clearly, she had dibs. Not that is bothered Ava.

"Kind of smells like a female, doesn't it?" Ava wrinkled her forehead and attempted to help her friend, but there were so many scents in the air that it was challenging to separate them. With a collection of alcohol, perfumes, sweat, and everything from gum to hairspray, it was difficult to pin point the one thing she was searching for in the crowd. As it turns out, she didn't have to because Mariah found him first.

"There he is," she muttered under her breath and nodded toward the corner of the opposite side of the room. A handsome guy in his twenties wearing a polo shirt and jeans stood back, while two less attractive men played pool. Ava noticed that he was well groomed, clean-shaven and appeared to take a great deal of pride in his appearance, but she sensed a self-consciousness that was highly appealing. He took frequent sips of beer and generally avoided making eye contact with anyone. Ava sensed that he could feel their stares, but he didn't look in their direction.

"I'm going over, want to come?" Mariah raised an eyebrow, while Ava shook her head.

"Not right now, I want to roam around a bit. I'll catch up with you later."

Both girls knew this wasn't true. Mariah would have the virgin out the door and in her bed before he even knew what happened. She worked fast. But it was okay. Ava wanted to seek her own adventure.

However the night proved to be dull. Regardless of the fact that it was a busy club and Ava had a few stimulating conversations, there was a part of her that just wasn't into it. At one time she thrived on finding her next prey and moving in for the kill, however lately she had lost interest. Now, her main goal was to learn about the immortals and to become one—and very little else inspired her.

Life as she knew it was dull and any conquests or goals outside of the immortal world weren't of interest. In fact, a part of her just wanted to run away from everything she knew and was familiar with in her lifestyle; she no longer wanted to live in a building full of vampires, she no longer wanted to live in this city, she no longer wanted to work at her current job. Her obsession with immortals quickly had prevailed over everything else.

A scent pulled Ava out of her drunken stupor and back to reality. It was another vampire. Not that it was unusual to find her kind at a nightclub, but this one was familiar—very familiar. But then it disappeared. Had she only imagined it? Just as she was about to leave for the night, it grabbed her attention again, and this time, she recognized it. It was coming up behind her, but the crowd was too thick for her to turn around. The scent was becoming stronger and that only encouraged Ava to move toward the exit so that she could make her escape home. Maybe he hadn't seen her?

But he did.

Outside, Ava rushed past a group of smokers that stood near the exit and down the pathway toward the sidewalk. However the sound of his voice caused her to stop in her tracks.

"Ava?" His gentle pleading tone tore down her defenses and she slowly turned to face him. Much to her surprise, Ava found Bryan wearing a vampire costume. She couldn't help but laugh at the irony.

"I see you decided to stretch your imagination when picking out a costume this year?" Ava quietly joked as he approached, his sky blue eyes centered on her face. In part, she hated herself for not being angrier with him, but at the same time, she was relieved to not have a similar reaction as she did their previous meeting.

He opened his mouth as if to answer, but instead his lips curved into a smile. Much to Ava's surprise, Bryan reached out and pulled her into a strong hug. It felt so good to be in his arms again, as much as she hated to admit it to even herself. For some reason she visualized Landon frowning upon her reaction, but quickly pushed the thought away and instead focused on the warmth of his body against her own. He was tall and her face was buried comfortably into his chest.

"I'm really sorry, Ava." His hot breath warmed her forehead and it caused Ava's heart to race wildly inside her chest. Her intense attraction to him was unmistakable and within seconds, Ava could sense his arousal, just as he would be able to sense her desire for him. It was one of the downfalls of being a vampire. There were some things you didn't miss, such as the tiny, almost minuscule droplet of water that fell from his lips and was sliding down her face. A normal person wouldn't have even noticed something about the size of pinhead but because of Ava's elevated senses, the droplet of liquid alerted her to an ultimate high, while Bryan's arms gripped her even closer. She was at such a heightened state of sexual longing that she almost hadn't noticed that his lips were gently kissing her face, his tongue barely gliding along her hairline. Suddenly, it didn't matter what he had done to her in the past; it was erased in the moment.

"I think we should go somewhere," Ava's voice became breathless and she suddenly felt a coldness grasping on her body, as Bryan abruptly let her go. He looked into her eyes and opened his mouth to say something again, but the words wouldn't come out. Finally his lips moved.

"Let's go."

The next few minutes were a blur. After finding his car in a nearby parking garage, the two climbed in and immediately clung to one another. Regardless of the awkwardness of making out in the front of Bryan's car, Ava was so swept up in the moment that she didn't care. But the sound of laughter in the distance pulled her out of lust-filled moment.

"What are we doing?" Ava asked after managing to move away from Bryan. He appeared puzzled; his eyes were full of disappointment and confusion. "We can't do this."

"Umm...I guess not *here*," Bryan appeared to be momentarily confused and finally glanced out the car window. "Let's go back to your place." And before she could even clear her head enough to reply, he stuck the key in the ignition and they were headed out of the parking garage and onto the street.

"No, Bryan, I don't think we should do this at all," Ava attempted to explain, as reality came rushing back to remind her of what he had done to her only a year earlier. "I just—"

"Ava, please," Bryan cut her off and suddenly appeared anxious. "You can't tell me that you don't want to spend tonight with me. I can feel it. I *know*."

"True," She regretted her answer, but she couldn't lie. Glancing down at her hands, she noticed they were shaking. "I just think—"

"Maybe you should stop thinking," Bryan calmly replied. "Maybe you should do what feels right, rather than what you *think* you should do. Maybe you should do what *you* want, not what Landon would say you should do."

"This doesn't have anything to do with Landon," Ava attempted to reassure both of them, but somewhere in the back of her mind she could picture Landon telling her to keep away from Bryan. But why would she even entertain the thought of listening? "It's just, it's cause when you left." She hesitated and the car was suddenly silent—completely silent—she had forgotten that Bryan owned a hybrid. "I was devastated when you left me last year. I was a mess."

"I know." The softness in Bryan's voice made all her defenses drop. "I *am* very sorry. I wanted to explain everything when I saw you last, but Landon hauled me aside before I even had a chance to say a word. He told me everything."

"He did?" Ava felt her hands nervously playing with the material of her costume. A nun? Now *this* was ironic considering she was with the very man

The Rock Star of Vampires

who had stolen a part of her innocence, when he turned her into a vampire. "What did he say?"

"Basically, that I was an asshole," Bryan replied and gave her a quick, desperate smile as they turned onto their street. They fell silent as they arrived back at the apartment building that they both called home. Neither said a word as they got out of the car and went inside.

Now close to midnight, everything was quiet. She half expected to find Landon waiting for them in the lounge area, but he wasn't. They entered the elevator and she noted that he hit the button to her floor. Neither said another word until they were in her apartment.

Closing the door, she turned toward him and she noted that his face was full of seriousness. He wasn't playing games this time. She could sense his honesty as he licked his lips and began to speak.

"I am going to be direct with you, Ava," He pushed his long, flowing cape aside—then in a sudden act of frustration, ripped it off and threw it on her couch. "I ran away. I was in over my head and I ran. I fucked up. I can try to explain it away a million ways, but that's the truth. I turned you into a vampire, carelessly I'll admit, then panicked and left."

"Sure, I was working on that film," he continued while sitting down on the arm of her couch. Tilting his head, his eyes looked up into her face. "But I stayed much longer than necessary. I could've been back sooner to visit, but I chose not to bother. I could've kept in contact with you too. I could give you some storybook, poetic reason why I didn't, but it wouldn't be true. And I'm not going to lie to you about that. I did the wrong thing and then, I left town again in order to give you some space. I only returned this soon to attend my aunt's funeral."

Ava nodded. She didn't have it in her to say a word.

"I was wrong, very wrong," Bryan said and cleared his throat. "I'm really, very sorry about everything. I'm forever thankful to Landon for helping you out *and* saving my ass."

"Saving your ass?" She felt her defenses climbing. Was this really what this was all about? Was he in some kind of trouble for turning her then not staying the expected amount of time, in order to help her with the transition?

"If the right people find out that I turned you and didn't fulfill my obligation, I could just 'disappear' like that." He snapped his finger to indicate his death. "Although I can honestly say I deserve it. I did a very bad thing, Ava. I honestly didn't realize the change would affect you so much. It didn't have such intense ramifications on me. I didn't turn anyone before and didn't know that it affects women more than men."

Neither did Ava. This was news to her.

"And you were fine when I left, not that it's an excuse," Bryan insisted. "Ava, I don't know what else to say, other than I am sorry. I wish I knew a way to make it up to you."

"There is a way," she slowly walked toward him, automatically sensing his lust for her. "You can tell me a few things."

"Anything." The words seemed to slowly roll off his tongue as he stared intensely into her eyes.

"You can tell me who you would've been in trouble with for leaving me," Ava answered, "And everything you know about the immortals."

Chapter Fourteen

Bryan appeared a little taken aback by her question and briefly considered it before answering. "You mean, *the* vampire. The man who runs the show?"

"First of all, how do you know it's a man?" Ava couldn't help but to challenge this belief. After all, even *she* had jumped to the same conclusion. Maybe they were all wrong. Why couldn't it be a woman?

"Oh, it *is* a man," Bryan assured her. "I don't know a whole lot, but I do believe it is a man."

"What if you're wrong?"

"I could be, Ava," he admitted with an impish grin on his face while he gave an innocent shrug. "I mean, I never met the guy, so anything is possible." He hesitated and searched her face. "Why so curious?"

"I just," Ava wasn't sure how to explain it and slowly approached him, but didn't get close enough to touch. It was probably better that way. "I just want to know more about the immortal vampires and I've been hearing stuff about the guy…I guess they call him the rock star of vampires?"

A smirk crossed Bryan's face and he looked down at his legs for a moment, then back into her face. "That's what they *do* call him. However, my understanding is that it isn't because he's the all-mighty power over all us vampires. It's his sexual prowess that has brought on that title."

"Oh," Ava felt slightly embarrassed. "I didn't realize-

"It's fine," Bryan shook his head and continued to speak in a gentle, flowing voice. "I understand. You are hearing bits and pieces of information and probably aren't getting a very clear picture of this man. Unfortunately, I can't really add very much and chances are, it's probably stuff you already know."

"Such as?"

"Ah," Bryan shook his head and glanced at a nearby table and appeared to be lost in thought. Easing back to lean against the side of her couch, he seemed hesitant to reply. "Umm...well, I know that he is the man who can make idiots like me disappear in a flash. I know that he frowns upon people telling our secret and even more so, if we turn them into vampires. So, I basically have already done two things that can put my head on the chopping block. I guess it all kind of balanced out."

"Maybe."

"Well, then again, maybe not," he continued shaking his head nervously. It was a less confident side of Bryan and one she wasn't used to seeing. "I guess, I can't write it off so easily. My point is that he frowns upon bringing more people into this lifestyle, whether it is mortal or immortal. Although, I am told that he especially frowns upon more immortal vampires."

"Why?"

"Cause there's enough in the world."

"Do you know this for a fact?" Ava automatically shot out another question. Her heart raced in anticipation of the answer. As it turned out, Bryan knew more information than some people and unlike most of the others; he was easier to talk to about it.

"Yeah, I mean you hear stuff, right?" He shrugged bashfully. "I was in Europe for a year, after all. That's where the majority of vampires are said to be."

"Really?" Ava felt her eyes widen in fascination. "And where else?"

"Ah, I heard a few are in Australia, some more in Asia..." He shook his head and paused. She had the very distinct impression that Bryan wasn't comfortable discussing the topic. "Honestly, I think they are on every continent but the most powerful and the oldest mostly live in Europe."

"Where in Europe?"

"Throughout," Bryan calmly answered her questions, even though the desire in his body was increasing by the moment. There were some signs that only she or another vampire would recognize as sexual arousal. It was a hint of something in his eyes, a slight scent arising from his body that the average person wouldn't notice, and a rise in temperature that caused a very faint pink hue in his cheeks. "But mostly in the UK."

"Why the UK?" She heard herself asking in a seductive voice and automatically wondered why she had done such a thing.

"That's just where they come from, Ava." He extended his hand, encouraging her to come closer. She hesitated.

"And in Canada?"

"Yes, they are in Canada." He grinned. "We're here, aren't we?"

"I meant, immortals?" She felt slightly frustrated. "Where are the immortals?"

"All the places I just mentioned," he insisted. "But also Canada. I'm not sure where or if they are even in this city, but they *are* in this country."

"I heard mostly larger cities?" Ava continued to throw questions at him as if to test his patience, but it was a test he always passed.

"That would make sense with what I know," he nodded. "If you were immortal, would you want to be roaming around a small town? A place where everyone knows everyone else's business? Not likely."

"What else do you know?"

"Unfortunately, not much else." He shuffled around uncomfortably. He attempted to make it look like it was due to the discomfort of the place he sat, but she knew better. "I just know they are all over the world and that their identity is a secret. No one can know that vampires exist and these people make sure that no one finds out."

"So you don't know where this guy who oversees us all is? How come we can't see him?"

"He doesn't exactly take appointments," Bryan joked and cleared his throat, noting the seriousness in her eyes. "I don't know where he is, Ava. I really don't. I honestly have done everything in my power to avoid this guy, I haven't exactly been looking for him."

"Do you know who would know?" She continued to push. After all, Bryan had connections all over the world, couldn't he find out?

"I'm not sure," Bryan replied. "I can try to find out from my friends, but I can't promise anything. They aren't any more likely than me to know."

"Do you know any immortal vampires, personally?"

He hesitated and it made her suspicious. "No, Ava, I don't know any personally. Just mortals like us."

"Are you sure?" She wanted to give him another chance to answer the question because she was sure the first response was not correct.

"I can't tell you anymore, Ava," he said and she could sense that the discussion was finished. "I wish I could, but I really can't."

"I have one more question."

"Go ahead."

"Why did you turn me?" It was something that had crossed her mind many times. Of course, she had begged him to, once learning his secret. However it didn't sound like it was something that was ordinarily done, regardless of the situation.

"I sensed something in you," Bryan answered gently and he once again extended his hand and unlike the last time, she slowly approached him. "I sensed a loneliness and it was something I recognized very well. I knew you were searching for something and I guess maybe I thought being a vampire would fill some kind of void in your life."

"How could you recognize loneliness?" Ava countered, recalling how popular he had been in high school. Bryan was the last person she would expect to understand how it felt to be completely secluded from the world. "Of all people, I doubt you truly understand loneliness?"

"Why not?" He whispered as she moved closer; his eyes shone as they looked up in to hers. Ava could hear his breath become labored and watched his pupils dilate. "What makes you assume I wasn't lonely?"

"You were always the most popular guy in high school. How could you possibly be lonely?" She thought back to the days when she sat alone in the school cafeteria while a small group of popular students gathered around Bryan, as if he were king of the universe.

"So? Ava, you really don't know much about my life." He clasped his hand in hers and squeezed it. His voice grew softer and there was an unmistakable vulnerability as he spoke. "There was much more going on behind the scenes when I was turned, it happened when I was very young and the popular person you saw in high school was a vampire. A vampire that was able to make the girls understand sexual pleasure like they never had before, that's why I was popular." He uttered the last few words with slightly elevated breath and he pulled her closer still, until she stood just over him. "Loneliness isn't something that is solved in a bedroom and it is the result of many years of neglect."

She silently nodded. He was right. In that moment, she had a new respect for him.

"After all, we are the world's orphans." He moved her closer still until their legs touched. A shot of electricity ran through her veins. "No vampire was brought up in a happy home, by stable parents and lived a normal childhood. You don't become this because everything is right in your world. A subconscious part of yourself is seeking it, just like you are seeking the immortal lifestyle now. The only difference is the immortal lifestyle is one step farther because clearly, being a mortal vampire isn't enough. And I truly do understand."

Gazing into his eyes, Ava knew he really did appreciate her situation. Maybe in a way no one else ever did. She felt every last defense fall to the ground.

"A part of you was calling out for me that night at the bus stop." He let go of her hand and slowly eased his arms around her waist. He was no longer capable of breathing normally; as he moved his face inches from her own and his hot breath caressed her cheek. At the same time, Ava felt his hands embracing her waist. His fingers dug into her skin and she felt all the desires from earlier in the night overwhelming her entire body.

"There was such a strong, intense loneliness and unhappiness inside of you, that I could feel that you wanted to be one of us." He spread his legs and moved her between them. She could feel the heat from his body mingle with her own, sending an uncontrollable throbbing inside her thighs. It was the combination of his hot breath touching her face; the warmth of his body and his labored breathing that was driving her crazy. She continued to stay focused.

"I could sense it immediately or I never would have approached you. I never would've changed you," Bryan continued. "We all send out signals even when we aren't aware."

"I thought it was because I was so naïve and innocent." Ava dully admitted. "That you could pull the wool over my eyes."

"Not at all!" he insisted. "True, I did sense an innocence with you but it was like an aphrodisiac for me. It wasn't some kind of game. I wasn't attempting to hurt you, even though I know I did. There was definitely something that was very different with you that I found incredibly attractive. I made a judgment call when I turned you. I honestly thought it was the right decision."

"Really?"

"Really, Ava." He drew her even closer. Her body was not touching the bulge between his legs as his hands slid over her hips. "I assure you, I did only what I thought you wanted me to do. Maybe I was wrong to take advantage of such a situation, but I just followed my instincts. And as a vampire, I don't have to tell you how strong our instincts are, now do I?"

"No, you don't," she replied as he pulled her into his arms and their conversation was over.

Chapter Fifteen

"So, there are a few things I don't understand," Ava whispered to Bryan in the dead of the night. She knew he was awake. The sound of someone breathing was very different when they were asleep; it was softer, gentle and pure. It was the only time any human being was in such a peaceful state that tranquility swept over them. It was something Ava had noticed almost immediately after becoming a vampire. "I still don't really understand why you changed me when you knew it was forbidden? You said there was sadness inside of me but what does *that* mean? Why me? Aren't there hundreds of miserable women in this city?"

"It sounds like there are a *lot* of things you don't understand," Bryan's voice was calm, relaxed and showed no judgment. It was one of things that Ava immediately had liked about him. Probably because it forced her to relax, which was something completely against her true nature. He cleared his throat and swallowed. "Where shall I begin?"

"Anywhere," Ava replied as she felt his fingertips gently running over her arm, while his eyes suddenly opened and glowed through the darkness. Normally such a gesture would've stimulated her senses and turned into a physical encounter; however, she was completely exhausted after the intense night that had followed their return home from the Halloween party. "Start wherever you wish."

Bryan cleared his throat and sighed loudly. Rolling over on his side, she felt his naked leg against her own and she sensed that he was hoping to create a diversion from answering her questions. However after a few minutes of silence, he finally began to speak. "First of all, I should tell you how I became a vampire. Maybe everything will make more sense, if I do."

Ava sensed a rare helplessness in his voice—it was like a lightning bolt shooting through her body, causing her head to swing around and she gazed at the man beside her. Bryan's eyes were staring into the dark and his face appeared serene and firm. "Please tell me everything." She felt the words flow from her lips, even though Ava made no conscious choice to say them. "Please?"

"Okay, I've never told this story to anyone," he began and momentarily closed his eyes. "It happened when I was still a kid. I was probably. . ." Bryan hesitated before continuing. "I was probably 16. It happened in the middle of the night. But the worst part is that I don't even remember it happening."

"Wait," Ava's interruption seemed to break him from a trance, his eyes shone back in her direction. "I don't understand. How did you not know for certain that it happened? And I thought you couldn't turn someone who was still that young?"

"You're not *supposed* to turn someone that young." Bryan corrected her and suddenly, Ava felt very naïve. Why had she taken that rule so literary? "But it happens. And in fact, I bet it happens a lot. It's just that the desire isn't there. You don't smell kids like you do adults, so they're usually out of risk because they aren't a temptation. But they aren't completely safe. No one is safe from anything in this world."

"Oh," Ava's voice was soft and child-like, which ironically was exactly how she felt after that comment. She also felt stupid.

"That's what I love about you," Bryan's voice was suddenly full of humor. "I love the fact that you have this innocent belief that the world always runs the way it's supposed to."

"I never said that I thought *everything* runs the way it should," Ava insisted in her defense. "I just thought there were some pretty clear cut rules regarding vampires."

"True, there are, but not everyone follows them," Bryan reminded her. "After all, I wasn't supposed to turn you or even tell you that we existed, but I did, didn't I? It happens and sometimes you sneak under the wire for your stupidity, sometimes you don't. It's a risk you take."

"So, does this happen a lot?"

"Turning kids? I don't know." Bryan snuggled closer to her and she could feel his hot breath on her shoulder. "I've never heard specific stories. I'm not even sure who did mine. There's a good chance they met an untimely death, but I can't be certain."

"So, what do you *think* happened, Bryan?"

"I'm pretty sure a babysitter did it."

"You had a babysitter when you were 16?" Ava started to laugh. "Are you serious?"

"Not *my* babysitter," He joined her by grinning. She could see his teeth as he smiled in the darkness. "My parents split up when I was fifteen and before the divorce actually went through, mom and I were kind of homeless for a couple of months. We went to live with my aunt Becky. Her husband was in the army and away at the time plus she had a newborn baby, so she kind of welcomed having my mom around."

"So the babysitter was actually for your aunt's baby?"

"Exactly," Bryan spoke slowly. "Sometimes she and mom would go out for dinner or whatever and I don't think she trusted a boy who just turned sixteen to baby-sit a newborn, so she hired some girl who went to college with my sister. I was just as thankful because I didn't want to be stuck changing diapers."

"It's funny, what you remember," Bryan cut into his own story and moved away from Ava—it wasn't far, but *she* sensed it. "I remember my mother commenting on how it was fantastic that Becky was helping out this college kid who needed the money, by hiring her as a babysitter. And yet, she made me what I am today. I became all the things my mother hated in my father. A womanizer who is irresponsible—isn't it funny how life works out?"

"You choose to be that way," Ava casually reminded him. "Only you can make that choice."

"I realized that—now," Bryan agreed. "But when I was 16 with raging hormones on top of the whole vampire thing, I became an animal."

"Your mom obviously didn't know what the babysitter would do to you," Ava pointed out. "And you don't seem positive it was her that did this to you?"

"I'm pretty sure," Bryan cleared his throat and moved closer to Ava, laying his face against her shoulder. "I had a dream that she was seducing and biting me. At least, I thought it was a dream until the next morning when I got in the shower and the water hit the back of my neck. It was like a jolt through my whole body. Every drop that touched my skin was painful and when I looked in the mirror, I saw the bruising and small cuts. At the time I hadn't realized what had happened."

"When did you start to feel that something was wrong?"

"I just started feeling really tired all the time," Bryan replied and Ava nodded. Most people would've written it off as a bad flu, had they not been aware of the change. It was a fatigue that was unlike any other. When a vampire's body needed blood, it created a physical drain that could be felt in every limb and Ava had even experienced some occasions where she was light headed. Many women who were not aware of their status just assumed it was a lack of iron in their blood that made them feel so exhausted. Many doctors, in fact *most* doctors, misdiagnosed it as anemia, thyroid issues or depression. Ava even heard of one incident where a woman had been diagnosed as having cancer—it just proved to her that doctor's really played a guessing game with people's health.

"So, what happened?"

"Mom dragged me to a doctor a few times," Bryan took in a deep breath and she could see his chest rise and fall. "Nothing seemed to help. She assumed it was stress due to the divorce and put me on anti-depressants. Or, should I say, she tried to put me on anti-depressants. I was old enough to know that I wasn't depressed and pretended to take them, but threw them out."

"So how did you know you were a vampire?"

"I actually didn't at first," Bryan admitted. "But as my senses became stronger, I just thought it was somehow linked to puberty or something. I didn't understand at all. I was horny as hell, but so were all my friends, so I didn't think anything of it. I could see and hear everything, but I didn't give it a lot of thought. Just assumed it was normal for all kids."

"And then one day, I was at a party," Bryan was lost in thought as he told the story, staring at the ceiling. "I was at a party with this chick. It was weird 'cause she stood out in the crowd like any vampire does, but at the time I didn't understand why. It was almost like a light surrounded her and the hair on the back of my neck stood on end. And I could smell this strange, scent that I didn't understand."

"She came up to me and we were talking and hitting it off and suddenly she asked, when I turned. I had no idea what she was talking about. She looked at me like I was crazy and said, 'A vampire?' and I laughed at her. I thought she was just high or something, but it didn't take long before it became clear that she knew something about me, that I hadn't even realized."

"What made you believe her?"

"She described everything so perfectly," Bryan responded. "The bruising, how I felt weak all the time, how my senses were intense, everything. She knew it all and it was too much of a coincidence. And when I still had some doubt, she told me to drink blood. She told me to pick up some chick that night and bite her, to make sure I tasted her blood and I would feel alive for the first time in months. I did what she told me." The room was silent for a few minutes before he continued. "She was right."

"The difference was tremendous. It was like I had my life back again. And the next time I saw this same chick at a party, we talked about it. That's how I began to learn about who I am now."

"Did you tell her the babysitter story?"

"Yeah, she pretty much agreed with me," Bryan replied and seemed to snap out of his trance-like state. "She thought that was when it happened. Especially when I told her about the dream and the bruising I found on the back of my neck, the next morning."

Ava nodded silently. She had the same bruising on the morning following her change. It was easy to understand why the entire ordeal would've been confusing for someone who knew nothing of his or her own vampire status.

It was one thing to diagnose a disease, but how can you diagnose yourself as something that wasn't even supposed to be real?

"The sadness inside of you," Bryan continued to answer her questions, while moving even close to her. "I think I sensed it even back in high school. And as strange as it might sound, I did relate to it. But there was too much distraction when we were both in school. When I saw you as an adult, something just told me that this might be the answer for you. Maybe it wasn't the perfect solution but maybe it could send you on a different path, one that opened your eyes to a whole new world."

"And you wanted to do that for me?"

"Yes," Bryan laid the side of his face against her shoulder and his long eyelashes fluttered against her skin. "And it was you, not any others because most of their misery was superficial and stupid. I could sense their unhappiness being related to their appearance, boyfriends and other ridiculous things. But for you, it was different."

"How so?" Ava's breath grew heavy as his eyelashes continued to brush up against her naked skin, in a rhythmic motion. She attempted to hide her desire for him by clearing her throat.

"It was just different in a...." He stopped and seemed to be choosing his words carefully. "I don't know how to describe it, but on a deeper level. It wasn't just a superficial scratch that would heal but almost like a deep cut that would leave a scar." Bryan admitted and stared into her eyes. "When I saw you at the bus stop that night, I knew that you felt no sense of hope, just complete despair. And I felt that you had nothing to lose by joining our world. I felt that maybe it was the answer for you, even though maybe it was a bit presumptuous of me. But I wanted to get to know you better and see if this was a lifestyle that would somehow improve your disposition."

Ava hadn't realized that Bryan's attempts were meant to save her and found it interesting. It was strange how differently both he and Landon looked at the vampire lifestyle. Landon would never suggest it as an option to save someone, but as a way to ruin a life.

"And now, I'm not always sure if I made the right choice," Bryan admitted as he moved his face close to her own, causing Ava's heart to race uncontrollably. "But at the time, it was the choice that I thought was the right one. I never really thought about the consequences or downfalls."

"I don't want to seem as if I don't take any responsibility in this situation," Ava brushed her lips against his face. "I realize that I asked you, begged you to be a vampire. I thought it was the right thing for me. I thought. . .I guess I thought the same thing as you."

But would she always?

Chapter Sixteen

Ava didn't want to get out of bed on Monday. It didn't matter that she just spent an enjoyable weekend with Bryan. It didn't matter that her new boss was very pleasant. It didn't matter that she was well rested on a beautiful, sunny morning. She had no motivation.

But eventually, she *did* get out of bed. Opening her window ajar, she had hoped to be inspired by some fresh November air, but instead discovered two familiar voices floating through her room: it was Landon and Bryan.

"...time for this. I have an important meeting with my agent in a half hour," Bryan said abruptly, the sound of a garbage truck almost drowning out his words, as it stopped across the street. "If you have an issue, you'll have to take it up with me later."

"No, I'm taking up *my* issue with you right *now*," Landon Owens spoke with such hostility, that Ava felt a jolt run through her veins and lurch into her heart. The frosty air caressed her body but she couldn't close the window yet. "I know you were with Ava this weekend and *you* know how I feel about that."

Bryan sighed loudly and in a voice that resembled that of a defiant teenager, his response was simple. "Yeah, I know."

"And yet, you did it?" Landon spoke with authority and for a moment, Ava couldn't help but compare his reaction to that of a parent.

"I'm not picking up the pieces when you decide to fuck off again and screw half of Europe," Landon snapped. "Don't you ever learn from your mistakes?"

Bryan once again sighed loudly. Ava could picture him running his fingers through the few curls that usually avoid the grasp of the gel he used every morning on his short, blond hair. His eyes were probably searching the area for an escape route, even though he knew that avoiding Landon was impossible. He was racking his brain for the right words, the perfect smile and the most charming and effective way to mollify this situation. Ava knew him well.

"Look, I understand why you have such a low opinion of me. I get it, I really do," Bryan's voice was calm. "But I don't have any kind of vicious plan in the works. This is a different time, a different circumstance and Ava has a mind of her own. She certainly wasn't forced to spend the weekend with me." He paused for a moment before throwing in the kicker. "And I only fucked my way through about a quarter of Europe, if you must know."

That's when Ava could hear the faint sound of his shoes against the pavement, as he walked away.

It wasn't until she was in the shower that Ava really thought about the exchange. Although it was somewhat flattering that Landon jumped to her defense, she wondered how he knew about her weekend with Bryan. What had he seen or heard? And for that matter, why did he think she needed someone to defend her in the first place? Although it was true that Bryan had left her in a mess the last time, it was also shortly after she had changed to a mortal vampire. And although Bryan's actions were irresponsible, it was a different situation. Would her one, most vulnerable moment, turn into the crayon that colored her entire life?

After getting out of the shower and putting on her makeup, Ava slowly dressed and eventually made her way to work. She had no appetite and in fact, the strong scent of coffee as she entered her office, was almost enough to make her want to vomit. Coffee hadn't irritated her in a long time, so clearly she was a little too sensitive that day.

A split second after tolerating the unpleasant scent, Ava was faced with Nisha's anxious eyes. It was clear that something was wrong because the attractive, Indian woman could not hide her emotions. It definitely wasn't the best way to start the morning.

"What's wrong? You look upset." Ava asked before the young woman had a chance to introduce her concerns. "Did something happen?"

"It's not *what* happened," Nisha whispered in a scratchy voice while her dark eyes expanded. "It's what is *about* to happen."

"Which is?"

"I heard that Ms. Lee is going to be fired." Nisha wasn't able to hide the sadness in her voice, while Ava had to bite her lip in order to hold back her laughter. The fantasy of doing cartwheels through the office briefly passed through her mind.

"But she...she's not even here now," Ava attempted to show no judgment in her reaction. It did seem odd that the company intern would even be aware of this kind of situation. Why would she be exposed to such sensitive information? "I don't understand."

"No one does," Nisha confessed with some panic in her voice. "But Derrick Johnston is coming here this morning and the rumor is that he's going to fire someone. Ms. Lee is scheduled to come in later this morning, that's why we think it's her."

"Really?" Ava felt her hope deflate. The fact that it was only a rumor gave her little comfort. Had she gotten her hopes up for nothing? But maybe there was still some hope for the morning. Perhaps she would have an opportunity to ask some questions of the immortal vampire, while Derrick was visiting their office. "So, Mr. Johnston will be here shortly?"

"Ye..Yes," Nisha appeared confused by Ava's reaction. "But aren't you worried?" She paused, and then hurriedly continued. "I mean, maybe it's not actually Ms. Lee. What if it is one of us that is about to be fired? Oh my God! I can't lose this internship. I need it for school. What if they are closing the office?"

"Nisha, come on," Ava couldn't help but to speak abruptly toward her coworker. She was such an intelligent lady but sometimes she said the most ridiculous things. "The CEO of the company isn't coming here to fire someone like *us*. You're an intern and I answer the phones, he couldn't give a fuck about us. And to be honest, we don't even know that he is coming here *to* fire someone. It doesn't make sense that he would bother stopping by at all. CEOs don't exactly hang around their companies."

"I know," She shook her head sadly and showed her puppy dog eye reaction. "I still don't want to see Ms. Lee fired. She was always so kind to me. I would feel terrible to see her go."

"She might have been kind to you," Ava thought about the fact that it was actually her own hex that had caused the former boss to fall down the stairs, and couldn't help but smirk. "But not me, so I won't exactly lose any sleep over it."

Realizing that her comments probably came across too harshly for the sympathetic co-worker, Ava quickly jumped back in. "I'm sure things will work out as they are meant to, don't worry. It may be nothing at all. We could all be overreacting."

But Nisha turned out to be right. Derrick Johnston rushed into the door shortly after her prediction, saying a brief hello to Ava, before heading into Matthew Crole's office. The door was automatically shut and a layer of tension hovered over the staff. Ava noticed the accountants finding various excuses to pass the closed door and glance toward it, then look in her direction, as if attempting to read her reaction. She showed nothing.

Ms. Lee hobbled in on crutches shortly afterward, all smiles and sunshine as if she were about to be crowned as Miss Universe. Almost an hour later she staggered past Ava again, this time with a grimace on her face; actually, she was *lead* out by one of the building's security officers.

Ava recognized just how ugly Ann Lee really was as she limped out the door. Her eyes were small, narrow and frown lines filled her pale face. Suddenly, the former boss's hair, clothes, everything looked pathetic and unattractive. She no longer walked with authority but in shame and Ava hated to admit it, but there was something about watching this woman suffer that she enjoyed. She couldn't help but shoot the former boss a smirk, to which she was a recipient of a glare.

Luckily, Nisha was on the phone in another office at the time. The last thing Ava felt like doing was trying to comfort her coworker over something she personally was happy about. Eventually Derrick and Matthew pulled each of the Anderson & Smith employees into an office and let them know that this 'incident' wasn't meant to become office gossip—any concerns over the 'dismissal of Ms. Lee' were to be brought to their attention and would be addressed. Ava was the last person to be spoken to and she assumed it was because she was the lowest ranking person in the office, but soon discovered there were other reasons.

As she approached the room where the two men sat, Matthew rose and quietly told Derrick that he would be taking the conference call in the boardroom. Smiling at Ava on the way out, Matthew closed the door and left her alone with the company's CEO.

"Ava, have a seat," Derrick pointed to the same chair she had sat in when they last had a discussion, the one where he advised her to remove the hex on Ms. Lee. "We must have a little chat."

She gave him a wary smile and sat down.

"Ava, you do realize that it is very rare for the CEO of a large company such as Anderson & Smith to visit any of its offices. In fact, it's almost unheard of and yet, here I am again." His dark eyes sparkled as he waved both arms in the air and she recognized his fragrance as an expensive men's cologne. "It will be the exception, rather than the rule. Today I had some business to attend to, which I have finished. Everything is now as it should be and I don't plan to return any time soon."

"But before I leave, I want you to know that I see you as a huge asset to this company."

"You do?" Ava blurted out, considering how frightened she had been of him only days earlier. Should she even trust him now? His sudden change in disposition was questionable.

"Indeed, I do!" He insisted and spoke to her casually, as if they were old friends. "Your heightened senses make you an asset and even though I once gave you *shit* for putting a hex on Ms. Lee, I now must thank you. As it turns out, the old bird was doing some creative accounting."

Ava's eyes flew wide out. "Really?"

"Yes, she was," He relaxed back in his chair. "And although any hostility you had toward her had nothing to do with this incident, I'm happy that your hex caused her to be away. It gave us a chance to review her work."

"See, if Ms. Lee had gone on vacation, she could've had time to cook the books. But where she was so suddenly relieved of her duties, Matthew quickly noticed that something was off and immediately alerted my attention to the issue."

"Wow!" Ava was stunned by the news. "But I don't understand. Ms. Lee knew you were coming to the office all last week, so wouldn't it make sense she cover her tracks then?"

"Somewhat, but we weren't planning to go over the books. We were just discussing the general function of this office. I felt like we weren't bringing in the business we expected, so I was here to find out why that might be," Derrick replied and then went on to explain, "I think it's important to occasionally do some investigating on my own, rather than send someone else to look into things for me. As it turned out, it was in my best interest to do so."

"And Matthew found out what she was doing?"

"Yes, although things looked on the up and up at a glance, there was something that caught his eye and well, here we are now."

"I guess everything works out in the end," Ava wasn't really sure of what else to say. Although she was still processing everything that Derrick Johnston had just told her, another part of her wanted to rush ahead and ask him questions about the immortals. She had several burning the tip of her tongue but was just waiting for the perfect opportunity.

"Indeed it does," Derrick replied and shared a grin with Ava.

"I am surprised though," Ava admitted. "My senses are usually pretty strong and I didn't sense any deception from her."

"Nor did I," Derrick shrugged. "And that puzzles me as well, Ava. How could something like this get past both of us? Especially you; mortal vampires still carry the human trait of intuition and that combined with all the other senses, makes you very quick to pick up on anything that is a little...funny? Would that be a suitable word here? Funny? Strange?"

"Both work," Ava assured him. "I didn't realize that mortal vampires had that power. I just assumed we had nothing over the immortals." She was relieved that he brought up the topic. Now they could ease into her questions—or, so she thought.

"But we do have some instincts, even though we are immortal," his eyes suddenly darkened, narrowing as he tilted his head. "And I know what you want and it's not going to happen."

Chapter Seventeen

"What?" Ava was taken aback by his comment. How could he possibly know what *she* wanted? Her cheeks became warm as he stared.

"Ava, I know that you want to become an immortal and it's simply not going to happen," He spoke to her sternly, with a trace of compassion in his voice. "These things are monitored and we have enough trouble keeping our secret as it is, without creating more of us that will be here forever. Mortal vampires are bad enough, but at least you people expire at some point. But immortals roam the earth forever and the more we have, the more likely it is that someone will learn our secret."

Ava wanted to say something but her throat felt dry and she couldn't form words.

"And I know you feel this way, not because I have clairvoyant powers," he reassured her, with signs of understanding in his voice. His eyes never left her face, as it now was burning up. "I know because word gets around the vampire community. The right people know that you want to make the change and we have been sternly informed that it was *not* to happen."

"But, why not?" She asked finally able to find her words. "Why *not* me? Who decides? I don't understand."

"See that is the thing, Ava. You are not supposed to understand. You aren't even supposed to know or question it." He folded his hands before him and searched her face. "Why do you want this so much? What, about this lifestyle appeals to you? Do you really think this is something you would want a year from now? What if its just a phase?"

"I don't know," she awkwardly admitted. Feeling stupid, Ava quickly jumped in with a rambling response. "I just feel like being a mortal vampire isn't enough. Something tells me that this is what I am looking for, that this is just what I need. I'm not content with my life right now and as soon as I learned about immortals, I automatically knew that this was the answer for me."

"What question is it answering for you, exactly?" Derrick appeared fascinated. "You do realize, we *never* die. You will watch as all those around you die. You will watch your idols die. You will witness things on this earth that you would've wished to be dead for, as I often do." He paused for a moment and Ava felt her face heat up again. She felt ridiculous and pathetic under his intimidating stare. "You must always move around, never stay in one place. Your entire life is a lie. And you can't stop it. Ever."

Her head hanging down, Ava knew he was right. Could she watch all her friends die? Could she live a secret life, moving from place to place, cautious to never get attached? Plus, did she want to see the world 100 years from now? Would it fill her with shame?

"You do realize you also can't marry unless it is another immortal vampire who knows your secret. It is too risky. You can never have children," he spoke gently. "It's not the solution; it just introduces a new set of problems."

"But I feel like I can be part of something much stronger than I am now," Ava attempted to explain in a child-like voice and quickly thought of what Benjamin once said. "I want to be one of those people who hides the secret, who helps to keep everything together. I want to explore the world and see everything it has and let's face it, one lifetime is never going to be enough to do everything I want to do. It is not enough time to read the books I want to read, see the places I want to see and experience the things I want to experience. I can live a million lives rather than just one."

"Perhaps you are only meant to do so much in your lifetime," Derrick's voice was calm and his words, to the point. "But although it has some positives, it simply isn't what you think. I believe you might be looking for answers in the wrong place."

Ava sighed loudly in frustration. Yet again, someone was talking to her as if she were a clueless child who couldn't think for herself—why did everyone seem to think she wasn't able to make this decision on her own? It filled her heart with frustration and sadness.

"You don't understand," Ava insisted, waving her hands around. "This isn't just some stupid phase for me. This is something that I *really* want." Her voice began to soften and she suddenly didn't care how much vulnerability she showed to this man, who was a stranger to her. "From the first time I heard of the immortals, something inside of me just sparked. A part of me that I never knew was there, suddenly felt alive. And I just knew that *this* was something I had to do."

"You are *so* young to be making such a big decision," Derrick spoke with sincerity in his voice, but at the same time, she knew he didn't understand her devotion.

She felt like no explanation would satisfy him and Ava wasn't even sure how to express what was in her heart. "Look," she began thoughtfully. "I've never been someone who really ever fit in. I didn't fit in when I was in school. I don't fit in this office," she gestured toward the closed door beside them. "I don't fit in with other vampires. Something inside of me just tells me that this is the answer. That being an immortal is where I belong."

Ava bit on her bottom lip and felt as though her explanation was falling short. It just sounded like mindless ramblings rather than a reason with substance. "Maybe I could put myself in a position to make the world a better place. Maybe I could feel like I have a purpose. I can't explain it to you in any words you might want to hear, but trust me when I say that this is what I want. That being immortal would be my home."

Derrick Johnston remained silent for a few moments after she stopped speaking, his face showing no expression one way or another. "You are following the wrong yellow brick road Dorothy and I have no power leading you to the wizard, so any arguments for this change are lost on me."

She nodded slowly. "Can you at least tell me more about the immortal world?"

"What is it you wish to know?" He shrugged. "I don't think there is anything I can add. You know that there are only a few of us roaming the earth. We make sure we are in positions where we can hide our secrets and that we move around enough that no one can discover ours."

"What about your powers?"

"Well yes, we do have some powers," Derrick nodded. "Not unlike your own, except more intense. Our senses are stronger so we can, for example, see things much farther away than mortal vampires. There really isn't much else to tell. That's why I don't understand what all the fuss is about."

"I feel like you aren't telling me everything," Ava surprised both of them with her confession. "I feel you are trying to downplay the entire thing to me."

"Oh, you do, do you?" He grimaced and became much more serious. "Look, the bottom line is that you cannot make the change unless an immortal changes you and we aren't in the position to do so, unless the one who leads us says so. And the likelihood of that ever happening is very small. It's rarely allowed."

"Under what circumstances would he?" Ava continued to push.

"I don't know the answer to that question," Derrick admitted. "In fact, it's been a very long time since this opportunity has been granted to anyone."

"Do you remember why he did, at the time?"

"Ah, hmm. . .." Derrick appeared to be in thought and his lips started to curve into a grin. "It was a very long time ago, however, I believe that it was because of a romantic relationship."

"You mean, like. . .a girlfriend?" Ava found herself stumbling over the words carelessly.

"Don't get any ideas, young lady!" His eyes were downcast while his eyebrows rose, in an almost seductive pose. A huge smirk covered his face and he seemed much more amused than made sense in their discussion. "That went over terribly, if I do recall so I don't anticipate it will happen again. And definitely not with *you*."

"Wait a minute!" Ava suddenly was hit with a thought. "You know who this man is, *don't* you?" Her eyes widened and suddenly she had no doubt what the answer was to her question. "You are speaking as if you know him personally, not that you just heard something in the rumor mill. You *know* who this guy is, don't you?"

"Ava, it doesn't matter because *you* don't know who it is and I don't plan on telling you." He quickly shot her down. "I am not in the position to do so anyway, this identity is to be kept secret, no matter what."

"I want to know who it is," Ava was determined. "I want to meet with him myself and tell him my wishes. I want him to tell me to my face that he will not allow me to become immortal and why. I want him to see that I'm serious. Is there any way I can convince you to tell me?"

"It's not a matter of me being willing to tell you," Derrick insisted. "It's more about the fact that I'm not *allowed* to tell you. See, this is one of the reasons why you would not suit the immortal world! There are very specific rules in place that you can't just break as you wish. One of them is that the identity of our leader is to be kept a secret. It's been like that for hundreds of years and isn't about to change just because you bat your eyelashes, giving me some story about why you feel you are one of us. I'm sorry if that isn't a help to you, but it's just the way it is."

With that, Derrick stood up and Ava realized that their conversation was being halted. She felt like her words weren't taken seriously and suddenly all her hope from the morning came crashing down at her feet.

"Can you at least talk to him, tell him that I would like to speak to him," Ava made a last ditch attempt to get her way. "Please let him know that I exist and that I want this more than anything. Please ask him to consider speaking with me."

"This person knows all the vampires!" Derrick was getting frustrated with Ava, his eyes becoming very dark and small. "It's a leaders job to know everything. Don't be such a fool, let it go."

"You make him sound like we are talking about Jesus!" Ava rebutted. "Or Santa Claus."

"You have more of a chance of meeting either Jesus or Mr. Claus than you do of meeting the leader of vampires, I will tell you that much!" He abruptly turned around and headed for the door. "I will pass on your message Ms. Ava but I assure you that your wishes will be ignored. I know your generation thinks you can snap your fingers on a whim and demand whatever it is you wish to have, but it simply doesn't work like that in the real world. And it certainly doesn't work that way in the immortal world. It is my advisement that you let this notion go and move on with your life. Find happiness somewhere else that is much more sensible and one day, you will forget this silly dream that you have to be an immortal."

She felt her entire body slump over as she made her way toward the door. It felt like the longest walk of her life, under his judgmental eyes.

"I would also suggest you to stop asking so many questions and poking your nose where it doesn't belong." He paused for another long moment. "I think you would do much better by asking *yourself* about this discontentment rather than focusing on a quick fix solution to your problems. Perhaps if you spent more time focusing on what you have in life rather than what you don't, life would be a much more pleasant experience for you."

Ava felt shaken by his words and humiliated by his overall tone. He spoke to her like an idiot who had no depth as a person, who had a perfect and sheltered life. She had experienced much more than many her age and yet he judged her as if she were completely clueless.

"I only wish there was a human side to me." His tone dropped and she thought his voice was shaking, even if just a speck. "If only I could trade spots with you, Ms. Ava, I gladly would and you'd quickly see that being an immortal can be the most devastating wish to ever come true!"

Her heart raced as these words rang through her head. There was something very emotional in his voice and she wondered where it came from. Was he right? Was being an immortal *not* the answer? Suddenly, nothing made sense.

Chapter Eighteen

Ava was despondent after her conversation with Derrick. Her one and only dream was to be immortal and he had made it perfectly clear that this was nothing more than a fantasy. It would never happen. The blade of finality had never felt so sharp, so excruciating in her life. Not even Bryan's abandonment of her a year earlier hurt this much.

There was usually something about a definite ending that gave a speck of comfort. Perhaps because it tied up loose ends and doused all fires and simply left you to recover. But this time, it just wasn't working for Ava. A part of her felt as if it was dying and all she could do was watch it waste away into eternity. She was powerless.

And it made her angry. Why were others always capable of having their dreams come true, but never her? How many times can you be defeated by life?

Her luck had turned sour after losing her parents. Being forced to live with a grandmother who had no maternal connection to Ava, made a terrible situation even worse. Feeling unwanted and tolerated rather than treasured, had broken her spirit. Ironically, Ava's only dreams as a child *was* to be loved. But even that turned into an illusion that evaporated before her eyes.

It always came back to pain. Even when she would rage about her own personal abandonment issues, pummeling at a punching bag in her high school gym, eventually she would weakly slide to the floor, drowning in frustrated tears. With agonizing moans rising from the deepest part of her soul and a flood of drops falling between gasping sobs, had anyone else wandered into the dreary room to witness such a scene they would've been dumbfound by her erratic behavior.

The tears usually lasted much longer than Ava realized and left her physically drained. She would eventually rise from the floor, remove her gloves and go into the ladies room to throw some cold water on her face. There, she would sorrowfully stare at the dirty mirror and into her own eyes. Silently she would gaze, feeling a rush of calm after the storm that had overtaken her body.

And it happened again and again: week after week, until something began to heal inside of her. It was a gentle, calming warmth that eased through her body, giving Ava a strength that she never knew existed. But a heart didn't completely heal overnight. It was only the first step in a long, difficult journey.

The school counselor had suggested boxing as a way for Ava to deal with her emotions. Not that it had been her choice to talk to the grey-haired old lady in the first place. It was assumed her dismal grades in school were only a reflection of her emotional life. But Ava knew it was much more complicated than that. And each time the older lady would ask Ava how she felt about her parents' 'passing', she wanted to scream *"How the fuck do you think I feel about my parents both being dead?"* But she never did. Instead, she went through the motions. As if the counselor was listening. As if she cared.

Although Ava enjoyed boxing, she would grow tired of it and eventually stop. She also lied to the counselor in order to get out of their regular sessions. It was sometimes easier to fake a smile and say the words people wanted to hear, than go into dark places that weren't ever truly appreciated or understood.

Her anger grew out of that same lonely place she had explored in her boxing days. Ava had no connection to anyone or anything. Of course, rather than abandonment, this time it was the sting of rejection. She had been open and honest with Derrick but it only lead to another dead-end road.

Had she spoken with the 'Rock Star' of vampires and *he* had told her no, then that perhaps would have given her some sense of closure. Had Derrick suggested a more balanced argument rather than a cryptic warning, perhaps the news would've been easier to swallow. But because she was being told an inequitable 'no' without any room to move, Ava felt like she had been handed an injustice. It was simply a brick wall placed before her and there was no way around it.

And so here it was a couple of weeks before Christmas and happy people were buzzing all around her, making Ava want to crawl into a hole and die. The fact that Bryan was back and constantly trying to show signs of affection, gave her no sense of comfort. Ava knew it wouldn't last. There was no future between them. Meanwhile since his return, Landon all but completely avoided her. It was as if he were angry with Ava for taking up with Bryan again. It didn't make sense and, his attitude only increased her frustrations. It felt as though she could not win.

Ava hadn't bothered to tell Mariah about her conversation with Derrick. It was simply too depressing to even talk about it. Their lunch date following that disappointing day was full of many silent periods and an overall dark mood that hadn't set well with Mariah. In fact, she made a rare Friday night appearance at Ava's door, holding two bottles of wine and a mischievous smile on her face. She was dressed in yoga pants and a comfortable t-shirt, much different from her usual office attire.

"Can I come in?" She appeared hesitant, as if there were a chance that Ava would say no, but her efforts had been appreciated.

"Of course, as long as I can have some of the wine," Ava cleared her throat and showed no signs of joy, with her hair pulled back in a ponytail and wearing a pair of Valentine's Day pajamas.

"Of course, I was planning to share," Mariah pushed past her friend and made herself at home, walking directly to the kitchen then a drawer holding the corkscrew. "Did you seriously think I was going to drink all this myself?"

Without hesitating for a moment, she quickly swung around with her mouth open ajar, "Never mind, don't answer that."

"I wasn't going to say a thing," Ava shut the door and dragged her feet into the kitchen, where Mariah was giving her full attention to the bottle of wine that had somehow opened at record speed. "I'm just surprised you're here."

"Why? We're friends, aren't we?" Her dark eyes searched Ava's face a little more intently than would be expected. "Isn't it normal for friends to visit one another?"

"Of course!"

"Oh good!" Mariah let out a sigh and began rummaging through the cupboard for some glasses. Finding them, she quickly poured them each a glass of red Australian wine and passed one to Ava, then downed the entire contents of her own in a second. Pouring another one, she added, "I was concerned that you were angry with me because you've been so quiet lately."

"Oh, what?" Ava took a small sip of wine. Appearing slightly confused, she finally gathered her thoughts after quickly scanning their last few conversations. "Not at all, I've just been preoccupied with some problems."

"I mean, I know I'm not always forthcoming—" Mariah hesitated and Ava wasn't sure what to say so remained silent. If her friend wanted to talk, she would not stop her. "I thought maybe it was me. But if there was something wrong, you know you could've talked to me about it." Mariah's huge brown eyes carried a rare innocence that few would ever see.

"I know, I just..I just didn't even know how to start," Ava stumbled through her words.

"Come, sit down," Mariah pointed toward the couch that was literally only steps away from the tiny kitchen. Grabbing a bottle of wine and her glass, Ava's friend wasted no time in going into the living room and sitting down. Ava followed hesitantly and wondered if she could talk about such a painful topic with her friend. Derrick's announcement felt like being diagnosed with a fatal disease to Ava. She didn't want her friend to think she was being extreme in her emotions.

"Did that jerkoff Bryan take off on you again?" Mariah attempted to predict the conversation before it began. "Please tell me he hasn't."

"No, actually, he's been great." Ava acknowledged, curling up at the end of the couch with her wine glass in hand. "And I hate to admit it but I almost wouldn't really care if he went away." For a moment she silently wondered if she would feel equally dispassionate about the immortal situation in the future, but quickly pushed the thought aside. It wasn't even close to being the same. "It's just not the same as it was the first time. *I'm* not even the same person that I was a year ago."

"The change will do that to you," Mariah gave her a comforting smile. "But then again, so does life, in general. It's good though, he holds no power over you, right?"

"Right."

"So then, what's going on?"

Ava took a deep breath and leapt into the story about Derrick and her inability to ever be an immortal.

"So, let me get this straight," Mariah finished her second glass of wine and was pouring a third, more generous glass, as she spoke. "You're telling me that you *can't* become immortal because this guy told you no? Are you kidding me?"

"No, it's apparently unthinkable that I even ask to turn because they won't even consider it," Ava stared into her wine glass. "I have no say in the matter."

"Neither does Derrick the dickhead!" Mariah spoke abruptly and in an instant, her innocent chocolate eyes became full of the same fire that Ava saw on a more regular basis. "Who the fuck is he? He can't tell you *shit!*"

"Well, he's an immortal, Mariah," Ava found herself slightly irritated by her friend's insistence that she had a say in the entire situation. "I can't become one of them if they won't allow it."

"But he's just *one* of them! He's not *the* top one of them," Mariah moved closer to Ava and pushed a strand of long hair behind her ear. "You're getting depressed because this one guy told you no? He's not in the position to make these decisions and from the sounds of it; he's just the messenger. Ava, you've gotta talk to the real guy: the so-called 'rock star' of vampires. He's the only one who can say no to you, all these other guys are just repeating his orders."

"But they are *his* orders!" Ava understood that her friend desperately wanted to make her feel better in this situation, but it didn't seem like she fully understood everything. It was kind to be optimistic, but cruel to give false hope.

"Well, you don't necessarily know that and also, I would rather try to convince him then some of these others guys," Mariah insisted. "I think you should push harder to find this leader and don't fuck around with this Derrick guy or anyone else. And how do you even know this guy is an immortal?"

"I'm pretty sure. I get a stronger sense with him. Trust me, you'd know what I mean, if you met him. It's completely different from all the vampires in this building," Ava answered while her brain continued to probe the question. She wasn't even really sure how to answer it. All vampires had a different impact but it was a little more difficult to pinpoint. "I think it's an intimidation thing with him. He makes me nervous."

"And none of the vampires here," Mariah waved her hand around, as if to suggest the entire building, "No one here makes you feel intimidated."

"I don't know if 'intimidate' is the right word, exactly. I just feel really uncomfortable," she replied while touching her chest to indicate inside her body. "I only felt that way a couple of times. The first was when Bryan returned."

Mariah nodded her head, rolling her empty wine glass around in her hand. "Which makes sense 'cause he had been gone so long after turning you."

"And the other person is Landon, but I think that's cause he came along during a very vulnerable time in my life," Ava reluctantly admitted something she didn't even want to consider. She didn't want to think about any feelings she had toward him. Especially considering they weren't reciprocated. "I guess 'cause of our relationship."

"Landon has a different, kind of vibe to him," Mariah reflected for a moment. "I've always noticed that but I just assumed it was because of his personality or because he's been a vampire for awhile. I think he was born that way or pretty close, so obviously it's totally different. He has said it's all he knows."

Ava slowly nodded her head. "Even he's said that he feels that I have no chance of becoming an immortal."

"But again, he has no say," Mariah reminded her, pouring another glass of wine for herself while Ava finished her first. "But hey, why not talk to him and maybe you can persuade him that you are serious. If anyone in this building can help you, it's probably Landon. After all, he is a pretty smart guy."

Feeling slightly encouraged by her friend's words, Ava nodded. Sometimes another point of view enabled her to see more clearly. Maybe things weren't so hopeless after all.

But deep down, she knew Landon would quickly extinguish her hope. He would never help her out with this goal.

Chapter Nineteen

Regardless of Ava's affection for her friend, to the rest of the world Mariah had not lost her edge. This became abundantly clear on the day she flew into the offices of Anderson & Smith, with a vehement presence that both startled and intrigued people in the waiting area. Ava actually witnessed an older man's eyes widen to about twice their usual width, as he stared at the fierce young woman. Beside Ava, Nisha stopped dead in her tracks, as if she couldn't physically leave the spot.

Catching herself before starting on a rampage, Mariah toned down her voice to the decibel of a shy child. "Would you be able to join me for lunch soon?"

Everything about her friend's disposition made Ava nervous. There was a strange mixture of subtlety and fury that was not going unnoticed by anyone else in the room, let alone another vampire who was able to sense the undertones of someone's mood. The intensity was gripping her, and Ava was relieved to look up at the clock and see that she was only ten minutes away from her assigned lunch break.

With a small, reassuring smile, Ava gave a slight nod and in the gentlest tone she could find, she replied, "Just a couple of minutes. Have a seat." Her eyes glanced toward the waiting area, where the older man continued to stare in their direction.

Mariah said nothing but gave a slight smile before making her way to the appointed area. Meanwhile, Nisha escaped the spell she was under and finally approached Ava with a fax in hand. "Is your....*friend* okay?"

Ava noted the strange way Nisha put emphasis on the word *friend* and having already adopted some of Mariah's tension, lifted her eyebrow in curiosity. "Yes." She spoke in the same conciliatory manner as she had just done with her anxious comrade, who was currently looking extremely distant and edgy in the waiting area; the older man continued to stare at her with intrigue in his eyes.

Feeling another tinge of irritation for a variety of reasons, Ava found herself repeating her words mindlessly.

"Yes, *yes,* yes! She's perfectly fine," Ava's last word came out as more of a hiss than anything else and apparently did the trick, because Nisha dropped off whatever was in her hand and rushed away.

Glancing toward the waiting room, Ava took a deep breath and attempted to concentrate on work. Her eyes watched the clock closely as every second seemed to drag out, and Ava felt much like a child waiting for recess. Finally, she grabbed her purse, stuck her head around the corner and quickly informed Nisha that it was her lunch break.

This should make for an entertaining hour.

Following her lead, Mariah calmly stood up and the two headed toward the door. Once the pair was in the hallway, her friend started to unravel.

"I'm ready to *fucking* lose it! You won't believe what happened to me this morning." Mariah began to spit fire almost as soon as the two reached the elevator and waited for it to open. Ava didn't have to ask what had just happened. She already knew.

"Calm down!" She attempted to comfort Mariah, gently touching her slender arm, as they stepped into the elevator. Fortunately, it was empty. Mariah wasted no time jumping into her story.

"The fucking asshole fired me! Just fucking fired me!" She thrust her arms up into the air while her eyes immediately darkened like clouds in the sky, just before a fierce thunderstorm moved in. "And I wasn't doing anything wrong! *They* were and yet, *I* get fired. Can you fucking believe that?"

Her last words shot out with no misgivings at the same time as the elevator door slid opened to a group of older, mostly Asian men. Not that this created a sense of shame or embarrassment for Mariah. Then again, very little did.

With her head held high, she walked out of the elevator and toward the main exit with Ava right behind her. She pretended to not notice the strange looks the two of them were getting. In a way, it was irritating to her because Mariah had every right to speak as she wished. Although it made sense that seeing someone in such professional attire probably created the illusion that she was passionless, always willing to wear the corporate mask, but that would be a very wrong assumption.

"I need a drink!" Mariah proclaimed as she swiftly pulled on her Ray-Ban sunglasses and headed out the door, her heels loudly clicking on the floor at a rapid pace. It was almost as if she couldn't get out fast enough.

Ava rushed to keep up with her and soon the two were outside in the chilly, yet sunny afternoon. It was only a little over a week away from Christmas and all around, decorations peaked out of windows and people rushed past them with shopping bags in hand. For those who had families, it was a warm time of year. For people like Ava and Mariah, it was irrelevant and cold.

"So *what* happened?" Ava finally caught up with her infuriated friend and grabbed onto her arm. "I'm not trying to piss you off, but this isn't the first time you've been fired and it wasn't like you even liked your job. So what, exactly happened? What did they do wrong?"

"They were *fucking* in his office while I was outside dealing with all the pissed off patients, who were waiting to see the doctor!" Mariah blurted it out fast and once again, had no concern for who was around her. This time it was a woman and her two young children, one of whom was giving a bug eyed stare to the lady using bad word. The mother glared at Mariah, who either didn't notice or didn't care. Ava assumed the latter.

"Are you kidding me?" Ava asked as Mariah entered the first pub they could find and quickly found an empty table at the back of the room. The two women hadn't even sat down when the waiter rushed over and gave them an almost creepy, sadistic smile and started to ramble off the days' specials.

"I'll have a double Vodka martini, shaken *not* stirred and just leave the menus with us," Mariah abruptly cut him off and nodded toward the table, as she pulled out a chair to sit down. Ava felt that the waiter was probably biting back his words as he efficiently placed the menus on the table in silence, and then walked away.

"Okay, let's calm down and start the story from the beginning," Ava mildly suggested. "So your boss was doing some girl from the office? Are you sure about that?"

"Yeah, the lazy one with the big tits and no brains," Mariah pulled her sunglasses off and flung them on the table. "Like he's been doing all along. I'm positive they are having a 'secret' fling." She signaled with her hands that she was quoting and shook her head in frustration. "Today I had patients practically piled in the corner waiting for Miss Tits and Ass to screw him, or whatever she was doing so that the rest of us could start our day and—"

The apprehensive waiter returned with her drink in hand, an amused look on his face. "Your drink, mademoiselle." He spoke with an accent that wasn't French and gently sat it in front of her. Ava noted that rather than show irritation, he appeared intrigued by Mariah. With a huge smirk on his lips, he turned his gaze toward Ava. "I'm sorry, I forgot to ask if you would also like something to drink."

"That's...ah, fine," Ava cleared her throat, noticing that half the martini was already in Mariah's mouth. "It was kind of more important that my friend got her drink first..ummm..." Ava cleared her throat and coughed. "You know what, I'll just have a glass of red wine for now, thank you."

Giving a professional nod, he once again rushed away and left the ladies to discuss the events of the day.

"So, I..I think I get the picture," Ava attempted to put it all together. "So your boss...he's doing one of your coworkers and *you* got fired?" Although playing innocent, she already suspected that it was Mariah's mouth that got her in trouble this time around. This wasn't her first rodeo.

"Yes, I'm certain he's been screwing this ditch pig since I started there. They have all these 'meetings' in his office and she follows him around like a pathetic puppy dog, always trying to get his attention in any way possible," Mariah appeared to be calming down slightly as the waiter dropped off Ava's drink and quickly took their order.

"There was only three of us working in the office today, and I had all the people just building up and waiting. We were like two fucking hours behind and I had to try to calm everyone down."

"And?"

"And when he finally came out and started to deal with all these patients, Tits and Ass decided that she needed a coffee break after their 'meeting'!" Mariah once again signaled the quotations with her hand, this time with overly exaggerated body language that made Ava grin despite the seriousness of the topic. "So I grabbed the doctor between patients and told him how I felt."

Ava noted that she finished this sentence as if the innocent employee, merely weighing in on a topic. She knew better.

"And it didn't go well?" Ava asked even though the answer was already quite obvious.

"And...it *didn't* go well," Mariah finished off her drink and glanced around for the waiter, who was nowhere in sight. "I need another drink; where *is* he?"

"Calm down, he'll be back soon," Ava was hoping to hold her back from drinking too much over lunch. "So what did you say to the doctor?"

"Granted, I probably didn't have the best timing," Mariah grudgingly admitted. "But I just told him the way it was. I said you held up patients for a long time and I had to cover for him. And that's fine but it's when he went on to lie about their *meeting*, that I sort of lost it a bit."

"And said?"

Catching sight of the waiter, Mariah mouthed 'another'. He quickly nodded, almost as if he anticipated her request before it was even asked.

"And?" Ava coaxed.

"And I suggested that he should fuck Tits and Ass on his own time, not when we have a million patients waiting outside."

"First of all, are those the exact words you used?" Ava asked but suspected it was, regardless of what Mariah answered.

"Well, I.... kind of. I mean, I don't think I said 'fucking' but I *do* believe I called her Tits and Ass."

Ava thought this entire situation would be funny, had it been a sitcom on television and not real life. Her friend didn't feel the need to censor herself in situations that induced her anger. Although a part of her admired this, another part knew it got Mariah in a lot of trouble.

"Really?"

"Trust me, if you met her you'd see what I mean."

"I have no doubt."

"Anyway, I," She hesitated for only a moment when the waiter dropped off their drinks with the smile of Cheshire cat. Once he was gone, she continued by repeating her comment from earlier. "I just told him to screw around with Tits and Ass on his own time and not when we're knee deep in patients that are pissed off at me for waiting"

"And he was mad 'cause I said he was doing ...*her*."

"Tits and Ass?" Ava repeated the nickname used for the Mariah's former coworker.

"Yes, and I..may have said some other things." Mariah quickly raised her drink and took a huge sip. "I mean it was after he said some things too."

"Which were?" Ava was drinking her wine much faster than usual. She felt as if she were in the front seat of an action packed movie.

"He acted offended that I would suggest he was ever unprofessional and that I would question his moral compass."

"Well, it isn't like he knows you are a vampire with big, vampire ears who can hear things through doors."

"I actually couldn't hear through the doors, but I'm not *stupid*. There are some things that are obvious when people are fuck buddies. Trust me, I know these things."

"He was offended and what else?" Ava asked watching her friend polish off another drink. The distressing situation hadn't affected her appearance, with not a hair out of place or a smear of makeup. Had Ava been fired, she would've looked like someone who had wandered out of a mental ward, with smudged makeup from crying and pale from the emotional upset.

"He suggested that he didn't have much respect for me because I constantly returned to the office smelling like booze. Total detractor from the fact that he is doing Tits and Ass of course, but he went on to get on his high horse about being offended by my comments and totally turned it around as if *I* were the bad one for making suggestions about his character!"

"That does seem like his natural defense in a situation like that."

"I kind of...lost it a bit and said that I had no respect for any man that would seriously stick their dick into Tits and Ass. I mean really!" Mariah suddenly looked sad. "I just couldn't help it, I was so angry!"

"Did you really say that part of it?" Ava couldn't stop her laughter this time.

"Yes! It was clear I was already as good as fired so of course I had to throw in an insult." Mariah shrugged. "Wouldn't you?"

"Well, I..

"The words just flew out of my mouth!" She ran a hand through her hair and for a moment, Ava thought she saw a tear in her eye but it was quickly blinked back. She couldn't help but feel there was more to this story.

"And that's when he fired you?"

"Yes," Mariah started to chew on her straw. "As *if* I had done something wrong. I had every right to voice my concerns."

"And then he fired you?" Ava repeated.

"Yes," Mariah suddenly lost her fire and slumped down in her seat. She stared at her empty martini glass, as if contemplating another one. Ava wondered if the alcohol had stolen some of her passion. "It's not fair."

Although Ava recognized how the timing of any words used in this conversation probably had a negative impact on this situation, she still sided with her friend and felt that it was wrong to put her in such an unfair situation. One of the disadvantages of being a vampire was having extraordinary senses that you weren't able to talk about and therefore you often could not create an argument for your side of many situations. You had no choice but to remain silent and accept things as they were.

And regardless of her tough exterior, Ava could see the misery in her friend's eyes.

But she couldn't help but wonder: did Mariah read the situation correctly?

Chapter Twenty

Winter had officially arrived and Christmas was only days away. While many of her coworkers were looking forward to a holiday season spent with loved ones, Ava was looking forward to time away from her coworkers.

Since her former boss got the boot and Matthew Crole had taken over the office, Ava had to witness all her female coworkers fluttering around him like a bunch of lovesick teenagers. Truthfully, he was divine with his dark eyes, perfectly groomed hair and radiant smile. It was very easy to understand why all the women wanted his attention.

Ironically, it was this same fact that turned Ava off. The idea of chasing after a man that had other women falling at his feet, seemed as appealing as fighting for that season's 'it' toy' at the mall—was it ever really worth the hype? Her personal experience with Bryan suggested that it was not.

Matthew grew on her as weeks went by. Always super friendly with a warm smile that seemed to light up a room, it was hard to really dislike the guy. But watching her coworkers attempting to out-cleavage one another every day, and trimming their skirt hemlines was getting a tad ridiculous. No wonder some men thought themselves' to be the best thing since sliced bread. It was simply a monster that women helped to create.

Now that Christmas break was looming, Ava could avoid her incredibly alluring boss, as well as the parade of oversexed co-workers that followed his every move. She had enough drama in her life without getting in the middle of that situation.

Instead she was home alone, as Bryan had left town once again. This time he was supposedly spending time with his dad and step-mom in Alberta, but Ava didn't really care. For some reason the original allure of his return seemed to fade as time went by. It wasn't that she didn't care about him, but it was becoming abundantly clear that their relationship did not surpass the bedroom (or wherever else they decided to have sex) and she found her original intrigue quickly fading. Perhaps it only happened in order to neatly close a door to the past.

Not that she would stop having sex with him if the opportunity arose in the future. But if he never returned again, she wouldn't be heartbroken.

Mariah was quite surprised to learn this fact. But not as surprised as she was to learn of Ava's disinterest in her current boss, whom had stolen a quick glance at a couple of days earlier, when she picked up Ava for lunch.

" I don't get it?" She sipped on a glass of wine, shaking her head. The girls were meeting in Ava's apartment two nights before Christmas to do a job search for Mariah. So far Ava's friend hadn't had any luck. Sitting on her living room floor, laptops on the coffee table before them, it seemed that the bottle of wine was receiving more attention than either of their well-intended searches.

"What do you mean you don't get it?" Ava set down her glass of wine so quickly, that it almost spilled on her laptop. She decided it was time to move it to the floor. "Even if I wanted to, I would have to wade through all the other girls and their ample cleavage and perfectly manicured fingernails. I just don't think I could do it and I don't want to be part of this whole... situation."

"Situation?" Mariah shook her head in confusion. "What are you talking about?"

"I just see these other girls chasing him around like dogs in heat and I find it pathetic. I don't want to be one of *those* girls, you know?" But after the words were out, she already sensed that her friend was probably not on the same page as her. She would've confidently pursued him from day one and paid no attention whether the other girls were interested in him or not. It would be irrelevant to her.

"I don't think you are giving yourself enough credit," Mariah insisted while flipping from one webpage to another, not really paying attention to the original task she had set out to do. It was a little frustrating to Ava, who was sincerely attempting to help her. Was this the same girl who had been so devastated to lose her job only a few days earlier?

"It's not that I'm not giving myself credit, but that I just don't want to play these games. It's too complicated when you're at work."

Mariah shrugged and grew silent, suddenly very interested in something on her laptop.

"Well, just look the situation with *your* boss and Tits and Bum—"

"Tits and *Ass*," Mariah corrected her. "And it's not at all the same thing. Their relationship didn't affect *them*, it affected me."

"But if I hooked up with my boss, maybe it would affect my coworkers."

"Ah," Mariah swung her hand dismissively through the air. "Who gives a fuck about them? That's not your problem."

"It could be."

"Anyway, the point is that you should consider it after the holidays," Mariah continued to push her point, while seeming somehow detached from the conversation. "Who knows *if* or *when* Bryan will return? He could be gone another year, you never know. And you even said yourself that it was losing some of its original fizz so, you know, why not?" She shrugged continuing to flip through webpages that had less to do with job hunting and more to do with shoe shopping. "It would make your job much more interesting."

"I can't argue with that point."

"Or there is always Landon." Mariah once again made the suggestion.

"Let's not go there again." Ava put her hand up to indicate 'stop'. The possibility seemed extremely unlikely since the two hadn't spoken in weeks. Probably not since Bryan's return and Landon's insistence that she would never become an immortal. It seemed they had nothing to talk about at that point.

"Oh come on!" Mariah teased, realizing that she was hitting a nerve.

Finishing the last of her wine, she pushed her glass aside and focused her full attention on Ava. "You mean, if he showed up at the door right now and asked you to hop into bed with him, you wouldn't consider it for a moment? Come *on!*"

"That would never happen," Ava dismissed the idea and avoided making eye contact with Mariah. "Besides, he is with Chloe."

"Oh I think things are almost done with him and ghoul girl. I saw them arguing in the entranceway earlier this week. It wasn't pretty."

"Well regardless, I don't think we will be revisiting those days." Ava replied dully.

"What exactly happened with you two that there is all this tension," Mariah pried with sparkling eyes, as if she were getting some juicy gossip. "How did you go from hot and heavy to barely speaking? I don't get it and you've never really told me what happened."

"I did something that was..." Ava searched for the words but she wasn't even sure how to finish that sentence. It wasn't exactly something she could voice to put herself in a favorable light, and she certainly couldn't reveal everything to her friend, regardless of how open-minded she was in these situations. Ava could not say the words out loud.

"Did you cheat on him?"

"No! Of course not!" Ava realized that her reaction was probably a little too swift. Looking into her friend's eyes, she recognized that Mariah was actually trying to strengthen their bond, but Ava simply could not tell her the truth. She instead opted to tell a partial truth.

"It was just stupid and pointless," Ava felt her defenses fall to the ground, like a weak kitten just learning to walk. If only *she* hadn't been so weak, perhaps things would've played out very differently.

"What do you mean?"

"It's kind of a long story," Ava stalled.

Mariah leaned against the couch and studied her with pensive eyes. "I am not exactly working right now, so I have all the time in the world. Tell me."

Taking a deep breath, Ava racked her brain and attempted to cherry pick the things she wanted to reveal. There were some secrets that were better kept to one's self. For her, this would be one of them. Rather than handing over the truth on a shiny platter, Mariah would have to settle for crumbs on a paper plate.

"We were getting along great. Things got intense very quickly. I mean, not just physically but emotionally. It was almost..." Ava searched for the perfect words. "....too much too soon."

"And?"

"We started to fight about little things. And then little things became big things." Ava fell silent for a couple of minutes.

"Then we had a final blowout fight and everything just fell apart." Ava shrugged as if she didn't know why—but she did.

"What happened?" Mariah looked completely engrossed in the story, while her fresh glass of wine lingered close to her lips. "Something big, I'm guessing?"

"I...we had this argument over something that happened at a restaurant," Ava tread carefully and felt some relief over the fact that she *was* being honest about that part. Yet, her mind reviewed quick flashes from that particular evening and embarrassment burned her cheeks. There was definitely no way she could tell the rest of this story. No way.

"It's....it probably won't even make sense to you cause it never made sense to me." Ava stalled.

"Just tell me," Mariah insisted. "Maybe I will understand."

Ava slowly shook her head. "There was this girl there. A very beautiful woman actually, who was our waitress. She was openly flirting with him and I felt a little angry but didn't say anything. He picked up on it and after she left, Landon commented that he could see I was pissed off. I agreed that I was and he insisted I had nothing to worry about."

"So as the night went on," Ava continued, carefully retracing her steps; she didn't want to get ahead of herself and let any important details slip. "She continued to come over, barely pay attention to me but flirt with him. One time she 'accidentally' brushed her boob against him, as she was walking away."

"Classy!" Mariah rolled her eyes. "I mean, I would do the same thing but not in that kind of situation."

Ava wasn't even sure that was true of her friend but simply smiled. The point was that Mariah was on her side and it felt good to have someone in her corner.

"Anyway, the topic came up a couple more times with me and Landon but it seemed as if he was bringing it up to needle at me. It almost felt like he was trying to pick a fight."

"Maybe he was?" Mariah pointed out.

"Maybe. Anyway as the night went on, Landon went to the washroom and was gone a long time. And I noticed that hot waitress was also missing in action so I couldn't help but to assume the worst. Especially since I saw her following him when he left."

"Sounds fishy...but might not mean a thing."

"I wanted to give him the benefit of the doubt but my own insecurities got the better of me so when he finally returned, I obviously asked what took him so long and he said he had a phone call. Just then the waitressed returned to drop off our bill, and ignored me while brushing up against him again."

"Wow, you must've been pissed." Mariah's eyes widened. "Did you say something?"

"Not until we went outside to his car and we got in a big argument over it."

"Ohhhh..." Mariah made a face and shrank back a bit. "I don't like where this is going."

"I know. Things got really hairy after that."

"And he lost it?"

Ava slowly nodded and remained silent. The story had shaped into a lie. She really didn't want to dive further into the topic. Although portions of the night were a blur, she was unable to lose the memory of the hurt in Landon's voice and frustration in his eyes. In that moment, she felt as though he would never forgive her. And even now, she still wasn't sure he had.

"But to be honest." Mariah said without stopping to consider the story. "I don't think that is all that big of a deal. Couples have gotten into arguments about far worse things and it seemed a bit ridiculous that he would get *that* angry over such a stupid little fight."

"He said that he was upset that that we didn't have trust in our relationship."

Mariah grimaced and took another long drink of wine. Shaking her head, she rolled her eyes and remained silent.

Ava felt terrible for revealing such a half-truth to her friend. That little argument was the tip of the iceberg that night and in fact, it was she that had ruined their relationship and *not* some minor argument over a waitress; at least, not *that* argument over the waitress.

Chapter Twenty-One

Ava could sense that something wasn't right with Mariah. It started around Christmas but became more prevalent just into the New Year. She was no longer the fiery friend she used to be, but much more subdued. It was somewhat unnerving. Ava knew that this was partially because the job hunt wasn't going so well—since few people were hiring right after the holidays—but was it something more?

Bryan's return in the second week of January managed to distract Ava from her concerns, especially when their relationship suddenly began to consume all her time again. She felt guilty for not checking in with Mariah more often, but also didn't want to interrupt her job hunt. There were times Ava grew frustrated with herself, questioning if she was being a very supportive friend.

"She'll be *fine*," Bryan's carefree attitude kicked in whenever Ava expressed her concern. "Mariah is too strong to be held down for long and plus, receptionist jobs downtown are a dime a dozen. It's just a bit slow right now cause everyone is getting back into the swing of things after the holidays."

Ava wished she could have the same relaxed and casual attitude that Bryan had, but then again he often was a little too *unconcerned* about the upcoming months and years. He never worried about the future or what it would bring, but floated from one day to the next with no stress at all. It was a trait that she envied but also, kind of resented. Did he not take life seriously at all?

Meanwhile, Landon began to make some occasional solo appearances in the lounge area of the apartment complex, but he never made reference to Chloe. In fact, no one was really sure if they were broken up or not, because she had been missing in action in recent weeks. Maybe she was visiting family for the holidays? No one was certain. The last person to see them together was Mariah and as she had indicated previously, they were in the center of a stormy argument.

Things were rolling along but as the days slipped by and January came to a close, Ava grew concerned when Mariah wasn't in touch with her for over a two-week period. She wasn't answering her door or phone, hadn't replied to text messages or emails and no one had seen her at all. The silence was deafening and Ava secretly feared something had happened to her friend. She lived alone and so there was no one to check in with for answers.

"Maybe she's just. . .I don't know, maybe she went on a vacation." Bryan shrugged when Ava expressed her concerns one Saturday afternoon. It was an unusually warm day in late January and the couple was sitting outside on his cramped patio, drinking coffee.

"That doesn't make sense when she's unemployed." Ava replied with a softness that could have been mistaken for intimacy between the two of them, but was actually her own overwhelming fears of the worst. Yet she couldn't help but be irritated by Bryan's nonchalant attitude towards Mariah.

"Maybe she got a job and is working weird hours or something?" Bryan shrugged and pushed back one of his blond curls that the gentle breeze blew out of place. "I think you worry too much."

She wanted to remind him that perhaps he didn't worry *enough*, but her own fears seemed to smother her frustrations with Bryan.

When she found both Landon and Benjamin in the lobby the next afternoon, Ava expressed her concerns. She explained how she was unable to get in touch with Mariah at all and gave details about her numerous attempts. The two exchanged looks and admitted that they had also not seen the young woman in recent weeks and had assumed she was out of town.

"I wasn't aware she lost her job," Landon leaned forward, conveying sincere compassion, while Benjamin appeared to be deep in his own thought and finally shook his head.

"You know, I don't believe I've seen her in weeks. Not since before the holidays," He took a deep breath and made a face. "I believe we might need to investigate to ease your mind. Let's hope it's nothing serious, but the girl isn't one to cower away in her apartment, now is she?"

"Should we call Samantha?" Ava nervously began to play with a strand of her wavy hair. "I mean, she...she might need to check her apartment in case something is wrong?" Ava felt her heart begin to race and her face grew warm. "Am I overreacting?"

"I think normally I would say yes," Landon said and paused for a moment. "But considering she isn't working right now and is still not answering her phone or door, I don't know. I think maybe we should at least pick Samantha's brain to see what she thinks."

"Okay, should I call her?" Ava searched his eyes and felt an unmistakable connection to Landon in that moment. In fact, his reaction was what she had been looking for while having this same discussion with Bryan, the previous day.

"I'll do it, Ava." Landon reached in his pocket and removed a Blackberry. Standing up, he walked away from both her and Benjamin, while tapping buttons on his phone. Ava glanced at the older man for some sign of hope, but he appeared to be reflecting her own reaction.

"Do you think she's okay?" Ava finally uttered. "Please tell me the truth."

He hesitated before nodding. "Absolutely! She's fantastic. Probably squirreling away some young lad and tearing the bloody crap out of him, as we speak."

Ava couldn't help but grin at his remark and he quickly did the same.

Landon returned and inspected the two of them, waiting to get their attention before revealing the news. "Samantha said the rent for February was paid however, she understood our concern and will try to contact

Mariah. If she cannot get in touch with her within the next couple of hours, she will let me know and come back to check in on her."

"Maybe she is just avoiding me," Ava's voice was child-like in response. "Maybe she will talk to Samantha."

"I..." Landon glanced at Benjamin and shook his head. "I doubt that's the case, Ava."

It was almost three hours later before Landon sent Ava a text saying that Samantha hadn't been successful either and was on her way over to check in on Mariah. Now Ava was really worried.

Do you think she's ok, Landon? Please tell the truth.

Yes!! But we need to make sure.

Ava met with Landon outside Mariah's door shortly afterward and together, they waited for Samantha to arrive and check in on her tenant.

"Maybe if you try?" Ava begged with her eyes. "Maybe she will come to the door for you?"

Shrugging, Landon loudly knocked at the door and rang her bell. "Mariah, are you in there?" When there was no reply, he gave Ava an apologetic look and shook his head. "If the entire building wasn't so soundproof, we would probably hear her through the door."

"Sometimes I can anyway."

"Sometimes, but her door looks pretty snug compared to some of the other ones in the building. Have you noticed any of her windows opened lately?"

Ava shook her head. "She rarely opens her windows. The smells and sounds from outside bother her."

For some reason Ava thought back to when she first turned and how every sound or smell was so offensive to her and yet, had she known at the time, it was due to the fact that a window was opened ajar. Had it been properly closed, it probably wouldn't have pushed her to the edge as it had and-

"Hi guys," Samantha appeared from the stairwell and gave them each a smile. The beautiful blonde was so warm and friendly with a girl-next-door appeal, that no one would've ever suspected her to be a vampire. The rest of them had some traits that were probably considered shady to the outside

world, but Samantha showed no signs of being part of a darker world. She looked as if she had fallen from a magazine ad for an organic brand of makeup, rather than someone who sought out blood in order to feel whole.

Just then the elevator door opened and Ava held her breath in hopes it was Mariah, but it was Benjamin. "Did you find her?"

"I just got here," Samantha gave him a warm smile. "How are you, Benjamin?"

"I'm quite well my dear. Not as fit as I was twenty years ago, but I am well." He nodded politely and gestured toward the door. "That one hasn't been around in quite some time and we are a little concerned about her well-being. We certainly don't want to pry but are concerned, as you can imagine."

"I do understand...." Samantha showed genuine concern and Ava admired her professionalism and how well spoken she was when addressing the issue. "I left a message earlier today and made it clear that I would have to check in on her if she did not call me back. I trust you all if you feel that something is wrong, I certainly would rather check in case she is injured or needs help."

Ava felt her heart pounding furiously when Samantha loudly tapped on the door. After waiting a reasonable amount of time, she finally slid a key into the lock and turned it. Upon opening the door, Ava was relieved that no foul smells came from the room but did note that their landlord's eyes grew in size. *Oh no.* Ava and the others stood back and were not able to see inside.

"Mariah, I hope you received my message earlier today," Samantha spoke both slowly and with a patient tone in her voice. Ava felt a chill crawling up her spine and she shook. Landon's eyes automatically landed on her and he silently studied her face. "I am not here to intrude on your privacy but your friends were quite concerned when they couldn't get in touch with you for a few weeks."

She pushed the door open a little farther to reveal Mariah sitting on the floor of her sparsely furnished living room, her arms wrapped around her legs and she appeared to be crying. Although her windows had been closed earlier that day, they now were open and long, flowing curtains frantically blew around. Only wearing a pair of shorts and an oversized t-shirt, Mariah was shaking.

She appeared to be in a daze; as if she didn't know they were all standing, watching her in disbelief. This was the same friend who was always strong and defiant and suddenly Mariah was a whole other person in Ava's eyes. She wanted to rush over and give her hug, but was afraid to enter the room. She had a brief flash of herself a year earlier, when feeling overwhelmed by her suddenly increased senses and feeling as if she were about to go mad.

"It's like a scene from bloody *St Elmo's Fire!*" Benjamin abruptly commented under his breath, and while Ava would've normally laughed at his reaction to the situation, the moment was much too grave. He was referring to one of the most notable scenes in the movie and she definitely understood why he made the connection. "I mean, that Demi Moore girl and—"

"Umm...Benjamin," Landon muttered while touching the older man's arm to indicate for him to not say anything else.

"Mariah," Samantha began to speak again. "Are you going to be okay, honey? You really don't look well. Is it okay if we come in?"

Mariah barely glanced at them, as if she just realizing they were there. She shook her head and let out a little cough, then cleared her throat. "Just Ava." Her voice was small and wouldn't have been heard, had they not been mortal vampires but everyone nodded their head and all eyes were on Ava.

"Are you going to be okay?" Samantha directed her question at Ava. "Is this going to be too much for you?"

"I will be fine." Ava reassured the others, even though she wasn't at all sure how to handle the situation.

"If she needs anything," Landon spoke up. "I'll be upstairs in my apartment." He pointed toward the ceiling then made eye contact with Ava. "I'll give you some privacy."

"As will I," Benjamin quickly jumped in. "If you need anything at all, I will be upstairs."

"Do you have blood?" Landon asked Benjamin. "I suspect she might be in need."

Ava nodded, knowing that not having blood for a long time was known to encourage or worsen a depression and was glad Landon thought of it in that moment.

"Yes, of course." Benjamin showed no hesitation. They all knew he bought some of the finest blood available through the VP. His eyes were now directed at Ava. "I will bring it to you immediately."

The two men walked toward the elevator and Samantha shot her a compassionate smile before doing the same.

Ava entered the room where the broken woman sat trembling and gently closed the door behind her. Mariah seemed unaware of the conversation that had just taken place in the hallway but completely lost in her own thoughts. Slowly lowering herself to the floor, Ava reached out and pulled her friend into a strong hug, while the woman who was always a pillar of strength, broke down and cried.

Chapter Twenty-Two

It was Landon who returned to Mariah's apartment with a small, dainty container that most people would've easily mistaken for some kind of energy shot. Without saying a word, he handed the blood to Ava and offered her a sympathetic smile before she gently closed the door behind him.

Mariah continued to cry in a near hysterical mode, while Ava stood helplessly in the middle of the room, unsure of the best way to deal with this situation. Was there something she should say? Was there something she *shouldn't* say? Her experiences in comforting or being comforted were limited. She finally decided to just sit on the floor beside her friend, and let her cry.

Eventually Mariah's tears began to subside and Ava watched as she wiped her face with the back of her sleeve. Finally identifying a way she could help the situation, Ava jumped up to locate a box of tissue. Unable to find one, she ripped a paper towel from a nearby roll and brought it to Mariah.

"I'm sorry, I wasn't able to find a Kleenex," Ava spoke apologetically, as she handed it down to her, relieved to receive a smile in return.

"It's fine," Mariah voice was soft, almost child-like. She quickly wiped her eyes then blew her nose. Shaking her head and clearing her throat, she added, "I don't have any. I already used them all." She nodded toward a nearby garbage can that was filled with bunched up tissues. An empty wine bottle sat on the floor beside it, with several more scattered throughout the apartment. Clothes were thrown over furniture, dirty dishes were on the counter and various papers were covering a nearby desk. The disarray was very out of character for Mariah, who was usually a neat freak.

"So," Ava hesitated in order to find the right words. "I tried to get in touch with you and I was getting worried. Did something happen?" Judging solely by the expression on Mariah's face, Ava felt she had picked the wrong words. "I mean, I..I can see something is wrong, I just…I.."

"No, it's fine," she rose from the floor and lumbered toward her couch, which appeared to be pushed much farther back than usual. Ava noted that Mariah had lost weight since they last met; her clothes hung loosely on her body. She sat down and stared at the paper towel in her hands. "I don't really have an explanation. It wasn't something specific that happened. It was just….it was just, everything. My life."

Ava nodded in understanding. Being trapped in an apartment all day, searching through endless job listings was probably enough to drive anyone crazy. Remaining silent, she slowly moved toward the couch and sat down beside Mariah. Staring down at her own hands, Ava realized that the small container of blood was still enclosed in her fingers.

"Benjamin gave me this for you," she held out the shiny, black bottle and a small smile played at Mariah's lips as she reached for it. "It might make you feel better."

She nodded in agreement and silently stared at it for a few minutes before twisting off the cap and drinking the contents. Ava saw some color return to her friend's cheeks, while a vague sense of life entered her eyes. She wondered how long it had been since Mariah had any, but didn't want to ask. Quite often, vampires would fall into a depression or become slightly irritable when blood was removed from their diet for too long. They were often the first to deny that it had any effect on their emotional health but at the end of the day, it really did. There were stories of vampires living in psych wards, diagnosed as cases of depression and bipolar disorder when actually, it was simply a lack of blood that profoundly affected their emotions.

"That helped, thanks." Mariah said and set the empty bottle on the end table beside the couch and turned on a lamp.

Taking a deep breath, she cleared her throat and turned toward Ava. "Thank you for caring enough to check in. It's been a horrible couple of weeks."

"Why didn't you call me?" Ava bluntly asked. "Why didn't you reply to my texts?"

"I just didn't," She shook her head and her eyes shot around the room, finally landing on Ava's face. "I didn't want to disturb anyone with my problems. I didn't want to admit that no one was interested in my resume or that I was afraid no one would be. I didn't want to drag anyone else down with me. And I guess I just got to the point where I was too depressed to even talk to anyone."

"I never saw this side of you." Ava tenderly admitted. "It scared me a little when I first arrived."

"You never saw it because I didn't want you to see it," Mariah confessed. A light from the nearby lamp silhouetted her face so beautifully, that it made Ava wonder if her friend had any idea how much she really *did* have in her life. Looks were minor compared to her tenacity and confidence, two traits that were worth their weight in gold. It just seemed as if she allowed a series of negative thoughts to take over. And who hadn't from time to time?

"Does this happen a lot?" Ava signaled toward disorder in the apartment. "I mean do you get depressed a lot?"

"Why do you think I drink so much?" Mariah attempted to smile but it fell from her face.

"But I don't understand," Ava gently admitted. "I see you as someone who has so much going for you, and I never would have expected you to feel hopeless."

"I don't know if I have very much going for me," she let out a short laugh. "I go through phases. It's just worse now that I'm not working."

"And the holidays," she continued, shaking her head. "I pretend that I don't care but it *does* bother me. I don't have family and outside of this building, no one even notices me at all. It's just a joke. My life is a joke."

"I think we all feel that way sometimes and I certainly know about not having family," Ava confessed and began to better understand Mariah's loneliness. It was something she had dealt with in her own way.

"But your family died. My family just doesn't care." Mariah spoke evenly.

"I have a grandmother, so I sort of do understand. She's not involved in my life at all." Ava struggled to relate and didn't want to insult her friend by comparing their situations. It always appeared that they were worlds apart; but were they?

"When's the last time you spoke with your family?" Ava hoped she wasn't prying with her question.

Mariah shook her head and for a long time didn't answer, but let her head fall back as she stared at the ceiling. "My dad? I'm not sure, but I haven't talked to mom since I moved."

"When did you move?" Ava was curious. This was a part of her life they had never discussed. Her friend's past was a mystery.

"I was 17? Maybe 18." Mariah replied, avoiding Ava's eyes and staring into space.

"That's young."

"Yup," Mariah agreed and glanced at Ava, a detached grin on her face.

"That must be difficult." Ava sympathized.

"It is," Mariah's quiet voice was beginning to disappear while her usual, stronger tone was starting to return. "I've only periodically talked to my dad since my parents split up, when I was around seven. I think the last time we actually talked was at a family funeral, when I was 18."

"You haven't been in contact since?"

"No."

"And your mom, you were 17?"

"Yeah, she kicked me out shortly after my 17th birthday," Mariah revealed, staring at the floor as if her memories were all outlined on the hardwood tiles." She thought I was trying to seduce her boyfriend."

"Why would she accuse you of such a thing? I can't believe she kicked you out!" Ava exclaimed, her eyes widening in alarm. "That's horrible!"

"Mom's main concern is having a man around," Mariah turned so that she was facing Ava. Her voice continued to gain confidence, while her eyes started to show some of their usual spark. "She had a birthday party for me and for some reason, decided to invite this guy too. I think that was an excuse to socialize with him because we never met before."

"That's kind of weird?" Ava wasn't sure how to reply.

"Tell me about it," Mariah ran her fingers through strands of her hair, attempting to get some knots out. "He was probably just in his late 20s, I guess? He was younger than mom. Anyway, her plan didn't work cause I guess he was watching me more than he was listening to her."

"Really?" Ava thought that was really strange and creepy, but didn't want to inject her thoughts at this point.

"Yes, I remember cause after the party, I overheard her on the phone complaining to her friend that he seemed more into 'the girl' than her." Mariah used her fingers to indicate quotation marks and rolled her eyes. "At the time it didn't occur to me that this adult would be checking me out or that my mother would be jealous. It just was all too weird."

Ava wrinkled up her nose but remained silent. She hadn't realized that Mariah's family was so messed up.

"Anyway, he showed up at our house a couple of days later. Mom was in bed with a migraine," she said while showing no expression on her face. "I figured he wouldn't stick around since mom wasn't available, but he kind of bullied his way into the house."

"I was just an awkward teenager and didn't know how to get rid of him, so I let him talk. He asked me about school, if I had a boyfriend, weird stuff like that." Mariah suddenly stopped talking. The room fell into a heavy silence and Ava was scared to ask any questions, so simply waited. She had a bad feeling about what was coming next, even before Mariah said the words.

"He umm...he kept talking and I guess he thought I was probably comfortable with him. I was trying to act mature, so when he brought up topics like going to the bars, having some drinks, I wanted to be all grown up and act like it was something I had experienced. " Mariah restlessly rolled her finger around one lock of hair, her eyes glued to the floor. "I was hoping mom would get out of bed. I envisioned her waking up and hearing his voice, then wasting all this time putting on her makeup or fixing her hair, so he would see her looking her best."

"And he finally stood up and I thought he was going to leave, I felt relieved and got up to walk him to the door, but he grabbed me from behind and covered my mouth. He told me if I screamed, he would slit my throat and that I was hardly an innocent virgin." Mariah stalled, licked her lips and hesitantly finished her story. "And then he raped me."

Ava closed her eyes and shook her head. Slowly opening them again, she had expected Mariah to be crying, but she seemed frozen. "I'm *so* sorry, Mariah. I don't even know what to say. I had no idea."

"I didn't exactly admit it to anyone. You're the first person," her voice was once again child-like and she appeared to shrink in her seat.

"My mother wasn't there to protect me. She actually caught us doing it and accused *me* of seducing *him*." Mariah curled up in the corner of the couch and started to rip small pieces from the paper towel that she used earlier to wipe her tears away. "She was putting on the defensive act at first, threatening to call the police on him. But it was a lie. Just a front to look like a good mother. A couple of days later, we had a huge fight and she called me a little whore and kicked me out."

"Unbelievable." Ava shook her head in dismay. Her grandmother wasn't looking so bad in comparison. At least she never threw her out on the streets.

"And a few weeks later," Mariah paused for a moment. "I discovered I was a vampire."

Chapter Twenty-Three

Mariah found a job. Ironically, she was hired to work at the same placement agency that she had approached to help her find employment in the first place. Apparently they were in dire need after their previous receptionist quit on a whim, leaving the entire office scrambling: in came Mariah, with her extensive background and a very professional image, solving two problems at once.

"Fortunately for me," Mariah relayed in a phone conversation with Ava, "They were kind of fucked, so they didn't have the time to check with my previous employers. Good thing I give a great first impression."

The girls had agreed that this wasn't a long-term solution for Mariah, but she needed some kind of work to pay the bills. It gave her time to explore the kind of job that would truly interest her.

Ava noticed an improvement in her relationship with Mariah after learning about her struggles as a teenager. She now saw her friend through a different set of eyes and recognized that her anger was often misplaced, stemming from a traumatic youth. All her experiences really spoke to why she was now such a strong, aggressive woman who had earned her right to be called a fighter. She had certainly dealt with her share of battles.

After being kicked out of her mother's home, Mariah stayed with a friend until graduating high school and officially getting out on her own. It was a topic she dashed through quickly, probably hoping to leave the past behind her. In fact, she only briefly mentioned her discovery that she was a mortal vampire but didn't elaborate any farther. Her life continued to be a mystery.

Then again, after dealing with a disappointing relationship with family, maybe she had a right to be a little detached.

Focusing on Mariah's issues allowed Ava the opportunity to avoid her own set of problems. But eventually she found her mind drifting back to all the questions about immortals. She wanted answers.

Mariah promised to help her, but only managed to knock on a lot of doors to get no answers. Bryan also said he would snoop around while on a location shoot in the US, but Ava didn't really put much faith in him. She knew Landon was also a dead end so instead started to do some research online and in the local library. It was a tedious and unrewarding task. Books only talked about the mythological creative as opposed to the reality. It made her question the reliability and accuracy of all information found in the library. If vampires had managed to manipulate information in the so-called non-fiction books, what else was incorrectly reported on a regular basis? How much was written by supposedly reliable sources contained the truth? It was a disturbing thought.

The Internet was almost as useless. Every site dedicated to vampires appeared to be created by those who wished themselves to be the dark creature of stories, rather than the reality of her kind. They talked about drinking animal blood and eating raw meat, things that were both unsafe and repulsive to any vampire she had ever known. The sad part, she realized, was that some naïve people would actually see these 'facts' as reality.

Pouring over a computer was a fruitless task that only wasted more of her time. There wasn't even a hint of authenticity on the Internet and it was clear that the immortals that monitored this kind of thing were very good at their job. The idea of vampires was made into such a ludicrous and exaggerated notion, that no one with common sense would even believe what was out there. Then again, that was what they wanted; for the world to believe that they were not real.

Ava wondered if she put a comment on social media whether someone who monitored such things would find her. She wondered if maybe her words would be viewed by the correct set of eyes and someone, *anyone* would help her out in her search of the so-called rock star of vampires.

Even the title was silly. The *rock star* of vampires: how ridiculous was that? Ava couldn't help but picture someone that was a cross between Captain Hook and Captain Morgan, severe and powerful in appearance, only with a certain arrogance that would repulse her. If he was so powerful, chances are he was also a dick. In Ava's experience, most people who held that much power were jerks.

She even thought of Derrick Johnston and how he walked through the office, like he was the most important person in the world. If he wasn't the leader and acted in such a manner, Ava cringed thinking about the guy who actually led them all. Was he evil like the devil? Was he all—powerful like God? Did he wear an Armani suit and have a flock of supermodels following him? The image she had in her mind was unpleasant. She knew if he were like that, he definitely wouldn't give her the time of day.

But she continued to search and attempt to figure out ways to find the information she sought. Anything was possible and she really had nothing to lose, did she?

Finally one day she decided that the best way to learn anything would be to communicate with Derrick Johnston again. After all, as far as she knew he was the only link she had to the immortal world. If he wouldn't talk to her, maybe he could forward her to someone who would. There had to be an immortal in the Vancouver area or somewhere in Canada? It didn't hurt to ask, and she wasn't too shy to do so.

Of course Mr. Johnston could be found in the corporate address book. Odds were good that he wouldn't even see her email. It would be read by an assistant who probably only forwarded a trickle of emails on to him. People at the top rarely had time for those on the bottom, even when they wanted to project the image of an open, reachable leader. Few ever really were.

Ava decided the best way to stand out was to make reference to the fact that they had already met. She spent as much time thinking about the subject line as the rest of the email, realizing that the trickiest part would be to even capture his attention. She finally decided to write— *regarding our meeting in Vancouver, Canada.* This would create the image that they had already established a business relationship and an assistant might see her email as having more value.

In the body of the letter, she simply said that she wanted to discuss something with him and would he, at his convenience, get in contact with her? She obviously didn't want to mention his vampire status but hoped he figured out that this was the information she sought. Then again, maybe that would make him ignore her email because he had been pretty clear that he would not help her at all.

She mentioned that she recognized he was busy, but maybe he could suggest someone in her area that she could discuss this matter with in the future? That seemed reasonable, didn't it? Hitting send, Ava sat back in her chair and wondered if he would ever see this request. The odds were against her that he would reply, if he did.

A few days went by and no response. She briefly wondered if maybe it would be a good idea to send another email and be more specific, but was hesitant to do so. After all, there was a dangerous side to Derrick Johnston and although Landon insisted that he would never hurt her, maybe he was wrong.

A couple of weeks passed and there was no reply. Bryan was reporting no new information from his end, while Mariah was coming up with nothing. Why was everyone being secretive? She was already a vampire—granted she was merely a mortal—but it wasn't like she wasn't aware of their secrets. Why not at least talk to her about the subject?

Deciding she had nothing to lose, she sent another email to Derrick. This time she noted in the subject line that she was attempting to learn information on the topic they had discussed previously. She commented in the email that all she asked was to have someone sent that she could discuss these matter with. She pointed out that maybe with some details that the idea of changing her 'position' may not be as alluring.

It was immature and clumsy, but Ava reluctantly sent the email that suggested that learning new information on the immortals would somehow relieve her desire to become one.

It was a lie.

But it was also a lie that captured someone's attention because her email wasn't ignored this time. Instead, she was surprised when Matthew Crole approached her at the reception desk on Friday morning. It was quiet day with few meetings and the phone barely ringing, so Ava found herself almost falling asleep in her chair. What he said woke her up.

"Can you come into my office for a moment?" He gave his usual, radiant smile and gestured for Nisha to replace Ava. "I would like to have a word with you."

Ava was a little nervous. She immediately wondered if Derrick Johnston had made a complaint regarding the two emails she had sent. Maybe she was in shit for bothering him? Would Matthew fire her? Her paranoia kicked in.

Silently following him into his office, she found a chair while he closed the door. There was a different vibe in the room now that Ann Lee was gone. It felt warm, friendly and welcoming. Once she was seated, he sat in his chair and made eye contact with Ava.

"So I hear that you wanted to discuss something with Mr. Johnston" His words sent a flicker of fear through her body. Maybe she had crossed the line. She also considered that Matthew might ask her to explain why she wanted to converse with Derrick. Obviously, she could not tell him that she was a vampire. "He personally emailed me this morning and asked that I speak with you."

Ava felt her heart thumping loudly in her chest and her throat became drier with each second that crawled by. She attempted to read Matthew's expression and wasn't sure whether he was angry or calm. He hid rather well behind his professionalism.

"Okay," was all she could manage, as she eased into the situation, attempting to read his words and body language at the same time. She wasn't getting anything.

"So, he suggested that maybe this was something I could help you with." Matthew's smile was sincere and she suspected that his words were as well. Ava searched her brain for some other possible reason she could use for contacting the company CEO. Maybe she could pretend to have career aspirations with the company? She could lie and pretend her concerns were regarding Ann Lee being fired?

Even if she were to entrust him to the truth, it would serve no purpose. Obviously, he was not a vampire so he *couldn't* help her with this situation but at the same time, how was she supposed to dismiss him without being insulting? It was a tricky situation and she felt her heart and mind racing simultaneously.

"You know, it's ah. . ." She hesitated and attempted to choose her words carefully. "It's not a big deal. I don't think..I mean I don't feel that you could help me."

"I can certainly try." He shrugged and carried a slightly indulging look in his eyes, as he leaned back in his chair. "So what's up?"

"Ah, you know, that's fine," Ava moved to the edge of her chair and felt her face burning. "It's not a big deal and I don't want to waste your time."

"I have all the time in the world and if I can't find your answers, I can find someone who might have them," Matthew assured her with a smile.

Ava was stuck. What the hell was she supposed to say to *that?* After all, this was her boss. There didn't appear to be any pleasant way to get out of this situation without looking like an idiot.

"How about I make this a bit easier for you?" Matthew seemed extremely casual with her and had an amused grin on his lips. "I know what your emails to Derrick are about and I know what you want."

Ava felt all the color drain from her face and she wanted to disappear. A million thoughts raced through her head. What did Matthew think she wanted to know? Did he know about vampires? If so, would she be in trouble with Derrick if she said too much? How the hell was she supposed to get out of this situation? Ava wanted to disappear.

"I know why Derrick has sent me to talk to you." He moved forward in his chair, leaning his elbows on the desk. "And he expects me to tell you that it's not going to work." After pausing for a long moment, he continued. "But he's wrong because it just might."

Chapter Twenty-Four

Ava remained silent. A million thoughts were running through her head, her instincts perched at the edge of a landing. What did Matthew Crole know? What the hell was going to take place?

"I know you are a mortal vampire." He said the words with a smoothness that indicated no judgment on the matter. His eyes roamed her body as if she had just changed in front of him moments earlier, and he was noting any alterations in her appearance. Ava remained silent, her breath labored as her thoughts jumped from one fear to another. Although there was no immediate indication that having her secret revealed would have a negative impact on Ava's future, the anxious brain always prepares for the worst.

"Derrick has informed me that you want to become an immortal and I was told, in a *very* firm manner, that I was to discourage you," Matthew continued casually, as if they were merely discussing their weekend plans. Ava felt her heart racing like wildfire and her throat suddenly became dry. He leaned back in his chair the same way he would if home in his Lazy Boy, rather than sitting in his office. "But I disagree and don't feel he has any right to stop you."

Ava remained silent. A part of her wanted to confess her own frustration and share the details of her difficult journey, but something made her stop.

Why would Derrick entrust so much information to someone outside this secret world? It didn't make sense.

"Nothing to say?" Matthew seductively raised an eyebrow while a smirk curved his lips. Leaning forward on his desk, he tilted his head. "You are a hard lady to read. I would've thought you had some comments or questions at this point?"

"I don't understand," Ava finally found her voice, although it was mild compared to its usual tone. "What *exactly* did Derrick tell you?" She attempted to remain expressionless and see what kind of explanation he had. She felt as though she were walking into a trap.

The smile finally escaped Matthew's lips and his composure became somewhat more serious, perhaps to reflect her reaction to this conversation. His lips appeared to be barely moving but yet, she could hear exactly what he was saying. "As I said, I know you are a mortal vampire. I know you want to become an immortal and he insists that you cannot."

She remained motionless while her brain frantically searched for how to reply to this comment. After all, no one else outside of the vampire world knew her secret—and it wasn't something she was prepared to share. This lifestyle was never to be disclosed to anyone other than those of their kind and the last thing Ava wanted to do was to break a sacred rule. There was no way Matthew Crole should know her secret. Did Derrick really tell him?

"What?" She found herself stalling for time and wondering how she would get out of this situation. What if he was tricking her? There was certainly no way that he was a vampire and yet he appeared very confident in his assessment of her life.

A grin once again covered his handsome face; his dark eyes sparkled gleefully as he watched her. "You look concerned."

"But you aren't a vampire." Ava challenged him, suddenly unsure of her own senses.

"That is right," he confirmed. His perfectly manicured fingers reached for an expensive pen on his desk: not because he was planning to use it, but to nervously flicker it. "The only reason I am privy to this secret world at all is because my mother is also a mortal vampire, just as you are. Derrick has been close to my family for a number of years and therefore we have always known of his status. In our household, we often had very open discussions on everything regarding the topic."

Ava opened her mouth to say something but only one word came out: "Oh."

"Actually both my parents were mortal vampires but the trait isn't passed on, as I am sure you know. Obviously, they couldn't hold this secret from me nor did they want to," Matthew rolled the pen between his fingers, occasionally inspecting it but for the most part he was very attentive to Ava, who remained quiet.

"I know you are skeptical of me," Matthew nodded and his face turned serious as he sat upright in his chair. "I shouldn't have been so glib about it when I brought it up but as I said, it simply wasn't a big deal in my family. Of course, we weren't allowed to speak of it outside our home, but we generally had many conversations about it. It wasn't a taboo subject, so I guess that I felt pretty comfortable bringing it up to you."

"Derrick told you this?" Ava felt herself start to relax, but she still remained hesitant to say too much. "I mean I understand that it wasn't a big deal in your home, but I still am surprised that he would share the information about me."

"I understand your confusion," Matthew gestured toward his monitor that sat nearby, to indicate having received an email. "Derrick contacted me this morning to discourage you from the immortal lifestyle, that's how I knew about it. I suspect he didn't want to talk to you himself in case you bombarded him with a million questions that he wasn't prepared to answer, and since I already know about your world, it makes sense that he would entrust me to talk to you about something that's clearly very personal."

"I guess." Ava's throat was still dry but she was starting to relax. Everything Matthew had said made perfect sense.

"I suppose that technically, he shouldn't have said anything to me either," Matthew finally set the pen down and looked her in the eye. "But I believe an exception was made this time."

"So," Ava felt stuck on a detail from earlier in their conversation and decided to bring it up again. "You said your mother is a vampire?"

"Yes, and so was my father before he died. But I am *not* one of you."

"But that doesn't make sense, does it? If both your parents were one..."

"It doesn't mean a thing unless they turned me. If it were hereditary, vampires would not be allowed to procreate. It's as simple as that," Matthew nodded slowly. "Of course, I'm assuming you already knew this?"

"Well, not exactly," Ava felt her face burning as she confessed this detail to her boss. The fact that they were even having this conversation at all was surreal let alone discussing pregnancy and children. "I was told that it was up to me if I ever wanted to have children, but it was something I should consider very carefully because I was a mortal vampire. At the time, I admit that I was so preoccupied with turning that it didn't occur to me to ask. In fact, it was the last thing on my mind. I just assumed it meant that I should try to avoid having kids."

"You *can* have kids and my assumption is that how you would handle explaining to them that you are a vampire, is what would make you possibly hesitate," Matthew's forehead wrinkled as he frowned and studied Ava carefully. "Didn't the person who turned you go over all this?"

"The person who turned me abandoned me shortly afterward," Ava quietly confessed. For some reason it caused her shame, even though she had done nothing wrong. There was still a part of her that felt it was her fault that Bryan had left during that crucial time.

"Wow!" Matthew's eyes popped wide open. "And he's dead, right? I'm assuming he was punished for doing such a thing. It's completely against everything the vampire culture believes in."

"He's not actually," Ava quietly admitted shrinking back in the chair. Once again, Ava felt like she was taking ownership for a problem that was not her own. "He was let go but I don't believe it went over well."

"It most certainly would not. Turning you at all would be considered completely unacceptable, let alone leaving you to go through it with no direction." Matthew shook his head and gave her a sympathetic look, causing her to cringe. "Wow, that's unbelievable, Ava."

"I know." Her voice fell flat and she felt like a child in the principal's office, even though she had done nothing wrong.

"My own father turned someone and well," Matthew paused briefly and his eyes looked up toward the heavens, a hint of unintentional frustration quickly passing through them. "That's quite another story. Needless to say, it did *not* turn out well for him."

"I am sorry to hear that."

"You shouldn't be," Matthew's voice barely spoke over a low whisper. "You wouldn't be, if you knew what he did."

Ava gave him a knowing look and neither spoke for a moment.

" I'm assuming someone took over where he left off? I would hope so?"

"Yes, a friend of mine did."

"That's good. I am relieved to hear that." His lips curved into a gentle smile. Unlike the exuberant joker that she had dealt with upon entering the room, Matthew's entire demeanor had changed somewhere in the midst of their conversation. He now reminded her more of a confidant. "Very good because from what I hear, the change is quite an ordeal."

"Can I ask you something?" Ava suddenly felt a burst of bravery.

"Of course."

"How come you never changed into one of us?" Ava was curious why their lifestyle wasn't at least somewhat intriguing to him, as it had been to her. It was her assumption that given the chance most would prefer to be a vampire; or would they?

Staring down at a piece of paper on his desk, his thoughts were clearly somewhere else as he shook his head. For a moment, she thought he was not going to answer.

"I had no interest at all. I still don't." His eyes jumped back up to meet Ava's and he tilted his head. "Not that my mother would have allowed it, had the idea ever seriously crossed my mind. She said it was the last thing they wanted for me and actually, it reminded me a bit of the communication I had with Derrick earlier today regarding you. He seems to feel that becoming an immortal would be the worst possible thing for you."

"He doesn't know what is good for me." Ava spoke defensively. "I want to at least have more information, so I can make the best possible decision."

"That makes sense but the problem is, that it's not information that you can easily get and also, you have to remember that it's not completely your decision whether or not to become an immortal. The approval comes from much higher up than Derrick."

"I realize that but first I want to learn everything I can and take it from there." Ava spoke honestly. "And if I am going to get a no, I would prefer it be from the person who makes the final decision."

"Fair enough," Matthew appeared restless as she sat forward in her chair. "And my point of this whole meeting, is to tell you that although Derrick insists that he is unable to help you and wants to completely discourage you from your mission, I believe that it's not up to him and you should first see what you can learn."

"Really?" Ava continued to be skeptical and in fact, was going along with this conversation to see where it lead, but hadn't expected much to come out of it. But if Matthew's parents were vampires, he might also know some information on the immortals and perhaps be able to help her out.

"You *are* a vampire, so it's not like you don't already know that your kind exist," Matthew shrugged as if it wasn't a big deal at all. "So why not learn what you can? Why should anyone have the right to stop you? Find out what you can and make an informed decision from there; but the point is, you should be allowed to make an informed decision."

Ava decided to be bold. "Do you think you can help me?"

Matthew pursed his lips raising his eyebrows playfully. "I can certainly try."

A smile curved her lips and for the first time in recent weeks, she felt encouraged. Perhaps someone was listening to her after all.

Ava hadn't realized how long their conversation had lasted until leaving the office almost an hour after first stepping in. One of the female coworkers that constantly prowled about Matthew with hungry eyes gave her a dark glare as she walked out and returned to the reception desk. Even Nisha gave her a questioning glance before silently getting up and leaving her alone. The last thing she wanted was to create office gossip but at the same time, it felt titillating to create some curiosity.

Maybe there were a few advantages to making friends with the boss, Ava decided.

Chapter Twenty-Five

A va's original reservations about Matthew Crole subsided as the day progressed. There was something about his striking smile that caused her defenses to quickly collapse to the floor and roll away, almost as if they had never existed at all. Perhaps her coworker's suspicious glances—that eventually turned to jealous glares—had helped to encourage Ava's ego to drop all misgivings about her boss. Regardless, she felt empowered.

Enchanted by the morning's activities, Ava sent a few messages to Mariah regarding her conversation with Matthew. She was surprised and disappointed when her friend barely responded to her news. She felt a stab of hurt that Mariah was so quick to fade out of her life, as soon as her own was back on track again. Then again, it wasn't all that long ago Mariah went missing in action, only to be found locked away in her apartment. What if her lack of communication actually indicated a bigger problem?

After a few days of occasional texts and no physical sightings, including their regular lunch dates, Ava expressed her concerns to Landon and Benjamin. The three had recently picked up their old habit of meeting in the apartment building's lounge area after work. It seemed that now that Chloe was out of Landon's life and Benjamin changed his schedule from doing *whatever* he did all day—he claimed to have 'various' investments: no one was really sure what they were, but it was said he was involved in the

Vampire Plus product line. Some even suggested he was partial owner of the company—their previous ritual was revived.

"Have you guys seen Mariah around lately?" Ava eased into the question, almost dreading the response. She watched the two men exchange curious looks and feared they thought she was being nosey, so started to ramble. "I mean, we usually meet for lunch or something at least once a week. Lately, she barely texts me and I guess, I was just worried that something happened. I hope she is okay."

Landon was the first to laugh. It was more like a sneeze or cough he had attempted to hold back, only to fail miserably. A smile curved his lips and a light shone from his eyes that told Ava that she had no reason to worry. But it was still a very *bizarre* reaction. Had she been out of line to say something? What was she missing?

"No, ah, I think she's perfectly fine," Landon assured her while his smile continued to grow. Ava raised her eyebrows and turned attention to Benjamin, who remained stoic.

"I do believe the girl is more than all right these days." He cleared his throat and glanced toward Landon, who was now smirking into his hand and avoiding eye contact with both of them. Was something going on with Landon and Mariah? Ava felt a twinge of irrational jealousy as she considered this possibility.

Benjamin pursed his lips and continued his thoughts, "In fact, I believe she's just found herself a brand new fishing hole and I suspect that is keeping her out of the light of day."

This was Landon's cue to throw his head back in laughter. Ava had never seen him so jovial and felt a little lost in the conversation. Meanwhile, Benjamin did not react at all, causing Ava to be even more confused about the entire situation.

"God Ben, dude, you have such a bizarre way of wording things. I mean, a fishing hole? Really?" He continued to laugh, his face flushed and his eyes full of glee. Landon actually had tears forming because he was laughing so hard and he quickly wiped them away and smothered a grin. "I just, I don't know...."

"Well, would you prefer I say that Mariah has found a new resource to whore around in? I mean, where I come from, we attempt to show some dignity," Benjamin teased and abruptly fell into hysterics, catching up with Landon's reaction.

Ava was stunned and felt a smile tugging at his lips as she watched the boys enjoy themselves. Were they seriously suggesting that Mariah was too busy hooking up with new guys to keep up with her old friends? The only 'new resource' she could think of would be Mariah's job, or was there something else going on in her life that Ava didn't know about?

"What are you talking about? What is the resource?" Ava cautiously asked the question, feeling slightly out of the loop. "I was just concerned that she was all right, but I guess that answers my question."

Landon once again and gave a short laugh. Benjamin was now attempting to conceal his amusement, raising his eyebrows and remaining silent.

"Oh yes, Ava, I would say she's *more* than all right." Landon assured her and before he could continue, Benjamin jumped in to add his two cents.

"If you didn't dawdle after work, little girl, you would have caught sight of your friend a bit ago," Benjamin was very theatrical in his gestures as he pointed first toward the door and moved his finger along to indicate the elevator, then toward the ceiling, implying Mariah's apartment. "She raced through here with another one of her young men. One of many recently, I might add. So if you have not heard from her as of late, it could be because she is up there, tearing it up with the buggers she is meeting at her new job."

Landon stopped chuckling for only a second before he was back at it again, although with a little less passion this time. "Again, Benji boy, you got a weird way of wording things." Then he turned to Ava who showed signs of their shared humor, a smile brightening up her face. "What he is trying to say is that Mariah has a reputation for being...social with new guys? You probably haven't seen a great deal of this side of her because she's been quieter in the last year. But she used to be very promiscuous."

"Maneater, I would say!" Benjamin injected his latest thought with a serious expression on his face. "That's what we used to call her back in the day: Mariah the *Maneater*."

Landon was no longer laughing but a smile still took ownership of his face. "It's true, Ava. We shamelessly referred to her as the 'Maneater' and well, we actually thought she was past that stage." He glanced at Benjamin, who was now shaking his head 'no'. "I guess not."

"Not at all!" Benjamin jumped right in, lowering his voice. "And we are *not* the shameless ones here. I suspect this temp agency brings in all sorts for her to pick through. She must be like a kid in the candy store."

The two began to laugh again and Ava found herself falling in line with her friends, not very surprised at this realization about Mariah. At the end of the day, all she cared about was that she was fine.

The three continued to talk until Benjamin rose from his chair and yawned, announcing that it was time to go upstairs. "It's been a long day for me."

And then he was gone, leaving Ava alone with Landon. They exchanged quick glances before she found herself looking down at her sleek, new pair of Michael Kors boots. Feeling awkward she looked back up again to see him watching her.

"So, Mariah really has been missing in action again?"

"Yeah."

"At least it's not like last time, right?" Landon leaned forward as if he was preparing to stand up, reaching for his laptop bag and momentarily avoiding her eyes. "Did you ever find out the issue last time that caused her to hide away in her apartment?"

Ava shook her head slowly, as her thoughts travelled back to that day. "I think it was just a combination of everything. First she lost her job, then she didn't see many prospects of finding a new one and of course, there were the holidays too. Sometimes it's just a matter of too much at once." She clearly wasn't about to reveal the confession Mariah had made regarding how her life as a vampire began. She wondered how many times this traumatic part of her past was reborn in the midst of a depression.

"That's good. As long as she is back to normal," Landon appeared relaxed and slightly hesitant about ending their conversation. "I just wonder if this is a bit of a step back for her. After all, she hasn't been like this in at least a year or more. It just seems strange she would pick up that old behavior."

"Hmm....I don't know," Ava confessed and bit her lip, feeling like this conversation was going on for just a *little* too long. This time, she stood up first and Landon appeared slightly surprised by her action, before doing the same.

"I was happy to hear that you are changing your mind about the immortal lifestyle. I don't want to upset you but I think it's better in the end if you move on," Landon suddenly commented. "I know it was important to you, but you must see that it is not a great idea."

"What?" Ava was slightly thrown by his comment. What made him believe that she had abandoned her original goal? She felt annoyed that he thought she was so flighty, like a child constantly changing her wish list for Santa. Irritation crawled through her heart and she felt the blood pulsing through her veins. "What are you talking about? I never said I let go of that idea."

Landon stared into her eyes and she refused to look away this time. He nodded slowly and suddenly appeared to have his attention drawn to the other side of the lobby. Ava glanced over and seeing nothing alarming other than a strange man talking on his cell phone, she assumed it was just to break up the intensity of their conversation.

"Well you should," Landon reiterated his previous belief, yet again. "I thought you had moved on because you haven't asked around lately and Bryan told me he thought you had as well."

Ava assumed that he said this in order to ease Landon's mind. Although he was back for short breaks, Bryan had been filming a movie in various locations and must've crossed paths with Landon during one of his brief returns. Ava knew for a fact that her on-again, off-again boyfriend was attempting to learn what he could, while traveling. Not that he often had the opportunity to learn anything new about the immortals, since it was such a secret world.

"In fact, I found someone who said he would help me," Ava bragged and quickly wondered if she should reveal such information. Landon would hate this and that was the biggest reason for even bringing it up. "And I hope to finally find the link I need."

"Ava, come on," Landon shook his head and turned toward the elevator. "I assure you that this person probably doesn't know as much as he claims.

He probably is some lunatic who thinks he is a vampire or is just playing you. It's very unlikely that you *just happen* to meet someone who can give you answers. Think about it."

Ava resented his depressing assessment of the situation and felt anger rising inside of her. His condescending manner sent fury through her body. Who was he to try to hold her back from her dream of becoming an immortal? Didn't he realize that his insistence was not changing her mind? Why couldn't he respect her decisions?

"Why can't you give me an ounce of support? Why is it so hard to believe that maybe there is someone out there who wants to help me?" Ava spoke with calmness in her voice even though on the inside, she was shaking like a leaf. Her heart raced and her legs felt heavy, like dead weight attached to her torso. "I don't understand. It's almost like you have no faith in me. I'm not an idiot. I just want answers."

"I'm not saying you are an idiot, Ava," Landon spoke earnestly and for a brief moment, she felt her defenses lower. Perhaps she had misread the situation. Perhaps he *was* actually in her corner. "I just think you are slightly naïve about this situation and you might be getting in over your head. I don't want you to piss off the wrong person. In cases like this one, it's generally smart to keep under the radar."

"I'm not naïve," Ava felt her eyes burning but fought back the tears. Why was he talking to her as if she were a child? Perhaps the fact that he had seen her at her most vulnerable had forever formed an unflattering opinion that would never be altered. "Just because I allowed Bryan to change me last year does not mean that I naively fell under his spell. I may have made that decision for the wrong reasons then, but it doesn't mean I am this time."

"Ava, I'm not suggesting that you aren't able to make your own decisions," Landon calmly insisted. "I just mean you are naïve about this situation. I don't think you fully understand everything involved and why it's not a good idea."

"It is up to me to decide whether or not it's a good idea," Ava corrected him. Her entire face felt tight, frozen in a grimace. "If I don't fully understand the situation it's because no one will tell me all the facts. Everyone is saying no, but not telling me anything more than biased accounts of why it is a bad idea and shutting doors in my face. That's hardly giving me credit. I'm not a child."

Landon's face remained calm but his eyes were full of sadness. He merely nodded as if to end any conflict between them. Ava felt her defensiveness slowly drain down to her toes as she stared into his eyes: they were full of warmth and caring and although she wanted to say something that would settle the storm brewing between them, she couldn't. She walked away.

Chapter Twenty-Six

A va woke up to the sound of pouring rain, as it pelted against her window. There was something invigorating in the air that March morning, sending an electric current throughout her body. She preferred to sleep in on Saturdays in order to maintain the delicate balance of a vampire's biological makeup, since there were apparently catastrophic effects on mortal vampires that did not comply.

But it was to no avail. She felt wide-awake and eventually just gave in to her restlessness and got out of bed. Glancing out the window, she observed the large raindrops pounding on the pavement below. Cars had their wipers on full blast as they drove by, while some people with no umbrellas held newspapers and other items over their heads, as they rushed along the sidewalk.

A cab stopped in front of the building entrance and Ava watched as Mariah jumped out of the back, wearing clothing that indicated a walk of shame, after last night's activities. A slinky little dress that left little to the imagination and the kind of stilettos that most women would never wear out while just running errands. With a smirk on her face, Ava couldn't resist sending her friend a quick text message commenting on her attire.

Do u always wear short skirts and high heels to the grocery store? That's where u went, right?

After a couple of minutes she got a reply

Don't be a smart ass. And stop spying from your window—creepy ;-)

A few seconds later,

Want to go shopping this week?

Ava quickly replied yes; she missed her friend and wanted to get the latest news. Although her recent activities indicated that Mariah was fine, something inside of Ava was questioning why she was on such a promiscuous streak. Although it didn't seem completely unlike her friend to do so, it was a little extreme. Then again, perhaps she was worrying over nothing.

Feeling content, Ava jumped in the shower and felt assured that the early rise might give a great kick-start to her day.

It didn't.

After doing some cleaning and catching up on emails, the afternoon started to drag by and a sense of loneliness filled her heart. Ava often felt that weekends and holidays were created primarily for couples and families, which left people like her out of the loop. Unless she was partying on Saturday night, Ava felt as if she had no role to fulfill.

She considered herself single because Bryan was hardly a boyfriend. Although she liked to give the impression that they were dating in a serious way, no one really believed it: not even her. He was off filming his small part in a low budget movie and was probably with a different girl every night, since they weren't exclusive. She was back in Vancouver, alone and pretending her life had more excitement than it actually did.

She thought about her dream to become an immortal and often wondered if Landon was right. Maybe it *wouldn't* fulfill her in the way she had hoped. What if it was simply her way of grasping at straws, rather than to admit that she had *no* future? Unlike other people, she didn't have dreams. She had no idea what she wanted to do with her life. Although Ava had various interests, none of them was something she was deeply passionate about and therefore, nothing seemed worth pursuing. She wasn't charismatic like Mariah or Bryan, she wasn't calm and patient like Landon, nor was she eccentric like Benjamin. She was just: what?

The only thing Ava really was passionate about was love. Perhaps because she grew up in a famine after her parents' deaths, she seemed to constantly look for something to fill the gap. Unfortunately, romantic love was practically non-existent and family was irrelevant. She considered herself an orphan.

Actually, Ava did have family but it only consisted of her grandmother. Neither of her parents had sisters and brothers, so no cousins, aunts or uncles and all other grandparents were dead. Under normal circumstances, Ava should have been close to her grandmother, considering she was her only connection in the world. However the older woman had no interest in such things and had grown bitter with age. Although always stern yet tolerable, she had taken a downhill slide after Ava's mother passed away: after losing her only child.

In many ways, the vampires were her family now. Most of them had little or no connection to relatives and some, like Mariah, preferred to not revisit that area of their lives. It was strange, Ava often mused, that vampires were usually the loners of every group. It was obvious that few of them really fit into any social setting and perhaps it was for the best. After all, no one was allowed to know the secret.

Ava started to feel confined and decided to go downstairs to see if anyone was in the lounge area. Perhaps Benjamin would be there to distract her with one of his lively stories; he was not.

She found Landon sitting alone.

Although initially hesitant to join him, he quickly caught her eye before she was able to sneak away and back to her apartment. Approaching him, she gave an awkward smile while he merely observed her in silence. She wasn't sure of how to take him or what to expect, after their last conversation.

"Hello," he gazed at her face, his eyes glowing dark. Landon's voice showed little emotion.

"Ah, hi," Ava quietly replied, seating herself in the easy chair across from him. He was holding a copy of *The Province* in his hand and closed it upon her arrival. Even with all the technology that his employer provided him with, he was still a landline, talk radio and newspaper kind of guy.

"So," Landon's voice became cocky as he set the paper on the table beside him. "Did your magic source of information give you the road map to the land of the immortal yet? Or do you have to make five easy payments before he tells you all the secrets he knows?"

Ava was hurt and almost stood up and walked away. Her face tightened into a grimace and she looked away in frustration, then back again. "Why do you assume that this person doesn't know what he's talking about?"

"Of course, it's a man, what a *surprise*," Landon mocked her, shaking his head. "A guy who probably knows the exact, right words to say to get you to do whatever he wants, in order to 'help' you find this information."

"That's *not* the way it is!" Ava felt blood rushing to her face, while her forehead wrinkled in anger. She hadn't exactly hidden the fact that her source of information was a guy and wasn't sure why it was suddenly relevant. His remarks were so condescending and cruel. "He isn't like that."

But wasn't he? After all, Matthew Crole had definitely become much more flirtatious in recent days. Hadn't their work relationship slowly evolved into something a little more playful?

"Not yet, but I'm guessing he will be," Landon was adamant. "So tell me what makes this guy such an expert, and why exactly were you talking to him about your status as a vampire in the first place? How many times do I have to tell you that we can't share such things with just anyone? You *did* say he wasn't a vampire, right?"

"I didn't tell him a thing," Ava angrily refuted. "I never have revealed the truth to anyone. He just knew."

"Come on, Ava, how could he *just* know?" Landon shot her a dirty look. His eyes grew even darker as they talked and it was obvious he was furious with her. It bothered her more than she would've expected. Why was his acceptance so important to her? It shouldn't matter what he or anyone else thought. But it did.

"He just did," she insisted, unsure if she should reveal the details. After all, what would he think of her if she told him about all her attempts to reach out to Derrick? "What difference does it make?"

Shaking his head in obvious irritation, Landon avoided her eyes for a few seconds before replying. "Look, you can do whatever you want, but my concern is that someone is leading you on a wild goose chase. Very few people have these answers. I mean, think about Benjamin and what he once said about looking high and low and finding nothing. Don't you find it a little suspicious that you have questions and then suddenly someone approaches you with the answers you were looking for?"

"Well I didn't actually get the answers yet and I think when you are determined, you can learn anything," Ava countered with fake confidence that almost convinced even her of this possibility. She couldn't look Landon in the eyes and simply glanced across the room, hoping someone would join them in the lounge to end this conversation. No one was around.

"Come on, Ava, you are smarter than that," Landon insisted. Sitting forward in his chair, almost as if he were reaching out to her, he tilted his head and searched her face. A sudden, intense energy between them translated into a physical sensation similar to a wave of heat. His desire for her was an unexpected element in their conversation that she chose to ignore.

"I think you need to be careful with this guy and really think about any information he gives you. I seriously question how he could know that you were a vampire or that you wanted to learn about immortals."

"Someone told him," she blurted out in hopes that Landon wouldn't think she was revealing the vampire secret to anyone. She played by the rules. "Another vampire."

"That's impossible." He gently reprimanded her.

"It is not."

"Then tell me the truth, Ava," Landon's face softened, his entire demeanor relaxing before her eyes. The heat between them lifted and was replaced by a gentle, comforting warmth. "What exactly happened? Tell me what took place and if I feel that you are being told the truth, I will back off and allow you to do as you please. I won't judge you or pry into your life anymore."

His eyes showed no judgment and it was clear that Landon was calling a truce. Ava was determined to meet him halfway and slowly nodded her head. "Okay, I will tell you."

Sitting back in the chair, Landon relaxed and watched her with interest.

"I was attempting to contact Derrick Johnston, the CEO of my company again." She watched Landon raise his eyebrows. "Don't worry, I wasn't talking openly about my reasons in the email, I just stated that we had to talk. I was pretty certain he would know why because he flat out told me he wouldn't help me learn about immortals and to forget about contacting the leader."

"Why did you want information about the leader?" Landon tossed the question at her. "And for that matter, if he already said no, then why did you feel he would change his mind?"

"I thought that he would feel differently after he had time to think about my side of things. I thought that it didn't hurt to try one more time and see what he said," Ava admitted, but even while saying the words, she felt defeated. "I was hoping he would decide to help me out. And as for the leader, isn't it that person who decides whether or not anyone can join the immortals?"

"Join? *Join?* " Landon spat out the words and began to laugh. "You make it sound more like an exclusive club than a never-ending lifestyle. Even that alone makes me feel that you don't see the seriousness of this situation."

"I do!" Ava insisted, growing frustrated. "I just worded it wrong. Sorry, *become* an immortal."

"And?"

"And I emailed him a couple of times and he didn't respond," Ava admitted.

"And he won't." Landon reassured her.

"But my boss, the guy who he got to replace the woman I-"

"Put a hex on?"

"Yeah, Ms. Lee," Ava smirked in spite of herself. "Anyway, he took me aside and claimed that Derrick had told him the entire story. He wanted Matthew to convince me to not bother and that it was a dead end."

"Because it is."

"No, according to Matthew it isn't and I have every right to find this information."

"But he is not a vampire?" Landon attempted to show no judgment, although his eyes told a different story.

"No, but he said he can help."

"Ava, come on," Landon began to smirk and shook his head. "You know he is feeding you a line of BS. There is no way Derrick would reveal such information to him, especially if he is not a vampire."

"He said that his parents are vampires and that Derrick is a friend of the family."

"And Matthew *isn't* a vampire?"

"No."

"Highly unlikely." Landon said decisively. "You've been had."

Chapter Twenty-Seven

Ava wondered what it was like to wake up in the morning and truly feel alive, with no sense of dread about the day ahead. She wondered what it felt like to wake up with a purpose, as if anything really mattered. But most of all, Ava woke up wondering what it was like to feel some kind of connection to something—to anything—in the universe.

And if her sense of defeat was even more heightened, it was because of a recent conversation with Landon Owens. While she had insisted that Matthew was sincerely attempting to help in her pursuit of becoming an immortal, he drained all her optimism by insisting it was simply wishful thinking on her part. What if he was right? What if Matthew was just feeding her a line of bullshit? Maybe he was playing a game with her.

Recently, the combination of everything was so overwhelming to Ava that she began to fantasize about leaving Vancouver. She could quit her job, escape the apartment complex and go somewhere new, somewhere unfamiliar. She wanted to run away and never look back. After all, did she really have anything keeping her there? Landon was cold in her presence and Bryan was rarely in town. With an uninterested grandmother and not even a pet, it seemed like this city wasn't really her home. Even Mariah was rarely around anymore—just as Ava felt like they were getting closer, her friend would disappear for weeks at a time.

But maybe there was still hope. Perhaps Landon was attempting to cast doubt in her heart so she would leave the immortal pursuit alone. But why did it matter to him? What difference did it make to his life if she were mortal or immortal? He clearly felt some sense of obligation to look after her as if she were a child that had been left on his doorstep. Landon wasn't responsible for her life and it was irritating to think that he wanted to control her.

She knew that things were about to get worse, when her grandmother made a surprise phone call one evening. Not recognizing the unfamiliar phone number, Ava picked up and said hello. She quickly wished she hadn't.

"Ava, is that you?" Edith Wolfe's voice was shrill and Ava automatically felt her entire body grow tense with anxiety. She was suddenly dragged back into her lonely childhood, one where love was nonexistent, brought up under judgmental eyes that viewed her as an imposition.

The two hadn't spoken in close to a year, so why was she contacting Ava now, out of the blue? Fear crept into Ava's heart and seeped through her veins. As much as she disliked her grandmother, this was the only family member she had left. What if she were ill? Without her, Ava was floating through the universe with nothing to anchor her ever again.

"Yes, it is me," she replied in an even tone, impressed that she was able to hide her discomfort.

"Good. I've been looking from hell and back to find your number," Edith gruffly remarked and cleared her throat. "A package arrived at the house for you. I'm not sure why it came here, but I can forward it to you, if you wish."

"Okay," she took a deep breath, her tension shifting to curiosity. Who would send something to her grandmother's house? "That would be great." Ava gave her grandmother the details, slightly surprised that she was interested in making this much of an effort for her, but decided not to question it. "Thank you."

"It will probably be a couple of days before I get it sent out," her voice became slightly frail as their conversation moved forward, causing Ava to feel a twinge of guilt for her original reaction to her call. On the other hand, this wasn't her first time dealing with her grandmother and therefore, she felt it was better to push her emotions aside. "If you prefer, you can come pick it up"

Ava did *not* prefer to do such a thing. Seeing her grandmother was not something she was remotely interested in doing at that time. How could she forget all the cruel things she had said to her over the years? Not to mention those said during their last conversation, when Ava moved out. Edith Wolfe had made it pretty clear that she was not welcome to return.

"No, that's fine." Her reply was more abrupt than she intended. Briefly considering an apology, Ava decided against it.

"Very well then, I will mail it as soon as I can," her grandmother sounded taken back by her granddaughter's tone and after a slight hesitation, she continued. "You know Ava, I am not young anymore and I do think we should keep in better touch in the future. Regardless of our differences we've had, you have no other family."

Ava wanted to bring up so many past events that contradicted any kind of warmth between them, but decided against it. After all, was it worth the fight? Perhaps she should simply agree. But when she attempted to reply, words refused to leave her lips and instead, she let out a small cough that broke the silence.

"I will be in touch in the future," the older woman suddenly said, before ending the conversation with a few pleasantries.

Once off the phone, Ava felt overwhelmed with sorrow. This exchange had opened an old wound. She felt pulled in two directions.

On one side, this was her grandmother, Ava's only living relative. What if she were to die before they had the opportunity to bury the hatchet? Maybe that's what their conversation was really about; had she denied her grandmother that opportunity?

On the other side, this woman had been bitter and miserable toward Ava during a time when she most needed her love and support. It left a huge hole in her heart, and in a way, she often wondered if it had set a precedent for all her relationships in her life. How could she form a solid bond with anyone if she hadn't experienced one with her own family?

Falling back on her bed, hot tears burned her eyes and slid down her cheek. Ava found her thoughts drifting back to the night when she stood on the rooftop, contemplating whether or not to jump. Had she made the wrong decision? Hadn't everything slid downhill from there?

No, it had been a nightmare *before* that day. But maybe Landon was right and perhaps she was looking for answers in the wrong places. Maybe being an immortal would make her more miserable. But why did she feel it was the answer? Why was she so drawn to the lifestyle?

But if she lived forever, Ava would eventually work her issues out. Life would make more sense as time went on. Things would be clearer. There was an inner turmoil that threatened to take away any peace from her world and yet, she was convinced that there had to be an answer.

And it was power. Hadn't she been denying all along that she was intrigued by the sheer *power* of the immortal life? Weren't they a step above the rest of the world in many ways? Had she thought the dominance would help to extinguish her own insecurities?

Taking a deep breath, Ava finally rose and pushed all thoughts from her head. Somehow, she managed to get through the rest of the evening by focusing on errands and a million other things that helped to preoccupy her thoughts, until the day turned to night.

Exhausted, she eventually fell asleep in her clothes and didn't awake until the next morning. Her apartment was completely silent and because her windows were closed tightly, she could hear nothing from the outside world. Even inside, no taps were dripping, the refrigerator didn't seem to be running and even the ticking clock wasn't as loud that day.

Shooting up in her bed, Ava momentarily worried that the power had gone out during the night and that was the reason for the silence. But a quick glance at her clock confirmed that all was well with the world and she had not overslept.

There was a peacefulness within her that she didn't understand, but wasn't about to question. For once, she was *not* going to pick it apart until an infection overtook her thoughts.

Quickly getting ready for the day ahead, Ava was surprised to find a message on her phone from Mariah, asking if she wanted to go shopping after work. Feeling like perhaps it was a positive sign, Ava quickly replied 'yes' and smiled at her phone.

The morning and afternoon flew by and before she knew it, Ava was in downtown Vancouver and waiting for her friend. They agreed to meet at one of Mariah's favorite stores, where the two would probably do more window-shopping than anything else.

"So, where have you been lately?" Ava asked when her friend finally caught up with her at a popular retailer. She didn't make any reference to her conversation with Benjamin and Landon, where they insinuated that Mariah was sleeping her way through the phone book. It was better to keep an open mind.

"I've been busy and a neglectful friend," Mariah smirked and dove into a cascade of stories involving some recent encounters with men she met through the employment agency. It was a great location for her to work because she had the advantage of learning something about the candidates, before making her move. She even managed to find a virgin in the mix. Leave it to Mariah to do so.

Ava smirked to herself, while thinking that it was probably appropriate to call Mariah a Maneater. Indeed, her stories suggested that her heart wasn't with any of these men she dated and although Ava appreciated her carefreeness, another part of her wondered if these flings were enough to make her happy. Sure, Mariah told the stories with such an arrogance and spoke about these guys as if they were merely puppets on a string rather than real human beings, but it felt as though this was a wall that she chose to hide behind, more than a bragging session.

"And so that's why I haven't been around," Mariah finally completed her story as the two strolled through the large, bright store. "It's been..well, busy."

She giggled and wandered toward the cosmetic counter, more specifically the perfume section. Checking out many of the overpriced bottles, Mariah finally decided on a fragrance that had a soft floral scent, with a touch of vanilla. It was very beautiful, but most of the other perfumes were making Ava's eyes water and burning her nose. She quickly excused herself and went outside for some fresh air.

"I'm sorry about that," Mariah eventually joined her with a bag in hand. The two headed for her car. "I guess scents don't bother me as much as you. Probably because I've been a vampire longer and managed to get accustomed to it."

"Yeah, I guess that's it," Ava agreed, glancing at the dark clouds overhead. The wind was picking up and blowing small papers and a few stray bags through the streets. People were rushing by them as if they weren't there at all and Ava suddenly felt very detached from everything around her.

"Are you okay?" Mariah asked with concern and Ava forced a fake smile, while nodding.

"Sure, everything is fine."

"Has Bryan been around lately?" Mariah appeared suspicious as the two walked down the street.

"No, he's still filming or *something*." Ava found herself emphasizing the last word of her sentence. "I don't really think about him a lot."

"What about Landon?"

"I try not to think about him at all."

Mariah let out an impromptu laugh. "Okay, that says something in itself. Did he piss you off again?"

"Nah," Ava exhaled loudly and avoided eye contact with her friend. She didn't really feel like diving into this subject any farther. It just felt draining to think, let alone talk about. She already knew what Mariah would say anyway. *Don't listen to Landon; you can do whatever you want.* But could she?

"Just the same old crap?" Mariah pried but Ava just nodded. "What about the hot boss?"

"Nothing really to report." Ava decided to not get into his offer to help learn about the immortals. It was clearly a hoax as Landon had suggested and besides, he hadn't approached the topic since the original conversation, so she was skeptical. "Sorry, my life is definitely not as interesting as yours right now."

Mariah shrugged. "Sometimes 'interesting' isn't all it's cracked up to be," she gave a quick smile while averting her eyes and Ava noted a rare look of vulnerability crossing her face. It was brief, but grasped Ava's attention. "Sometimes happiness is more important than all the drama and bullshit we get caught up in."

These were not the kind of words that Ava normally expected from her friend, so was left speechless. The two didn't talk the rest of the way home.

Chapter Twenty-Eight

It was foggy. For a brief moment, she was unable to focus her eyes but once she did, Ava quickly recognized the dark, murky waves that surged nearby. Night skies made it difficult to see clearly, but there was something haunting about their mechanical motions that made her both slightly nauseous and nervous. She took a deep breath of the fresh, salty ocean air in hopes of calming both of these ailments. It didn't work.

Closing her eyes, she felt the nighttime chill that propelled shivers throughout her body, causing her legs to become weak, while her torso shook uncontrollably. There was a frostiness that clamped onto her exposed skin and swirled through her hair, up her sleeves and down her thin t-shirt.

Standing on the shoreline, she felt an aggressive ocean pushing powerful waves against her feet, leaving them suddenly wet. Looking down, she noticed that her thin pair of flimsy summer shoes gave little protection against the water that splashed over them. Ava was about to move away when something caught her eye. A white object was jumping around between the waves and stood out in the darkness of night.

Regardless of her physical discomfort and intense fear of what she might see, Ava felt that it was beckoning her to come closer, as it floated toward land. Had it been something that fell from a boat? Perhaps it was from another country, caught in a hellish storm and floating toward the British Columbia coastline?

Ava felt hesitant to move any closer but at the same time, she fell under its spell and couldn't look away. It was white, dancing around in the ocean as if to tease her, refusing to release her eyes until she had the article in her full view.

It was a piece of clothing. Perhaps a blanket or random fragment of material that was held captive by the ocean's waves. It continued to move toward Ava, becoming more visible by the second. While at the same time, there was a pleasant feeling erupting from Ava's chest that quickly turned to a euphoric explosion throughout her body. It was a kind of happiness she had never experienced before and yet, it didn't seem to belong to her but instead, to the object that was moving in her direction. She felt an authentic smile curve her lips, gently and with ease as if it were the first real smile of her life.

She saw it.

And then she saw it clearly.

It wasn't just a piece of white material in the water.

It was Mariah.

Appearing to be alive, her eyes wide open and her crimson lips in a peaceful smile that caused Ava to no longer be plagued by coldness but instead, a comforting warmth poured through her body. There was no longer a storm in the ocean. There was no more fog in the skies. It was a clear day and her best friend was floating in the indigo waters.

Her feet no longer wet, Ava moved closer to get a better look at Mariah, who was clearly fine, but unaware of what was going on around her. She was wearing a white blouse that hugged her full breasts, exposing a black bra underneath and slender waist below it. A long, black skirt clung to her lean legs and her feet were bare. Mariah's hair cascaded beautifully, one single strand sticking to the side of her serene face.

Ava found herself completely drawn into this scene and bent down to get a closer look at her friend. It was the most beautiful vision she had ever seen in her life and yet, it wasn't exactly something she would ever be able to express. There was just a glimmer in her friend's eyes, flawlessness in her complexion and a natural beauty that seemed to radiate from her entire body. Leaning down, Ava felt a wonderful light that bathed her own body and took away any chills that were remaining from moments earlier.

She didn't understand and yet, Ava felt that it wasn't necessary that she did. There was an unmistakable bond that grew without words and serenity that could've easily filled the entire ocean. The warmth grew more intense until Ava felt a droplet of sweat spring from her hairline. It was the brightest sun she had ever viewed in her life, surrounded by a deep shade of orange in the sky that reminded her of flames. The colors were vivid and alluring.

The warmth only increased. Her entire body was now sweating as she stood upright and for some reason, it crossed her mind that it was nice to have her flimsy shoes now. But as she looked at her feet, Ava suddenly felt her eyes jump back to Mariah in the water and she was disturbed to see her floating away.

Abruptly, she jumped up and put her arms out, as if she would somehow be able to reach for her friend, who was quickly disappearing out of her sight.

Startled, she felt like a spirit was jumping into her body and her eyes suddenly opened. No longer on a beach but sitting in her bed, she focused on Bryan removing his clothes on the other side of the room. Their eyes met and he merely smiled. Stunned, Ava threw the covers off her perspiring body and slowly put together what was happening around her. It had been a dream. And this was real.

"What are you doing here?" Ava could barely whisper when she finally did speak. At that moment, she wanted nothing more than to be alone with her thoughts. The mystical dream that had just taken over her entire being was disturbing to her, its impact left her feeling confused and disorientated.

For a brief moment, she considered discussing it with Bryan but figured that it would be a waste of time. He would merely tell her it was 'just a dream' and that she was overthinking it, then probably attempt to have sex with her: a concept that held no interest for her that night.

"I just got in. I finished shooting and ah, I felt like I should come home." He sounded slightly apathetic compared to his usual self and Ava felt that had it been a better moment, she probably would've inquired if something were wrong.

Lying back down, she didn't respond to his comment. After stripping down to his boxers, he stretched his bronze body to showcase every muscle before heading to the bathroom. Ava closed her eyes and immediately fell back asleep.

She slept soundly for the rest of the night.

The next day Ava was still haunted by her dream. She awoke to Bryan's hot breath behind her, causing the hairs on the back of her neck to stand on end. Rising out of bed, she got ready for work. She moved around the room, quietly hoping not to awake him: not because she was concerned for his peaceful slumber, but because she wasn't in the mood to talk.

After arriving at work, she still wasn't in the mood to talk. Unfortunately, Matthew arrived shortly after her and beamed his usual bright smile.

"Ava! Just the girl I wanted to see. Can you come into my office for a moment?" She didn't reply but quietly followed him into the next room. Nisha gave her a questioning look as she passed and Ava pretended not to notice.

After his door was shut, Matthew cheerfully began to ramble on as if he had been awake for hours and felt excited to be alive. It was something she did not understand. He arrived at work like this every morning. Did he have some wonderful lover ushering him into each day or was he simply just a morning person?

"I got some news for you regarding the immortals and I—"

"Look," Ava put her hand out as if indicating he should stop. "I'm just going to be straight with you right now. I was talking to someone recently who told me that it is impossible for two vampires to have a child, who isn't one. Are you being straight with me?"

"Two vampires are discouraged from having children for obvious reasons." Matthew seemed to relax his excitement of seconds earlier, but remained pleasant and friendly. "But as I told you, mortal vampires aren't *born* that way. I shouldn't have to tell *you* that Ava. My parents wanted to leave me to make my own decision and that was, to not become a vampire."

His comment embarrassed her. Of course it wasn't true. Landon's entire presence was always so intimidating to her that she apparently fell under his spell and took his word even though, it really didn't make sense. After all, she was a vampire and had not been born into it. Not one vampire she met was born into it. They always had a story about how they turned and it never started with 'my parents were vampires...'

"I'm sorry," Matthew's voice softened. "I didn't mean to be condescending. I'm just surprised you'd believe that story. I hope I wasn't being rude."

"No," Ava's voice was soft as she stared at her hands. Finally looking up, their eyes met and she saw compassion in his. She smiled and he did the same. "It's not your fault. You're right. I did know better and the person who told me this was very clear on the fact that he doesn't want me to become an immortal. In fact, he is always discouraging me, so I shouldn't be so naive."

"I hate to tell you," Matthew pulled his chair up closer and leaned forward on his desk. "But, it sounds like he is trying to shake your confidence. Of course you knew that already, Ava. Perhaps it is in your best interest to not speak to this person about the immortals. We all have people who would rather keep us at a level that makes *them* comfortable, not that the other way around. It's unfortunate, but it's reality for most people."

"It's not the first time," Ava admitted sheepishly. "He often makes me feel like I'm on the wrong track, like turning into an immortal would be the worst possible thing for me."

"Why does he have such an issue with you becoming an immortal? Is he an important part of your life? Maybe a boyfriend?" Matthew raised an eyebrow and relaxed back in his chair, a look of interest on his face.

"No, just a guy I've known for a long time." She used the words that most innocently summed up Landon. It wasn't as if she was about to tell Matthew how they met or the significance he had had in her life. "He um... he's also a mortal vampire and actually wishes he wasn't even that, to be honest. But it's weird because I feel that he's sincerely concerned for me."

"Regardless, you should be able to get the information you need to make an informed decision. That's generally how I take on life and I think it makes the most sense," Matthew emphasized. "After all, you could find out all the information you need to know and not be the slightest bit interested in going ahead with it."

Ava doubted that but nodded. "Or, not be able to move ahead in the end."

"True but regardless, I think it's only fair you have all the information first and I have something new for you," Matthew regained his original excitement and Ava felt herself caught up in the moment. "I talked to my mother last night and she would be willing to help you out, if she can."

"That's great."

"She also said that there is a lot of talk in the vampire world lately," Matthew appeared to be hesitating, as if carefully picking out the right words. "I know she has mortal vampire friends, but only Derrick is immortal."

He stopped and looked into Ava's eyes for a long moment before continuing. "But she made a few interesting comments in our conversation. She said a lot of mortals have been inquiring on the immortal lifestyle recently. I don't know if this is just a group of your friends trying to help you out, or if that means you're not alone in your dreams to live forever. Mom said she wasn't too certain either and that maybe you might want to keep a low profile for the time being. Just to be safe."

"Now *you* are sounding like my discouraging friend!" Ava teased but there was definitely truth to her statement.

"I'm not finished," Matthew raised his eyebrows and reached for his coffee on the edge of his desk. Inspecting the contents, he quickly set it aside again. "My mother believes that the immortal world is actually very small and that no one has changed in years. It has been suggested that because of the rising interest in vampires through the media that perhaps more immortals need to be out there, making sure that the secret is kept safe. Many feel that it will only grow worse in the coming years."

"That does make sense," Ava shyly replied. "But I doubt that the immortal world will change their mind. It sounds like they are pretty stubborn about allowing new people to become one of them."

"You might be wrong about that, because apparently someone in the immortals is really pushing to add one more person." He hesitated and appeared to be reading her reaction. "Because of the growing population, the fact that the Internet has made the world much smaller and the growing interest in their kind, they may need extra people to help monitor and guard the secret."

Ava felt her heart suddenly fluttering and her eyes widened.

"And you never know, it could be you."

Chapter Twenty-Nine

"It doesn't make sense," Mariah insisted shortly after the two sat down for dinner on Friday evening. They were at a popular chain restaurant located in the city's downtown area. It wasn't a trendy place favored by Vancouver's social elite, but it served delicious, healthy food and cheap drinks.

"What doesn't make sense?" Ava asked casually, noting the dark circles under Mariah's eyes. In fact, her entire appearance was slightly haggard compared to her usual stunning and flawless look.

"Landon." Mariah declared, acting agitated and glancing around the restaurant. "Why was he trying to convince you it's impossible for two mortals to have a kid that wasn't a vampire?"

"I assume because he wanted me to question how trustworthy Matthew is," Ava answered with a shrug. She was slightly embarrassed by her own ignorance on the topic and didn't really want to discuss it any farther. The two had already talked about it on the way to the restaurant.

"Maybe he meant it would be difficult to hide from your child," Mariah rambled, as if she hadn't heard Ava's explanation at all. "Maybe he just meant that the child would probably grow up and want to be a vampire, because it would seem like the most normal thing to do?"

"I don't know," Ava replied, shaking her head. This wasn't the Mariah she was used to at all. Her usual brazen self was drowned out by a nervous energy that only grew as she talked. To balance it out, Ava continued in a calm voice. "I'm sure I misunderstood and he didn't want to mislead me."

"Maybe he sees it as a moral issue," Mariah anxiously suggested, picking at a hangnail. "Landon *is* Mr. Moral, so that would make sense. I can understand because I've also wondered how I could hide it from people that are important to me."

"For example, I once fell in love with someone who wasn't a vampire and I truly didn't know whether or not to tell him," Mariah quietly confessed, then fell silent as a waitress dropped off a glass of wine each.

Ava could see that Mariah was suddenly very upset and wondered when this relationship had occurred. Should she ask questions or wait for the story to unfold? Mariah was normally very secretive, so it would make sense not to push the issue. Both fell silent.

"I believe," Mariah slowly began, while gently running her finger over the rim of the wine glass. "I believe that most of us become a vampire when we are young and don't see the possible consequences. I think maybe that is why Landon is suggesting that you give up the dream of becoming an immortal. Maybe what appears to be a great idea now may not so great in the future?"

Ava slowly nodded.

"I'm not saying that you should absolutely forget about it and stop seeking answers." Mariah stared into Ava's eyes while she continued to fondle the glass. She still hadn't taken a drink from it. "But maybe-

Just then, Ava saw Mariah's glass tip over and the entire contents spill on her friend, who sprang from her seat and grabbed a napkin. She attempted to dab the wine off her black dress, while Ava grabbed every other napkin on their table and passed them to a frantic Mariah.

The waitress rushed over to help and soon, someone else appeared with a mop in hand, cleaning the wine off the floor. Ava watched her friend's even facade quickly dissolve and she thought tears were forming in the corners of Mariah's eyes. That wasn't like her at all.

The waitress and Ava both asked Mariah if she was okay but she didn't respond, but instead grabbed her purse and bolted toward the exit. Ava was left stunned, unsure of what to do; she quickly apologized and reached for her purse to pay the bill. Apologizing a second time, Ava then rushed out the door and looked around for Mariah. She was nowhere in sight.

The two women had taken Ava's car to the restaurant so she didn't want to abandon Mariah and go home. She sent a couple of quick texts then briefly wandered around the area looking for her, but to no avail. After about 20 minutes she attempted to call her but there was no answer, so she sent one last text saying she was on her way home.

Back in her apartment building, Ava dropped by Mariah's place but there was no response. Feeling very concerned about how something as simple as spilling wine could upset her friend so much, she finally sent one last text, before retreating to her apartment. There was little else she could do.

Bryan was watching television when she walked through the door. Muting the sound, he turned his attention to a defeated Ava, as she removed her boots.

"I thought you and Mariah were going for dinner? Did she bail on you at the last minute?"

"Kind of," Ava moved toward the couch and sat down, then quickly recounted the story, leaving out their conversation at the restaurant.

"That doesn't sound like Mariah," Bryan's comment was much more tender than Ava had expected, but she found herself ignoring the sentiment behind it and avoiding his eyes. There was something different about her on-again, off-again boyfriend in recent visits and she couldn't quite put her finger on it. But she didn't really want to and in fact, she found herself growing tired of him. She briefly wondered if her lack of interest only managed to incite a newfound attentiveness for her, but she quickly dismissed the idea.

"No, it doesn't," Ava glanced at her phone once again to see if Mariah replied to her texts but she had not. She could feel Bryan's fingertips gently caress the back of her neck while his breathing increased in excitement. Frowning, she sat her phone on the nearby coffee table and looked back at Bryan's begging eyes. "You can continue watching whatever you have on, I don't care. I think I am going to take a shower."

"Actually, I was wondering if we could hang out for a bit," Bryan continued to stare at her with a pitiful look that created a guilty feeling within her. She was kind of wondering why he wasn't spending time in his own apartment but didn't want to say anything. She was starting to regret those blissful days when she gave him a key. "I've barely seen you since I got back home a few days ago."

Ava nodded and tried to relax her body. She felt slightly guilty for her frustration with him and gave Bryan a small, apologetic smile. "Sure."

"So, how have things been while I was away?" His question was awkward and Ava attempted to lighten up in case she had somehow contributed to that feeling.

"Fine, busy."

"Have you found out anything more about the immortal thing?" Bryan seemed to relax and his hand once again slid over the back of her neck and to caress just under her collar. She couldn't deny that his playfulness was making the blood rush to various areas of her body. But she had to remain focused on their conversation.

"Well sort of, " Ava thought about Matthew's recent comments as Bryan's warm fingers gently moved a little farther down her shirt. "But nothing that's really important. I keep hitting walls more than anything."

"Yeah, that's what I wanted to tell you," Bryan spoke seductively, as if the topic of their conversation was somehow a turn on. "I keep hitting a lot of walls too and someone recently told me that I should stop asking so many questions. They didn't really suggest it as a threat to me but were insistent I let it go. I think you should be careful, just in case."

Ava raised her eyebrows as she thought about his words. She wasn't surprised. That was the message she seemed to get from almost everyone except Matthew, which concerned her. Perhaps this really was a dead end street. What if her search was a dangerous one?

"My understanding is that it's not something that can easily happen," Bryan's hand switched from under her neckline to the bottom of her shirt, his fingers tracing underneath to just below Ava's bra strap. He began to knead a little harder than before, sending a less than subtle message about his desires. His breath changed slightly in a way that those who weren't vampires wouldn't notice, but she did. It made her think of him running his hands over her, about his hot breath on her neck and-

He made another comment but she was lost in thought and missed it. "What?" She cleared her throat. "Sorry, my mind was wandering."

He let out a small snicker, clearly aware that he was distracting her as his hand continued to move to the closure of her bra and with one swift move, unsnapped the clasp and releasing the tightness that had grasped her chest all day long. He didn't hesitate to continue running his hands up and down her back in a soft, slow motion that was comforting and erotic at the same time. She turned to look into his eyes.

"I think you are getting close. Really close to something….big…" His pupils became large and engrossing and she had difficulty focusing on what he was saying. Her libido was not interested in facts or logic in that moment. Her throat grew dry as his fingers quickly left underneath her shirt to roam into the back of her thong.

"Is it really that big of a deal to become an immortal?" Bryan appeared to weigh his words carefully, as he moved closer to her body and she could smell his arousal as he neared. "I was thinking about it and it just seems like you would have to live this secret life, so it would be difficult to ever get close to anyone again. I don't know, maybe I just don't fully understand where you are coming from." His long eyelashes fluttered rapidly as his hand began to move over her hip, teasing her as they wandered toward the front of her pants, only to quickly move away.

"I see what you mean but there is a whole other side to all of this," Ava finally found her voice, even though it was small and breathless. "You get to live forever, to be young, forever and live a very full life. You have time to learn from your mistakes and travel the world, try everything there is in life. You can't possibly do all that in one lifetime."

She felt she had made a great case until Bryan shattered it with one sentence.

"You aren't *meant* to do everything in one lifetime." His hand was caressing her thigh, causing Ava to let out a small moan as his mouth quickly found her neck, ending their conversation. It didn't matter in that moment. It couldn't have mattered less as he sent waves of intense pleasure through her body, reminding her why their relationship continued, even though it was far from healthy.

It wasn't until later that night, as she lay awake while Bryan slept beside her, that Ava began to replay his words. *You aren't meant to do everything in one lifetime.* She had heard those exact words in the past. Wasn't it from Landon? Were they right? Was she really not meant to do everything in this lifetime? Was it matter of choices that highlighted certain areas and not others?

Ava didn't know.

It was a dream that was close to her heart, so there had to be a reason for her wanting it. She wasn't even sure of the deeper reason that drove this desire. It was something stronger than she had ever felt before and yet, Ava couldn't put it into words. The closest would be to suggest it was her destiny but even that sounded like the ranting of a delusional and inexperienced woman.

Checking her phone once again, Ava noted that Mariah had still not replied to her text and left no phone messages. She grew concerned and briefly considered dropping by her apartment again but decided against it. Maybe Mariah needed some time alone and would tell her what was going on tomorrow. After all, it was clearly more than a spilled glass of wine that was upsetting her.

It was an unsettling night and Ava felt defeated and eventually fell to sleep. She felt very low lately and assumed it was from lack of blood. Sure, vampires did drink from one another but it didn't always have the components needed because of their limited diets. Still, Bryan's was very rich blood that provided her with what she needed for now.

Another night. Another dream.

Chapter Thirty

Walking through a dark forest, she was searching for Mariah. All around her, trees hovered, branches and sticks protruding from the ground, causing each step to be treacherous and uncomfortable. She treaded with caution, in fear of sinking into the soggy earth. She was uncertain of how she had arrived or how she would get out.

The cold, damp air filled her lungs and sent a chill to every corner of her body and Ava wanted nothing more than to be home, covered in a thick, warm blanket, rather than roaming through the eerie woods. Each step sent her farther into the darkness, a mysterious allure pulling her deeper into the gloomy assortment of trees. Heaviness formed in her chest and drained her body as she continued to trudge forward, pulling her tired limbs along as if they were dead weight.

Stopping momentarily, Ava glanced over her shoulder and had the overwhelming sense of being followed. It was almost as if she were trapped in a maze. With each step, she felt more hopeless and discouraged in her search for Mariah. What if she did not want to be found? What if she wasn't even here in the first place? How would Ava escape?

And then she saw it.

Hanging from a tree was the body of an old, frail woman, a noose clasped around her neck. She wore a long, flowing dress that resembled something from a hundred years ago, with no shoes on her feet and a scarf on her head. Long, straggly hair hung in front of it, hiding her pale face, while her lifeless body swayed slightly.

Ava stopped dead in her tracks and although she opened her mouth to scream, nothing came out but a deafening silence that was captured within the forest that surrounded her. Unable to move, feeling that both of her feet were nailed to the ground, Ava began to panic. Hot tears ran down her face, her stomach churning at the repulsive sight. Just when she felt it couldn't get much worse, the lifeless head suddenly fell to the ground in front of her. Ava closed her eyes, not wanting to see the horrid sight. When she slowly opened them up again, it was to see Mariah's face staring at her.

That's when she woke up screaming.

"Ava!!" She heard her name and took a moment to realize that Bryan was sitting beside her in the bed. Her heart raced, sweat trickling from the back of her neck to the base of her spine. It wasn't until she looked into Bryan's eyes that she realized the full impact of her reaction on him. He appeared to be almost as frightened as she felt in her dream.

"Ava, are you all right? I never heard anyone scream like that in my life." He carefully placed his hand on her arm, as if fearful that she would push it away, when in fact, she welcomed it.

Ava slowly nodded, running her hand through her damp hair, glancing toward the nightstand in hopes of finding a glass of water. As if he read her mind, Bryan jumped up and quickly disappeared into the kitchen. She could hear the tap running and the cupboard door opening and closing. Sitting back in her bed, she took a deep breath.

When Bryan returned, she noted he was only wearing his boxers and a concerned look on his face. She looked away, not wanting to create an intimacy between them in that vulnerable moment. But at the same time, she was relieved to not be alone after that horrible nightmare.

Reaching for the glass, her hand still shaking, Ava managed to get it to her mouth and take a few quick sips. Her heart rate began to slow and suddenly she felt a chill in the air, where there had been perspiration only moments earlier. The scene of Mariah hanging from the noose was too much especially with how their conversation had ended earlier that night.

Setting the glass of water down on the nightstand, she whimpered a quick 'thank you' to Bryan before reaching for her phone. Glancing at it quickly, she saw that Mariah had not replied to any of her texts from earlier that night.

"Was it about Mariah?" Bryan sat on the edge of her bed and watched Ava return the phone to its original place. Grabbing the water again, she quickly finished it before returning the empty glass to the nightstand.

It was just a dream. It doesn't mean a thing. Let it go.

"Yes, it was horrifying. The worst dream I've ever had in my life." Ava finally revealed. "She was dead. Mariah was dead."

"It's just a dream, Ava." His words were gentle and for a moment, Ava felt as though she could hear Landon's voice speaking, rather than that of her boyfriend. There was a soothing quality that had only managed to arise in recent weeks, something she never would've expected from Bryan Foley. "You can't take it too seriously."

"But it felt very real," Ava whispered. "Too real. And she still hasn't got back to me. I mean, that whole thing at the restaurant tonight—" She stopped and shook her head. "She was acting really weird. It wasn't like Mariah at all."

"It sounded kind of over the top." Bryan had compassion in his eyes as he reached out for her hand and gently squeezed it, giving a weary smile. "Actually, it sounds like she overreacted." He shrugged innocently. "Has she mentioned anything that has been going on lately? Maybe something happening at her new job? Boyfriend problems?"

"No she hasn't, but we didn't really get a chance to talk tonight." Ava shook her head and recalled the limited amount of conversation that they did have; even that was a bit odd. "And maybe she won't. Maybe she doesn't trust me."

"I doubt it's a matter of trust. Come on, you guys are like best friends. If she doesn't tell you, chances are she just isn't ready to talk to anyone about whatever is on her mind." Bryan reassured her, leaning in to kiss her on the cheek, before pulling her into a hug that Ava felt completely disconnected from, and she wasn't sure why. Her thoughts were still attached to Mariah; wherever she might be.

The next morning, she woke to discover that Bryan was gone. Hadn't he mentioned something he had to do? She felt guilty for not really caring but at the same time, maybe she just wasn't being fair. Perhaps he was sincerely trying to capture her heart and she simply wasn't letting him in. But could she trust him? Could she trust anyone?

Checking her phone once again, she saw no messages and so she texted Mariah one more time.

I am really worried about you. Please text back so know u r ok

Taking a quick shower, Ava decided to throw on some clothes and head to Mariah's apartment to see if she was home. But her efforts were to no avail when no one answered the door. Where could she be? It wasn't as if Mariah was great at answering her door or replying to messages, but her reaction at the restaurant the previous night was pretty erratic. Plus Ava was still feeling very rattled about the nightmare that had awoken her in the early morning hours. Maybe it was just a dream, but it was quite unnerving.

Hesitantly, she decided to check the lounge area to see if either Benjamin or Landon were around. Finding it empty, she briefly considered either texting or dropping by Landon's apartment but decided against it.

"Ava?"

Hearing the soft, feminine voice behind her, Ava was full of hope when she swung around; but it was not Mariah saying her name. It was Chloe.

Noting the surprise in her eyes, a smile burst over Chloe's face and she shrugged. "I know I haven't been around for a while. But I'm still here."

"Oh yeah, I haven't seen you in ages. I was wondering where you were." Ava managed the insincere comment and noted that the brunette had gained weight since their paths last crossed. Her makeup seemed slightly tamer, her bangs cut shorter in a very blunt, severe style that screamed dominatrix or burlesque dancer. She wore a low cut t-shirt that draped over her breasts, making them somehow look bigger; apparently that was one of the places where she gained weight, Ava thought uncharitably.

"Yeah, I was away visiting family over the holidays and it became a longer stay than I originally intended because I wasn't feeling well," she admitted. "That's why I'm all fat now." She gestured toward her own stomach and smiled affectionately at Ava. It was almost like talking to a stranger, since the last time they met. She seemed more centered, more grounded.

"Oh," Ava managed and wasn't sure how else to respond to this comment. Besides the fact that she was preoccupied, there was an even bigger part of her that didn't want to share personal information with Chloe. It wasn't as if they were ever friends. "I hope you are feeling better."

Chloe took this second insincere comment as if it were true and nodded with a smile on her face. "I am *much* better. Maybe someday we can go for a glass of wine and talk more about it, but right now I'm going to drop in on Landon and see how he is doing. Maybe surprise him."

Ava had no doubt he would be surprised. Just then Bryan walked in through the main entrance and approached them. It was a welcome interruption that allowed her to avoid responding to Chloe's invitation.

"Chloe?" He asked and she quickly swung around and flew into Bryan's arms as if they were old lovers reuniting. Then again, knowing Bryan, maybe they were. Feeling even more awkward, Ava briefly considered trying to make a dash for it and sending a warning text to Landon, but figured it would be too obvious.

"Where have you been?" Bryan seemed more excited to see the femme fatale than Ava was, and since Chloe currently had her back to her (and Bryan didn't appear to remember that she was even there at all) Ava took advantage of the moment to send Landon a swift text.

Chloe's here. On way to see u.

Within seconds she got a reply.

Thanks.

Then again, maybe he wanted to see her. If Mariah had been with Ava at that moment, she wouldn't have felt the need for pleasantries and probably would've said something snarly about Chloe or her weight.

As she quickly checked her texts again, Chloe swung around and raised an eyebrow. "Did you want to join us for coffee? Oh sorry, you were busy texting someone." Her self-serving grin was just too much for Ava.

"Oh sorry, I'm looking for Mariah and was just checking to see if she had texted me back."

"Hmm.." Chloe tilted her head as if she were interested and glanced toward Bryan, her hand still touching his shoulder. "I haven't seen her, but I just got back last night."

Ava nodded. Bryan tilted his head with a look of compassion in his eyes. "Still no word from her? I bet she's fine. You know Mariah, always lands on her feet."

"Well, I think I will skip coffee and search some of her haunts." Ava knew that there really wasn't any place she could go to find her at that time of the day, but was willing to grab on to any excuse in order to get away from Bryan and Chloe. A little hurt that her on-again, off-again boyfriend appeared to be very excited to see Chloe return, she faked a smile and wished them a fun morning.

Heading back to the elevator, she sent another quick text.

Landon, she took off with Bryan for breakfast. Have you seen Mariah?

She was almost back to her apartment when he replied.

Good thanks for warning. No, no Mariah. Why?

Long story

Will we have to call Samantha again?

Ava recalled the day that she, Landon and Benjamin all stood outside her best friend's apartment, waiting for their landlord to drop by and check in on the despondent tenant. Mariah had been hiding inside and avoiding them all. Would she really do something like this again?

I hope not.

She waited a few seconds and as she reached her apartment, her phone beeped again.

Keep me posted. I will let you know if I see her. I'm sure it's nothing.

I'm not so sure. Will tell you more later.

Once inside her apartment, Ava decided to crash out in front of the computer and watch a movie or somehow occupy her mind. However she barely had her Mac turned on when someone was at the door. Assuming it was Landon arriving to find out the entire story regarding Mariah, she slowly made her way toward the door and swung it open. It wasn't at all what she expected.

Chapter Thirty-One

Ava was stunned when she opened the door to find Edith Wolfe on the other side. As a child, her grandmother's dark, penetrating eyes were soulless pools that expressed no compassion or humility. But for the first time in her adult life, Ava saw something different. They now displayed a vulnerability that caused her to take a step back and rethink her position.

"Ava?" The older woman's voice was as sharp as always, but no longer threatening. She was dressed in casual clothing that covered her thin frame; a pair of reading glasses rested on the top of her head. Her hair remained a flattering shade of blonde combed into a soft bob, and she tilted her head to one side, her hazel eyes gazing at Ava with curiosity.

Edith Wolfe often commented on how she had earned her age and didn't feel the need to look like 'an old fool pretending to be young' but with only a few fine lines on her face, she certainly didn't appear to be in her sixties. In fact, most people probably would've guessed her to be in her late 40s.

"Grandmother?" Ava was still stunned to find her only living relative at the door. They hadn't spoken in person since Ava moved out, over a year earlier.

"Well, aren't you going to ask me in, or do you have a young man here?" She curtly asked and then proceeded to make her way into the apartment, without an official invitation. Ava closed the door and quickly swung around to see if any of Bryan's stuff was within view but fortunately, it was not. The last thing she wanted to talk about was their current situation.

"No, I live alone," Ava decided that this was the easiest route to take, as she watched her grandmother make her way to the couch and sit down. She glanced around at her surroundings and appeared to be satisfied.

"Nice place you have here," she remarked, placing her purse on the floor. "Small, but in Vancouver anything that isn't the size of a closet is ridiculously overpriced. I don't understand why young people still flock to this city; the cost of living certainly cannot be justified."

"But you live here, grandmother," Ava couldn't help but comment as she joined her on the couch.

"Yes, but I bought a home here back when the prices weren't outrageous and I'm certainly not in one of the trendy areas of the city, so it's not quite the same thing," she retorted. "But I'm old and it's just easier to stay put."

Ava nodded, not really sure how to respond to that comment.

"So you must have a decent job to pay for this, especially if you live alone?" The old lady attempted a hesitant smile and Ava didn't have the heart to tell her that had it not been for the money left by her parents, she wouldn't be able to live where she did.

"I do. I work at Anderson & Smith."

"Oh yes, the accounting firm. I've heard of it. Are you studying accounting?"

"No, just doing reception for now." She hoped that this wouldn't lead to a long discussion on what should be done with her life.

"Well it's a start," Her grandmother nodded. "Everyone needs a start and you are still young. You have loads of time to decide on what you want to do with your life."

Ava shared a smile with her grandmother, surprised by her casualness regarding the subject. This same woman had hounded Ava constantly about her education and future plans when they lived together. Of course in retrospect, maybe it was out of fear that Ava would rely too heavily on the money that her parents left her. With this thought in mind, she felt herself relax a bit.

After asking her grandmother about such things as her friends and health -partially to keep inquiries about her own life aside, but mostly because she wasn't sure what else to talk about—Ava couldn't help but wonder what had brought on this visit. It was very random, just as the phone call from her had been a few days earlier.

A part of her felt guilty for not feeling a connection to her grandmother. They only had one another and that realistically should've made their connection even stronger but in fact, it was quite the opposite.

Landon once told her that family was just a word used to describe people that lived together, nothing more. Cynically, he had insisted that it was because of mainstream media and Disney movies that people had a ridiculous belief that blood relatives automatically felt an emotional connection. After Ava inquired about his own family, he went into such a rant that she decided it was probably better to avoid the question in the future.

Sitting beside her grandmother at that moment, she began to understand why he made this suggestion. Ava felt the same kind of awkwardness that she had when sitting beside strangers on the bus. It felt like she was somehow at fault, or it wasn't 'normal' because the two weren't bonding. Was Landon correct? Did she only feel the need to have a relationship with her grandmother because the unending media propaganda? Was it realistic at all? Landon believed all individuals were put on this planet to learn about themselves and to help bring knowledge to others. He did not believe that family necessarily fit into that equation.

"Do you mind if I have some water?" Her grandmother suddenly spoke up to break their silence.

"Sure," Ava jumped to her feet, but not fast enough for her grandmother who was already up and halfway to the kitchen.

"Do you have bottled water, dear?" She asked, and much to Ava's horror, flung open the refrigerator door and stuck her head inside.

Ava panicked. Her vials of blood were in there. Although most vampires preferred the taste of warm blood, it was necessary to keep it cool until just before it was consumed. Of course, Ava rarely had any visitors to her home other than people who were also vampires, so it never occurred to her to keep it safely hidden in the back of the fridge or out of view.

"I don't see any water, but what is this?" Edith inquired, automatically zoning in on the one thing that Ava had hoped to keep secret from her. Standing erect, she stepped back and twisted her face, as if reacting to the vials sitting in the middle of the top shelf.

Great!

"Oh, that!" Ava laughed self-consciously and was impressed by her own quick thinking. "That's a new energy drink! My friend Landon is marketing it and got me in a test group."

"It looks like vials of blood." With a distasteful expression on her face, she gave her granddaughter a questioning look. "Is that supposed to encourage people to buy it?"

Ava jumped toward her cupboard and grabbed a glass to pour some water in. Turning on the tap, she gestured toward the sink. "We have a water filtering system throughout the building, so I don't buy bottled water." She eased into a smile. "As for the energy drink, it's something new that they are testing out in vials because of this whole vampire thing that everyone is into now. You know, the movies and books. Some company decided that they would try to profit off it but the energy shots aren't very good."

Ava poured her grandmother a glass of water and was relieved to see her close the fridge door, while inspecting her granddaughter's face. "Are you sure it's an energy shot and not some drug that you young people like to play around with? I saw something about that once on one of those news specials. I think they said that whatever it is came in a vial"

"No, are you crazy? I would never do drugs!" Ava insisted as she passed her grandmother the glass of water. "No, it's just energy shots. They aren't labeled yet because they don't want the testers to know the company involved, so they won't have preconceived notions before answering the questions. It makes sense. I've only had one and it really wasn't my thing, but I told Landon that I would at least try them and do the test group thing. I mean, you know, it pays too."

"Don't drink too many of those things!" Edith Wolfe took a sip of her water and stayed in the kitchen, despite Ava's hopes to get her back into the living room and away from the blood, in case she decided to inspect it again. "I read in the paper that people are sent to the emergency room because of all the caffeine in those things. Especially if mixed with alcohol. It's terrible."

"I know they aren't really my thing." Ava turned toward the living room, but stopped when she noticed her grandmother wasn't following her. "But like I said, I get paid for the test market, so it's not a big deal."

"Money isn't everything," her grandmother lectured, continuing to drink her water, as she watched Ava closely. "In my day, if you wanted energy you just ate healthy meals and went for a brisk walk after dinner. But then again, your generation is much different than mine. And I understand that it is a much more fast paced lifestyle than what I had in my day."

Ava smiled and glanced down at her feet, not really sure of how to respond to this comment. Sometimes she felt as though her grandmother could see right through her and it was unnerving.

"Yeah, it's true." She finally decided to agree. "It is a different generation and things are pretty crazy sometimes."

Silent for a moment, her grandmother finished her water and left the empty glass in the sink. "Well, I must be moving along and finish my errands for the day." She headed back to the living room and much to Ava's relief, picked up her purse that had been sitting beside the couch.

"Oh yes, I almost forgot to drop off your package that arrived at the house." Her grandmother unzipped her modest, leather purse and reached inside. Pulling out a thin packet, she quickly inspected the address and handed it to Ava, who had just followed her out of the kitchen. "This is for you."

"It's weird that it went to your place," Ava commented, noticing that there was no return address on the envelope. She was curious but decided to wait until her grandmother left to see what was inside. "I don't know what it would be."

"Probably some legal documents from your parents lawyer." her grandmother guessed as she pulled her keys out of the purse and zipped it up again. "I figured it would be faster to bring it to you myself rather than take the time to mail it again and wait for God knows how long for it to get here. It might be important."

"Well, thanks," Ava replied. "I should have just dropped by your place to get it."

Her grandmother gave her a crooked smile, raising one eyebrow. But her eyes were still sharp in their reaction and almost sent an opposing impression. "It doesn't matter now, it's here with you. That's all that matters in the end."

She headed toward the door, almost as if mentally checking off another errand from her task list. Having had a pretty superficial discussion about both her and Ava's life, it hardly felt like they were related at all. Ava wasn't sure if she wanted to create a bond with her grandmother. Did she really want a relationship with her, or was it simply what she felt she was *supposed* to do?

"I will be talking to you in the future," her grandmother piped up one last time as she turned the doorknob. No good-bye or hugs, just a matter of fact response to their meeting. It didn't matter that they hadn't seen each other in over a year. Then again, it didn't matter when they *did* see each other every day, so why should this be different?

"Thank you for this," Ava held the thin packet up in the air and watched her grandmother's eyes as they glanced at it quickly while nodding, then she escaped out the door with no more comments or pleasantries.

Once the door was closed, Ava waited a long moment to open it. Instead, she stared at the writing, wondering whom it belonged to and turned it around for any indication of where it came from, but there didn't appear to be anything. There was a postmark but it was so faded that Ava couldn't see it.

She tore it opened to find an envelope inside. It looked like an invitation- a bit of a disappointment. She half-heartedly opened this one last envelope to find a card. Pale yellow in color, it centered on a drawing of a little girl on a swing. She wore a cute, blue and white dress and an oversized hat. The child looked very content and at ease with the world while nearby, a squirrel watched her curiously.

Weird.

Assuming it was something from one of her grandmother's friends who had long forgotten her age, she opened the card to find a chilling message.

**Discontinue your pursuit to become an
immortal or someone will get hurt.**

Chapter Thirty-Two

Ava froze. After rereading the words several times, she went through an array of emotions, from overwhelming fear to a jolt of regret. Maybe Landon had been right all along and she should've just left this alone. Why *did* she want to become an immortal? Was it *this* important?

But then curiosity crept in and she wondered who had sent this letter. And why to her grandmother's house? Who would even link her to that old address now? Could it be traced? Who cared *this* much to scare her?

Suddenly feeling so alone, Ava sank to the floor, hot tears burning her eyes. Why did life have to be so hard? Why was she being blocked from this world that intrigued her so much? What was she supposed to do now? After working so meticulously to learn about the immortals, only to throw it all away because of this threat: this *one* piece of paper. And she had fought against people like Landon so hard because he-

. . .because he didn't want me to become an immortal.

Filled with anger, Ava wiped away her tears and jumped up from the floor. With paper in hand, she flew out of her apartment and frantically ran down the stairs. Practically racing to Landon's apartment, she felt like a crazed woman who was seeking her target. All her suspicions pointed to him being the one who sent this package to her grandmother's house, or if not, knowing who *had* sent it.

A weary Landon answered the door, with a large cup of coffee in hand. His eyes searched her face as he listened to Ava's rant regarding the letter, why she thought he sent it and how furious she was that such measures were taken. Remaining relaxed and silent as she spoke, he gently ushered her into his apartment and closed the door. His composure caused Ava to feel like a raving lunatic and she took a deep breath to calm down. Fighting back her tears, Ava turned away from him as he spoke.

"I'm sorry this happened to you, but I assure you it wasn't me," Landon's words were soft and comforting, causing her to completely drop all defenses. As much as she hated to admit it to herself, Ava was relieved for this assurance. She didn't want to think that Landon would actually do something like this to her. In fact, it *didn't* seem like something he would do; however, from a logical point of view, he was her loudest protester in her pursuit of an immortal lifestyle.

"Then who was it?" Ava could barely voice a whisper. "Who would do this to me?"

Landon shook his head and silently reached for the letter in her hand. His eyes studied it for longer than was necessary, almost as if he thought he'd discover the answers to their questions, but he once again shook his head and passed it back to her. "Do you have the envelope? Was there a postmark?"

As he took another gulp from his cup, Ava sighed loudly and frowned. "It was too faint to see. I guess it doesn't matter anyway." Feeling as though she had hit another dead end, she plopped down on his couch and considered her options. Should she just forget about it? Did it really matter if she found out where the letter came from or who sent it?

Glancing at Landon, who calmly observed her while continuing to drink his coffee, she suddenly wanted to be like him; at peace, relaxed, unconcerned about the future. She wanted to wake up in the morning with a feeling of tranquility and enjoy a cup of coffee, rather than living in this anxiety-ridden hell she was a part of now. Was her goal to become an immortal really worth the frustration that she was constantly feeling? Did she want to continue carrying around this heaviness that was lodged in her chest? What if she just let it all go? Would it flow away or would things fall into place? An unexpected peacefulness surrounded her like a warm bath when she considered it, making her feel that she was on to something.

Ava decided that maybe she should return to her own apartment to contemplate these questions. She already knew where he stood on the issue and his current subdued state was suggesting that any interest on the subject was lacking. With that in mind, she rose from the couch.

"I'm sorry, I should go," Ava awkwardly broke the silence. "I shouldn't have come here."

"No, it's fine," Landon's voice had a sudden jolt of energy and walking over to join her, he gestured for her to sit back down. "I can understand why your first reaction was to assume it was me, but I assure you it was not. I've been very vocal about my feelings on this topic, but I've always done so to you directly, not in a silly letter and I wouldn't even know where your grandmother lived." He shrugged and stared down into his coffee. "It almost seems like someone who is supporting you in person, but clearly feels differently than what they say."

"Maybe," Ava rubbed her eyes and felt like completely dropping the topic. She didn't even want to think about it anymore. She didn't want to deal with it. "I don't know."

"What about the immortal you met a few months ago? The CEO of your company that was hanging around." Landon suggested. "You said he was discouraging you as well. Maybe he heard you were doing some snooping around and wanted to frighten you?"

"Maybe." Ava felt depression creeping in and although she really wanted to return to her apartment to be alone, it occurred to her that Bryan would probably show up with his bright exterior and that was the last thing she wanted to deal with at that time. Even worse, he could show up with Chloe.

"I guess it doesn't matter anyway," Ava finally spoke in defeat. So many words were swirling in her head and it felt like a huge puzzle that couldn't be solved. "It is completely out of my control."

"Ava, if I thought it was something that was good for you, I wouldn't try to discourage you." Landon spoke candidly and his amber eyes searched her face for a moment, before he looked away. "I just really don't think it would be a good thing for you or *anyone*, really. Everything I've learned in my research about immortals guarantees that it's not the answer you think it is."

"Then why do I want it so bad?" Ava asked the question that she had been unable to answer herself. "Why does it matter so much?"

"Because you think it *is* the answer to what makes you unhappy, but it isn't." Landon's assurance was full of sincerity and kindness and in that moment, she knew he was right. Maybe she had to step back and take an honest look at her life and consider what really drove this need to be an immortal. Wasn't there a powerful sadness that had captured her heart for so long now? Had she thought that being an immortal would fill that gap?

"I think you really should search inside of yourself to get the real answers before you make such a drastic change," Landon continued avoiding her eyes. "It's not like you can become immortal and go back if you decide that it wasn't the answer. It's not like moving to another country, then deciding that you want to return. It doesn't work that way."

"I know," Ava replied softly, staring at the paper in her hand. She felt like a silly child and Landon was the adult, attempting to explain a life lesson. It was pathetic, but was he right? It was as if the words he had been repeating to her again and again suddenly made sense. Perhaps it was because she finally gave them consideration.

"I just don't want to see you make that mistake. I never was trying to hold you back but I found it frustrating that you wouldn't listen. It wasn't as if I wanted to ruin your life, I was trying to tell you that I know a lot about this subject and that's why I felt it wasn't in your best interest." He took another drink of his coffee, only leaving a few drops in the bottom of the cup. "Maybe six months from now you will feel very differently about everything. But at least wait to see."

"But what if I want it more six months from now?" Ava cautiously inquired. "What if I still feel the same way and I'm not any closer to finding out the answers."

"I think we will cross that bridge when we come to it," Landon advised earnestly. His smile was small, but sincere and Ava felt her entire body relax in his presence. She felt shame and guilt for making accusations against him.

"But right now, it's too soon. Life is a journey and you have to see where it takes you, not the other way around."

Ava silently nodded and felt a collection of fears and concerns slowly start to dissipate. It wasn't something she had to impulsively decide in that moment and then forcefully pursue. She'd always been in such a hurry throughout most of her life, maybe it was time to slow down and carefully unwrap one present at a time. There was no frantic rush to the end of the race but simply a comfortable walk that could lead anywhere. It was great to have goals. It was great to have dreams. But the best gift of all was in knowing that she didn't have to fight an uphill battle to get to them. Maybe life met you halfway.

Neither said a word and Ava eventually decided to leave.

"Just take it easy, Ava," he gently recommended. "Stop panicking about this and don't ask any questions. Maybe if you back off a little, the answers will come to you without you having to chase them down. That's my advice."

Feeling engrossed in the raw emotions that Landon had helped dig up; she decided not to return to her apartment. Bryan would probably be back from his morning adventures with Chloe and she simply wanted to be alone with her thoughts, rather than rehashing them to someone else.

Mindlessly, she wandered toward the rooftop, where she could ponder many things, including her conversation with Landon. Even her grandmother's visit earlier that day had brought back old emotions that she thought had been long buried. Although the older woman seemed somewhat aloof with Ava, she was still not as harsh as memory had suggested. She wondered if her memory had greatly distorted the image of her grandmother, or whether the older lady had changed in the past year.

As she reached the rooftop, Ava recognized a fragrance. A soft, floral scent met her on the stairway and beckoned her up the short stairway leading to the top of her building. Cautiously, Ava climbed to the top step, inhaling the smell that she recognized as the perfume that Mariah had recently purchased, while the two girls were shopping. Had she been upstairs that day? Was she there right now? The fragrance was pretty intense, which suggested she had been there recently.

Ava almost didn't see her. Huddled in a corner, wearing the same clothes as she had when they met for dinner the previous night, Ava could see the wine stain on her dress. At first, she thought Mariah was sleeping until her eyes suddenly sprang open and looked up at her friend.

"Are you okay? Have you been here all night?" Ava immediately squatted down beside Mariah, who stared back with a vacant look in her eyes. "I've been trying to find you. What happened at the restaurant?"

"It's not what happened back there," Mariah's voice was weak and shaking. "It's my life. It's a complete mess."

Chapter Thirty-Three

Ava didn't know what to say. She wasn't sure how to process her own afternoon, let alone help Mariah out. Although she certainly had no issue being a friend, she was growing slightly frustrated by these dramatic disappearing acts that were quickly becoming Mariah's signature move.

But no! This was her friend and Ava was just being selfish. Mariah was clearly deeply troubled and needed someone who cared. Besides, she would do the same for Ava if the tables were turned.

"I don't understand," Ava murmured, feeling the coldness enclose her body. Was she the only one who noticed the damp, chill in the air? Had Mariah stayed on the rooftop all night, wearing only her dress and heels? How many other times had she done the same thing? Ava wasn't sure what to ask, so settled on the one question that would most likely open the floodgate. "What happened yesterday?"

Mariah avoided Ava's eyes. Staring down at the stain on her dress, as she ran her finger over the remnants of wine from the previous night. It almost felt symbolic in some way, but Ava couldn't grasp why. With an indication of vulnerability in her voice, she eventually began to speak.

"It's not what happened yesterday, Ava. It's a lot of things that I haven't told you about. Yesterday I just woke up feeling like I couldn't pretend anymore. My life isn't fine. I'm not fine." She finally looked up into Ava's eyes; her makeup had disappeared, and with it, a layer of deceit had also been removed. "I haven't been for a long time, even when I tried to tell myself otherwise."

"So, tell me everything," Ava made an effort to show compassion, but heard a sense of frustration in her own voice. She felt guilty for being insensitive and was relieved that Mariah didn't seem to notice. Then again, how many times had Ava attempted to contact her in the last day, only to be ignored? This scenario seemed to repeat itself, almost as if Ava was supposed to chase after her friend, as though the simple act of reaching out wasn't enough. It was draining. But she attempted to push her frustrations aside and understand Mariah's sorrow.

"There's just so much to tell," Mariah shook her head and looked away once again. "I haven't been completely honest with you."

"About?"

Taking a deep breath, Mariah moved a strand of disheveled hair from her eyes. "To start with, I wasn't honest about why I got fired from my last job. I lied about everything."

"Why?"

"Pride. I didn't want you to know what a loser I really am," Mariah admitted, hugging her own legs; as she leaned forward, she looked like a lost little girl in Ava's eyes. And although she should've been angry by this confession, she found herself empathetic instead. "And when you hear why, you will see why I *am* a loser."

"You are *not* a loser, Mariah." Ava reassured her and was relieved to only hear kindness in her voice this time. "Please, just tell me everything."

"The truth?" Mariah raised her eyebrows. "I was in love with my boss. Deeply in love with him, in love in a way that I hadn't ever thought was possible. He was the most amazing person I ever met in my life and I couldn't get him out of my head." Tears formed in her eyes. "We never dated. In fact, I had no definite proof that he felt the same way. There were times I thought he did but I wasn't sure if I was misreading his kindness or seeing what I wanted. It was very confusing but I felt embarrassed and so I never mentioned it to you or anyone else before today."

"It wasn't an instant thing, it happened over time. I wanted to forget about him and push it aside so many times, but it wouldn't go away." Mariah looked as if a weight had been removed from her shoulders and suddenly she appeared even smaller in Ava's eyes. "I lied when I made it sound like he was this asshole, I was just angry. And the girl I called Tits and Ass, I was jealous of her because I could hear through the doors and I knew he respected her more than me. I think he thought I was just some pathetic receptionist who couldn't get a better job. And here he was, a doctor. Someone who was educated and respected, perhaps in a way I never would be."

"There was nothing going on between him and the girl. Nothing that I could see anyway," Mariah sighed loudly and paused for a moment, closing her eyes and finally opening them again. "But she was the type I figured he would prefer. Beautiful. Perfect. Elegant. The kind of woman he could go to one of his rich, society dinners with and not be embarrassed. Someone who was intelligent and had a super hot figure, while I had nothing to offer him and although there were times he was really nice, there were others he would walk by the reception desk in the morning as if I wasn't even there."

"He sounds like an ass."

"But he wasn't," Mariah was insistent. "I tried to tell myself that too. I tried to tell myself that he didn't really matter or that he wasn't a good person. But then he would say something to me or do something that suggested he did care for me in the same way that I cared for him. He would make me feel like I mattered to him and all my doubts would disappear and I would be back at square one again."

"Did you ever tell him how you felt?"

"I did," Mariah's face became very tight and her eyes watered. Ava began to wish she hadn't asked the question at all. "The day he fired me."

"Did he fire you because you told him how you felt?"

"Kind of," Mariah admitted and her face released all its tension, tears streaming from her eyes. "I went to work early that day. I had decided the night before that I would finally tell him the truth about how I felt and stop being so scared. And he acted weird, uncomfortable, as if I had said the most outlandish thing ever. As if he was embarrassed by *my* confession and he was trying to find a way to nicely tell me he would rather be dead than with me."

"I don't think that was the case, " Ava quickly injected. "I think you probably just took him off guard."

"But it didn't matter, he didn't care and that's all I got out of his response. He made it clear that he would never feel that way about me and never had. It was like a knife to my heart. I didn't know what to say or do, so I just walked out of the office and went to the washroom, trying to compose myself. I didn't know if I should quit or what to do in that moment. I just felt confused and alone." She began to cry even harder and wiped her eyes with the material of her sleeve. "It was one of the worst moments in my life. I never felt so humiliated and heartbroken at the same time. I felt devastated and yet, I had to walk out there and work? I didn't think I could do it but at the same time, I was frozen and couldn't react at all."

"So I went to the front desk and opened the office door, as I always did every morning. Patients arrived right away. The girl I call Tits and Ass showed up all super happy and friendly, with her boobs practically hanging out of her shirt as usual and I just sat there thinking that he would prefer a girl like her, rather than me. And that if I looked like her or was her, he would've been delighted to hear my confession." Mariah stopped crying and fell into thought for a moment. "She went in his office to say good morning and I heard the door close."

"Unlike what I told you before, I don't think they were screwing but I could tell they were close and that made me jealous. Also, they didn't take hours, only a few minutes but the words I could hear through that door almost destroyed me," Mariah confessed. "He told her what happened and said he didn't think I should be working there anymore because it was inappropriate. Tits and Ass actually took my side, which kind of pissed me off more, and she tried to explain to him that it was better to just wait and not make a rash decision."

"And that's when he said it." Mariah's face showed disappointment and defeat. "He said he thought I was 'unstable' and that he didn't want to push the wrong buttons and have me react in some crazy way. He said that he thought I was an alcoholic and that maybe he would recommend I start a program. Then he said that he actually thought he would insist that I did, if I wanted to save my job."

"Oh my God!" Ava knew that her friend had issues but thought that the doctor's words were a bit harsh. In her mind, he was an asshole but judging from the look in Mariah's eyes, she still held a lot of respect for him and took his words to heart.

"Mariah, that isn't true," Ava rushed to reassure her. "You aren't unstable, no more than anyone else. He's a doctor. He's all about facts and science, he probably has no real compassion. It's normal to have feelings for other people, that don't mean you're crazy. It's not like you were stalking him or anything."

"No, of course not," Mariah sniffed. "But I think he was right. And that's why I disappeared for a while over the holidays. I kept thinking and thinking about that day and it just worked against me because I began to wonder if my life really was that meaningless and worthless—if I was really that meaningless and worthless."

"Mariah, don't say that!" Ava insisted. "Please, don't take his words to be the truth because they aren't. Listen to me; I'm your friend. He doesn't really know you."

"But that's the point, you are my friend, so you aren't going to tell me I'm crazy. In fact, you probably don't see it. He is someone who has nothing invested in my life so he is being honest."

"No, Mariah, please don't see it that way."

Almost as if she hadn't heard this last comment, she picked up her story again. "He took me aside at lunch time, after the last appointment left for the morning and said he felt that a series of things made him 'uncomfortable' with me working in the office and that my confession was the final straw. Then, he fired me."

Ava fell silent. That was not the right thing for her boss to do, but she wasn't sure how to make her friend see this very point. Suddenly, she felt guilty for being so frustrated with her earlier in their conversation. She had no idea how hurt Mariah must've felt or how keeping it a secret was slowly tearing her apart. No wonder she had grown so despondent since being fired.

"And I went away, got a new job, thought I could leave it all behind," Mariah confessed. "I really, really thought I had moved on and then the other day, I went out to the drugstore to pick up deodorant and there he was, with another girl. A beautiful girl, she was probably twenty years old and flawless. He didn't even see me because he was so wrapped up in her. She was everything I was not. Young, perfect body, perfect face and I felt like more of a fool than ever before."

"Please don't do this!" Ava pleaded. "Don't measure yourself against this other girl and don't give his words so much power. Just because he said them doesn't mean you have to believe them."

"But he was right." Mariah looked away, nervously running her fingers over the stain on her skirt as she bit her bottom lip.

"Mariah, if there is one thing I have learned lately, it's that sometimes what we think we want, isn't necessarily the best thing," Ava tried to carefully explain her feelings to her friend. "I think sometimes we get attached to an idea without really looking at it closely. He clearly was *not* a good person. A good person wouldn't have fired you for something like that, or made you feel inferior for being honest about your feelings. I don't think you should let it drag you down. He's not worth it. No one who makes you feel bad about yourself is worth it."

"I know, but I can't help it," Mariah admitted. She slowly pushed herself up from the ground, and Ava followed her. Walking to the edge of the rooftop, Mariah stared into the distance and pointed at one of the tall buildings that towered over their own. "See that place with the glowing orange near the top, that's where I worked. I used to go there every morning and look forward to just seeing him. I haven't been there in months and he still has a hold over me. How pathetic is that?"

"You will move on and forget him," Ava assured her. "It is going to take some time, but I promise it will happen. One day you will see things differently."

"No," Mariah shook her head. "I've tried to hate him but when I go to bed at night, it's always his face I see in my head and his words that go through my brain. He's not the first person to call me unstable, so there is obviously some truth to it."

"No, Mariah, there isn't." Ava insisted, her voice quivering when she saw the hopelessness in her friend's eyes. If only she knew the best words to convey her message, but it was like trying to push through a brick wall. This man had somehow managed to tap into Mariah's insecurities and rip them wide open. "Please, don't listen to him or anyone who puts you down. It's more of a reflection on them, than it is on you."

"My mother used to say it too, way back when I was a kid." Mariah's voice was child-like as she continued to stare off into the distance.

"She *was* wrong." Ava was adamant. "You have to stop believing what everyone else is saying about you. Sometimes people who are hurt themselves try to hurt other people. You have to let it go."

Mariah didn't respond but silently stared at the building that had the orange light shining on top. If only Ava had known what she was thinking.

Chapter Thirty-Four

Her conversation with Mariah depressed Ava. She wasn't sure whether she was choosing the wrong words, or if they were simply being ignored because nothing was getting through to her. It almost felt as though they were floating around the surface but not connecting with the intellectual part of Mariah's brain. Had she been in a rational state of mind, it would've been clear that the doctor was an asshole and not worth all this misery.

But love did funny things to people and caused them to see wonderful traits that didn't really exist. Hadn't she done the same thing with Bryan? Even after he turned Ava into a vampire and left her to fend for herself, she still cared for him, even secretly hoping that he would someday return to sweep her off her feet.

Maybe everyone had a pathetic side at one point that longed for someone who would make a terrible mate. Maybe everyone had a fantasy that they would never admit to another human being. Maybe everyone hoped that the person they were in love with would swoop in, and say those magical words that they longed to hear. Didn't everyone ultimately bear some shame for where their hearts occasionally took them?

They ended their conversation with a promise. Mariah promised Ava she would keep in touch daily. No more disappearing. No more avoiding text messages or phone calls. No more self-loathing, secretly in her apartment and hiding from the world. From now on, she would stay in regular communication with Ava, and the two would talk about any issues as they arose.

It really was the only way that Ava knew how to handle the situation. She hoped that her words would eventually sink in to Mariah's head, especially after a good night's sleep, but she couldn't be sure.

Mariah did keep her promise and checked in regularly, so Ava began to feel more comfortable and sensed that perhaps unloading her feeling was exactly what was needed to move on. Ava considered how torturous it must've been for her to walk around with such a terrible impression of herself, sincerely believing that she was unstable. Although it was clear that Mariah did have some emotional problems, who *didn't* at some point in their lives?

Ava did a lot of thinking for the next few days. She wasn't only thinking about Mariah, but also about her conversation with Landon, regarding the immortal lifestyle. It was easy to see how she would get locked in an idea and stubbornly not let go of it, even when it seemed to be counterproductive.

But another side of her was curious about all the secrecy. It was obvious why they did not want the average person to know the truth, but why not a mortal vampire? And why had she received the threatening note? Who sent it? She considered every possible person and weighed all the evidence but over-thinking the concept was only driving her crazy.

Maybe she would never know the answers...

There was something very compelling about the idea of living forever. She could take advantage and move all over the world, see everything there was to see and learn about herself over time.

But there was the other side as well. What if she married and had to watch her husband age and die, only to continue her life? She didn't know if she could handle watching *anyone* in her life age and die, knowing she would live forever. What if she wanted to have children? There was something fundamentally wrong with the concept of immortality.

Although her heart had not completely let go of the idea of becoming an immortal, she decided to put her dream aside and to see how she felt about the idea in upcoming weeks. Maybe it wasn't meant to be.

As spring slowly ended and summer was only days away, Ava started to feel differently about her life. As her fixation with immortals faded, she began to notice other things going on around her: little things that she hadn't noticed when she was obsessed with her future, rather than focusing on her present. After all, wasn't life supposed to be about living in the moment?

One of the things she noticed was how attentive her boss was toward her at work. Originally, she just assumed it was because of the vampire thing that he was helping her out with, but as she let that dream slide, something told her that there was more to their connection than a mutual interest in the topic. He *did* talk to her a little more than the other employees and maybe, she decided, that was the reason why many gave her strange looks whenever Ava would walk out of his office. It was often just her stopping in for a quick hello. But then, she would worry about what others thought and avoid him for days.

Bryan was constantly out of town and in fact, she hadn't really seen him since his coffee date with Chloe. Since Ava had little respect for Landon's ex, she assumed that the two probably hooked up and it was the only diversion Bryan needed to forget about her. He went back to the set shortly after that last visit and hadn't returned to Vancouver since; at least, not to Ava's knowledge.

It kind of hurt her to think that she was just the 'fill in' when no one else was around. It made her feel a pain that she wanted to deny, along with any feelings she had for him, but deep down rejection always hurt. There was no way around it.

Somewhere along the line, her life had completely turned upside down and Ava wasn't sure how, or if, she would get it right side up again. Maybe change was good but it was also *scary*. Life had a weird way of hurting her when it changed and it was a lesson she had learned the hard way, again and again. The first of those changes was when her parents died. Then when she moved in with an unwelcoming grandmother. And finally, when Bryan made her a vampire then ran off to leave her during her weakest hour. There was a clear theme running through her life and it was certainly one of rejection. Ava decided that it would never happen again. She wouldn't let it.

The only person who hadn't rejected her was Landon, but she still had managed to ruin that situation. Her fears and insecurities were like a crowbar that pushed them apart, little by little, until he was completely out of her life. She had accused him of cheating on her when deep down, Ava wanted to pretend that she was the innocent victim. It was an unfair accusation, which she had hoped he would go out of his way to prove wrong. Instead, he was deeply offended and hurt by her words and then later, Ava's actions. She had reacted because she thought it was a way to hurt him back. It had backfired on her.

And she had deserved it.

No one ever stayed. They just found reasons to leave.

Although the thought of always being alone was excruciating, there was some relief in knowing that nothing and no one held power over her. No one could reject her if she wasn't in love. No one could take something away from her if she didn't have it. If nothing meant anything to her, then there was nothing to rip away from her and really, rip from her heart.

Ava decided that she could only count on herself.

But then something unexpected happened. Her grandmother started to occasionally phone. Actually it started out with text messages. At the age of 65, she decided to purchase her first cell phone for 'safety reasons' and after a few technological stumbles, learned how to text. And although she wasn't crazy about it in the beginning, often complaining about people who were too busy 'playing around on their phones' rather than making eye contact, she quickly became one of those people. She sent Ava a message every day. Then it was a couple. Soon, it was ongoing throughout the day, starting at 7 a.m.

It was kind of nice. The messages were often nothing very exciting—about the weather or something on the news—but it was nice to see her grandmother make such efforts. Eventually she grew tired of her new skill and decided to call Ava instead.

"Well, I can say I know how to do it now," Edith Wolfe gruffly asserted. "And that's good enough for me. I will text you now and again, but I would rather hear a human voice than take all day to type out a message."

Ava admired her initiative and was surprised that their conversations went so smoothly. It was much different from the days she remembered from her childhood. The old lady had certainly changed for the better. Then again, maybe it was actually *her* that had changed.

Their nightly conversations quickly became an unexpected routine and were much more pleasant than Ava had anticipated. Life sometimes took some very interesting turns.

Ava also attempted to spend more time with Mariah. She seemed to change as well.

Where Ava's grandmother became much more tolerable, her friend became a mellow version of her former self. But it was an unsettling tranquility that concerned Ava. She couldn't put her finger on it, but it felt as though Mariah had lost all her passion for life. Had she not known better, Ava would've suspected that her friend was on some kind of antidepressants that were meant to drain the life out of people, until they not only weren't depressed anymore, but simply felt nothing at all.

While Ava was relieved that she was not witnessing the manic side of Mariah that worried her so much, she wondered if this was better. It didn't seem like an improvement to not care at all.

Once again, this felt like a question that Ava should've been asking herself.

It occurred to her that it was no coincidence that they were close friends. Fate had brought them together, because at the end of the day, their struggle wasn't all that different. In fact, they were more alike than different. Her own life was fueled by sadness, while Mariah's was filled with anger.

And yet all around them, women walked by in their designer clothes, with smug, cold expressions and expensive sunglasses and handbags, acting like they had the world by the seat of its pants. These were the people who had once intimidated Ava, but then again, wasn't Mariah once one of those same women who arrogantly walked into a room as if she owned it: the same girl who had cried hysterically on the rooftop not long ago, emotionally raw and vulnerable.

Maybe people weren't all that different after all. They wore a mask or carried an attitude but maybe it was to distract and divert attention from what they really wanted to hide, similar to an illusion performed by a magician. Maybe that was the secret behind life. And maybe, she had only started to scratch the surface of what others had so carefully hidden away.

Chapter Thirty-Five

There was a dark feeling in Ava's heart that she could not escape. The fear of trusting was so entrenched in her body that it was nearly impossible to know where it started and where it ended. It ran through her veins and reached every fiber of her being. It was in every hair follicle and every drop of sweat that grew in her hairline and the back of her neck. It was ingrained in her brain and heart to never fully trust anyone—*ever*. And much like a criminal attempting to flee prison, she felt like a hostage in every area of her life.

But that wasn't abnormal. Didn't everyone feel that way? Wasn't fear really there to protect us from danger? So maybe, that meant that danger was never all that far away.

One of the reasons Ava continued her relationship with Bryan was because it was safe. She cared about him but didn't love him. It was also one of the reasons why she sabotaged everything with Landon because he actually did mean something to her. And she knew these facts about herself but she also didn't know how to reverse them and live like a normal person. Maybe she never would be *normal* in the sense that the rest of the world thought was ideal.

Ava knew that she and Matthew shared a secret bond that made her slightly uncomfortable. He was curious about what made her tick and that indicated to her that he cared about Ava as a person. Sometimes she thought it was just general curiosity, perhaps an attempt to learn about his employee. But deep down, she knew there were other reasons for his curiosity. It was unsettling; unlike most other people, she wasn't able to hide from him because they worked together. Was that the real reason why people didn't form relationships with coworkers? Perhaps it was the reality that they would have to see each other in an environment that was much more controlled than on a social level. Work was like another planet, a place where people put on a mask painted by a corporation that indirectly insisted that you not really be yourself, while on the clock.

At any rate, Matthew was anxious to talk to her on that particular Tuesday morning. Ava walked past the usual curious stares as well as those full of contempt, in order to reach his office. It was becoming more awkward every day.

"Do you see *that?*" Ava automatically posed the question after shutting his office door and heading for the chair across from him. His face was full of astonishment as their eyes met, as if the entire idea that their regular conversations were creating office gossip was a shock to him. He was too intelligent to be that naïve. "Everyone is looking at me like I'm the office whore!"

A smile curved Matthew's lips and his eyes sparkled under the dull, florescent lights. Chuckling as he avoided her reaction, he shuffled papers around his desk and shook his head, his composure dismissive. "Ava, you are most *definitely,* incredibly paranoid. I'm sure that if anything, the vultures are all waiting at the door wondering if you are in some kind of trouble that I'm always calling you in here. I seriously doubt that anyone thinks that you are here servicing me in any way."

Ava felt her face burning and she reluctantly sat down. "Come on, you *don't* see how they look at me. It's not like they have pity in their eyes, they seriously are looking at me as if there is something going on here."

"Maybe *you're* the one who is thinking that there is something going on here." He raised his eyebrows seductively and grabbed his cup of coffee from the corner of his desk. Taking a big swig, his usual jovial teasing was consistent, his good mood contagious. His spirit was constantly light and it was....well, it was very unusual to her reality.

"That's not what I'm saying," Ava was slightly defiant in her reaction. She sat up a bit straighter and found herself growing frustrated with his impish grin. "I just can tell by the way they look at me that they are thinking that something is up cause I'm in here more often than any of them." She gestured toward the door. "Plus it isn't like anyone can see into the office." Ava glanced at the solid walls and door that surrounded them.

"I get what you are saying, Ava. I am not going to lose any sleep over what those people either do or don't think, and neither should you." Matthew set down his coffee cup, a new smile lighting up his face. "I do, however, have some information for you that might be of interest."

"You do?"

"Yup, talked to my mother last night and mentioned that you were getting hate notes in the mail." She noted his demeanor was slightly more solemn, now that the topic was of a more serious nature.

"Well, there was only one note, but yeah," Ava agreed. "It was warning me to back off."

"Yes well, mom thought that was kind of weird. She said you certainly weren't the first person to look into becoming immortal so she was surprised that you received a threat." Matthew leaned back in his chair, tapping one hand against the opposite one, while searching her face. "Any idea who sent it?"

"Your friend, Derrick?" Ava guessed. "He was pretty persistent that I leave it alone and stop wanting to be an immortal."

"Well he's more a friend of the family than *my* friend," Matthew corrected her and rocked back in his chair. "But no, I don't think it was him. As far as he is concerned, I have *you* under control. If he were to bother at all, it would've been long ago."

"What do you mean you have *me* under control?" Ava's voice rose much higher than she meant it to and she looked away in embarrassment.

"I mean, he's been asking about you and I insisted that you were no longer looking into the immortal lifestyle. I told him I thought you were caught up with a mortal boyfriend or something and he accepted that and no longer sees you as an issue."

"When did this happen?" Ava's voice was sharp. "When did you have this conversation about me?"

"A few days ago." Matthew reached for his coffee cup again. "So don't worry about him. I don't think he would threaten you anyway."

"Hmm."

"But my mother seems to think that the fact that you were threatened at all suggests that you were pretty close to something big," Matthew pulled his chair ahead and he leaned forward on the desk. "In fact, she feels that maybe you were pretty close to discovering the top person in that entire.... situation? The so-called 'Rock Star' of vampires." He put both hands up and simultaneously bent two fingers to indicate he was quoting. "If there is actually such a thing."

"You don't think there is?" Ava got caught up on this fact rather than the more vital piece of information and quickly wished she hadn't brought it up.

"Well, who knows, right?" Matthew shrugged as his face twisted in doubt. "I mean, there are so many stories that you never know what is and isn't true. About vampires in general, there is so much misinformation out there that it wouldn't surprise me if there was within the actual community as well."

"I suppose."

"Regardless, mom feels pretty sure that something is up that you got that note." He sighed loudly. "And being a mother, she sent the message for you to be careful."

Ava smiled and didn't respond.

Their meeting ended shortly after he delivered this news and Ava made her way back out to the reception desk. The suspicious look Nisha gave her irked Ava.

"What?" Ava snapped.

"Nothing," She was quick to shake her head and put her hand up defensively. "You guys just have a lot of meetings."

"I know."

"Is everything okay?" Nisha's eyes were sincere, and Ava felt her defenses falling. It wasn't her fault that some of their coworkers were suspicious and it wasn't fair to take it out on this sweet, Indian woman.

"Yeah, we are just talking about.....career advice." Ava lied. "You know, do I really want to be a receptionist for the rest of my life?"

"It's a stepping stone," Nisha reassured her genuinely. "Hopefully he can help you."

Ava nodded and felt bad for being abrupt with Nisha. Her inability to trust people was too intense at times especially when someone really did have the best intentions.

Ava waited till no one was around to text Mariah to let her know what Matthew had told her that morning. She couldn't wait to pick her brain on this bit of news.

The day was really dragging and at one point, Ava considered saying that she was sick in order to leave early. She couldn't keep her mind on work and felt antsy after her conversation with Matthew. Was she really that close to the truth that someone felt threatened? Was it someone in her life that sent the note? And why to her grandmother's place? It didn't make sense.

Checking her phone again and again, she grew frustrated when Mariah wasn't replying to her texts. She began to worry that her friend was pulling another one of her famous disappearing acts and texted her again.

Is everything ok?

By the end of the day she had a simple reply.

Fine

There was no response to Ava's news. She wondered if maybe it wasn't such a big deal after all and left the office at the usual time. With a strange twinge in her heart, she arrived home and automatically knew something was wrong. It was a sinking feeling that she would never forget. But as she glanced around the building, nothing seemed amiss. Spotting Benjamin in the lounge area, she hurried over and nervously asked him if anything was going on.

"No, young lady," Benjamin was holding a newspaper in hand and appeared completely at ease. "I don't believe there is. All is quiet today. Why do you ask?"

"I don't know," Ava leaned against the back of the chair that was opposite Benjamin's seat. "I just have this weird feeling, you know? As soon as I walked in the building."

"You women and your bloody intuition. Drives us all batty," Benjamin teased and returned to his paper. "You may ask Landon, I believe he's upstairs."

"No, that's fine." Ava started to walk away and then hesitated. "Hey ah, Benjamin? Have you seen Mariah today?"

"Yes, I believe she sauntered in about fifteen minutes ago." He raised his eyebrows. "Problem?"

"No, I'm just paranoid," Ava began to walk away again.

"Wretched intuition." She heard him muttering under his breath as she walked away and knowing his comments were light hearted, Ava smiled while approaching the elevator.

Chapter Thirty-Six

She felt energized when she woke the next morning. Matthew was right. Ava had received the threatening note because she was getting too close to the truth, and someone was hoping that fear would be a deterrent. Ironically, if she had *not* received the letter telling her to back off, Ava would've grown weary of the fruitless investigate and stopped searching. But now she felt closer to learning the identity of the 'rock star' of vampires, Ava found a reawakened interest in her pursuit. In fact, she could hardly wait to get to work and tell Matthew her decision.

Unfortunately that didn't happen as quickly as she anticipated. Due to a police incident, traffic was tied up in the downtown area and transit was overextended, mostly because many vehicles were unable to take their normal route. Since she lived within a reasonable distance from work, Ava decided to save herself the frustration and walk.

Once arriving, she quickly discovered that most of her coworkers were in the same boat and even clients were going to be late. In fact, the only person in the office was Matthew.

"What are you doing here?" She stuck her head inside the doorway.

"I work here." He shot her a mischievous smile. "What are *you* doing here?"

Ava rolled her eyes and smiled in spite of herself. "You *know* what I mean. Because of this accident or whatever." She pointed toward the window while entering his office, then sat across from him. "It doesn't look like anyone else is here."

"You are," he grinned. "From the message you sent earlier, I thought you wouldn't be here this soon, but you're only, what?" He glanced at his computer. "Ten minutes late?"

"I walked."

"You're definitely getting a gold star from me!" His voice sounded unusually flirtatious. "Everyone else has called in late. I wonder how many are actually tied up in traffic and how many are tied up with another cup of coffee and a great excuse."

"It's hard to say." Ava smiled. "So um, I was thinking about what you said yesterday about me getting close to learning something about the immortals and that's why I got the threatening note."

"Yeah?"

"And I think I am going to continue my search." Ava slowly admitted. "Not necessarily because I *want* to be an immortal now but because I want to learn who is behind all this and what it's all about."

Matthew leaned against his hand and for once appeared slightly tired. "I'm curious, why go to all this trouble if you have little interest in being one anymore? Or is that just a story you're telling both of us, until the right time?"

"It's hard to....hard to explain," Ava found herself stuttering over the words. "I see it as a plan B."

"A plan B?" Matthew titled his head and raised his eyebrows. "What *is* that?"

"A plan B if I don't feel like my life is going as I had hoped. I want to..ah.."

"Live longer?" Matthew began to chuckle and then pretended to be serious. "Yup, that makes sense if you aren't happy, find a way to never die."

"I can't explain. Maybe I am not even sure myself," Ava smiled self-consciously. Rising from the chair, she pointed in the direction of the door. "I can hear people down the hallway, coming in this direction."

"You and your super, vampire ears." Matthew grinned, glancing down at a sheet on his desk while reaching for his coffee. "You will have to explain this to me better later on."

"I will," Ava promised and headed toward the door. "I just feel that if I screw up with my life it allows me to go back and fix it, then become the person I want to be."

"Maybe," Matthew looked up to make eye contact with her just as Nisha arrived at work. "Maybe you should be doing that anyway."

She was relieved that their conversation ended on that note because if it hadn't, Ava wasn't at all sure how she could respond. Preoccupied with her own thoughts afterward, she was disappointed that the original high from that morning had so quickly faded away. It was around ten when she glanced at her phone and wondered why Mariah hadn't sent her a text yet. Feeling a stab of concern, Ava decided to send her a quick message.

Hey. Did you get tied up in traffic this morning?

Sending the text, Ava figured that Mariah would've probably heard about the traffic jam and automatically used it as an excuse to call in late and get some extra sleep. The idea made Ava smile. Mariah was just ballsy enough to take that risk, whereas she herself, had practically ran to get to the office on time.

By noon, she was more than happy to accept Nisha's offer to go out to lunch first, while her coworker looked after the reception desk. Matthew's words followed her out of the office, bellowing at Ava while she walked down the street. It wasn't the first time it was suggested that she live the life she wanted, immortal or not. Unfortunately, it wasn't always that easy. For example, what about her parents? Hadn't they wanted to do many things before they died?

Immortality was a reassurance that she would always have time. It was her safety net. Most people wouldn't understand and she couldn't possibly expect them to because their own lives were so very different. Experiencing her parents' death at an early age made life seem so much more fragile and caused Ava to question her own mortality.

Entering a nearby coffee shop, Ava suddenly remembered to check her phone to see if Mariah had sent a text to her yet, but there was nothing. New fears flooded her mind and she worried about the delicate woman who had been hunched over on the rooftop only days earlier, crying hysterically over a man that didn't love her. What if Mariah was doing the same thing that very morning? What if she had broken her promise to contact Ava, if something was wrong? It wasn't unlike Mariah to cower away in her apartment and avoid her texts. People were creatures of habit and tended to return to what was familiar.

After a quick sandwich and coffee, Ava slowly made her way back to work and hoped the afternoon went faster than the morning. Upon her return, Nisha practically flew out the door as though she were feeling as confined by the office as Ava was. Matthew's door was closed, which meant he was with a client, and everyone else appeared to either be gone for lunchtime or unavailable.

The afternoon dragged by slowly and Ava was only too happy to leave at 4:30. The only positive aspect of the day was when Nisha confided that she had been permanently hired on at Anderson & Smith, now that her internship was completed. Although Ava was certainly happy for her coworker, there was a part of her that was also depressed. If only she knew what kind of career pursuit would fill her with the same excitement that Nisha was feeling that afternoon. Would Ava ever have that experience or would she continue to float through life with no direction?

Feeling discouraged and depressed, Ava decided to walk home rather than use the city transit. She wanted some time to be alone, to think. Travelling by bus usually did little to improve her mood, especially when constantly being pushed and shoved in every direction by people with no manners or consideration.

Checking her phone as she walked, she found a series of text messages.

Three were from Landon, each one indicating that he had to talk to her and trying to find out what time she would be arriving home. That was odd. Landon rarely texted her at all, let alone with such urgency. This was a concern.

The next one was from Bryan, something she hadn't expected. It was more or less just to check in and say hi, but it was so rare for him to do so that Ava was somewhat suspicious. Her on-again, off-again boyfriend wasn't much of a texter: he usually used his phone to play games or catch up on emails.

The next three didn't have a number. Ava wasn't sure if it was blocked or some kind of error. Glancing at that quickly, she felt her curiosity peak but the anonymous text messages didn't make sense.

Did you get my last message?

Do you not hear me?

Give up

Ava just assumed it was someone who put her number in as an error. It was clearly a series of texts that were meant to go to someone else because they didn't make sense. She put her phone away and tried to forget about Landon's message.

It was hard to believe that she had started the day off feeling optimistic and strong. Ava's spirit was now depleted as she turned up the street that led her home. It was on the way that she felt another vibration in her purse and stopped to check her phone. It had no caller ID.

Let go of your immortal dream!!!!! It won't happen!

Ava felt her heart racing wildly in her chest. This seriously could not be happening! How did this person locate her cell number? Scrolling back to the three other anonymous messages, Ava wondered if they were all connected.

She glanced around suspiciously, suddenly frightened that she was being followed, but no one was paying attention to her as they rushed in all directions.

It was with shaking hands, she texted back.

Who is this?

She immediately received an error message. The text wouldn't go through for some reason. Ava's legs felt shaky as she hurried the rest of the way home. Maybe Landon could help her solve this mystery since he worked for a cell phone company. Fortunately, he was in the lounge area when she arrived at the apartment building. Their eyes met and his mouth opened, as if he were about to say something.

"Landon, I'm getting threatening text messages now," Ava spoke nervously as she approached him. Today he sat alone with his laptop bag on the floor beside him. His eyes searched her face and he didn't reply. She noted that he was much paler than normal, as he licked his lips and pointed to the chair across from him, indicating for her to sit down.

Her heart pounding in dread, Ava automatically thought that the text messages were just the tip of the iceberg. What was he about to tell her? Had someone broken into her apartment? Was there a threatening package left outside her door? Would she go upstairs and-

"Ava, I'm taking what you are telling me seriously, but there is something else I have to talk to you about immediately. It's unfortunately some bad news." Landon hesitated and she noted the sadness in his eyes. Anxiety continued to grip her and she bit her bottom lip in anticipation of what he would say. She prayed that she would be able to handle whatever happened next.

"What? Oh my God! What's going on?" Ava heard her voice shaking and felt a sudden heat wave overcome her body. When he finally answered her question, Landon's voice sounded like it was drifting away.

"Ava," his voice was hoarse and weak. "Mariah's dead."

Chapter Thirty-Seven

Ava was speechless, her throat bone dry. Both her arms had suddenly turned to lead and felt weighed down on each side, like concrete. There were no tears. She was too shocked to cry. Too shocked to form a word. Her legs trembled and it was ideal that Landon had waited until she was safely in a chair to deliver such horrific news. There was an echo all around her and everything sounded like it was a million miles away. She could feel her stomach heave with anxiety and her heart pounded madly, as if it was racing to stay alive.

It couldn't be true.

Landon would never lie.

Landon would *never* lie.

Ava licked her lips and attempted to speak but felt herself lodged in silence. She could hear Landon speak but couldn't make out his words. Her thoughts were going a mile a minute and she felt her head involuntarily shake.

"No, it's...no," Ava finally got some words out. "No, she texted me last night. She's fine. It must be someone with the same name, some kind of mix up-" Ava desperately reached into her purse and with a shaky hand, removed the phone and carelessly hit a few buttons, attempting to find the text that would prove him wrong. "It was a mistake. She's just hiding somewhere. You know how she is. It's..."

Unable to make her hands work properly on the buttons, she sat the phone on her lap and looked up at Landon. With pity in his eyes, he silently rose from his chair and picked up his laptop bag. Swinging it over his shoulder, he moved toward Ava. Gently taking her phone with one hand, he offered his other one to help her off the chair.

"Let's go to your apartment," he said kindly. Ava grabbed her bag and stood up. She glanced around and noted that some of the other apartment building residents were arriving home and gathering in small groups to talk.

They are talking about Mariah. They are talking about how she lived here.

No! Mariah *lives* in this building; Ava silently corrected herself because it was obviously a mistake.

She couldn't remember walking to the elevator. Lost in her own thoughts, Ava simply followed Landon's lead until they were back in her apartment and he closed the door behind them. He sat quietly beside her on the couch.

Taking a deep breath, Landon turned toward her and spoke in a soothing, yet serious voice. "Ava, I'm sorry, it isn't a mistake. Mariah is dead."

Tears flooded her eyes. In her heart, she knew there was no way Landon would lie to her. There was no way he would get his facts wrong. There was no way he would be telling her this unless he was sure it was true. And so, she listened to every difficult word he had to say.

"Samantha called me earlier today and asked me to speak to you." He stopped and cleared his throat, staring into space as if trying to find the right words. "The police contacted her because she's the landlord linked to her address ah….she um, she said Mariah went to work today and she was fired. Something about checking some old references that weren't good and they think," he paused and took a breath.

"Her last boss really had a lot of issues with her," Ava sniffed, as tears slid down her cheeks and dripped from her chin. She thought about her rooftop conversation with Mariah regarding the doctor. She wouldn't normally betray someone's confidence but the words came pouring out. "He um….he thought she was either unstable or an alcoholic and fired her."

"That seems like an overreaction," Landon muttered, appearing deep in thought before looking back into Ava's vulnerable eyes. "There's no easy way to tell you this, Ava. She walked into traffic and the police think that it was on purpose." He hesitated to allow Ava time to process the information. "She walked in front of a bus and the driver couldn't stop in time."

Ava's expression grew more pained while she slowly nodded to indicate that she already knew. As soon as Landon announced Mariah was dead, Ava knew in her heart that it was a suicide. Clearly, the recruitment agency had checked her previous employers, including the doctor that Mariah was in love with and received unpleasant reports back. They fired her and when added to Mariah's recent depression, this was the final straw. Ava didn't have to be convinced and she could no longer deny it, all the facts fit together too well. And yet, she wanted so badly to be wrong. She wanted Landon to be a liar. She wanted Samantha to have made a mistake.

Ava barely noticed Landon leave the room to find some Kleenex until he was holding the pink box out to her with an apologetic smile on his face. Quickly grabbing two, Ava began to wipe the tears from her face. Landon sat the rest beside her and headed for the kitchen, where he poured her a glass of water.

Meanwhile, Ava glanced around the room, picturing Mariah everywhere. She was at the kitchen counter, opening a bottle of wine. Then she sat on the floor in front of the coffee table, searching for jobs on her laptop. Smiling, laughing, confidently speaking: it was hard to reconcile this Mariah with the Mariah who was so desperately in love with a man that she believed the horrible stories he insisted were the truth about her. Anger replaced a little sadness, but not for long.

"The police talked to Samantha?" Ava asked, hoping to piece it all together.

"Yeah, um. . .they wanted to confirm she still lived here and asked some questions. They said that was why the street was closed this morning. She had an early meeting before their offices opened because they feared she would overreact in front of clients." Landon returned to the living room, setting the glass of water on the coffee table in front of Ava. He sat back down beside her. "They wanted to know if she had any emotional problems. I don't know, but maybe they checked her apartment. She didn't really say."

Ava nodded silently. She thought back to that day they talked on the rooftop. Had there been anything she could've said differently? It was such a tragedy.

"I'm sorry, Ava. I know you were close." Landon placed his hand on her back and gently rubbed it. "I wish I didn't have to tell you all this, I really do."

"It's fine," Ava managed before her voice cut out. Clearing her throat, she felt overwhelmed with the many thoughts and memories racing through her head.

"I don't understand why her boss would say she was unstable. I totally don't see how he would come up with that conclusion." Landon began to think out loud. "That seems so drastic and cruel. And I can't believe that Mariah, of all people would stand for it, you know? She wasn't normally someone who took shit from anyone. She always seemed to be such a fighter."

Ava nodded and took a deep breath. "Mariah was in love with her boss and when she told him, he fired her. She overheard him tell someone else that he thought she was unstable."

Landon remained silent for a moment. "Wow, that's a pretty drastic reaction on his behalf. And why would he automatically think she was unstable? I don't get it. Did something else happen?"

"I don't know," Ava answered honestly. "I guess I didn't really think about it. Even if it had, it wasn't a fair label to put on her. Then again, it can be dangerous when people start to believe what others say about them."

"Regardless, there was definitely more going on than we realized."

And with that the two fell silent for a few minutes. Ava appreciated the fact that he didn't leave her, even if they didn't speak at all; it was comforting just to know he was there.

"Landon, I think I failed her," Ava confessed, grabbing another Kleenex from the box. Although she had stopped crying for the moment, she could feel tears lodged in the back of her eyes, ready to pour out at any moment. "I feel that maybe I wasn't there for her enough. I told her to come to me but even when she did, I didn't always know what to say or the *right* thing to say."

"Ava, you weren't her shrink," Landon gently reminded her, now rubbing her shoulder. "And even if you were, you couldn't have prevented what happened today. I know you feel that it was just this guy situation but I assure you, it was so much more than that going on to make her do something so drastic. It's never just one thing. One thing can set a person off, but it's not just one thing that causes someone to make such a severe reaction. Maybe other things were going on or something happened in the past."

Ava thought back to Mariah's confession of being raped as a teenager. It was clear that even though it happened years earlier, she was still carrying around that painful memory with her everyday. Why hadn't Ava recommended that Mariah talk to a professional? She hadn't meant to casually just sweep that confession under the rug as if it was a minor event. Had she made light of it in any way? Ava wracked her brain wondering how she could've dealt with every situation differently. Maybe it would've made the difference.

"I still feel that I should've done more. Maybe I should've recommended she go for professional help."

"Ava, don't do this," Landon spoke sternly this time. "Don't put this on yourself. You couldn't have stopped her. She knew what she was doing and chances are, this plan was in her mind already, long before this morning."

"Do you think so?" Ava felt tears returning to her eyes.

"I do," Landon assured her. "I'm positive you couldn't have done anything."

Landon stayed with her until long after seven that night and finally rose from the couch to make his way home. Ava watched him with a sense of dread and before he reached the door she called after him.

"Can I crash at your place tonight?" She felt small, like a child who was asking permission to sleep in her parents' bed after a nightmare. Ripping the tissue that was in her hand and feeling like there was no way she could face that night on her own; she was relieved when he said yes.

"Just come by when you are ready," he offered a small, sympathetic smile and headed out the door.

Ava continued to sit in disbelief before eventually rising from the couch and going into the bathroom. Running hot water into the sink, she quickly washed her face and pulled her hair back into a ponytail. Sighing, she thought about work the next day and realizing that she was in no condition to go in, decided to call Matthew to tell him the news.

Even as the phone rang, she dreaded talking to him, fearing he would be all giddy and clownish like he usually was in most situations. But he didn't answer and she left a voicemail instead, quickly explaining why she would not be able to go to work the next morning.

Much to her surprise, he quickly returned her call.

"Ava!" He seemed breathless on the other end of the line. "I'm sorry, I just got in from a run. My God! That's terrible news. I'm sorry about your friend." His voice was full of sincerity and compassion. "Please take off any time you need, just keep me posted, okay?"

Their conversation ended shortly after and Ava slowly got her stuff together for the night.

She was no longer crying but simply felt weighed down by the entire situation. It was slowly starting to process as she walked down the quiet hallway and entered the elevator to Landon's floor. Like a zombie, she knocked on the door, her mind a million miles away as he opened it and welcomed her in.

"Did you have anything to eat?" He took her bag and carried it into his bedroom, setting it on the floor. Ava opened her mouth to ask why he did that, when he cut her off. "I can get you something. I have some vials in the fridge too."

"No, I really don't want anything, thanks." Ava's voice was hardly more than a whisper. "I think I just want to crash out if that's okay with you, see if I can get some sleep. I am actually fine on the couch."

"It's okay," Landon shrugged bashfully. "I can sleep out here. I already have all my stuff for the morning together in the bathroom and you know, it's fine."

"Thank you." Ava managed a puny, pathetic smile before going in his bedroom and closing the door.

Chapter Thirty-Eight

va felt refreshed when she woke. Half conscious, half in dreamland, she had temporarily forgotten that her best friend died the previous day, and that she was currently sleeping in Landon's bed. She felt free and relaxed, as the sun peaked through the curtains, gently touching her face. Her mind was not yet full of thoughts and her heart not overflowing with anxiety and fear. With heavy lids, she closed her eyes and drifted back to sleep.

When she finally woke again, Ava's eyes were dry and her vision slightly blurred. After blinking a number of times, she was able to focus on her surroundings and for a moment, her thoughts wandered back to the wonderful times she had spent with Landon in this bedroom. So many lust-filled nights and loving moments flowed through her mind.

And then they were gone.

Reality came barreling through her soul, stealing the warmth of a blissful memory and replacing it with the coldness of truth. That was in the past. Landon's love was long gone and Mariah had just died.

Swallowing back her sadness, she stayed in the cocoon of warm blankets, careful not to move an inch, while the previous day rapidly replayed in her mind. Had this really happened? It felt like a nightmare but the fact that she was in Landon's bed confirmed that her recollection was true.

The apartment was silent and one glance at the clock indicated that Landon would have already left for work. Had she not heard him moving about in the kitchen earlier or was that part of a dream? She glanced around his room, as if to find a way to distract her thoughts. Everything was exactly as she remembered. Landon's view of life was to keep things simple and this was greatly reflected by the limited amount of clutter on his dresser and in his closet. He had the basics and nothing more.

Feeling nosey, she glanced at the nearby nightstand and decided to see what was inside. A book. Glancing at the cover, she saw that it pondered the possibility of a third world war. Depressing. A lone stick of gum slid around as she returned the book to it's original place and closed the drawer. Not much there. Ava glanced at the nightstand on the other side of the bed and decided to check it out too.

Condoms.

Finally getting out of the bed and turning up the covers, Ava left the room to find sunlight shining through Landon's living room. It energized her in a way she wouldn't have anticipated. If Mariah hadn't died the day before, Ava doubted she would feel this alive. Did it take someone's death to reignite life? Was it a reminder to appreciate and cherish one's time on earth? Ava felt as though she was viewing the world with a new set of eyes.

Wandering to his kitchen area she considered how it was not unlike her own, small and cramped with little room to move, but big enough for someone who had little interest in cooking. She quickly spotted a note on the counter with her name on the top.

Ava,

Stay as long as you wish.

L

A smile curved her lips as she put the note in the pocket of her shorts. It appeared that this death had softened the tension between them and perhaps this was a gift that came from such a horrific event. Had Mariah's demise brought her and Landon closer together? He had definitely gone over and above what was necessary in this situation, attempting to comfort her as much as possible. Maybe their issues seemed a lot less important in the grand scheme of things. She hoped that was true.

Thinking about all the messages Landon had left on her phone the previous day, Ava returned to his room to send him a text to thank him for his kindness and hospitality. Pulling the phone out of her bag, she quickly forgot her original plan as she stared at the screen, carefully rereading the day old messages. She wondered if Bryan knew about Mariah's death. Was that why he sent her a random text? Perhaps she would call him later. Her eyes then landed on the anonymous texts. The same messages that had scared her the day before were powerless today. The last 24 hours proved that Ava could deal with anything on her path and that included the immortals and their scare tactics.

Then she saw Landon's text saying he had to talk to her as soon as she arrived home. Now she knew why.

Mariah is dead.

Once again, there it was. Ava moved to the couch and sat down. Suddenly, any sense of well being that she had felt moments earlier completely drained from her body and disappeared.

Why did she do this?

What was Mariah thinking yesterday morning? Did she suspect something was wrong when the recruitment agency called a meeting with her before office hours? Why hadn't she told Ava about it? How had she acted when they fired her? Was she crying, screaming, acting erratically; or had she calmly risen from her chair, walked out the door and thrown herself in front of a bus? What was her thought process in that moment? Why didn't she stop, take a deep breath and give herself time to rethink the situation? Why hadn't she called someone? What was said in this meeting that was the final straw?

Then again, had she made this rash decision as soon as she left the meeting? Ava wasn't even sure what time it happened. There were just so many questions. Unfortunately, no answer would be satisfying or would ease the sense of loss she felt.

Ava thought back to their last few conversations. There was definitely a change in her friend. There was a lack of passion in her eyes, a sedated version of the person that Ava used to know. Although a part of her was relieved to see her friend's newfound calmness, it had been slightly unsettling to her. But she simply wrote it off as a phase. After all, everyone went through different stages from time to time. How could she have known what was going through Mariah's mind, if she didn't choose to share it?

At that moment, Ava felt her emotions change. No longer feeling a sense of guilt or shame, a rapid explosion of anger passed through Ava's heart. Why *hadn't* Mariah shared her sorrow? Why hadn't she at least given her friends a chance to help her? Why didn't she call someone that morning, rather than allowing misery to take over? Had she just decided to take the easy way out? She had promised Ava that she would contact her if there were a need to talk. She had *promised* Ava she would call if she needed anything. She had *promised* Ava that she would be okay. Had Mariah simply said those words to humor Ava? Did they mean anything at all or had she planned this all along?

The combination of questions and segments of conversations with Mariah in the past, increasingly began to take over Ava's thoughts at an accelerated pace until she couldn't take it anymore. Rising from the couch with her phone in hand, she rushed into Landon's bedroom and grabbed her bag. She had to get out of the apartment and go somewhere, anywhere. She had to leave these thoughts behind before they sent her into her own private hell. It was definitely a dark place she had the misfortunate of visiting many times and certainly couldn't let herself be pulled back into, not even for Mariah.

As she left the apartment, still wearing a tank top and shorts from the night before, Ava wasn't counting on seeing anyone in the short trip back to her apartment. With her own key in hand, she gently closed Landon's door before exiting. Barely making it to the elevator, she was checking her phone while waiting for the door to slide open, when a voice interrupted her thoughts.

"Bloody terrible news yesterday," Benjamin's voice startled her and Ava abruptly turned around, dropping all her defenses. Lifting her hand to her heart, Ava closed her eyes for a quick moment.

"You scared the crap out of me, Benjamin." She ignored the opening elevator door and walked a few steps toward him, as he stood in his doorway. She could see his wife in the background, glancing in her direction and quickly rushing away. "I didn't hear you open the door."

"And with your vampire ears?" Benjamin attempted a small joke to lighten the mood, as he always did in terrible circumstances. "I was thinking about the day we had Samantha come over and check in on Mariah. At the time, I wasn't sure if we were jumping the gun but now, I think we made the right decision. Perhaps, my dear, your instincts picked up on something that the rest of us did not."

Ava hadn't even considered this possibility until that moment and silently nodded in agreement. With this thought in mind, she started to turn back to the elevator and then suddenly stopped. "Benjamin, do you *really* think maybe we helped her that day? I can't stop feeling like I failed her, otherwise wouldn't she have called me yesterday morning?"

Her eyes pled with him to give her the truth even though she was frightened to hear it. Had Ava been so wrapped up in herself that she had somehow missed her best friend falling apart right in front of their eyes? She knew Benjamin wasn't one to pull any punches. He would tell her the truth.

"Ava," he moved away from his door but yet, didn't quite reach her in the hallway. Tilting his head to an angle, she could see concern in his eyes. "There is nothing you could have done. You tried your best to be her friend but don't take on the responsibility of her death. She made a decision and sadly, it wasn't a good one. But her mind was obviously not thinking clearly. Don't take this on yourself. You did everything you could, I'm *sure* of it."

"Now," he continued. "Do I feel that we stopped her from hurting herself that day we had Samantha go into her apartment?" Benjamin slowly headed back to the safety of his doorway while considering the option. "I do." He nodded his head and thought for another moment. "I really do. I think that it's very possible that she had considered the idea at that time. Judging by what has happened since and what I saw when Samantha opened the door that day, it was clear that she was in a bad way. It didn't just happen overnight. These things rarely do."

Ava nodded slowly. He was right.

"The fact that we may have helped, even back then," Ava paused and stared at the phone in her hands. "It makes me feel a bit better somehow."

"Then take it and run," Benjamin nodded, as he went back into his apartment and turned to look at her. "That's my advice to you. Take it and run."

Ava nodded and headed toward the elevator, where she hit the button for her floor. Behind her, she heard Benjamin's apartment door close at approximately the same second that her elevator opened. Walking inside, she carried with her the thought that maybe they had somehow helped Mariah. But had it been enough?

Take it and run.

Arriving home, Ava decided that she would take a quick shower and get out of the apartment. It didn't matter where she went or what she did for the rest of the day, it just mattered that she got out into the world. A world where people were alive and hopeful, where there was energy conducive of the living surrounding her and hope for the future. She had to get away from here, where her thoughts would creep into a dark place and may have more encouragement to stay rather than to escape. She wouldn't go down that road again. She saw where it could take her.

Chapter Thirty-Nine

Things slowly returned to normal. It was just a different kind of normal.

Mariah's apartment was emptied and cleaned. All signs that she ever lived there were long gone when Ava decided to walk through the vacant rooms, thinking about her departed friend. She was hoping that some little trinket would have been accidentally left behind; an earring or a necklace, not anything of monetary value but something Ava could take, purely for sentimental reasons. But there was nothing. No sign that her best friend had ever even lived there at all. It was a bit surreal.

She was disappointed. Of course logically, it made sense that everything of Mariah's would be removed from the apartment. Between family picking up her stuff and the cleaners that followed, someone would notice had anything had been misplaced. It had been Ava's fantasy that just like in the movies and television, she would walk through the rooms and something shiny would catch her eye, a piece of jewelry or special souvenir on the floor or behind a door; but it simply wasn't in the cards. It wasn't realistic.

Each room was an empty soul that no longer mattered and it caused Ava to collapse on the floor and start to sob. For some reason, wandering through the same apartment that she and Mariah had shared everything from tears to laughter in, only to find it completely bare was almost as difficult to deal with as the actual death. It was a finality that was engulfed her in such intense pain that resembled nothing she had ever felt before in her life. Even her parents' death hadn't felt this difficult and Ava wondered if it was because she had been so young at the time; perhaps children are more resilient than adults. Perhaps it was because her parents were older than she, whereas Mariah was close to Ava's age. Then again, she realized the very nature of death is such that it's different each time it is dealt with.

Suicide. The word sounded too clinical, as if someone merely passed away of a disease of the body, rather than a grief of the mind. Where did such a word come from and who decided that it sounded proper for someone's desperate act to leave this earth? It didn't seem to truly capture the intensity of such a grief-filled act.

But it was a word she was hearing a great deal. After all, Mariah's death had been front-page news in at least one local newspaper, if not them all. Ava hadn't the heart to even look it up to see and frankly, she didn't want to know. The only reason she was aware of one of them was because she noticed it lying on the table in the lounge area one day, when she wandered down to talk to Samantha. Her landlord quickly removed it after seeing Ava burst into tears at the sight of the story, which detailed more about the interruption to traffic and interference to people's early morning commute, than the fact that a life was now over.

But to Ava and many others who lived in the apartment building, it was a real person's choice to end their life, not just a big story to start off the evening news. It made Ava wonder how many times people forgot that the murders and tragic deaths reported by emotionless reporters on the evening news, were actual *real* people to their families and friends. The same people, who held up traffic because they jumped off a huge building in the downtown area or walked in front of a bus were human beings that lived, loved and dreamed just like the viewer on the other side of the screen. They went to work every day, fell in love and hugged their children, just as everyone else. And yet on the local news, they were reduced to the same status as an actor playing a tragic character on a nighttime soap opera.

Ava thought about these things a lot in the following weeks. She thought about death and how short life really was, how grief can take over your mind until you allow it to convince you that death is the only answer to every question. Had Mariah felt that all her problems were that unsolvable, that her life had no value or meaning? Although Ava started the grieving process in a state of sorrow and anger, eventually her frustration with Mariah's decision faded and escaped her. It wasn't that hard to believe, and as much as she hated to accept it, there were signs that her friend considered this action long before it had happened.

But Ava couldn't spend all her time thinking about it. The entire concept was too much weight to carry around daily and although she felt it was necessary to always remember her friend and the value of life, at the same time it was really clear that dwelling on it could drive her crazy, if she let it.

Ava's friendship with Landon changed during the mourning process. Not only had he broken the news of Mariah's death and offered her a place to stay that first, horrible night, but he was around much more often than he had in months. There seemed to be an invisible wall that dropped between them and although she couldn't put her finger on it, there was definitely a change in the energy between them. Where there was once tension and distance, there was now a bond that they had never experienced before, not even in the early days when they first met and had a physical relationship. She felt at peace in his presence.

People in the building that never spoke to Ava before started to say hi to her in the elevator, some even shared stories of their memories of Mariah. Her friend would have been so surprised to learn that many people had a very positive view of the young woman and even more, were shocked by her actions. It wasn't just Ava who viewed her friend as being strong and confidant; apparently it was something that most people saw in Mariah. Unfortunately, it now appeared to have been more of an act or a mask to cover the sorrow that was really inside.

Some other acquaintances were considerate during her time of despair. Chloe stopped by her apartment offering condolences and Ava secretly smiled, knowing that Mariah had often referred to the unusual, young woman as a 'ditchpig', but maybe they were both wrong about her after all. Benjamin was also regularly checking in on Ava, something he had never done before unless they just happened to run into one another. He would drop by with stories of his 'younger' days back in Europe and spin, what Ava believed to be, very tall tales of him escaping everything from jealous husbands to mobsters and police. It was entertaining.

Bryan attempted to come home more often and Ava felt as if she clung to him at first but eventually figured out that their relationship was definitely coming to an end. Had she more strength, perhaps Ava would've approached the topic on one of his short, occasional visits but it just wasn't in her to do so during those specific times.

Probably the biggest surprise at all came from her grandmother. The same woman who was once very cold and not a part of Ava's life, was quickly making many steps in the right direction, possibly to make up for her lack of interest in the past. Once she learned of her granddaughter's young friend committing suicide, the elderly lady made a point to drop in to visit when she could or call on a regular basis. She did not leave it to text messages when it came to this very serious situation. That surprised Ava.

During the first few days after Mariah died, her grandmother warned her to not hold on to any anger surrounding the circumstances. Although she reassured her that it was a normal part of grieving, Edith Wolfe also insisted that it was a phase that should be left quickly in order to move on to the actual sadness involved with death.

"Ava, I spent many years being angry over your parents' deaths." Her comment came as a surprise during one particular phone conversation. It was probably about three days following Mariah's suicide and things were still very fresh in Ava's mind. "I spent years being angry with them for selfishly taking a vacation, with the pilot who flew the plane and even with God for taking their lives away, but there comes a point where you have to accept that being angry isn't going to save you from the heartbreaking sadness. And it *is* heartbreaking but you have to go through it before you can move on to the other side. You can't sit on it and let it fester forever because it does you no good to do so. And if you don't listen to another piece of advice I ever give you, I insist that you at least listen to this one. Life is too short. Please don't stay angry with a ghost."

Ava accepted her words eventually, after rejecting it initially. "But this was different from my parents. It was suicide. She decided to take her own life. She knew it would hurt everyone in her life. Why wouldn't she just reach out to someone, anyone."

"Perhaps she did," her grandmother remarked thoughtfully. "And perhaps you helped keep her on this earth longer than you realize."

Ava knew that Benjamin had made a similar comment to her in the past and maybe they had a point, but at the same time...

"But why didn't she call that morning," Ava heard her own voice get caught in sorrow as the anger began to melt away with each word that followed. Tears burned her eyes as she repeated the question she thought again and again. "Why didn't she call me? At work, even? I don't care. I would've tried to help. She knew that too."

"Ava," the older lady's voice was gentle on the other end of the line. "No one can answer that question. Who knows what kind of catatonic state her mind was in at the time? We don't know what she was thinking in the moment. We don't know what happened just before she did what she did. We don't know what happened even *days* before she died. That's the problem, we *don't know* and all we can do right now is guess.....and guess and guess and drive ourselves crazy, playing a guessing game that has no answer."

She fell silent for a moment and Ava stopped crying. She knew her grandmother was right.

"We don't know, but we can try to understand, because we have all been in a desperate moment where our lives seemed hopeless. The only difference is that she reacted, probably quickly and without thinking. Probably with no thought to those she would leave behind or how things might improve if she just gave life a chance. It's not an easy situation to understand, believe me, I know. And no one would tell you otherwise but at the same time, we can only guess. And usually our guessing is way off. People are far more complex than a simple explanation."

"I know," Ava managed to whisper into the phone. "I know."

"You have to, no, you *must* think of the good times you shared. The smiles, the laughter, the joking and have that at the center of your mind," she persisted thoughtfully. "Always remember Mariah's smile and the sound of her voice. Focus on that, not on her death. Never on her death, because it was such a very small portion of her overall story. The biggest portion was her life."

Ava nodded and smiled.

Chapter Forty

I t wasn't easy to return to work on Monday. In fact, it was the last thing that Ava wanted to do. It was her preference to hide in the safety of her apartment, locked away from the rest of the world; the same world, that Mariah had decided she could no longer face at all. Maybe those feelings were not so difficult to understand, Ava considered.

As she headed to Anderson & Smith on that warm, July morning, Ava thought about how much everything had changed in the past year. Such a silly, immature girl had once walked in these same shoes, even as recently as a month ago. Just flittering through life with no real goals or plans. Then again, she had been so fixated on becoming an immortal that perhaps her tunnel vision made Ava blind to everything else. The world now looked very different.

She feared that her coworkers had learned of her best friend's death and dreaded a series of intruding inquiries. However, upon arriving at work, this wasn't the case. As she walked through the door, lowering her head, Nisha was already there and welcomed her with a surprising question.

"Hey, how was your vacation?" She smiled cheerfully, as if Ava had just finished the most joyous and pleasant experience of her life. It threw her off guard for a moment, but she quickly recovered and bounced back into the moment.

"Oh, I...it was okay," Ava offered a hesitant grin, glancing toward her boss's office door. It was open and she could see Matthew's eyes focused on the reception desk. Ava tried to act as normal as possible, however, not quite getting into a wonderful vacation mode frame of mind, she instead found a way to excuse her strange behavior. "I guess I'm a little tired."

"That's understandable!" Nisha gave a bright smile, before launching into a long-winded story about her last vacation and essentially was connecting to being more tired upon return. The merriment in her voice was slightly irritating, so Ava busied herself with making a cup of coffee while she listened, hoping the conclusion was soon on its way. It dragged on, but she did her best to fake an interest, while her mind was actually a million miles away.

"I have a *ton* of work to do, so I'd better get to it. We will talk more later." Nisha assured her while grabbing her own cup of coffee and rushing away. Ava felt guilty for being irritated with her coworker. Her intentions were good, even though the happy chatter was a little too much to endure so early on Ava's first day back. She had been so lost in her own dark thoughts recently, that being reintroduced to anything that wasn't a heavy topic was a shock to her system.

"Good morning, Ava," Matthew seemed to automatically take over where Nisha left off, as he approached the reception desk. She felt more relaxed with him since he was aware of the true circumstances that had taken her away for almost a week. It felt freeing to not have to hide her unhappiness when he prompted a conversation.

"Hi," She spoke quickly, signing into the computer and clicking onto the mountain of emails that were waiting for her. Picking up her cup of coffee, she gave Matthew her full attention and turned her chair in his direction.

"Can I speak to you for a second?" His voice was gentle and he casually gestured toward his office. "It won't take long and we will see if a client comes in." He made reference to the fact that he was planning to leave his door open during their conversation.

Without saying a word, Ava set her coffee down and rose from her seat to follow him into his office. Expecting that a client would enter the front door at any moment, she didn't even bother to sit down, and following her lead, Matthew didn't either, but instead perched on the edge of his desk.

"Ava, I didn't tell anyone why you were out." His voice lowered to little more than a whisper and he followed her eyes, as they uncomfortably glanced out toward the main entrance. "I didn't tell them about your friend because it was obviously a personal matter and in order to not raise suspicion, I said you had a few days of holiday to visit a relative in town. I hope that is okay."

"Yes, of course," Ava replied in her most professional tone and deep down, she appreciated the thoughtfulness of this gesture. Although Mariah had stopped by the office on various occasions, Ava was pretty certain no one would have known her name or made the connection to the tragic accident in the downtown area. Almost a week had passed and Ava was doubtful it was still on most people's minds. "I appreciate that."

"It's a private matter," Matthew gave a compassionate smile. "How are you doing? Do you need more time off or anything else I can help you with?"

"No, I don't think there is anything anyone can do at this point," Ava answered honestly, and watched him nod to show understanding. "Not unless you can turn back time."

"I only wish I could," Matthew reassured her with sincerity in his eyes. "I think we all wish we could at some point in our lives."

Ava rewarded him with a small, grateful smile and nodded. "That's true."

The rest of the day went slowly and Ava fell into autopilot mode. It was simply the only way she could endure her return to the fast-paced office. It surprised Ava when interactions with various clients seemed to actually lighten her mood, but at the same time she had very powerful moments that reminded her that Mariah was gone.

At lunchtime, Ava made a point of avoiding any spots that she and Mariah used to frequent. Tears formed behind her sunglasses when she considered that she would never again sit across the table from Mariah, while her friend downed glasses of wine and talked about the hot guy across the room or how much she hated her job. There was simply no one else with her spark, her special flare.

Luckily, her coworkers were all too busy to really ask her any questions about Ava's 'vacation' and eventually the day came to an end.

Just as she was about to walk out the door, Matthew called her back and asked her to step into his office for a moment. Clients were long gone and the only people remaining were a few employees finishing up their work. Ava would have preferred to escape but out of courtesy, dragged herself into his office.

"Thank you, I know this must've been a difficult day for you," Matthew smiled and shut the door behind them. She sat in an empty chair and placed her purse on the ground. "I will keep this brief."

"That's fine," Ava's voice sounded child-like and she wondered if she appeared as fragile as she felt at that moment. Opening her mouth to say something more, she hesitated and changed her mind. Matthew noticed her reaction and took a few seconds before saying anything more.

"Ava, I just wanted to know if you've had any more threats since we last spoke?" He raised his eyebrows and sat erect in his chair, as if preparing himself for her answer.

Had she had any more threats since they last spoke? Ava felt like her brain was clouded and the fog wasn't about to lift anytime soon. He watched her, his head tilted slightly and she knew it was time to respond.

"No, I don't think so," She spoke truthfully while her brain frantically searched for the answer to his question. Everything from the past week was fuzzy and although there had been a couple of threats, she felt that both had occurred previous to Mariah's death.

"That's good. The last thing you need right now is something else to worry about." His sincere compassion made Ava feel more depressed. Every hug, smile or attempt to show her kindness she had received in the last week caused a burning in her eyes and often, tears were quick to follow. It was amazing how horrific events brought out the softer side of people and Ava wondered why life in general couldn't prompt the same reaction, without something terrible having to happen first.

"Did you ever figure out who was sending them?"

Ava shook her head no. It was something she hadn't thought about for days and she wasn't sure she even cared. It was clearly someone who knew that she was getting close to learning too much but at that point, she no longer was concerned.

"I don't really care about any of it anymore. Learning who sent the messages, becoming immortal, learning about them," Ava shook her head as if it all seemed completely irrelevant. So much had changed in a week. How could she explain that to him? "Does it even matter? It feels so insignificant now."

"It did matter to you and it may matter again," Matthew reminded her and stood up from his chair, indicating it was time to end the meeting. "I just want you to know that I will be here if you ever need any more assistance. I may not be the most helpful person in the world, but I have some resources that I can look into."

Ava gave a quick nod and rose from her chair. Once at the door, she felt a warm hand on her back and she quickly turned around to meet Matthew eye to eye. The warmth in his expression surprised her. He was standing so close that she could feel his hot breath on her skin, and his voice felt like it was melting in her ears.

"In the meanwhile, if there is anything I can do for you, don't hesitate to ask." His words were gentle and Ava felt her heart race at the suggestion behind his offer. She opened her mouth to respond and once again, no words came out. "Just let me know."

Ava nodded and slowly left his office and then, her workplace.

As she walked home, she considered her feelings on Matthew's suggestive parting words. Was he trying to insinuate something more than a boss/employee relationship or had it just been her imagination? Her thoughts automatically flew to Mariah and *her* feelings for an old boss. Maybe it was those same feelings that had contributed in ruining her life. It sounded so dramatic but they were definitely a factor in what had pushed her over the edge. The work environment complicated things much more than they normally would be, had they not worked together at all.

It wasn't a risk that Ava could afford to take.

Chapter Forty-One

Life moves forward. It doesn't matter what kind of tragedy or heartbreak we meet along the way, time continues to trudge ahead—with or without our cooperation.

Ava's reluctance to appreciate the warmth and beauty of summer day stemmed from a combination of grief and guilt. So many things were a reminder of the time she spent with Mariah. Her friend's death resembled a bad breakup that weighed heavily on her heart. Restaurants, pubs and shops they would visit together and even subtler things like a song, would bring tears to Ava's eyes. It didn't matter how often she reminded herself that it was unhealthy to live in the past, Ava couldn't seem to stop herself. Was this the proper way to mourn?

She sought articles about death online and turned to various spiritual books at the local library, but each only brought her temporary and slight comfort. It didn't change the fact that Mariah had committed suicide and left behind so many unanswered questions.

The day would eventually come when Ava felt her sadness begin to lift. It happened as she was browsing at a clothing store and spotted an outfit that Mariah would have loved. She felt her lips curve into a smile that shone directly from her heart, but this was rapidly followed by guilt; her friend was dead and here she was, in the middle of a store, grinning like a moron.

But then she remembered what her grandmother had said about Mariah's life being much more than her final moments alive, and reluctantly allowed herself to feel a moment of peace.

Ava was also surprised how the tragedy continued to stir up memories of her parents' deaths. After all, they were tragically ripped from her life at such a young age. Sure, she had been sad and cried heartfelt tears at the time, but for some reason they were nothing compared to the ones she cried for her friend. It didn't make sense really and she reluctantly brought up the subject with Landon one evening, as they sat in the lounge area of the apartment complex. The topic was reborn after learning the surprising news that another vampire from overseas would be taking residence in Mariah's old place.

"It's different for a lot of reasons," Landon responded gently, as if he was concerned that the wrong words would cause her to frantically collapse in tears. "You were much younger when your parents died so you were more resilient and I guess, your understanding of death was probably a lot lighter. When we are young, I think we have more faith in a higher power and the universe, so we don't see death as the catastrophic event that we view it as adults."

"What do you mean?" Ava was puzzled by his explanation. "I saw it as pretty catastrophic at the time, I just wasn't as upset."

Landon hesitated for a moment. "Okay, so, when I was a kid, my grandmother died. I was upset, of course because she was one of my favorite people in the world. But at the same time, I just accepted it for what it was and moved on."

"As adults we don't do that," Landon continued. "We tend to over dramatize events that hurt us and I think, it's because of a mislead belief that this shows more devotion."

Ava shook her head to show she didn't follow him at all. She knew he wasn't attempting to make light of the topic but for some reason, she wasn't able to understand what he was suggesting.

"For example," Landon spoke slowly as if processing his thoughts while he spoke. "You can rethink memories of times spent with Mariah, you can go over and over those final days and try to look for clues that she was thinking of ending; her life, you can cry or get angry and to a certain degree that's normal, but eventually, you have to let it go and when you do, it's not because you suddenly don't care. It just means you learned to accept her death."

Ava slowly nodded, her eyes downcast as she considered the millions of thoughts that bombarded her since Mariah's death. It was almost like hitting replay repeatedly and hoping to find a different solution but instead, feeling drained by the entire experience. She somehow thought that going over the details again and again would be helpful in accepting the death and moving on, but it only made her more emotionally frazzled.

"Then why does it not feel right to let it go?" Ava's voice was small, childlike and she felt as if her entire body was shrinking in the chair.

"Because you have this belief, as many people would in your situation, that dwelling on it and feeling completely miserable is somehow showing more dedication to Mariah and how much she meant to your life. And it doesn't." He fell silent and tilted his head, carefully watching Ava. "It shows no more loyalty to carry around a heaviness in your heart. And when you are a kid, you recognize that because a child has a much more simplistic view of the world. It's only after we become adults that we adopt these misleading beliefs."

Ava felt a weight falling from her body, as if his words were releasing the grip that this death had on her since it happened. Was he correct? Had she felt that the longer her own grief existed that it somehow showed more respect toward Mariah's life? That she hadn't forgotten her friend? That she hadn't stopped caring?

"Of course you are still going to think about her sometimes and miss her, maybe even cry but you don't have to walk around with this monkey on your back every day," Landon explained. "It's not going to bring her back. She made the decision to end her own life and it's sad, it's terrible...but it's not *your* burden to carry."

"I," Ava started to speak but her throat felt dry and she stopped. "I just feel like...maybe...maybe I could've done something differently. Maybe I should've—

"Ava," Landon abruptly cut her off. "You couldn't have done anything.

She wasn't knocking at your door, asking for help. You were there for her many times and she wasn't always very responsive, you even said that a few times. You weren't responsible to chase her down, beg her to tell you what is wrong. It was up to her to come to you and all you had to do was make yourself available and make it clear that she *could* approach you, if she needed help."

Ava silently nodded.

"Do you think you did that?" Landon asked. "And I want you to *really* think about my question before you answer."

Ava did and considered all the times she had texted her friend, knocked at her door and sincerely tried to be there for Mariah.

"Yes," An unsettling anger crept into her heart, blazing a fire through her body. "And she almost never accepted. I shouldn't have had to chase her down and *beg* to help her."

Landon recognized her change in moods and quickly reacted. "Ava, don't get angry either." His words seemed to deflate her frustrations like a pin bursting a balloon and she sank farther down in her chair. "We don't know what she was thinking and we never will. Don't get angry with her for not *letting* you help her, be *proud* of the fact you were the kind of person that reached out and tried to help. A lot of people wouldn't have made that effort and regardless of her final decision, I have *no* doubt that she knew you were there for her."

Ava felt tears well up in her eyes but unlike those that she experienced in the days and weeks earlier, they weren't full of frustration and self-pity. This time, they were erupting from a peaceful place that promised that there was hope around the corner. Landon was right, she could always remember Mariah for those last few horrific days and her dramatic suicide, or she could remember the beauty of her smile and the sound of her laughter. Hadn't her grandmother said that as well?

Later that evening, Ava sat alone in her apartment. She lit a candle and replayed her conversation with Landon. He was right. He was *so* right. Every word he said truly resonated with her and she felt such relief after their conversation that she decided to send him a quick text to thank him again. Although his words had had an effect initially, they had since run much deeper into her spirit and it was almost as if they set her free. Not just freeing her from her sadness in regards to Mariah's death, but maybe something more, something she hadn't realized was there before that day.

Grabbing her phone, she quickly did a directory search but rather than hit 'L' for Landon, her finger somehow slipped and instead hit 'M'. Mariah's name was the first one to show up and Ava stared at it for a while, Landon's words from earlier that day flowing through her head. Mariah was gone. Any trace of her being alive had vanished. Someone had removed her Facebook profile as well as any other social media that Mariah had joined. Ava knew it was time to delete her from the contacts, but that simple action was far more difficult than she had originally imagined. With tears in her eyes, Ava hit 'edit' and removed her name.

Setting the phone down, she took a deep breath and decided that the text to Landon would have to wait. She needed a few minutes to resonate the many thoughts that were in her head and finally lay them to rest. Deleting Mariah didn't mean she didn't still love her best friend, it simply meant she now accepted her death, and it was time to move forward. Landon was right. She had to feel pride for reaching out to Mariah and doing everything she knew how to in that moment.

Exhaustion suddenly crept in; Ava lay down on the couch, closed her eyes and fell into the most restful sleep she had in years.

Chapter Forty-Two

Sometimes our hearts heal while we sleep. It's almost as though a spirit much greater than ourselves gently caresses our soul while we're in dreamland, removing all the impurities and sadness that have overextended their stay. Perhaps the spirit can recognize that a lesson has been learned, a phase has now finished and our soul is ready to mend. It's a mystical thing that isn't easy to understand but when the time is right, we sense it.

Ava woke the next morning feeling free. It was as if all her anxieties had been lifted while she slept, leaving her with a satisfying sense of emptiness. It wasn't that she didn't care about Mariah or everything that weighed heavily on her heart, it was more of a feeling of comfort that was unusual. She couldn't remember the last time she felt such a sense of peace. The detachment took away the invisible ball and chain that she had been dragging with her for most of her adult life, especially since Mariah's death. It felt nourishing but very unfamiliar. It was like walking through a world she never knew existed.

At first she assumed that it was just her groggy state that had temporarily released her from all the anxieties that usually clamped onto her heart. Hadn't Ava always felt plagued with worries and fears, ever since she was a teenager? Clearly something was amiss and once it found its place back, all the familiar unpleasant emotions and thoughts would find their way home, as if only on a short vacation.

She made some tea, sat in silence on her couch, sipping the delicious brew and enjoying this newfound inner peace. And as minutes ticked by, Ava began to realize that so much had changed in just one night. Her usual need to grab her cell phone and check text messages was replaced by a yearning to open the curtains and stare at the clouds, as they hung low over the mountains in the north. Had they always been so beautiful and perfect? Why did she feel it was the first time her eyes truly saw all the colors that surrounded them, the trees in a nearby park and the beautiful blue skies?

She thought of Mariah and wondered if there was a heaven. Ava was skeptical about religion but *did* believe that everyone had a spirit. Where had Mariah's soul gone, after it emerged from her deceased body? Was it aimlessly roaming the earth or did it die with her body? Was it a ghost floating through her old apartment building and various familiar territories? Was she in the room with Ava in that moment?

Nervously, Ava glanced over her shoulder, fearful that Mariah would be standing behind her in amusement over such a thought. But the room was empty and the tiny apartment suddenly seemed much larger than it ever had before that day.

This strange disconnect was a bit eerie for Ava. As much as she loved the freedom that seemed to come with it, she did wonder if it was right to feel so emotionally detached from her own life. Was she having some kind of breakdown? Was this *normal?* Had she died in her sleep? Was *she* a ghost wandering through her own apartment? Shaking her head, Ava grinned at the absurdness of that thought and returned to her kitchen to refill her coffee cup.

The sun suddenly shone through her window and Ava felt inspired to go outside and do something—she wasn't sure what—but the sunny skies were calling her to join nature, and she was a willing participant. For now, having not showered or fully gained her energy, she opened her window. Often reluctant to do so because it had no screen, Ava just felt the need to breathe in the fresh air and hope nothing repulsive was anywhere close at hand.

The air was warm, the smell much fresher than Ava had expected and she felt energized as she closed her eyes, feeling the rays of sunlight reach for her through the glass. A soft, almost unnoticeable object caressed her cheek, causing Ava's lids to fly open and she glanced around. Was it a bug that had entered the room? She didn't see any sign of such, but then something in the corner alerted her attention. Ava saw an object flickering across the room. Turning abruptly, it almost was if her eyes were a few seconds too slow.

Swinging in the other direction, she unsuccessfully attempted to 'catch' whatever was teasing her senses. Ava was ready to dismiss her earlier instinct and return to her comfortable spot on the couch when suddenly, she saw it; a beautiful, orange butterfly was fluttering about, momentarily landing on various locations, only to leave and continue its exploration of the room.

Ava felt frozen. Slowly backing up against the wall, as if watching a play that was in middle of an act. The butterfly showed no sign of shyness as it explored the open concept between the kitchen and living room, hovering near the bedroom but quickly returning to where it first had arrived. Although it was fickle in its pursuit of location, Ava felt her heart race upon seeing the beautiful insect suddenly land on the picture frame that enclosed a photo of her and Mariah together. Her mouth falling open in astonishment, a chill went up Ava's spine, as she watched the butterfly rise from the photo and flutter out the window.

She couldn't move and although a part of her wanted to cry at the beauty of the moment, a voice in her head asked her why. Logically, it probably didn't mean a thing. But deep inside, Ava knew differently.

Rushing to the window, she closed it once again and her eyes scanned for the butterfly outside, even though she knew it was long gone. And for some reason, Ava felt as though everything at last had come full circle.

After she took a shower and dried her hair, Ava thought to check her phone. She found it on the nightstand, where she had left it the evening before. She felt little interest in connecting with the outside world; unfortunately, it was a necessary evil.

She ignored a text message from Landon, asking her if she wanted to go for an early morning hike with him. Glancing at the clock, she figured he would've been long gone by that time.

The next message was from Bryan. He was planning his return to town that day. In fact, he was probably back already, judging from the timeline illustrated in his brief message.

Ava sighed heavily and crashed back down on her bed. She had to talk to him about their relationship and dreaded having that conversation. She just wanted to spend some time alone. Maybe go for a walk, relax with a good book or watch a movie on Netflix. No conversations. No interactions.

But it didn't work that way. A couple of hours later, engrossed in a new book, she heard someone at her door. She briefly reflected that it wasn't necessary to answer it, but then decided that it was probably time to face things head on. She rose from her chair, but Bryan was already using his key to get into her apartment.

Predictably, he bounced into the room, much like Tigger from Winnie-the-pooh, full of smiles, energy and light. Ava felt a sense of jealousy fill her and wished she could muster such emotions and excitement toward her own life, but she quickly brushed it aside, offering him a pathetic little smile and her voice sounded timid when she said hello.

"So, what's going on? How's life?" He continued to smile brightly, attempting to embrace her but Ava quickly moved away. His face lost some of its radiance but not much, and he tilted his head. "What's going on?"

Although she knew he was referring to her mood, Ava wasn't fully sure of how to explain the strange emptiness that she had awaken with.

"Nothing." She walked toward the couch and sat down. Bryan did the same, his eyes innocently searching her face. Suddenly, she felt terrible about ending their relationship. He had been so supportive after Mariah's death, often checking in on her and showing compassion. Even though he fluttered around absently, much in the same way the butterfly had done earlier that day, Bryan really had no ill intention and in fact, he probably had not one enemy in the world. There was a naivety about him that could've been easily misread as stupidity, but Ava knew better.

"Look, I'm just going to get right to the point." Ava felt so differently about her life at that moment, that her sensitivities were probably at an all-time low. "I don't think that this is working out." She watched the smile slowly disappear from his face. "I'm sorry, but I just feel that this isn't a good time for me. I can't be in a relationship right now. I just need time to get my life together and figure out what happens from here."

She recognized that her words weren't making sense, but Ava also knew that she had nothing more to give. No thoughts, no ideas, no input. There was just a blank slate that couldn't process anything in that moment.

"I thought," Bryan looked down at his hand. "I thought that things were improving with us actually, I thought that since I got back, that we were getting closer."

"I just," Ava stopped and watched his eyes search her face. "I'm sorry. We will always be connected because you were the one who turned me. I think that maybe we are taking that connection and misreading it to be something much more than it is. You are a free spirit and I am still trying to learn about myself and figure out my life. I don't even know who I am now."

Bryan was calmly trying to process her words and the sadness in his eyes stabbed Ava with guilt. "I think you are probably just upset. I mean it hasn't been that long since Mariah died and I can see how that could be stressful, so if you need some time to be alone, that's cool."

Although it was her instinct to interrupt him as he spoke, she decided to wait and allow him his opportunity to speak, before replying.

She silently shook her head no.

"I'm sorry, there is no easy way to say this but my heart is just empty right now and I don't think that." She hesitated for a moment. Would she feel differently someday? Was he correct to think she was merely upset and not thinking straight? "I don't know what's in the future, I can't think that far ahead. But right now, I can't and I don't want you to get your hopes up that anything will change in the future."

He nodded, taking a deep breath and smiled sadly. "Okay, I understand." Without saying another word he rose from the chair and slowly walked out the door.

Chapter Forty-Three

Ava was haunted by the look in Bryan's eyes when she broke up with him. Although their relationship had never been ideal, it hadn't been horrible either. It wasn't as if he made her life miserable and in fact, it was his charismatic personality that she missed the most in the days that followed their breakup. His enthusiasm and energetic vibe was exactly what had held them together for so long. But it wasn't love, so was there really a foundation for their relationship?

Ava spent the rest of the weekend questioning whether or not she had made the right decision. She even considered talking to Bryan again, perhaps explaining herself in a less clumsy fashion in order to make him understand better, but he was gone. Not answering his door, she eventually found photos on Facebook of him partying in Los Angeles with a group of attractive people that she didn't recognize. It stung a bit at first but then Ava realized that this was how Bryan dealt with things. He had to keep moving. He had to keep running away from anything that was uncomfortable. After all, hadn't he done that after turning her into a vampire, two years earlier?

She began to move on from Mariah's death and finally felt free from the guilt that originally consumed her. Ava accepted that she had done everything possible to help her friend and that there were simply some questions that would never be answered. It was time to forgive and let it go.

Life had a way of teaching lessons that were needed, and losing Mariah had taught Ava that happiness was a state, rather than a destination you desperately tried to reach. How many times had she thought nothing else mattered, other than becoming an immortal? She was convinced that her happiness depended on that one thing. How silly she had been.

Ava hadn't realized that Landon felt a connection to her struggle. He knew all the signs quite well and silently watched from a distance, occasionally checking in, but usually preferring to stand back and wait. He felt that grief was a personal and private thing that everyone worked through differently and that Ava would manage, in her own way. But if she ever needed him, he would be there.

Landon stopped in his tracks. Arriving home from work, he almost didn't notice Ava sitting alone in the lounge area. She looked so small in the chair that it almost concealed her delicate frame, as her solemn face stared out a nearby window. She didn't even turn around as he approached and he felt hesitant to ask what was wrong.

"Ava?" He spoke gently and she slowly turned her head and stared at him with despondent, caramel eyes. He could sense the darkness surrounding her, similar to the time when Mariah died, and it made him nervous. Landon sat across from her and carefully placed his laptop bag on the floor, attempting to show no judgment. "What's going on?"

"Ah, nothing," Ava shook her head dismally and he noted that she wore less makeup than usual, while her clothing was bland and dull. Her dark hair was pulled back in a bun, as if she had been rushed that morning and didn't have the proper amount of time to get ready for work. "I wasn't feeling well so I left work early today."

"Didn't make it upstairs yet?"

"No, I thought I would sit here for a while and think about some stuff. It's weird, I couldn't bring myself to go up to the apartment." Ava glanced down at her hands and he noted that she actually looked physically ill. He could sense a heaviness around her that only increased with their conversation. "Sometimes those four walls feel like they are closing in on me."

Landon briefly considered making a comment about the size of his apartment and how it often made him feel smothered, but decided against it. Her mind was elsewhere and he decided it was probably much more helpful to listen, rather than add to their conversation. He was worried but did his best to conceal it.

"Did something happen today?" He decided to throw in the question to get a sense of what he was missing. Perhaps she was simply under the weather.

"No," Her voice sounded upbeat for a moment and gave him hope but her eyes told him a different story. "I just have been doing a lot of thinking lately about my future and what I want."

"And?"

"And I know for sure that I no longer want to be an immortal," Ava answered with such a emotionless voice that Landon almost wished that they were continuing to have the debate on whether or not it was a good idea. At least that would suggest some passion toward the topic—any topic— rather than complete apathy. For all the times he had wished to hear those words from Ava, he certainly wasn't enjoying them now.

"No?"

"I mean, I still want to learn more about them," she was quick to throw in. "I would like to know who this so-called 'rock star of vampires' is, but I don't want to become one. Which is ironic; you would think that Mariah's death would make me more determined to live forever but instead, it makes me want to just be normal."

Landon didn't find it strange at all. Death had a strong impact on the living.

"It's funny because when I was miserable and hated my life, I wanted to be an immortal," Ava continued, her lips briefly lifting into a slight grin at her own comment. "And now that I have a whole new perspective on life and death, it no longer appeals to me. It just wasn't the answer."

"Maybe because you realize that being an immortal will force you to live through mourning again and again, through every decade and lifetime."

Landon suggested as he leaned forward, attempting to understand her position. "It's hard enough to deal with things in one lifetime, let alone again and again."

"Yeah, but maybe it gets easier." Ava considered, glancing at the floor and then to avoid eye contact with Landon, her attention was switched to across the room.

"I doubt it." Landon spoke honestly. "I don't think something like this ever gets easier for anyone."

Ava nodded, remaining silent.

"I heard you and Bryan broke up?"

"Yeah," Ava finally turned her attention back to Landon. "It was going to happen eventually anyway, it was just a matter of the right time."

"What made that day the right time?" Landon was intrigued. He had always thought Bryan had put Ava under his spell, just as he had with many women, making them unable to see the vacant person that lay beneath his bright, shiny exterior. He was always tuned into his performance side and although Landon originally thought Bryan was purposely trying to be deceptive, it eventually became clear that the young actor was functioning on the only dimension he knew existed. There were no other sides of his personality except for the socially acceptable one that people would be drawn to, so that was the role he continued to play. He couldn't have been more lost and that, Landon was certain, would lead him down a very dark path.

"I don't know," Ava gently admitted. "There was just something about that day that said it was time. I just couldn't pretend anymore. I guess sometimes you have a connection with someone, but it doesn't mean you are supposed to *be* with them, it just means...nothing." She finished the sentence dreamily.

"I think it means something but maybe that phase was over in your life. You aren't the same person you used to be," Landon spoke candidly. "You've changed a lot in the last few months, anyone can see that. You're transforming into a butterfly." He joked and noted the shocked expression on Ava's face. Not knowing about the beautiful creature that flew into her apartment not long ago, drifting around the room and finally ending on a photo of her and Mariah together, he flinched. Had he misspoken? Landon had no idea that Ava briefly had considered telling him the butterfly story but changed her mind, feeling that some secrets had to be held close to the heart.

Ava jumped back into the conversation with more confidence. "Lately, I've been thinking that maybe I should move. Maybe start over somewhere new. I am so confused that I don't even know where I want to go or what I want to be doing, for that matter. The only goal I've had for the past year was to learn about the immortals and now that I no longer want to become one, it's almost like I have nothing to look forward to or to work toward. I'm not excited about anything in my future and a part of me is afraid that I never will be again."

"I think you will be," Landon insisted. "I think you just need some time to absorb everything and one day, you'll just know. It'll hit you when you are ready and when the time is right. You just have to be patient with yourself."

"I have never been patient with myself," Ava admitted with another little smile, but somehow this one shone a little brighter than the one from the earlier portion of their conversation. This time she had some light in her eyes, giving Landon hope that maybe things would soon take a positive turn.

"My grandmother wants me to move back in with her and I'm considering it," Ava's confession took Landon by surprise. "I just feel very disconnected from everything right now and for the first time in years, we seem to be really bonding and getting along. And she's not young; maybe I need to consider spending more time with her and getting away from all the memories in this building. Think about what I want to do with my life."

"But won't moving in with your grandmother tip her off about the vampire thing," Landon's voice hinted at some unexpected emotion. Was that the real reason he didn't want her to leave? "It would be hard to hide in the same house."

"Nah, I think I can get around it," Ava admitted and laughed. "Believe it or not, sometimes *I* forget about it, I've become so used to being one."

"It's really not a big deal," Landon reminded her. "In fact, I have to say that only new vampires really see it as a huge thing, the longer you are one it is just normal. Contrary to everything on television and in the movies, being a vampire is pretty irrelevant and just simply a part of life for some of us that we become accustomed to. Otherwise, it's life as usual."

"Yeah, it's funny you guys used to talk about that with me," Ava seemed to move more in his direction as she spoke. "About how being a vampire was so exaggerated and highlighted in culture now, that it was only a big deal to those who believed all the fiction surrounding the lifestyle."

"It glamorizes it, makes it sexy," Landon chuckled shyly, quickly looking toward the entrance. "Being a vampire is like the tattoo version of lifestyles. It looks cool, so you think you are too. If only they knew that to those who live it, it's not a huge deal at all. It's kind of like all those people in the world who want to be famous or rich and when they succeed, are disappointed about how very ordinary their lives actually are, and being a vampire," Landon slid to the edge of his seat and began to slowly stand up, "is exactly the same thing. It looks glamorous and exciting on the outside, and really not so exciting on the inside."

"It's true, I see that now."

"No one ever sees it in the beginning," Landon spoke compassionately and picked his laptop bag from the floor. It was time to leave. He could sense it. "But maybe you should seek out this 'rock star' just to put an ending to this story. Maybe it's time the truth is revealed."

"I think....I think you're right."

"But," Landon started to slowly walk away, still looking over his shoulder. "I think you should also be prepared. Just as vampires may seem all shiny and bright on the outside to those who aren't one, maybe this rock star will end up not being the sparkling star that you expect."

Landon left her with a seductive smile and new questions in her head.

Chapter Forty-Four

"I hope you enjoy Chamomile tea," Ava's grandmother flew in the door with two medium cups from a nearby coffee shop, stuffed in a carry out tray that included napkins, milk, sugar and spoons. Her grandmother made it a habit to never leave an establishment without everything she felt was owed to her. Whether or not she used it was irrelevant. As she always taught Ava, it was all about the principal of the matter.

"Yes, I do, actually," Ava quickly shut the door behind Edith Wolfe and followed the elegant older lady into the kitchen, where she promptly removed the cups from the holder they were enclosed in and sat each on the counter. "Damn! I forgot to ask for honey." She shook her head in irritation. "You can rarely get sugar and milk with your beverages, *forget* about honey!" She dramatically waved her hand in the air and Ava recalled how the two had hardly spoken, only a few months earlier. It was strange how quickly their relationship had changed.

"That's okay, I think I have honey here," Ava walked toward the cabinet but her grandmother was already shaking her head no.

"It's fine, I am happy with the tea just as it is." She removed the cover from one of the cups, allowing all the enclosed steam to seep out. "The point is that I should've asked for some. With the price they charge for a simple cup of tea or coffee, I want to make sure I get everything that they are willing to give me." She stopped and thought for a moment. "I would take a coffee pot and a bucket of hot water, if they were willing to give it to me."

A smile tugged at Ava's lips when she thought of her dainty grandmother dragging a bucket of water out of the high-end coffee establishment, and didn't dare make a reply.

"I hope you weren't heading out," Her grandmother surveyed Ava's clothing—which consisted of a pair of Tinker Bell pajamas—then shook her head. "I guess not?"

"Nah," Ava shrugged and glanced toward the window that was still closed despite the hot, summer afternoon. Where would she go? What would she do? "I might later," she lied.

"Still, you young people are pretty casual with wearing your pajamas at all hours of the night *and* day." Her grandmother wandered to the sink and put a quick splash of cold water in her tea, before putting the lid back on. She didn't wait for her granddaughter's reply but made her way into the living room, sipping her tea. Ava picked up her own cup and followed her grandmother to the next room.

Edith Wolfe's comfort level with Ava had greatly increased, as she sat on the couch and brought her feet up restfully to her side. She wore a pair of nylons on her feet but still seemed to avoid having more than a fraction of her foot actually touch the couch.

"I guess we are just more carefree now," Ava attempted to explain the pajamas thing and sat at the other end of the couch, turning to face her grandmother who nodded in understanding.

"Just promise me I am dead in the grave before you start wandering around the grocery store on a Saturday afternoon wearing those.' She pointed toward the yellow and purple Tinker Bell ensemble. "I was just getting a few groceries and saw a young woman running around the store as if it were her living room. My God, it wasn't as if she were a young child and even then...." Her words drifted off and she took a sip of tea.

"I promise I will wait till you're dead before I go out in public with my pajamas," Ava couldn't help but share her grandmother's grin. "I thought you hated shopping on Saturday afternoons."

"I usually do but I have a hair appointment a little later," she replied.

"My girl is only in a couple of days a week now so I have to catch her when she is free." Her eyes shot around the room and behind Ava, as if looking for something. "That's a lovely photo and you and your friend. That's the girl that passed, isn't it?"

Ava knew the one she was referring to because it was the *only* picture she had on her walls. "Yes, that was the two of us last year."

"Very nice that you have that now," her grandmother replied. "I know I took a picture of your parents just before they went off on their trip years ago, and I was always thankful for that one time, I actually remembered to keep batteries in my camera."

Ava glanced down at her untouched tea and her mind shot back to the old Kodak camera from her childhood, back before the digital age had taken over. Although, it hadn't become a part of her grandmother's life until she absolutely had no choice but to make the change. She hated technology but attempted to follow it. Now she took photos with her phone.

"I remember that night *and* that picture," Ava recalled the last get together they had as a family with her grandmother, just before her parents left on the trip that took their lives. "It's hard to believe how long ago it was."

"Time moves forward even when we don't." Her grandmother's remark surprised her and for a moment, Ava's eyes darted toward the older woman, assuming that she was making a reference to her current state regarding Mariah. But this was quickly dismissed.

"When I think of all the time I was angry about your parents death and terrible, absolutely *terrible* I was with you, I shudder." Her words shocked Ava. Although she had expressed anger about her parent's death in the past, it was the first time she had even come close to admitting how unfairly she had once treated her granddaughter as a child. Ava couldn't speak.

"I was so incredibly angry at everyone back then and it was wrong," Her grandmother spoke apologetically and gave an awkward smile to Ava. Her fingers nervously played with the lid to her cup of tea and her eyes glanced down to observe them. "It was so wrong of me. But I thought the world was to blame for taking my only child away so young, so tragically. I was in complete shock for so long and suddenly I had a granddaughter who was by all means as shocked as me and yet; I couldn't explain it to you. I couldn't answer your questions, like why did it happen? Did someone do something wrong? Did your parents know they were going to die?"

Ava recalled all the questions she had asked that seemed so insensitive to a grieving mother, but at that time she had never experienced death before and was confused by each and every element of the event. She pictured each second of the plane crash and became obsessed with any television show that featured a crash of any kind. It was almost as if she had to understand every aspect of the situation before she could mourn. How had she forgotten the terrible questions she had asked?

"I didn't even understand it myself and I grew so frustrated because of my own pain, my own confusion and anger. My own denial was so strong at first that anyone asking me about their death only enraged me, because I wasn't yet ready to accept it." She confessed and took another long drink of her tea. "Not that it is easy to this day, but at least I have it in better perspective than back then. But what a horrible tragedy."

"It was," Ava agreed in a child-like voice.

"But we move forward," her grandmother insisted. "We get stronger and there is clarity with time. And there will be for you as well, after you've had time to process your friend's death."

Suddenly the old lady was on her feet, purse in hand and walking toward the door. "And I must leave you now and attempt to find some form of parking downtown that isn't outrageously expensive. If I can get close enough to the salon, my girl usually pays it for me."

Ava jumped up behind her and with tea in hand, followed her to the door. "Oh. . .okay then."

"But I will see you soon," The old lady leaned in to give her a quick hug and swung open the door and abruptly stopped. "Oh dear, there is an envelope outside, I almost walked on it." She leaned over and picked it up, glanced at it and quickly passed it to Ava. "That's strange, don't remember seeing it when I came in."

"Oh, it's probably my mail going in the wrong box again." Ava shook her head. "I swear that our mailman just throws everything into one of the mailboxes downstairs and hopes to get it right. Whoever got it probably just left it for me." She noted that the envelope had no return address. "Probably junk mail anyway."

"Well, let's hope not, " Her grandmother gave a quick wave and rushed away.

Once alone in her apartment, Ava tore it opened to find a thick piece of paper and at first, she was certain it was blank. However after opening it she did find three little words

Stop asking questions.

And then on the bottom

It's not worth your life.

Another threat! Ava felt her blood run cold and she quickly scanned the envelope for any clue as to where it came from, who sent it, anything! But there was nothing else on the paper, nothing unusual on the outside of the envelope.

Unlike the time before, Ava quickly regained her composure and took a deep breath. It was someone trying to scare her. Maybe it was someone in the building who had overheard her conversation with Landon or knew she was still asking around about the immortals. But what difference did it make? She had been very clear recently that it was just idle curiosity and that she no longer had any interest in becoming one.

Rushing to the nearby table, she found her phone and quickly sent Landon a text. When he didn't reply, Ava briefly considered going to his apartment but then changed her mind.

On Monday she would talk to Matthew again. And this time she would insist he find out some real answers.

Chapter Forty-Five

"I think whoever sent you this is full of shit," Matthew growled after hearing Ava's story on Monday morning. He appeared a little more edgy than usual, and it even occurred to her that perhaps she had picked the wrong time to spring this on him. After all, it was before the other staff had arrived to work. "It's very weird."

"I don't exactly think *weird* is the word I would use in this situation," Ava could hear her own voice grow shaky as she spoke, something that didn't go unnoticed by Matthew. He raised his eyebrows slightly, while his pupils dilated and lips opened as if they were about to allow a few words to slip out, but decided to wait. In that moment, she felt incredibly attracted to him and felt the sexual tension quickly fill up the entire room. She decided to remain silent.

The sun was suddenly shining brightly through the window and for some reason, was causing Ava's eyes to burn as she stared at Matthew. He was so beautiful, with long eyelashes and large, dark eyes. She wanted nothing more in that moment but to run her fingers through his hair, but stopped herself, shaking away the thought. "They...whoever it was, threatened to kill me."

"I think it's just a to scare you." Matthew seemed convinced of his beliefs but continued to stare into her eyes, as if it would somehow allow him to read her thoughts. Fortunately, he could not. "I really don't believe that you are in any danger, Ava."

"And if you are wrong?" She tilted her head and felt very vulnerable in that moment: both to whomever left the note and Matthew. She hated feeling this way and struggled with these emotions. "What am I supposed to do, go to the police and say the top vampire is threatening to kill me?" Her hands flew dramatically in the air while her eyes doubled in size to create affect. At the same time, she couldn't help recognizing the humor in the situation and a grin escaped her lips. "Seriously?"

"Ava, other than talk to Derrick again, there is really nothing that I can do. I was sure that my mom would be able to help you out, but we really are coming up empty on this and I just…. I understand your frustration because I feel it too." Matthew appeared preoccupied and she felt as though he was hoping for nothing more than for her to leave the office. "Listen, I am going to be heading out later this week for a business trip, and Derrick will be at one of the meetings that I am scheduled to attend. I will just tell him about the threats you are receiving and ask him to let whomever know that you are not attempting to become an immortal any longer."

"But I still want to learn more about them…" Ava felt her voice drift off as she watched Matthew's expression turn to frustration. "Okay, just please, please let him know to call off the dogs. I….I don't care about any of this anymore. I just want them to leave me alone."

Ava gave Matthew a small smile before standing up, and quietly exiting his office. Clearly her hands were tied and at that point, did it even matter anymore? The thing she didn't understand was why there was so much of a threat now, considering that she had backed off the subject. It didn't make sense and regardless of Matthew's assurance, she wasn't feeling very safe. She just wanted it all to go away.

Landon was also of little help. Although he always offered her a place to stay if she didn't feel safe, he also made it clear that he didn't believe that the immortals would give her any trouble, since she no longer sought their secrets. In fact, even on the night that she fearfully reported a note was delivered to her door, he seemed slightly passive on the phone and it almost appeared that he was entertaining company at the time, therefore his physical desires were probably greatly overlapping any friendly concern he had for her.

Feeling depressed and discouraged, Ava's thoughts grew more and more mournful throughout the day. She was exhausted from a lack of sleep all weekend. Every sound frightened her and yet, she was almost as scared when it was silent. What if immortals were capable of slipping into a room without even being detected? For the little bit of information she had uncovered about their kind, still left her with a lot of unanswered questions.

Fear had a way of entrapping its victims until it was almost impossible to breathe. Try as she might, nothing could make her forget the letter that she had since read, reread and inspected for clues, over and over again. Nothing had changed since it first sat in her hands, other than the fact that her fear had turned to terror. Her thoughts raced excitedly and molehills quickly turned to the most enormous mountains that protruded over any other before them.

Talking to people like Matthew and Landon, who thought little of the whole ordeal wasn't helping the situation. They treated it like a silliness that had gotten out of hand, nothing more.

It was on her way home that same day, that thoughts of her deceased friend suddenly crept up on her once again, weighing her down with multitudes of sadness, spiraling into a darkness that surrounded her heart. Sometimes she felt like the only person who hadn't forgotten about Mariah. Knowing that her friend had no relationship with her family, Ava wondered if anyone else even cared at all. Sure, there was a funeral and all the expected formalities that accompanied death but sometimes she felt as though she were the only person in the world who remembered Mariah's confident and smug smile. Perhaps it was because she had also saw the broken version of this same woman that she was able to see the three dimensions that Mariah had often worked so hard to hide. Her presentation had always been that of an aloof, cold woman who feared and cared for no one except herself.

Ava often thought of the man that had broken Mariah's heart. Had he even cared how much his rejection hurt her? His words had been torture but then again, she often had to remind herself that it was only one side of a two-sided story. And the more she allowed her mind to scan through the details and eventually bounce back and forth like a ping pong ball, it only made her feel worse

Ava felt some comfort in not being alone, so she stopped in a store on her way home, browsed through the racks of clothing even though she had no intention of buying anything at all. Nothing caught her eye. And the anxious salesgirl that approached her looked defeated as soon as she realized this fact.

Although it was just as likely that an immortal would approach her in public as at home, at least there were too many people around for a stranger to attack her. Knowing that immortals wanted to remain as invisible as possible, it seemed to be the best choice. After all, no one took her seriously, so what was she supposed to do?

It wasn't until she left the store and crossed the street to get a tea at her favorite shop, that Ava realized that there was a message on her phone, as well as a couple of text messages from Landon. Her first instinct was to ignore them, frustrated by what she viewed as his general lack of concern for her, but after purchasing her tea, she instead sat down in the quiet café and texted him back.

They exchanged messages. He wanted to know when she was returning home. Feeling completely apathetic, she sank farther into the comfortable chair and attempted to ignore the message, choosing instead to stare out a nearby window. She watched people as they walked by, often preoccupied with a conversation or talking on their phone. Everyone had a place to be. She didn't.

Eventually, she tapped her phone and it sprang to life again. Rereading Landon's last message, she allowed her fingers to slowly glide over the face and reply.

I don't know

Send

Watching the dark clouds gather overhead, she wanted to curl up in this comfortable chair and never leave. Just sit and watch the people going by, some glancing in at her curiously, most not noticing her eyes observing them. She wondered what it would be like to be someone else at that moment. To have another life, wouldn't it be nice?

Her phone vibrated and she glanced at it.

I need to talk. Text when you are on your way.

At first, she didn't care. So what? Landon thought he needed to talk to her. But then her thoughts returned to the day that Mariah died and even though she didn't want to return to that dark place, a part of her feared that he wanted to share bad news with her again. Landon rarely sought her out and when he did, it seemed to be for an undesirable reason. Her mind racing, but her body simply exhausted she didn't want to move an inch.

People walked into the coffee shop, purchased a beverage and left. No one else was seated.

Everyone else has somewhere to go

After finishing her tea, she reluctantly rose from her seat and headed toward the door. The lone employee looked up from a newspaper he was pretending not to read and grinned at Ava, as she headed out the door.

Back out on the street, she felt like she was in the middle of the jungle of people. Everyone was rushing in various directions, bikes whizzed by as if she were in their way, while traffic appeared a little more backed up than normal. Ava just wanted to go home, soak in a hot tub and forget about the world. She was already dreading her conversation with Landon. It wasn't that she didn't appreciate the times he had helped her but she simply felt worn out and exhausted by everything that had been going on over the past few weeks. Maybe she needed a vacation, she decided.

Entering her apartment building with a sense of dread, she remembered that she was supposed to text Landon back but hadn't bothered. Glancing toward the lounge area, she realized that it wasn't necessary, since he was already waiting for her.

He gave her a self-conscious smile and watched her wearily wander toward him, her eyes begging him to make this fast and painless.

"I'm sorry to bug you," he replied, noting her expression. "I went up to your apartment for a second and found something by your door." He reached for an envelope that was sitting beside him on the couch. "I wasn't sure if it was another note and I didn't feel right just leaving it for you, in case it was something serious."

Silently, Ava curved her lips into a smile and reached for the envelope, she opened it and stared. With no expression on her face, she passed it to Landon.

The questions end here unless you hope to be reintroduced to Mariah on the other side.

Chapter Forty-Six

Through the darkness, she could hear him breathe. Gentle and rhythmic, there was something intoxicating about the image of Landon in such a peaceful state that made Ava intensely attracted to him. She envisioned running her hand over his chest. Stirring him awake, his eyes tracing her fingers as they lightly ran over his navel and past the waistband of his boxers. His breath would increase while his chest would rise and fall faster, working against a force that rose inside of him and was waiting to explode in an intense passion.

But Landon was in the next room, alone, while Ava lay awake on the couch, staring at the ceiling. He had invited her to stay for a few days until things were settled with the immortals, just for her own peace of mind. Ava wearily agreed, unsure if it really would matter where she was if they chose to 'get' her, but she decided it was probably easier to just go with the flow. However, she *did* insist on sleeping on the couch this time so that she wasn't an imposition.

"I can just slip out in the morning and get ready for work in my own apartment," she had suggested as a simple resolution for any concerns about sharing the bathroom during the hectic early morning hours. It was Ava's preference to navigate the morning routine in her own space. "Besides, I don't want to inconvenience you anymore than I already have."

"Staying in my apartment isn't exactly an inconvenience," Landon protested with a quick shrug, glancing around the room as if surveying the environment. "It's not like you haven't stayed here before."

Although he could've easily been implying the last time she was there, on the night after Mariah's suicide, there was a seductive lure in his eyes that was suggesting an earlier time when they had been intimate. It took her off guard, but within seconds, Ava managed to convince herself that it was her own imagination leading her in that particular direction.

"I know and I do appreciate it," Ava felt confident in her reply, nodding with a smile on her lips. "I just would feel better if you were able to sleep in your own bed, plus if I leave early in the morning, I won't wake you." She referred to the fact that it was necessary to walk through the living room in order to leave his apartment.

"As you wish," he finally agreed to the arrangement.

Wide-awake, she now lay on the couch; fully aware of every breath he took from the other side of the closed door. Feeling an unexpected desire for him, she briefly wondered if Bryan was home alone in bed. Perhaps she could distract herself with him for the night. Although it would help subside the physical desire for the moment, wouldn't she continue to want Landon each and every time they were together in a room?

If Landon awoke now, Ava was certain he would be able to sense her desire for him and she'd be embarrassed. Would he be able to hear the subtle sound of her fingers as they ran under the waistband of her underwear? She did so as quietly as possible incase he awoke to hear as they gently stroked the warm, smooth skin that she wished he was touching in that moment. She thought back to the days when his tongue would work powerfully where her own fingers now touched, while she would squirm in anticipation, gently rising and falling to increase the pleasure that rang through her body. Her moans were soft in the beginning, growing louder as she reached climax, something she held back now.

Still very alert to any sound that would indicate he was awake in the next room, Ava worked diligently to achieve a sensation even slightly relating to the one in her memory, but knew it would never match. She thought about how he drank blood earlier and how that made for a stronger physical reaction to sex, and wondered if he had done that in hopes of such a night? Her other hand slid under her shirt and fondled her right nipple which was hard, sending more sensations through her entire body. Gyrating her hips, she knew her body wanted more but she had to remain quiet. It was merely relief when she finally felt the strong pulse against her fingertips.

Her heart thumping loudly in her chest, Ava thought the release would enable her to sleep. It did not. Moments from that day were still flashing through her mind as if she were watching fragments from a previous episode of a television show. But she remained uninterested. It was strange to feel unattached and unconcerned about all the things that used to worry her. Perhaps her intense attraction to Landon was merely a distraction.

She was relieved to wake before Landon the next morning and slip out of the door. Although it was unlikely he would sense her desire for him, Ava wasn't about to take any chances and rushed back to her apartment, where she immediately jumped in the shower. How could she continue to stay in his apartment? Maybe, Ava decided, she would just tell him that she wasn't scared and would be fine in her own place.

Deciding to put it on the backburner for now, Ava quickly got ready and headed for work. Rushing out the front door of her building, she almost ran past Landon, who stood on the sidewalk staring at his phone. He quickly looked up and Ava felt herself blush, afraid he knew the reason for her leaving so abruptly that morning.

"Well hello there!" He smiled at her innocently, tilting his head in curiosity. He was handsome but at the same time, Ava felt a little silly for feeling such a strong desire for him during the previous night. Feeling the warmth of embarrassment fill her cheeks, she quickly looked away and pretended to check for something in her purse. "I was a little concerned when you were gone this morning. I thought maybe something was... wrong?"

Ava noted the hesitation in his voice and suddenly felt as if she were being rude when avoiding his eyes. Clearly, he had no idea why she was feeling uncomfortable and it would look more obvious if she continued to act so shifty. So she looked straight into his eyes and gave a gracious smile.

"No, I'm sorry, I should've left a note or something," Ava admitted. "I just wasn't sleeping well and finally decided to go home and grab a shower. I should have let you know."

"It's ah...it's okay, I was just about to text you, actually. " His amber eyes showed no sign of looking away and Ava convinced herself that he had no idea what kind of thoughts had been going through her head about him. Thank God vampires weren't able to read minds. How humiliating would that have been?

"Oh thanks. I'm sorry, again, for not being a little more considerate." Ava shook her head, quickly grabbing her sunglasses from her bag to hide her eyes, even though it was a dark, dreary day. He continued to silently stare and flashbacks the previous night of Ava's hands caressing her own skin were vivid in her mind. Had he heard? What was he thinking in that moment?

"I probably shouldn't hold you up," she awkwardly spoke and he finally looked away, sliding his phone into his front pocket.

"Yes, I really should get to work." His smile was unusual, almost hesitant yet curious at the same time. What was he thinking? Maybe she was just being paranoid.

"Me too," Ava briefly considered finding an excuse to not return to his place that night but decided it was a topic that didn't really have to be addressed at this time. She said a quick good-bye and headed in the opposite direction of Landon, who had to catch the Sky train.

The day flew by. Matthew was out of the office for the rest of the week, so she couldn't discuss the latest note that had been left for at her door. Not that it would really matter. What more could he say? She just hoped he was able to talk to Derrick and he could get word back to whomever was doing this, that she was no longer interested in the immortals. In that moment, she couldn't have cared less and no longer wanted to learn anything more about them. In fact, even when Landon had speculated the previous night that perhaps it was someone in their own building leaving the notes, Ava didn't care. At one time, her brain would've examined all the appropriate evidence and she would have made guesses about who was involved but not now. She didn't care. It didn't matter. She didn't even want to think about it.

On the way home from work that day, Ava again considered how she would avoid staying at Landon's place for another night. She knew he would be insistent on it but she honestly felt pretty safe and didn't think there was any real threat to her life. Besides, could she lay on his couch one more night, fantasizing about his tongue gliding over her body? At least at home she could find a more satisfying way to live through her fantasy without the embarrassment of him catching her in the midst of a lustful thought.

Yeah, there was absolutely no way she could stay at Landon's again that night. The decision was made.

But it didn't stick.

Landon stopped by her apartment for a visit around dinnertime and was pretty adamant that her 'crack head' ideas of staying home alone were ridiculous.

"You were *threatened*, Ava! What do you not understand about the fact that another note insinuated that you could be killed?" Landon began to rant immediately after she attempted to gingerly give him her opinion. They were standing in her living room and hadn't even made it to the couch before their argument began. "You have to assume that the threats are real and not take a chance."

"But you even said that maybe there isn't much you could do if an immortal showed up," Ava quickly reminded him. Turning her back on him, she headed for the kitchen and reached for a clean glass in her cupboard. "Plus they have threatened me before and I never had a problem."

"This one was a little more persistent," Landon made a fair assessment and she knew he was right. Ava could hear his voice getting closer as he followed her into the small kitchen area, where she poured herself a glass of water. Briefly glancing in his direction, she saw him leaning against her stove. "I think it's better to be safe than sorry. In fact, if it makes you feel better, I can come here and stay rather than the other way around."

Ava briefly considered the idea. "I don't think I need any protection at all."

"I know that's what you think and you could be right," Landon spoke evenly and shrugged. He had changed out of his work clothes and was now wearing a pair of jeans and a t-shirt. Without meaning to, she found herself glancing at his crotch and immediately looked away, hoping he hadn't noticed. "Let's just not take the chance and stay at my place until this Mark guy from your work-

"*Matthew*," Ava corrected him and took a sip of water.

"Whatever," Landon shook his head dismissively. "The point is that it will be settled soon and you can get back to a normal life and you'll be safe again. But for now, just humor me, please. Let's pretend that I might know what I am talking about."

Ava reluctantly nodded as she drank some more water.

"In fact, you can sleep in my bed this time." Landon spoke in a matter-of-fact voice and Ava had to look away quickly incase he could somehow read her eyes. "I don't mind sleeping on the couch, so don't worry about it. And chances are you won't wake me when you go to leave in the morning."

"Are you sure?" Ava heard herself ask and she bit her bottom lip.

"Definitely," he spoke earnestly and headed toward the door. "So, get your teddy bear and pajamas and come to my place whenever you are ready."

Ava smiled as she watched him leave. Maybe she would take a bath before she went to his place tonight. Just incase.

Chapter Forty-Seven

The second sleepover at Landon's proved to be less of a challenge. Unlike the sensory alerts of the previous night, the musky fragrance of his sheets didn't become an aphrodisiac to Ava. Although she did experience an unexpected feeling of comfort being enfolded in his blankets, as she listened to the soft murmur of his television in the next room. She felt safe, like a child tucked into her parent's bed after a horrible nightmare, protected from a world of monsters and scary creatures.

Her subconscious mind was persistently reminding Ava of her carnal desire for Landon. Although she attempted to ignore her thoughts, they only grew more powerful. It had happened at work earlier that day, while trying to concentrate on emails but instead her mind was floating back to the previous night on Landon's couch. Now as she slipped into a gentle slumber, Ava had no idea it would soon be interrupted by erotic visions that felt incredibly real, as they flowed through her mind.

It wasn't delicate and beautiful, like a fantasy in a romance novel or Hollywood movie. There was no seduction this time; no build up in excitement, but Ava's dream seemed to start right in the midst of some very erotic intercourse. On all fours, she could feel him inside her, aggressively pumping while her body shook from the impact, her hair fell in her face while involuntary sounds escaped from a deep place inside, one that she hadn't even known existed. Every cell in her body was on edge and she closed her eyes and squeezed tightly as he pushed deeper inside her and pulled her torso into a more upright position. She suddenly felt his teeth sinking into the skin that met with the back of her neck. As his tongue and lips worked simultaneously, greedily ingesting her blood, she gasped loudly. His fingers roamed her body, squeezing, roughly caressing while his breath was hot on her neck, panting behind her ear. Reaching her peak, she found herself making loud sounds that could've been easily mistaken for sobs rather than intense passion and fulfillment.

She felt her body collapsing forward in exhaustion, while his did the same on top of her, his heart pounding furiously against Ava's back. Hot liquid ran down her thighs and slid toward the sheets beneath her. In that moment, Ava had never felt as blissful and slowly turned her head around—but it wasn't Landon who had just brought her to this point of exhilaration—it was Matthew.

They didn't make eye contact. He was still carefully licking the bite he had made on her back, oblivious to anything else in that moment. That's when something else caught her eyes. Landon was in the room, standing back and watching with interest. Much to her surprise, he held no judgment or anger in his eyes. He didn't look turned off by the encounter but at the same time, he didn't exactly look turned on either.

Ava opened her mouth to say something but no words came out. She felt a soft, thin tongue tracing down her back while fingers ran back and forth over her nipples. Turning around to say something to Landon, she was surprised to see him silently removing his clothes, as if he wanted to join this encounter. However something had changed. Matthew was no longer behind her but a woman. Her large, round breasts rose and fell with each breath and she appeared engrossed with Ava's body, her fingers tracing it as if measuring every inch of her naked flesh.

Ava's eyes flew open and she jumped up in the bed. Her heart raced and her clothes were drenched in sweat as she quickly realized it was a dream. The gentle murmur of the television in the next room told her that it was still early but her eyes were too tired to check her phone.

What did this dream mean? Was this about her attraction to Matthew?

Was she about to disappoint Landon once again? Was it simply her own mounting desire for Landon that was holding her hostage?

No. Ava knew what the dream was telling her. She knew who the woman was and why Landon was involved. It was something from the past that had been sitting in a corner, collecting a mountain of dust; but it wasn't going away. The time had arrived to air it out.

The next morning, she was relieved to once again wake before Landon, so she could return to her apartment. The television had long been turned off and everything was silent when Ava snuck past him on the couch. A blanket draped over his midsection, his naked chest slowly rising and falling, as he appeared to be in a deep sleep. Ava left, gently closing the door behind her. She would send him a text to confirm everything was okay, when back in her place.

Once there, she quickly removed her clothes and climbed into the shower. Her mind returned to the night of her big fight with Landon. It was so long ago but it still didn't give her an excuse to pretend it didn't happen at all. It was time to face the music and to apologize. She slowly dried herself after the shower, still deep in thought. If only she knew the right words to say.

Ava felt a chill in the air as she walked to work that morning, signaling that fall would soon be on its way. She smiled and slid on her sunglasses, suddenly feeling very light and hopeful. In a few months, this wretched year would be complete. A new beginning was around the corner. It gave her hope.

Her spirits however, started to deplete after a long day at work. As she came closer to having an open discussion with Landon, she started to dread his reaction. Things had been going so well between them in recent weeks and she feared approaching the topic would ruin it. Would he accept her with forgiveness? Was this the right thing to do?

Ava felt a chill swoop up her jacket as she returned to her apartment building later that day, causing her to shiver as she took a quick glance around. Benjamin was sitting alone in the lounge area and he immediately caught her eye. Without giving it a second thought, Ava drifted toward him.

"Well well, look at you," Benjamin dropped the newspaper onto his lap and carefully inspected her with a mischievous glint in his eyes, a smile playing over his lips.

"Yes, look at me," Ava quipped with a sardonic grin on her face. "And look at *you!*"

"Well there isn't much to look at here, I'm afraid," Benjamin said, folding his newspaper into small portions. "Just my normal, everyday life. A little bit of this, a little bit of that, keeping up on business news." He tapped his hand on the newspaper. "One must always be aware."

"One must." Ava agreed and reluctantly sat across from him, feeling a little too preoccupied to really get engrossed in a conversation.

"And speaking of keeping aware," Benjamin sat the newspaper on the empty seat beside him and raised his eyebrows. "I couldn't help but notice that you have new sleeping arrangement in recent days. That's an interesting turn of events for you, Miss Ava."

With an embarrassed smile, she shook her head, avoiding his eyes. "It's not what you are thinking, Benjamin."

"I wasn't *thinking* anything, was simply making a passing remark." He spoke dramatically, holding his hands both up to imply some form of innocence. "I merely was suggesting that perhaps you had a *blast* from the past?"

Ava wasn't sure how such a blasé comment could strike her as so dirty, but it somehow caused blood to rush to her cheeks and she was lost for words.

"It's quite nice to *stomp* on familiar grounds once in awhile," Benjamin continued with such innocence in his voice that a stranger wouldn't have caught on to what he was suggesting. "You already know the *lay* of the land and it's quite refreshing, wouldn't you say, Ava?"

"I'm staying there because I had threating notes left at my door again," Ava felt the need to enlighten him but she did so in a calm tone, not at all showing or feeling any hostility to his constant teasing. "I am sorting it out but for now, I guess maybe it's smart to have someone around, just in case."

"Yes, I bet he is all around *you*, Miss Ava." Benjamin continued to playfully torment her. "But at any rate, I'm sure you are in....good hands?"

Ava couldn't help but laugh at Benjamin's final remark as he stood up and she did the same. "Thanks for your...concern?"

"But of course, I'm always concerned for thy neighbor," Benjamin spoke earnestly as the two headed for the elevator. "I do believe there is something about that in the bible, am I right?"

"I don't spend many Sunday mornings in church," Ava confessed. "So, I can't tell you."

"I bet you are pretty indisposed on Sundays mornings." Benjamin followed her into the elevator.

Back at her apartment, Ava found a text message on her phone from Landon. He was going out for about an hour but would let her know when he arrived home.

Ava frowned, automatically heading to her kitchen to pour a glass of wine, to calm her nerves. She was really looking forward to getting this confession out of her system, to clearing the air with Landon once and for all. If he was angry, it was a cross she would have to bear but regardless, it was time to do the right thing.

She grabbed her glass with one hand and the bottle with the other and made her way to the living room. Placing the bottle on the coffee table, she sat down on the couch and put her feet up.

How would she go about this apology?

Landon, remember the time we had the horrible fight and broke up? Remember how I insisted you were ogling that waitress and made an excuse of a work call, in order to meet her in the back? Remember how I said I could tell you how much you wanted her. . .well, here's the thing. . ..

Ava closed her eyes and shook her head. How was she supposed to do this? How was she supposed to tell Landon the truth? How was she supposed to confess that it was *her* and not him that had been completely out of line that night? Would he hate her? She was ashamed and embarrassed at her own weakness.

It happened during her early days as a vampire. Although months had passed and Ava had been able to finally get a grasp on her five senses most of the time, there were still incidents where a scent would make her vomit, a sound would cause her head to ache or a physical sensation would be much more powerful than she had expected. . .and that's what got her in trouble on that particular night.

Landon had taken her to a popular chain restaurant on an evening that the two were already feeling some tension in their relationship. It was at that point where things were kind of losing their original excitement and Ava was still attempting to grasp the concept of her new life. It actually started off as a boring night but it quickly took a change in direction.

The restaurant was unusually quiet, allowing a very attractive and scantily clad waitress—who introduced herself as Paige—to spend more time and attention on their table than Ava would've preferred. The tension increased after the waitress 'accidentally' brushed her breast against Landon, as she leaned across the table to sit down a glass of water. The waitress then gave her a raised eyebrow that Ava perceived as taunting, causing jealousy to flicker and she abruptly left the table with an excuse of visiting the ladies room, in order to escape.

She was barely in the quiet sanctuary of the restroom, when Paige walked in behind her. Closing the door, Ava was stunned when she proceeded to lock it. Assuming that she was about to be involved in an argument, she felt the hairs on the back of her neck stand up. "What are you doing?"

"I wanted to talk to you alone." Paige told her, with no indication of what was to come next. She tilted her head and smiled. "I'm not hitting on your boyfriend, I just thought you should know."

Ava nodded slowly and was surprised to discover that they were surrounded with a scent indicating sexual arousal. Swallowing hard, she felt blood rushing through her body as her own desires crept up on her unexpectedly. She had never felt attraction to a woman before and felt her defenses immediately crumble. This woman was very alluring with a natural, yet beautiful face. Her figure was what Ava considered 'ideal' to most women, curvy and slender at the same time. There was an innocent, girl next-door appeal about her that was mixed with a simmering sexuality that was rare.

Paige inched closer to her and hesitated, as if to see Ava's response. There was an unmistakable heat between their bodies and without even giving it a second thought, Ava instinctively leaned forward and felt the waitress' lips touch her own. They were soft and warm, gently brushing Ava's mouth in curiosity. She could taste vanilla on the tip of her tongue;

a sweet scent filled her lungs and her body suddenly became very aroused, drawing her closer to the stranger. She wanted to touch her.

Ava felt herself succumb to her physical desires, their lips locked together more intensely as her hands were gently running up and down the smooth skin on Paige's arm. She heard a soft moan escaped her throat and things got a bit out of control.

Unlike in the movies or any porn flick Ava had ever viewed, things weren't slow and seductive but quite the opposite. Both of them were greedily exploring the other's body, as if in fear of not taking full advantage of this mutual attraction. Paige opened her blouse and quickly placed Ava's hand on her right breast, moaning gently as she squeezed it while at the same time, Ava felt Paige's hand run up her thigh and into her skirt. Neither was shy, as they touched, caressed and kissed each other everywhere, almost as if they were stuck on fast forward. They were gasping, moaning and eventually pulling their pieces of clothing back on in a rush, acting as if nothing was abnormal about their long disappearance.

Landon hadn't noticed anything was unusual and simply became furious with her for 'having a hissy fit' and avoiding him for almost twenty minutes.

Had it been twenty minutes?

Ava was stunned that she had made out with a girl, something she hadn't ever considered before that night. Feeling guilty over her own actions and confused about her sexuality, Ava found herself accusing Landon of cheating on *her*. She said the words without thinking, automatically shamed by the pained expression on his face. But it was too late. The words were spoken and couldn't be taken back. That was the beginning of the end.

Chapter Forty-Eight

I t hadn't exactly gone as planned. In fact, she couldn't have possibly predicted how the night would end.

Ava thought and rethought every word she would say to Landon. Although it probably didn't make sense to bring up the past, she felt compelled to make the one confession that could easily rock the boat on an already calm shore. But it had been a secret that was bursting at the seams and its admission was long overdue.

Standing outside his door later that night, Ava took a deep breath before knocking. Changed into a perfectly faded pair of jeans and a grey hoodie, Landon appeared relaxed as he answered and quickly ushered Ava inside.

"Come in, come in. Don't mind the mess." He offered approaching his kitchen, where everything from breakfast cereal to banana peels and a milk carton were on the counter. Upon closer inspection, she noticed crumbs, a stack of opened mail and flyers also scattered in the confined area. "I was hoping to get things cleaned up before you got here but it's just been a crazy day."

"Everything okay?" Ava felt hesitant as she approached, something that was not missed by Landon.

"Yeah, everything's great." Landon said, hurriedly throwing out empty containers and quickly grabbing a cloth to wipe down the counters and pile his mail in one corner. ""Why? What's up with you? Did you get another letter or something?"

"No, nothing like that."

"You're acting kind of weird, like something is up," Landon's eyes glowed like a cat's from across the room, as he attempted to read her. "Are you sure everything is okay?"

"Actually, no." Ava said and cleared her throat. "Could I talk to you about something?"

"Sure, what's up?" Landon asked as he put his hand on her lower back and guided her to sit on the couch with him. She suddenly felt her heart racing; all the words she had rehearsed in her mind were long gone.

"I want to talk to you about when we broke up," Ava said hesitantly and searched Landon's expression, but found no answers. "I want to clear the air on some stuff and I think it's long overdue."

"Okay, but it really doesn't matter anymore." Landon informed her. "I think that is all water under the bridge."

"But there is something you should know."

"We fought because you accused me of messing around with the waitress," Landon quickly recounted it as if time hadn't passed at all. "I think you now realize that I didn't do that."

Ava opened her mouth to reply but he quickly cut her off.

"But clearly a lot of shit was going on at that time. You were still new to the vampire life and we both have grown up a lot since then," Landon spoke as if *he* had been rehearsing his words all day, not the other way around. "It is over, forget about it."

"But there is something you don't know." Ava told him and could tell her words concerned him. "I did something that night that was wrong. I felt weird about it so I overreacted."

He remained silent and so Ava took a deep breath and launched into the story. She decided to not get into the specific details other than to explain her unexpected attraction to the same waitress that she had accused Landon of ogling. Blood rushed to her face as she went on to explain their bathroom encounter and she could barely look him in the eye.

"Wow, I hadn't expected that," Landon gave an awkward smile that she wasn't able to read. "Umm, I guess it is normal for a new vampire to have a much more intense physical reaction to someone they were….umm, attracted to and so, *you* like, messed around with that waitress?"

"Yes." Ava said in a small voice and felt her body pulling back slightly, as if afraid of an attack of words. "I'm really sorry, Landon. I know that it was still cheating even though it was a girl."

"Yeah, I suppose it would still be…I mean, it was," Landon awkwardly ran a hand over his face, briefly closing his eyes. "I just am…surprised, that's all."

Ava bit her lower lip and wondered if she had made the right decision. She wasn't able to read his reaction and didn't know what to do or say next. "You know," her voice was soft, unsure of the words until they fell from her lips. "I can leave, if you want."

Landon immediately started to shake his head, even before the words were out of her mouth. "No, of course not. I don't want you to leave at all. I'm sorry, I just, I'm trying to process…I mean, I can't believe that you and that girl…"

Ava looked into his eyes and gave a helpless nod, hoping that he would understand. Hoping that he wouldn't hate her. "I can't justify it. I was angry with you, still grappling with all these changes with my senses and I did something incredibly stupid."

Landon opened his mouth as if he was about to say something, and then stopped. Ava made a quick decision and rose from the couch. "I should go. I really think it's not—"

"No, don't go." His voice was barely audible as he stood up and carefully reached for her hand. His fingers brushed Ava's skin, gently caressing it, as his breath grew labored. She felt a pull toward Landon as his eyes slowly inspected her body. She wore a simple cardigan over a white tank top and pair of fitted yoga pants. Moving closer to Ava, his dilated pupils hesitated on her neck and in one rapid swoop, Landon lurched forward and sank his teeth into the delicate skin.

Ava let out a loud moan when his sharp teeth dug through her flesh, momentarily causing the room to spin and everything to go dark, as he hungrily sucked blood from her body. His hands grazed her naked skin, one gliding over her face while the other roamed under her top. She felt blood rushing to meet Landon's tongue her heart pounded in excitement that set a fire down her body, rapidly igniting the vulnerable skin between her legs.

Slightly faint, she was enveloped in his arms as he held her more tightly, his hot breath overflowing, warmth throughout her body. Her legs felt weak as he moved her onto the couch. Ava rested her head on the soft pillow and watched Landon quickly remove his hoody, followed by the t-shirt underneath, and throw them to the floor. His jeans quickly joined the pile, leaving only a pair of dark boxer shorts.

Climbing on top of Ava, she felt mesmerized as his mouth started on her belly button and ran its way up, while his hands worked together to unclasp the bra strap in the back. She silently helped him remove her clothing; pulling off the cardigan, tank top and finally the bra to toss on the ground. The clothing had barely touched the floor when Landon's mouth reached for her left breast, hungrily drawing it into his mouth, his hands sliding down her stomach and into her pants. Her body arched slightly, meeting with his fingers, feeling they were more of a tease than providing her with any true pleasure. His tongue was now doing the same with her nipples, barely licking them. Ava felt as though she was being tortured; her desires were much greater than the inadequate sensations she was receiving.

Moaning softly, Ava's head fell back and closing her eyes, she felt Landon's mouth returning to her neck. Ava pulled his body tightly against her own as his teeth and tongue worked into the bite he had previously made; she could feel his desire for her strengthen not only in his heavier breath but also the jutting bulge in his underwear. She awkwardly slid her hand into Landon's boxers in hopes of encouraging him to be less gentle with her, but within moments, her hand quickly slumped Ava's body fell back into a dizzy stupor.

He left her neck and she could feel her pants being pulled off as the cold air and the sensation of Landon's tongue aggressively attacked the most pleasurable spot on her body. She gasped, her head continuing to spin, pleasure running through her lower body. As her body filled with intense gratification, she brushed her fingers over her hard nipples. Suddenly, things took a switch.

Landon was kissing her mouth, the taste of her body still fresh on his lips and she suddenly had the desire to taste him, but her head was spinning. He stopped.

"Shit! I drank too much of your blood!" His words seemed to flow around her and Ava couldn't speak. "Ava, you need some blood right away. You're white as a ghost."

She opened her eyes and everything was blurry. Feeling weak with sudden exhaustion, she watched Landon jump off the couch and the next thing she knew, fresh blood was running to the back of her throat. A warm sensation filled her body, starting in her chest and working its way through every inch. She felt vital and strong. In fact, her strength grew more and more powerful, causing her eyes to widen, seeing an exhausted Landon leaning over her. His eyes were burning through her and she felt an overwhelming primal urge that was unlike anything she felt before; she wanted to devour him.

Lunging forward, noting he was completely naked, this time it was Ava to sink her teeth in his neck, causing Landon to gasp loudly, saying her name as if he were begging. He weakly fell on top of her, submitting to her moment of dominance until she moved away from his neck.

"Sec." His hot breath stroked her face and he reached to a nearby table. "Let me drink some more blood."

Knowing that Landon had just had a substantial amount after biting her, she was surprised that he was now looking for more. Without saying a word, their eyes met and he quickly commented. "You'll see."

After drinking the contents of a small, vial-like bottle Ava felt him finally slide in between her legs, causing her to let out a gasp as he simultaneously stuck his tongue deep into her ear. Slowly at first, he thrust himself into to her, sending pleasurable sensations, and finally giving satisfaction to her longings. He picked up the pace, pushing in farther more rapidly while his tongue slid into her mouth and his lips hungrily took hers, muffling her shaky gasps of pleasure. Ava lifted one leg in the air, as the other fell off the couch and to the floor, allowing Landon to move in closer; but it wasn't quite hitting the spot.

Releasing his mouth, she pulled her body up and softly pushed Landon onto his back. Obediently following her lead, he watched as she straddled him. Ava finally felt she could unleash the strong longing that was hidden in a secret place, waiting to be touched, releasing her to the highest level of satisfaction. She lowered herself onto him, riding while he reached for her breasts and closed his eyes, soft moans pouring from his lips. She rotated her hips one-way, then the other, repositioned herself and finally she found it; the itch that she could never quite reach. She picked up the pace, voraciously raising and lowering her hips, while Landon's hands dropped to her thighs, anchoring her body. As she leaned slightly back and moaned loudly in intense pleasure, he did the same, his fingers digging into her skin. Her breasts bouncing, her hair sticking to the sweat on her face, she used the back of the couch to hold on to for support. She couldn't believe how fiercely her body was working against Landon's or that he seemed to be at the pinnacle of sensations in that moment with her, his eyes squeezed tightly together in extreme concentration.

She was overtaken with her release. It was forceful and her heart pounded like a jackhammer when she found it; heady sensations filled her body and she let out a high pitched moan just as Landon roughly clamped onto her thighs and an unfamiliar sound rose from deep inside his body, one she had never heard another man make before in her life.

Suddenly feeling sweaty and slightly embarrassed, Ava climbed off an equally exhausted Landon who just watched her, mesmerized by what had just taken place. Her legs felt too wobbly to go beyond the couch—which was fine—there was no place she would've rather been.

Chapter Forty-Nine

"I tried to catch up with you earlier in the week, but you weren't available," Matthew's surprise phone call on Saturday afternoon was a welcome occurrence. Although she knew he would get back to her regarding his discussion with Derrick Johnston, it was her assumption that conversation wouldn't take place until sometime Monday morning. "I had some information that I wanted to share with you and I figured you would prefer to hear it as soon as possible."

"Thank you, I appreciate that." She was sincere in her praise, but fortunately there had been no more warnings since earlier in the week. Plus Ava was so absorbed in her rekindled relationship with Landon that she hadn't really given the immortal thing any thought in a few days. "So, you talked to Derrick?"

"Yes, I explained that you were no longer looking into being immortal and he agreed to make sure that the word got back to the right people." Matthew assured her.

"Great," Ava breathed a sigh of relief. "So this is done then?"

"Not quite."

"What?' She wrinkled her nose and glanced at a wine stain on her coffee table. "Don't they get that I don't care? I just want to move on with my life."

"Well, here's the thing," Matthew hesitantly continued. "Derrick believes that this so called 'rock star' of vampires wants to meet with you."

"What?" Ava wasn't sure if she should laugh or cry. After all of *this*, now he wanted to meet her? Was this some kind of joke? "You can't be serious!"

"I actually am very serious." Matthew insisted and paused for a moment. "I don't know the when and where, but that's what Derrick told me. Perhaps he was mistaken though or you know, maybe it just won't happen. Either way, I think you are safe from any future threats."

Ava wasn't so sure of that, but she remained calm and simply thanked Matthew before hanging up.

What if he plans to threaten me in person next time? Why would he want to see me now?

Ava gave a heavy sigh, sincerely wishing she hadn't opened this can of worms in the first place. Knowing that Landon was tied up for most of the afternoon, Ava decided to get busy and clean her apartment. If she were preoccupied, perhaps it would ease her mind until he returned and they could talk it out. Ten minutes later, someone knocked on her door.

It was her grandmother.

"Oh, hi," Ava was taken slightly off guard as she stepped aside to allow Edith Wolfe to enter the room. "Did someone let you in downstairs?"

"Oh yes," Her grandmother smiled sweetly before making her way across the room to the couch. She sat down as Ava shut the door. It always amazed her how her grandmother got into the secure building with such ease. "I think it was a young lady who knew I was here to see you. I guess it's a small enough building that people kind of get to know everyone else."

"Well, somewhat," Ava agreed joining her on the couch. "I have my small group of people but I guess everyone in the building sort of knows one another enough to at least say hello."

"Very good." Her grandmother nodded. "Having a strong group of people around you is very important. I certainly know about that."

Ava smiled but remained silent. She didn't really know her grandmother to have a lot of friends and all her close family were gone, so it wasn't clear whom she was referencing with that comment. "I see."

"No dear, I don't think you do," Ava's grandmother raised an eyebrow and her expression softened, much like a child who knew they were in trouble. "I have been holding some secrets from you and I'm afraid the time has come to reveal them."

Ava was dumbfounded by her remark and fell into an awkward laugh. "What?"

"The reason I came here today was," she stopped briefly and scanned Ava's eyes before continuing. "I decided to tell you the truth about a matter that I know is very close to your heart. At least, it used to be."

"To my heart?" Ava was growing concerned. Did this have something to do with her parents? Perhaps her grandmother had held back some information about their death?

Edith Wolfe took a deep breath and with her usual confidence said. "I know you are a vampire. I know you have been for a couple of years and I know that you have been searching for information on the immortals."

Stunned, Ava didn't think any words could've possibly hit her any harder; that was, until her grandmother continued.

"I know because I am one. I'm an immortal."

"You're a vampire?" Ava was shocked by this confession and shook her head in disbelief. Too many thoughts were transpiring from this impromptu announcement that it was difficult to know where to begin. "But that's impossible, I would know. I would sense it."

"You *would* know and you *would* sense it, if you hadn't known me for your entire life." Her grandmother showed poise as she went on to give an explanation. "Since you have known me since birth, how could you possibly distinguish anything that was 'off' about me. Besides, no one expects an older lady to be a vampire. After all, it's not 'sexy' or 'glamorous' like in the movies, is it?" A simple smile slid across her lips. "In a way, that's better because it helps to keep me under the radar."

"I..I don't understand," Ava was still in a state of disbelief. Was she *really* sitting in her living room, having a conversation with her *grandmother* about how they were *both* vampires? This couldn't be happening. A million questions raced through her mind and with each, a logical answer quickly followed.

"I should start from the beginning." Her grandmother spoke in a matter-of-fact voice, remaining calm, despite the alarmed look in Ava's eyes. "But first, I will make us some tea. I think you may need some right about now."

She quickly set to work, making them both a cup of chamomile tea. Ava sat alone, mulling over a million questions. This conversation was completely surreal to her and so many things didn't make sense.

A few minutes later, the two sat comfortably on the couch, each with a cup of tea in hand. Had someone looked in at that moment, they never would've known by Ava's face that a huge bombshell had just been dropped.

"How can you drink tea?" Ava asked the first question that sprang to mind, even though it was probably one of the least relevant. "I mean, if you are immortal, why would you eat or drink anything. I've seen you do both many times."

"Why wouldn't I?" Edith challenged her granddaughter. "We certainly do not need the nutritional value of food but we can eat it, just as anyone. It just simply goes through our systems and has no bearing one way or another."

Ava reflected that her grandmother had always had a trim figure and never gained a pound. Then again, she had always eaten like a bird so she had just always assumed that was how the two sides of the story connected.

"But, if you are an immortal...."

"Many of the rules you think apply to immortals simply don't," her grandmother informed her. "Obviously, we can walk, talk and do pretty much anything anyone else can. Why not eat? Why not drink? We cannot get drunk off of alcohol. We get nothing out of consuming food. We must never go to the doctor for any reason at all. There are many things we do to keep under the radar and just because a hot cup of tea may not taste the same as it does for you or someone else, I still enjoy the warmth of the liquid and the memories of how it used to sooth me before I became a vampire."

Ava fell silent, attempting to absorb all this information. It was completely different than she had expected. Then again, what *had* she expected: certainly not her grandmother to make such a confession to her.

"Without getting into the entire story of how I became an immortal, I will simply say that I have been one for many years. I promise to elaborate on that portion of the story at another time." She took a sip of her tea before enclosing it in her hands.

"I returned to Canada around the time your mother was born. She was obviously not mine, since an immortal cannot bear a child but I adopted her from a close friend who was quite ill throughout her pregnancy and unable to look after the child."

"It was love at first sight and I vowed to always do everything I could for my little girl but unfortunately, the one thing I couldn't do was keep her alive." Ava noted the sadness in her grandmother's eyes as she quickly looked into her cup of tea. "One of the reasons for my bitterness for so many years after your parent's death is because I had sacrificed a lot by adopting a child. Of course, I would eventually have to find a way to leave because I could never tell her the truth about my status. There were so many little details that I would have to hide from her and becoming a parent wasn't something that I did lightly."

"So when she was taken away, I felt it was to punish me. I spent many years being very bitter about it, as you know and that's why I decided to tell you the truth today." Her grandmother took another sip of her tea and fell silent for a moment. "I knew you were a vampire for quite some time and wanted to be an immortal. When I learned this information and thought of the heartache I've had over the years, I said there was no way that *anyone* was to ever allow you to become one of us. It was bad enough, in my view, that you were a vampire at all but being an immortal, would simply be too much."

"I attempted to scare you with those silly notes and text messages. I know now that I went too far." Her grandmother took a deep sigh and shook her head. "My dear, you can live a million lives and still make stupid decisions, just like you were new to the world with no experiences to learn from at all. I'm proof of that but at the time, I panicked when you were getting so close and figured it was better to put you in fear, rather than make you become something you did not understand."

"But I probably would've came to the same conclusion if you had told me the truth long ago," Ava calmly suggested. "It was actually the fact that everyone was so secretive that made me want to learn more but if you had told me your story sooner, maybe I would've reconsidered."

"I thought about it many times, don't you worry." Her grandmother finished her tea and set the cup on the nearby coffee table, pausing for a moment. "But I originally didn't feel it would be a good idea to tell you the truth. It wasn't until Derrick Johnston approached me regarding this earlier in the week that I changed my mind."

"You know Derrick?" Ava was surprised. "I suppose, there aren't many immortals, so you probably know one another."

"Well yes, while that is true that there aren't many, I know Derrick because I know *all* the immortals." Her grandmother's face actually seemed to brighten when she shared the rest of her news. "Child, I am the head of the bunch. *I'm* the so-called 'Rock Star of vampires.'

"But-

"But it's supposed to be a young, virile man?" Her grandmother's face lit up into a smile and she shook her head. "That rumor has been swirling around for years. It amused me, so I let it continue and grow. The truth is that men don't always run the world, they just like to think they do."

"So you…you're *it*," Ava asked in a small, child-like voice. "You're the person I've been searching for all this time? You're the one who….ah, who.."

"Runs the show? Yes." Her grandmother only hesitated for a moment before continuing. "I oversee them all."

"So, is it true that immortals run the world?"

"It is true, but once again it is far less glamorous than you may think." Her grandmother wryly advised her. "And that's another reason why I didn't want you to join the immortal world. It's quite insidious and corrupt. I'm sorry to say, Ava that you may have romanticized the immortal vampires and I am here to let you know that we simply aren't the beautiful link in a chain. We are the frustrating clasp that is there to hold everything together, but nothing more."

"I don't understand."

"You're a smart young lady, look around you. Watch the news. Read some books." Her grandmother chose her words carefully. "The world is not lead by well-meaning individuals who want to save the environment, help the poor or improve people's quality of life. If that were the case, children

312

wouldn't be starving in third world countries and people wouldn't be dying of diseases with hidden cures."

"But why not change that?" Ava could barely hear her own words and she felt as though she were drifting through the room. Nothing about this conversation felt real. "You have the power."

"It's not that simple, Ava." She sighed. "It's much more complicated than that, I have the power over the vampires, I don't have power over the vultures."

Ava was stunned. Clearly, there were some things that she didn't understand. Apparently, things were more complicated than she originally thought.

Maybe the grass wasn't always greener on the other side.

Chapter Fifty

S he could smell him. His fragrance was so strong that it became apparent to her from the moment he walked in the door. It didn't matter that she was in a crowded grocery store, full of Sunday afternoon shoppers. It didn't matter that she couldn't see him with her eyes.

He was nearby; that was all she had to know.

The last couple of weeks had been a rude awakening for Ava. Her grandmother's confession had taken a few days to fully process but when it did, she felt as though a weight had been lifted from her chest. Instead she was filled with a freedom that Ava had never experienced in her life. It was like she had entered a world that was slightly frightening, but at the same time, allowed her to view things with a brand new set of eyes.

The fact that her grandmother was part of this secret world was astounding. She was the last person Ava would've ever suspected. Perhaps for the very reasons Edith Wolfe gave; she was older and people liked to believe the world of vampires was one created for the young and beautiful. It was a myth that everyone had believed for so long that they were incapable of seeing it any other way.

Learning the truth about immortals seemed to take the glittery shine off her original perception. Her grandmother explained that they actually weren't the exciting underground heroes she had thought. Immortals were very preoccupied with power and greed; they not only sought the challenge of manipulating some of the largest companies in the world, but often the world itself. Having lived many lives, they often felt superior to all others and were narcissistic enough to believe that they knew what was right for the universe. They were often wrong.

"Why do you think the world is such a mess?" Her grandmother calmly pondered, leaving Ava equally as curious. "My control is much more limited than you probably believe it to be. My own power lies with keeping secrets about vampires and for which, they must listen to me. But that is where it ends. Beyond that aspect of things, I have no power over their decisions affecting the rest of the world."

Fortunately, there weren't many immortals on the earth. Although her grandmother wouldn't give her an exact number, she was clear on the fact that only 'a handful' roamed the world and they always kept their ear to the ground, making sure that their secret remained throughout time.

"The Internet age has posed some new challenges, but nothing we cannot handle," Her grandmother insisted with certainty. "I have experts who are on top of this and for that, I'm thankful."

"What would happen if the world did find out about us?" Ava wondered out loud. "Don't you ever worry about the mortal vampires springing the secret?"

"Yes and no." Her grandmother casually shrugged. "It's not exactly a believable story so most would question the vampire's sanity and as for the rest of us, we would make sure their story didn't stick. I cannot tell you how or why, but we *are* always on top of it. Consider us a powerful force regarding the secret."

Ava didn't bother to ask any further questions about that because it seemed unlikely she wanted to learn the answers.

"Besides, it is strongly believed that if they learned about us, we would be captured and held against our will." Her grandmother sighed. "I believe the government wouldn't want people to know we existed. I mean, with our altered senses alone, we could pass on our powers and eliminate the need for entire industries. Of course, that's a little extreme, but it's truly possible."

Ava knew she was right. For example if most shared her own amplified vision, she was certain the optical industry would be all but eliminated.

With a vampire's dislike for processed sugary and salty foods and preference for organic, entire food companies would be at their knees—not to mention that people's health would improve as a result and the pharmaceutical corporations would have less illness to contend with, depleting their profits. With their intense sense of smell, many products full of chemicals exhibiting strong scents would lose their appeal. The list of professions and companies affected by such 'super powers' would definitely make vampires an undesirable group to have in existent.

"But even with our strong senses, many people wouldn't want to be a vampire," Ava suggested to her grandmother after she pondered the many aspects of society that would be affected, if everyone had the same abilities as they did.

"True but in a pinch, they might." Edith Wolfe raised her eyebrows. "Sickness and fears have a way of changing people and their opinions on a lot of things. For example, being an immortal vampire may repulse someone until they're on their deathbed and feel it's their only option. Then they would sell their soul for it."

Ava nodded. There were so many things she had never considered. It was an entire world opening up to her with many vivid colors and dark corners she hadn't expected to find.

But it wasn't just the immortals Edith knew about; it was also about the mortals.

Her grandmother was privy to a great deal of information. She had long known about Ava's choice to become a vampire. As it turns out, a great deal of time that they hadn't been in contact was because Edith Wolfe was upset about Ava's drastic decision to join the dark side, but eventually she learned to accept it.

"But I always followed your life," she had insisted. "I always was aware of what was going on with you, even though you didn't know it."

Ava was surprised to learn that her grandmother had become involved in a few occurrences after she turned into a mortal vampire. One of them was to send Bryan away after she turned. Had Ava known this months earlier, she would've been devastated but her grandmother's explanation now made a great deal of sense.

"That boy," Edith shook her head and rolled her eyes. "His intentions are good, believe it or not but his brain is in the wrong place. I could see that and although I shouldn't have gotten involved, I felt it was necessary that he be removed from the picture because he was definitely not going to give you the comfort you needed during that time."

Ava's grandmother had secured an acting job for him and when he abruptly took it rather than fulfilling his obligations, she immediately realized that it was time to bring someone else into the picture.

"I wanted the best for you and Landon was the perfect fit. He has a solid conscience and wouldn't leave you to suffer but he was also very educated in this area, able to be a strong support to you during the difficult transformation period." Her grandmother was apologetic about 'butting in' but insisted that Bryan's assistance would be problematic. "I sincerely feared that he would inadvertently supply you with the wrong information because the person who changed him was extremely sloppy."

"He told me the story," Ava spoke softly. "I do understand why you did what you felt necessary."

"The 'lady' who changed him is no longer part of our world. An imbecile who was a weak link in our chain." She didn't go so far as to suggest the woman had been killed and Ava decided it was better not to ask. "It was hardly the boys fault but he was warned a couple of times that his clumsy behavior was unacceptable. I believe he has since got the point."

"This is what immortals deal with," her grandmother shook her head and attempted to make a joke. "And to think you wanted to be part of it, to police the ones who are like dysfunctional children running about with such an important secret."

She also revealed that Landon had arrived on the rooftop after a bad dream, on the same night Ava had weakly climbed the stairs with the decision to end her life. Unable to sleep, he mysteriously arrived at the decision to get some fresh air. Of course, Edith had somehow manipulated the situation but Ava could hardly hold that against her. In the end, she had made the correct choice and although Ava's eyes could see that clearly now, she probably wouldn't have at the time.

"I hadn't done so in hopes of creating any kind of romantic relationship with him," her grandmother assured her. "I don't manipulate that kind of thing, but I just saw him as a compassionate and caring individual who would help guide you through the various stages of becoming a vampire. He was to step in for Bryan's incompetence and after doing so, I knew that he would always have one eye to you, even if you weren't close in the future."

"You were right about that." Ava confirmed. "So very right."

The two talked long into the afternoon and Ava felt a strong bond that had never existed in the past. Although it wasn't obvious at the time, Ava was finally beginning to heal from the many things that had once polluted her heart. After years of feeling unwanted and unloved, this new perspective of her life was like seeing a light for the first time. But she had one more thing she had to ask even though it was a difficult question. She inquired about Mariah. Ava feared that she had been eliminated.

Upon hearing the question, her grandmother shook her head for a minute before replying.

"Such a sad situation," she commented and for a moment, Ava thought she wasn't going to continue with the topic. "That young woman had many secrets, Ava. There is so much about her that you never knew at all. In many ways, she was her own worst enemy. In many, *many* ways."

"Did something happen the day she committed suicide?" Ava felt a lump forming in her throat, fearful of what more her grandmother would say.

"Suicide?" She raised an eyebrow and shrugged. "I suppose it could have been."

"What?" Ava felt her skin turn cold.

Her grandmother's eyes stared into her granddaughter's and she seemed hesitant to go on. "I'm not saying it wasn't on purpose. I'm just saying that only Mariah knows what was in her mind in that moment. Only she knows the circumstances surrounding that day."

"She was always so strong." Ava shook her head. "It never made sense that she would commit suicide."

"In every circumstance comes a decision. Some are good, some are bad." Her grandmother pondered. "When you turned to a vampire, I decided that Bryan wouldn't be a good person to help you through the change. In that circumstance, it seemed like the best decision. Maybe it was or maybe it wasn't. Perhaps helping you would've forced Bryan to grow up. Regardless, I had to make a decision."

"In Mariah's circumstance, *she* made a decision." Edith Wolfe gave a sad smile. "The strong often can't accept the fact that they are sometimes going to be very weak."

Ava remained silent. Pain filled her heart once again, wondering if these words applied to Mariah.

"Of course, you also have to ask yourself something." Her grandmother said. "Do you really think that Mariah was ever all that strong?"

The question had stayed with Ava ever since it was asked. Had she truly ever known her best friend? How much of her life had been in secret? All the times she would mysteriously disappear, where had she gone? Her life was hardly an open book; at least, not yet. But maybe someday, it would be. Time would eventually answer all questions.

Ava pushed aside these thoughts, finally finding what she was looking for in the grocery store. He was in the pet food aisle. Wandering the aisles, Landon made eye contact with Ava and a smile suffused his face.

Eventually, everything comes full circle.